LEARNIN' THE ROPES

by

SHANNA HATFIELD

D1524726

Learnin' The Ropes
Copyright 2012
by Shanna Hatfield

ISBN-13: 978-1477643570
ISBN-10: 1477643575

Shanna Hatfield
shanna@shannahatfield.com
shannahatfield.com

To those who are willing to take a chance,
chase their dreams,
and make a difference.

Books by Shanna Hatfield

FICTION

Learnin' the Ropes

Grass Valley Cowboys Series
The Cowboy's Christmas Plan
The Cowboy's Spring Romance
The Cowboy's Summer Love

QR Code Killer

The Women of Tenacity Series
The Women of Tenacity - A Prelude
Heart of Clay
Country Boy vs. City Girl
Not His Type

NON-FICTION

Savvy Holiday Entertaining
Savvy Spring Entertaining
Savvy Summer Entertaining

Lesson One
Location, Location, Location

"Git yerself out of thet durn city and into God's country."

Tyler Lewis read through the classified ad a third time, trying to decide if he was desperate enough to apply for the open position.

Leaning against his truck door with the paper propped on the steering wheel, cold seeping into his back from the rain-splattered window and hunger gnawing at his insides, he concluded he was, in fact, that desperate.

Wanted - Good mechanic able to work on a variety of equipment in Harney County, Oregon. Certification a plus. Wages congruent to experience. Room and board included. Must like animals.

Ty took a deep breath, quickly typed a text message and hit send to the number in the ad before he could change his mind.

If someone had told him a year ago he would be living in his pickup, unable to find a job, and willing to do just about anything that was legal to make a few bucks, he would have laughed in their face.

That was before the garage where he worked for the past seven years decided to lay off all but their newest mechanic to cut costs. Ten months later, Ty had $486 left to his name and everything he owned was packed into his pickup.

Let go with a promise that he would have his job back as soon as business picked up; the once-busy garage in a Portland suburb went out of business within a few months, leaving Ty no hope of being re-hired.

Applying for every open mechanic job he could find, he interviewed for positions doing everything from janitorial work to flipping burgers and couldn't get hired on anywhere. There were way too many people in the same sinking boat.

Five weeks ago, he gave up his apartment and moved into his pickup. With rapidly dwindling funds, he sold all of his furniture and anything else he didn't need which left him his tools, clothes, and one box full of mementos from his childhood.

Although it was expensive, the one thing he refused to give up was his iPhone. Without it, he would be completely cut off from the rest of the world. It served as his phone, computer, camera, radio, filing system, and number one job-hunting tool.

Wondering if he'd lost his mind for responding to the latest ad, he was Googling information on Harney County when a tap on the glass at his back startled him.

Looking through the water streaks, he grinned and rolled down the window.

"Hey, you might melt out here," he said to his sister, Beth, as she stood under a huge umbrella.

"Not likely," she said with a smile. "Come inside and have some dinner with us, Ty. You'll freeze out here tonight. The weatherman said it might even snow."

"In Portland? You're talking crazy," Ty said, stuffing his phone in his pocket and getting out of his truck. Locking the door, he followed his sister across the street and up to the tiny studio apartment she shared with her husband Nate. Ty tried to hide a smile as he watched Beth waddle off the elevator and down the narrow hallway. Eight months pregnant, she was definitely looking the part.

Opening the apartment door, the smell of baking bread made Ty's stomach grumble in anticipation. Beth gave him a narrowed glare.

"Did you eat anything today?" she asked, as Ty helped her take off her jacket and hung it on a peg by the door.

Hanging his coat next to hers, he nodded his head.

"What did you eat?" Beth asked, not quite believing his response, knowing he would sometimes only eat one meal a day.

"Half a granola bar." Ty said, not making eye contact.

Beth sighed and turned into the kitchen that was smaller than her former storage closet. Nate lost his job seven months ago and they gave up their former spacious apartment to cut costs.

She handed Ty a piece of bread slathered with peanut butter and jam before returning to her dinner preparations. Leaning against the wall between the kitchen and the main room of the apartment, Ty ate the sandwich as slow as his starving stomach would allow and watched his sister.

Waiting eight years to start a family, both Beth and Nate wanted to make sure their careers were stable and they could adequately provide for a child. The week after they found out she was expecting, Nate came home with the news he'd been laid off from his job as a technical engineer.

Employed as an office manager for a busy dental office, Beth had great benefits and a good salary. Even with her income, they were forced to give up their nice apartment and move into this tiny studio until Nate could find another job.

After months of Nate's applications being rejected, they both were worried about what would happen when the baby arrived. Beth originally planned to take three months of maternity leave, but now she was thinking more along the lines of two or three weeks. Nate might have to become a stay-at-home dad if things didn't turn around soon and none of them could begin to think how they would squeeze a baby into the cramped living space.

From the entry door, there was the tiny kitchen to the left. A hallway to the right led to the bathroom which was separated from the living and sleeping area by a long double-sided closet that essentially made up a divider wall.

Ty looked around the open room, taking in the couch and small television, the one end table with a lamp, the small kitchen table surrounded by chairs, and the big king-sized bed that took up the bulk of the floor space. Even if he felt right about intruding into Nate and Beth's home, which he didn't, there wasn't room for him.

Stepping back into the kitchen, Ty leaned against the counter and watched Beth stir something in a big pot. The mouth-watering aroma of chicken and herbs filled his senses. The last good, hot meal he'd eaten was with Beth and Nate four days ago.

Getting odd jobs through friends and acquaintances, Ty was mostly paid in cash. He saved what he could, but always bought a few bags of groceries and brought them over to Beth and Nate. In trade, she cooked him a hot meal while he made use of the bathroom, taking a long, hot shower and stretching out on their couch for an hour or two.

Without a home of his own, he sometimes parked across the street from Beth's apartment when he wasn't out job hunting or hanging out at the library researching jobs.

Since it was February, it was too cold and wet to stay outside much. He would certainly be glad when spring arrived. Winter was definitely not the best time to be homeless.

"What can I do to help?" Ty asked, washing his hands at the sink, ignoring the pangs of hunger that ripped through his stomach.

"Set the table?" Beth asked as she peeked into the oven, holding her hand under her rounded belly as she bent over. Before she could stand up, a gasp escaped from her lips and she gripped the counter.

"You okay, sis?" Ty looked at her in concern as he dried his hands. If she went into premature labor, he was the last person she wanted to be around. He couldn't stand to see a woman cry, suffer, or be upset.

"Yeah, the baby is pretty lively today, is all," she said, grabbing Ty's hand and holding it on her stomach. He left his palm where she placed it and could feel tiny little kicks against his hand.

"I tell you, he's going to be a first-class kicker on the football team," Ty said, smiling at thoughts of his future nephew.

"She could also be a ballerina or a soccer player," Beth said with a twinkle in her brilliant blue eyes, the exact same shade as Ty's.

"So have you and Nate finally settled on names?" Ty asked as he gathered up plates and silverware, setting them on the table.

"We've got the list narrowed down to a dozen each."

"Wow, that is real progress," Ty teased, putting the butter dish and napkins on the table.

He and Beth both looked up as Nate came in the door, tired and dejected. Nate spent his days filling out applications, participating in interviews, and trying to drum up some interest in his resume. The past few months he grew accustomed to hearing he was overqualified, too experienced, or they couldn't afford someone with his skill set. Those doing the hiring didn't even give him a chance to say he'd happily take a huge cut in pay just to be employed.

Hanging up his coat and putting his umbrella next to Beth's, he gave her a warm hug before extending a hand to Ty.

"Hey, bro, good to see you," Nate said, loosening his tie and unbuttoning his shirt.

"You, too, man," Ty said. "No luck today?"

"No. You either?" Nate asked as he carefully brushed off his suit jacket and hung it in the hall closet.

"Maybe," Ty said, leaning against the wall between the kitchen and the rest of the open apartment so both Beth and Nate could hear him.

"What's 'maybe' mean?" Beth asked, sticking her head out of the kitchen to look at Ty. "Care to expound on that?"

"I fired off an inquiry for a mechanics job in Harney County. The requirements were pretty vague, so I'll see if I get a response," Ty said, nonchalantly.

"Harney County? Isn't that somewhere in Eastern Oregon, in the middle of no-where?" Beth asked while Nate changed his clothes in the bathroom.

"Southeast, I think," Nate said as he reappeared, wearing faded jeans and a sweatshirt. "What would you be doing?"

"I'm not exactly sure. Do you have yesterday's classifieds?" Ty asked as Beth brought a basket of hot rolls to the table. The steam escaping from around the edges of the napkin caught Ty's attention and he shoved his hands in his pockets to keep from snitching one.

Nate pulled the paper out of his briefcase and gave it to Ty. Snapping it open, Ty scanned down the column of ads, placing his finger on the one listing for a mechanic. "This one," he said, handing the paper to Nate.

"That is vague," Nate said after reading the ad twice. "Based on the qualifications, you shouldn't have any problem. You've been a certified mechanic for what, eight years?"

"Nine. I got my certification the day I turned twenty. It was quite a celebration," Ty said with a cocky grin.

"I remember that," Beth said, smacking Ty on the arm. "If Mom had known about your little after-party antics, she would have boxed your ears."

"Yeah, she would have, but you were always good at keeping me out of too much trouble," Ty said, waiting for Beth to sit down before he took his seat at the small table. Scrunched into the corner by the kitchen, the table was laughably small when he and Nate, both over six-feet tall, sat around it. They'd gotten into the habit of extending their legs in opposite directions to keep from bumping knees under the table.

Ty studied his sister and felt love and tenderness tug at his heart. Two years his senior, Beth always mothered and protected him. Their mother, Toni, was wonderful and loving, but she worked multiple jobs to keep a roof over their head and food on their table.

From information he and Beth pieced together over the years, their mom fell in love with a no-good loser. He was a good-looking bad-boy type, oozing charm and telling her whatever she wanted to hear. Toni married him, thinking he would settle down and change his ways as they started a family. He played at being a husband, but preferred drinking, gambling and carousing to acting like a grown up. He tried to be a father after Beth was born but when Toni announced she was pregnant with Ty, the jerk disappeared. They never heard from him again.

Ty thought that might have been part of why Beth waited so long to start her own family. She wanted to make sure Nate was going to stick around, but he was one of the good guys. Ty knew despite their current financial situation, Nate would take good care of Beth and their baby.

"This job description says you must like animals. Have you ever been around animals?" Nate asked as they enjoyed the delicious chicken soup Beth served for dinner.

"One of my friends had a dog and Mom let us keep a stray cat for a few weeks once. I liked them both just fine," Ty said, buttering another warm roll. He'd have to find a way to buy more groceries to pay back for what he was eating tonight, but the food tasted so good.

Nate nodded his head. They went on to discuss some places they applied for jobs that day. Ty just finished his second bowl of soup when his phone buzzed. Pulling it out of his pocket, he was surprised to see a text message in response to his inquiry about the job.

Looking up, he smiled.

"What's that about?" Beth asked, curious.

"It's about that job. They want my full resume and references by tomorrow morning," Ty said, trying not to get excited. Turning to Nate he grinned. "Can I use your laptop for a few minutes?"

"Sure, man. Let's help Beth with the dishes and then you can prepare to dazzle these people with your extensive experience and credentials."

Ty laughed and helped himself to another roll.

After the dishes were done, Beth sat on the couch working on a baby blanket she was trying to crochet, while Nate and Ty sat at the table with the laptop computer. Having gone through the routine multiple times before, Nate created a folder on the computer for Ty so he could easily attach his resume and references to emails. Ty could have done it all from his cell phone, but it was a lot easier to sit at a computer and type out a cover letter.

When he finished, he asked Beth to read the letter. She suggested a few changes which he made before sending off the information to Lex Ryan of Riley, Oregon.

"Maybe this will be the one," Beth said, placing a warm hand on Ty's shoulder and giving it a squeeze.

"I hope so. Although I'm not so sure I want to move too far away from you, especially with the baby coming soon," Ty said, honestly. He had no idea how far this job would be from Portland, so the three of them pulled up a state map and found Harney County. By zooming in on the map, they finally located the tiny dot that marked Riley. It was really out in the middle of no-where.

"Good grief, Ty. That looks like a lot of open country. What if you get eaten by a bear?" Beth asked dramatically.

Ty and Nate both laughed.

"I don't think I need to worry about wildlife or bear encounters. I'm not going to the wilds of some third-world country. Besides, let's see if I even get an interview before we get all hysterical."

"Good point," Nate said, hugging Beth to him. "How about a game of Clue?"

As Ty sat playing the board game, he realized being destitute really changed your attitude about a lot of things. At 29, he never pictured himself sitting crammed into a corner playing a silly board game with his very pregnant sister and her husband and actually enjoying it.

One good thing he could say about being broke and without resources was that it made you appreciate the people who loved you.

Beth talked Ty into spend the night on their couch. It was too short for him to be able to completely stretch out, but better than trying to sleep in his pickup. It was also a lot warmer. Peeking out of the miniscule balcony window the next morning, Ty was shocked to see a frosting of snow covering everything. He smiled to himself, thinking Beth was right once again.

Taking note that Nate and Beth were still asleep, Ty quietly took his things to the bathroom, enjoyed a hot shower and dressed before bundling into his coat and heading outside. He walked down the street to a bakery and bought them all muffins and hot coffee, returning to the apartment just as Beth came out of the bathroom, dressed for work.

"Told you it would snow," Beth said triumphantly as Ty set the muffins and coffee on the table. Taking off his coat, he offered her a grin and helped her get plates and napkins. By then, Nate was up and the three of them ate breakfast before Beth left for work.

"What are your plans today?" Nate asked as he sat sipping his coffee and eating another muffin.

"I thought I'd try going to some of the bigger car dealerships again to see if any positions have opened up since the last time I checked," Ty said, slowly drinking his coffee. It was too early to start going door-to-door and too cold to sit out in his truck for any length of time. "How about you?"

"I heard a rumor that a new facility was opening in Woodburn. Thought I'd drive down and check it out. If I can get a contact name, maybe I can get my foot in the door before they fill all the positions," Nate said, finishing his coffee and getting up from the table. He and Ty did the few dishes from breakfast and left them in the drainer to dry.

Shrugging into his coat, Ty gave Nate a slap on the shoulder as they stood at the door.

"Thanks for letting me crash here last night. I might have frozen outside," Ty said, opening the door.

"Thanks for coming in. You know Beth worries about you. You're always welcome, bro," Nate said as Ty waved and walked down the hall.

Before he had a chance to make the dealership rounds, a friend called and asked Ty if he could come over right away to do some work on a car.

Ty arrived at Jeff's house to find his wife's car dead in the garage. It didn't take long to determine the problem. Calling Jeff, he offered an estimate on the cost of parts. Jeff gave him the go-ahead so Ty purchased the parts with his credit card and had the car back together and running smoothly by the time Jeff arrived home for lunch. Taking the car for a quick test drive, Jeff stopped by the bank and made a withdrawal, paying Ty for the parts and throwing in a nice chunk of change for his labor.

Inviting him in for lunch, Ty accepted and they visited for a few minutes before Jeff headed back to work.

Ty deposited the cash needed to cover the credit card expenses into his bank account then pocketed the rest, planning to buy some groceries for Beth and Nate later that afternoon. He was waiting in line to leave the bank parking lot when his cell phone buzzed with a text message.

Pulling back into a parking space he read the text from Lex Ryan about the job in Riley. According to the message, Lex was impressed with his experience and references and wanted to conduct an interview. Ty needed to call someone named Swede at four o'clock if he was interested. He would also be receiving a list of questions Lex wanted completed and e-mailed back before four if that was possible.

Ty quickly changed his plans and drove to the library. Going inside, he sat down at an empty computer station, opened his email account and completed the questionnaire from Lex.

At first the questions didn't seem like anything out of the ordinary, but toward the end of the two-page document, a few of them caught him off guard.

He answered them as best he could, confused and somewhat unsettled by the questions:

Are you afraid of dogs?
   No
Do wide open spaces bother you?
   No
Can you live without access to modern conveniences?
   Yes

Ty didn't know how he could have access to any fewer conveniences than he did living in his pickup, but decided it was best not to offer that opinion.

Are you willing to relocate to a rural atmosphere?
   Yes

How bad could it be living in the country? He'd gone for many drives outside of Portland and enjoyed the gentle rolling hills of farmland. It seemed peaceful and nice. He could adjust to that, no problem.

The final question Ty classified as downright bizarre:

Will it bother you to live in a house with the rest of the hands without access to a nightlife or eligible young females?
   No

A guy living in his truck doesn't have a night life or dating scene and there are no eligible females who want to hang out with a man who is homeless, so it didn't bother Ty in the least to answer that question honestly.

The reason behind the question did, however, give him a moment of pause before he hit send.

He needed this job, though, and if Mr. Ryan had a few quirks, so be it.

Staying at the library until time for his phone call, Ty found a quiet corner and pulled a small notebook out of his coat pocket. He used it to keep track of all sorts of information and wanted to have it handy in case he needed to take any notes from the call today.

At two minutes before four, he punched in the number and the phone was answered on the first ring.

"Rockin' R Ranch," said a voice that sounded like it chewed gravel for breakfast.

"Hi, this is Tyler Lewis. I was asked to call this number at four today and speak with Mr. Swede," Ty said, trying to use his best professional phone manners.

"I'm Swede and yer right on time. And it's jes Swede, no mister needed," Swede said. "The boss asked me to interview ya since I'm the one ya'll mostly be workin' with, so let's git 'er done."

Swede asked Ty a number of questions about his skills, experience and training. Ty got a little worried when Swede asked if he'd ever worked on farm equipment. Ty honestly answered he had not, but added that he could fix everything from lawnmowers to semi-trucks.

Sounding pleased, Swede went over the list of questions Ty answered earlier that afternoon via email.

"Are ya sure ya can live somewhere thet's remote without much in the way of a social life?" Swede asked. "It's all guys around this place and it's a long way to town if yer lookin' for some Saturday night action."

"I haven't had much of a social life since I lost my job, Swede. I don't see that the location will make much difference in that," Ty said, badly wanting this job. He didn't care if it was in Timbuktu; he needed to be employed for his own sanity and sense of self-worth, not to mention the money he could give to Beth and Nate until they got back on their feet.

"All right, then," Swede said. "Let me talk with the boss and one of us will get back to ya."

"Thank you, Swede. I appreciate the opportunity to interview with you."

"No problem. Talk to ya soon."

Ty hung up the phone feeling like the interview went well. In a moment of self-deprecating humor, he realized if he did land the job, he was all packed and ready to go.

Looking at his watch, he hustled out of the library to the grocery store, filling a cart with fresh fruit and vegetables along with cuts of beef and chicken. As a splurge, he added a strawberry cheesecake from the bakery, Beth's favorite.

Arriving at her apartment building, he lugged the groceries to her door and rang the bell. She opened it, surprised to see him.

"Hey, I didn't expect to see you again for a few days. What are you up to?" she asked, stepping aside as he came in the door and set the grocery bags on the kitchen floor. "What's all this, Ty?"

"Jeff hired me to fix Geena's car today and paid in cash. Thought I'd just restock some of what I ate yesterday," Ty said, putting groceries away. He felt Beth tug on his arm and looked down into her tear-filled eyes. She attempted to give him a hug around her wide girth, making them both laugh.

"You are such a good brother and good man," Beth said, swiping at the tears that trickled down her cheeks. "Thank you."

"You're welcome. How about you feed me dinner and we'll call it even?" Ty asked, taking the cheesecake out of the grocery bag and waving it in front of her. "I even brought dessert."

"Always did know how to get around me, didn't you," Beth teased, as she put the cheesecake in the fridge, looking forward to the treat. "Did you hear back about the job?"

"I did. I had to answer more questions via email and I had a phone interview with the ranch foreman. You should hear the way he talks. It sounds like he swallowed glass, the way his voice is all raspy and rough."

"But the interview went well?" Beth asked as she slid a casserole into the oven and set the timer.

"I think it did. He seemed a little hesitant when I said I'd never worked on farm equipment, but I have yet to meet a vehicle I couldn't fix, so I'm not too worried about it."

"That's wonderful, Ty. I'm keeping my fingers crossed," Beth said, helping Ty put the last of the groceries away. "You really think you've got a shot at this?"

"I hope so, although I'm not so sure I'm going to like the location," Ty said, leaning against the counter and accepting the cup of hot coffee Beth handed to him. "Swede, that's the foreman's name, said it's about a five-hour drive from Portland."

"Well, that's not so bad. You could always visit on a weekend, couldn't you?" Beth asked, making herself a cup of tea and motioning Ty toward the couch. Sinking down on the cushions, Beth let out a tired sigh.

"Swede said the closest town is Burns," Ty said, trying to remember where Burns was located on the map they looked up last night. Pulling out his phone, he Googled Burns and browsed a few web pages. Showing a map to Beth, he grinned. "At least it is on a major highway, so you can put your fears at rest of me being eaten by a bear."

"I really hope you get this job, Ty, but I'm going to miss you so much. I… we'll…" Beth choked back a sob and brushed at tears. Taking a deep breath and releasing it, she turned a watery smile to her brother. "Sorry. I know how well you do with emotional women, but I'm eight months pregnant and it comes with the territory."

"I'll forgive you this once," Ty said with an understanding smile. They chatted until Nate came home and the three of them discussed plans for the next day while they ate the warm and filling chicken casserole Beth made for dinner.

Ty was setting the cheesecake on the table when his phone buzzed. Reading the text message, he let out an excited whoop, causing Nate to nearly drop the dessert plates he was getting from the kitchen.

"I got the job!" Ty said, high-fiving Nate and hugging Beth. "Lex Ryan, that's the owner, said I can start anytime. I guess I'll plan on leaving tomorrow."

"Dude, that is so awesome," Nate said, cutting big slices of cheesecake and passing them around while Ty sent a text to Lex Ryan saying to expect him tomorrow afternoon.

"Congratulations, Ty," Beth said, smiling through her tears.

Patting his sister's hand, Ty gave her an excited smile. "This will be a good thing, sis, just wait and see if it isn't."

Ty was up early the next morning, taking a quick shower and dressing before hustling out to order breakfast while Beth and Nate still slept. He came back in and quietly set the food on the table, careful not to wake up Nate who was still sleeping. From the water running in the bathroom, he could tell Beth was up and getting ready.

Looking at his watch, he knew she was running ahead of schedule this morning. He resigned himself to a teary goodbye from his sister. When she came out of the bathroom a few minutes later, she gave him a tight hug, which sent the baby into a flurry of end-goal worthy kicks. Ty laughed as he placed his hands on her stomach and savored the last time he'd get to feel the baby kick before he actually got to meet the little one in person, whenever that may be. It could be a few months before he made it back to Portland. By then the baby would no longer be a newborn.

That thought made his throat tighten with emotion. He and Beth were close. They grew up that way and were even closer since their mom died of pneumonia six years ago. They were all the family the two of them had in the world, other than Nate, and that bond was very special. It was important to Ty that Beth's baby could get to know him, but that might be difficult from miles and miles away.

"Well, little mama, I think we should eat breakfast before it gets cold and then I'm going to hit the road," Ty said, holding her chair as Beth sank down at the table. Nate got up and joined them. The guys tried to joke and keep things light-hearted, but Beth's quiet sadness lingered around the table.

Quickly cleaning up from their meal, Ty made sure he gathered his few meager belongings before he gave Nate a brotherly hug and thanked him for all he'd done for him in the past years.

He hugged Beth again, inhaling her scent that reminded him so much of his mother. Setting her back, he studied her long and hard, realizing for the first time that she looked like a replica of their mom from her warm brown hair and oval face to her small build and short stature.

"I don't think I ever told you how much you remind me of Mom, Bethie," Ty said, hugging her again. "You're a beautiful person and I know you're going to be a fantastic mother."

"Thank you, Ty. I'm really going to miss you," Beth said, swiping at her tears. "Promise you'll stay in touch."

"I promise. As long as I've got cell service, you can call or text me anytime," Ty said, carrying his small duffle bag out the door and waving one last time. "Be well and be safe. I'll let you know when I get there."

Before his own emotions got the best of him, Ty headed out to his pickup. Filling the tank with fuel put a sizeable dent in his wallet as he headed south out of Portland. Following the signs, he turned southeast toward Bend and found himself there a few hours later. He filled up with fuel again and ate a quick lunch, although it wasn't quite yet eleven.

Getting back on the road, he continued driving southeast on Highway 20. As the pine trees and neat little farms gave way to mile after mile of sagebrush and open land, Ty thought he may have reached the end of the earth. Looking back, forward, right and left, all he could see was sagebrush and more sagebrush interrupted by the occasional craggy rocks and straggly looking trees he thought might be junipers.

Swede wasn't kidding when he said the landscape was a little different.

As he drove up to a tiny store by a sign that said "Welcome to Riley," Ty stopped to stretch his legs. Going inside the store, he asked about the Rockin' R Ranch and the guy working the cash register grinned as Ty paid for a cold soda.

"I know the folks at the Rockin' R. The Ryan family has been in this area forever. Poor old Lex passed away last fall after that awful cancer got him, but Lex Jr. is doing a right smart job of running the place now. Been trying to hire on a mechanic and a housekeeper. I'm guessing you're applying for the mechanic job."

"That's right," Ty said, not feeling particularly chatty with the loose-lipped clerk.

"Well, good luck to ya," the man said, slapping Ty on the shoulder. "You're built for the job, but so were the last two. Together they didn't last more than a week."

Ty suddenly wondered what he'd gotten himself into. If he had to turn around and drive back to Portland, he didn't think he had enough cash left to cover the fuel.

Not sure what to say, he didn't need to worry as the clerk rattled on about the ranch and how to find it. Lex, Lex Jr., Ty corrected himself, sent him directions last night, so he wasn't too worried about finding the place. He had the address programmed into his truck's GPS system, along with the emailed directions.

Giving a word of thanks to the clerk, he got back in his truck and drove a few miles further east on the highway before taking a right. According to the directions, he was supposed to drive three miles then take a left. Two more miles, he would take a right and another mile should bring him to the ranch house.

Lex indicated a possibility of not being home today and gave direction if no one answered at the house, to call Swede on his cell phone.

Ty noticed after he turned off the highway that the road, though paved, had not seen any maintenance for quite some time. Following the turns, he soon found himself bouncing down a gravel road, surround by snow-covered fields and pastures filled with red and white cattle.

Ty smiled, wondering if these were the animals he was not supposed to fear. They looked pretty harmless to him.

As he pulled into the ranch yard, it was hard not to be impressed. A huge Victorian house painted a shade of pale yellow with white and dark green accents was the focal point, complete with wrap-around porch, gingerbread trim and a yard enclosed by a white-picket fence. What appeared to be a garage, in the same shade of yellow, sat off to the side of the house toward the back.

A small but tidy looking cottage-style home and a sprawling ranch house were off to the left of the main house with a hulking red barn, machine shed, large shop and various outbuildings across an expansive open area from the two houses.

Parking his truck, Ty got out and smoothed down his jeans before straightening his sweatshirt and jacket. Running a hand through his thick, wavy brown hair, he realized he probably should have gotten a haircut before he left Portland. It had been weeks since he last had his hair trimmed and it was getting pretty long.

Walking through the gate in the fence, he strode purposefully down the sidewalk, up the porch steps and to the front door of the house. Ringing the bell, he waited, listening, but didn't hear any movement inside. Opening the screen door, he knocked on the wooden door and still heard nothing.

Deciding Mr. Ryan wasn't home, he pulled out his cell phone and turned only to find a huge, furry animal staring at him from just a few feet away with a bunch of sharp looking teeth bared his direction.

The crazy questions about liking animals were starting to make a lot more sense to Ty as he carefully backed up against the front door.

Lesson Two
Dog is Man's Best Friend

"A good feller needs a good dog."

If the shaggy beast eyeballing Ty was a dog, it was without a doubt the largest he had ever seen. He briefly wondered if it was some sort of mutated horse from the sheer size of it, but the shape of its face and body made him think it was a canine.

Not sure whether it was friendly or sizing him up for an afternoon snack, Ty decided there was no way he could beat the thing back to his pickup. Carefully raising his phone he called Swede.

"Swede, this is Ty Lewis. I'm standing on the front porch of the house and no one seems to be home."

"Welcome to the Rockin' R Ranch, Tyler. Ya must 'a made good time this mornin'," Swede said. "Come on down to the barn. I'm workin' inside the big double doors."

"I'd be happy to, but there is an animal here on the porch and I'm not sure it wants me to move," Ty said, warily watching the four-legged monster as it took a step closer to him.

"Thet's Baby," Swede said with a laugh. "Sit tight. I'll be right there. She generally don't bite. As long as she ain't growlin', ya ought 'ta be fine."

"Thanks," Ty said, sliding his phone into his pocket. He took little comfort in the fact that the animal didn't generally bite. Did that mean she did on occasion? Was he going to be an exception? He listened and realized the dog wasn't making any noise. Not growling was good.

Moving slowly he dropped his hands to his sides and tried to relax, making a loose fist and slowly holding it out for the animal to smell. If it was a dog, he knew from past experience, they liked to sniff a hand before they got too friendly.

"Hey, Baby, is that your name? Huh, girl?" Ty asked quietly, trying to keep his nervousness from his voice. "Are you a dog, Baby? Is that what you are?"

Apparently the animal decided at that point she liked him and lunged forward with what Ty could only think was a smile on her face. She engulfed his hand with her big slobbery tongue and pressed against him until he had to put a leg out to brace himself against her weight.

"Well, ain't thet somethin'," Swede said as he came around the corner of the house and jumped onto the porch. "Baby don't take to strangers. In fact, she's purty protective of the house and Lex Jr. Git down, Baby. Be a good girl."

The dog grinned at Ty and sat back on her haunches, wagging her massive tail and whining.

"Ya must be Tyler. I'm Swede," the older man said, sticking his hand out to Ty. Ty swiped his hand back and forth on his jeans to get off the dog slobbers before taking Swede's gloved hand.

"It's nice to meet you, Swede, and please call me Ty," Ty said, eying the dog. "Is that really a dog?"

"Sure is. Baby's a Kuvasz. A Hungarian dog bred to guard livestock. Baby weighs purt near a hundred and twenty-five pounds. She can take down a grown man if she's of a mind to. Lex Sr. brought her home when she was jes a lil' bitty ol' thing, so she's protective of the family and the ranch. Looks like she decided ya'll was part of the family. Thet hasn't happened before."

"Oh," was all Ty could think to say when the dog sidled up next to him, pushing against his leg again and whining. He patted her head and scratched behind her ears, earning himself a few good whacks from her tail.

"Stay, Baby," Swede ordered the dog as he walked Ty back out to his pickup and climbed in the passenger door. "Let's head over to the bunkhouse and git ya settled in. Boss doesn't expect ya to start until tomorra' so you can git the lay of the land today."

"Good," Ty said as he drove the few hundred yards to the large ranch style house. Gathering up his suitcase and a duffel bag, he followed Swede in the door and was surprised the inside of the bunkhouse looked like a very nice home.

The front door opened into a huge room that offered a gathering area with a big-screen television, a desk with a computer, several couches, and overstuffed chairs to the right. To the left was a well-appointed kitchen, complete with a long counter and barstools as well as a large dining table surrounded by eight chairs. A hallway began at the end of the great room and ran the length of the house.

There were six individual bedrooms with three bathrooms that made up the rest of the house. Each bedroom was set up with a full-sized bed, a dresser, closet, and small desk with a chair. All linens and bedding were furnished.

Swede showed him to a bedroom at the end of the hall, across from a bathroom. The bathrooms were small but each housed a nice sink with a medicine cabinet and vanity mirror, toilet and shower.

Swede went over the list of rules for living in the bunkhouse which included picking up after yourself, doing your own laundry including sheets and towels once a week in the laundry room behind the kitchen, taking turns with the cooking and general cleaning of the bunkhouse while the boss was trying to find a new housekeeper, and no smoking or chewing inside the house. No pets were allowed including anything that crawled or slithered.

All hands were welcome to use the computer in the front room but if the boss found out anyone downloaded anything of a questionable nature, it was grounds for immediate dismissal.

"There's also no drinkin' on the job. If ya want to do that, ya'll have to take it into town. The Rockin' R is dry," Swede said, giving Ty a narrowed gaze to gauge his reaction to this news. "There is also no cussin' or swearin' in front of the boss."

"Not a problem," Ty said. He'd never been a big drinker and his mother cured him of cussing by the amount of soap he ingested as a kid when she'd shove a bar of it in his mouth any time he said a word she deemed inappropriate.

"Good. Ya work Monday through Saturday and have Sunday off to do whatever ya like. The boss also gives paid holidays includin' four days fer Thanksgiving. Bet you didn't expect that?" Swede said with a cackle. "Ya git health insurance and start earnin' vacation time after ninety days. From mid-February to October, we need ever one here unless it's an emergency, so don't go plannin' a summer get-away. The boss pays us ever two weeks."

Vacation time? Health benefits? Had Ty missed that part of the interview conversation? He was so excited at the prospect of being employed, especially with a job that provided room and board, he didn't even dream there would be other benefits.

"That sounds great," he finally said, nodding his head at Swede.

"The boss has some paperwork for ya to fill out. It's on the desk in yer room. If ya have it ready in the mornin' that would be great," Swede said as they walked back down the hall toward the kitchen. "We take turns cookin' breakfast and supper. As soon as the boss finds a new housekeeper, we'll be off kitchen duty. Generally, we eat a sandwich or whatever fer lunch. There's a sheet in the kitchen by the wall phone that shows who is responsible for cookin' duty each day. I think the boys added ya in the rotation for the coming week, so ya might want to check that out. We eat breakfast and supper at straight up six. If yer cookin' ya can leave yer work an hour and a half early to come git the meal ready. The days ya cook, ya also do the dishes. Any questions?"

"How many other people work here on the ranch?" Ty asked, curious as to how many people shared the bunkhouse.

"There are seven of us, counting Lex Jr. The boss is gone today, but should be back tomorra' so you can meet then. The rest of the guys, ya'll meet tonight at supper. I live in the foreman's house, but do all my eatin' here," Swede said, opening the door. "When ya get yer things settled, come on down to the barn and I'll give ya a quick tour of the buildin's then take ya to the shop."

"Thanks, Swede. It won't take me long," Ty said, following him out the door and back to his pickup.

"Take your time, son. No hurry," Swede said then walked back toward the barn.

Ty carried another load of his belongings to his room and returned for the final boxes, wondering about the age of the ranch foreman as he put his things away. Swede moved like a man in good shape, maybe mid-forties, but his face said he was closer to his late-sixties by the lines and weathered skin.

Finishing with his meager belongings, Ty changed into a set of older clothes and put on the lace-up steel-toed boots he used to wear to work. He sent a quick text message to Beth letting her know all was well before walking out the door toward the barn. Feeling like whistling, he refrained, afraid it would bring Baby running his direction and he wasn't sure he wanted to get too friendly with the dog yet.

It was too bad Baby had other ideas.

Not wanting to oversleep his first day on the job, Ty set his alarm for five and was up, showered and dressed long before breakfast was ready. He liked the men that worked on the Rockin' R.

The four other residents of the house comprised the crew of the Rockin' R Ranch. Two brothers in their mid-twenties, Cal and Keith Harvey, were identical twins except one had a mole on his right cheek. An older man named Gus Anders, and a young kid Swede introduced as Jimmy Clarkson rounded out the interesting bunch. They were a friendly lot without being nosy and Ty appreciated that fact. He liked his own space and after almost a year of being unemployed, he had gotten used to being alone and not having anyone to talk to.

Jimmy made a warm and filling breakfast, even if it wasn't all that flavorful. Ty followed the foreman out the door after they all put their dirty dishes in the sink. Swede gave each man his orders and they all seemed to know what to do.

Turning on the lights in the big shop, Ty marveled again at the well-equipped building. Fit with a variety of quality tools, the shop featured two large work bays; big enough he could have parked two semi-trucks side by side and still had ample room.

Plenty of counter space, a large work bench with two stools, a big sink for washing parts and a bathroom along with a microwave and fridge made it Ty's idea of a perfect set up. Big windows on each side of the shop would let in plenty of light, although this early in the morning, he needed the overhead lights on to see.

From what Swede said, Lex Sr. had performed all the mechanic work for the farm. When he "took sick" he tried to keep up, but was unable half-way through the season. Evidently, the crew barely limped through their final harvest and nearly all the equipment needed repaired and back up in working order before the spring farm work started. Swede said they were down to one running tractor although it appeared there were three of them parked outside. Most of the machines were completely unfamiliar to him, but he realized he'd know each one intimately before he was through with the repairs.

Going to a filing cabinet, he found just what he was looking for - owner's manuals for several pieces of equipment. Some of the collection looked like they'd been around a while, but others were less than ten years old.

Thinking about the cost of some of the pieces, Ty decided the Rockin' R Ranch must turn a good profit to be able to afford not only the equipment but also the hired help and building maintenance.

He was shocked to find out he would be paid $1,500 a month in addition to his room and board.

Ty wondered if Lex Jr. was really hard to work for and had a difficult time keeping employees or was just plain crazy. Either way, he planned to make the most of this deal and send all the money he could to Beth and Nate.

He should be able to save quite a bit in a short time since it didn't appear there was much to spend his money on out here in the middle of nowhere, especially since the only bills he was going to have were his cell phone bill, fuel and insurance for his truck and any personal groceries he wanted to keep in the shop. Thankfully, his truck was paid off before he lost his job or who knew what kind of vehicle he would have been forced to drive.

His mom taught him early on to save money, pay cash when possible, and not rack up debt. Although he'd been tempted many times in the last several months to live off his credit card, he resisted and now he was glad. Envisioning all the things he could help buy for Beth and the baby, he smiled as he sat down on a stool at the bench and started reading about the tractors sitting outside.

He learned quickly no radio stations got reception in the shop and made a mental note to grab the speakers for his phone when he took a lunch break. The shop was too quiet without a little noise.

When Swede popped in at half-past nine, Ty decided he was ready to tackle whatever needed worked on first. Swede opened the big bay doors and drove in a huge tractor, gave Ty a pat on the back, and wished him luck.

"The one thing I never learnt was mechanic stuff," Swede said. "The other boys barely know which end of a screwdriver to use, so yer on yer own. Don't forget to take an hour break at lunch. I'll check on ya in a bit and let ya know when the boss is back."

Ty soon figured out what was wrong with the tractor and started working his way into the problem. Although he had never actually fixed a tractor, his varied experience with all different sorts of projects gave him a solid working knowledge. With the help of the owner's manual, it didn't take him long to find the problem or figure out what was needed to complete the repair job.

Making a thorough inspection of the shop, he realized there weren't any parts on hand and wondered how they went about getting what they would need. Looking at his watch, he realized it was nearly noon, so he shut off the lights, closed the door and walked in the direction of the corral by the barn where a pickup and horse trailer were parked and all the hands were standing together.

Walking behind the gathered group watching a horse run around the corral, he counted cowboy hats and realized there was an extra one in the bunch. If this was the boss, he was kind of slender and small-built for a rancher. Ty guessed him to be close to six feet tall with the boots and hat, but his shoulders looked narrow and the big chore coat he had on hung loosely on his frame.

"Thet's a fine lookin' stud ya brung home, boss. The mares are gonna be puttin' on quite a show for him," Swede said of the horse Lex had gone to Nevada to purchase. Turning to say something to one of the hands, Swede noticed Ty standing behind the group and motioned him forward. "Ty, come meet the boss."

Ty took a step forward as the boss turned around and greeted him with a dazzling smile that made his heart jump to his throat. Even with the hat on her head, swallowed up in the oversized coat, Ty quickly noticed the boss was a very beautiful woman with green eyes, smooth skin and rosy lips.

Sucking down his surprise, he stuck out his hand, "Nice to meet you. I'm Ty. Ty Lewis."

"We're so glad to have you here, Ty. I hope everyone made you feel at home," Lexi Ryan said as she shook the warm, strong hand of her newest employee. She should have asked for a photo along with that resume. She might not have hired the man if she'd known he was going to be so good-looking.

Ironically, the comments Swede just voiced about the stallion she brought home could definitely apply to the man standing in front of her. No doubt the first trip he made into town would result in every single female for a fifty-mile radius finding some excuse to come out to the Rockin' R Ranch to fawn over him. As it was, she was finding it hard to think of anything except the big, gorgeous man holding her hand captive with his.

Ty forced himself to let go of the soft hand with the long fingers that was sending sparks of electricity shooting up his arm.

"Thank you for hiring me," he said, trying not to stare at the person Swede referred to as Lex Jr. What a ridiculous name for a woman, especially one with such an attractive face. Other than her being tall, there wasn't much else he could surmise about her shape beneath the big coat.

"Are you settling in okay? Do you need anything?" Lexi asked, trying not to be too obvious in her perusal of their new mechanic. She thought she could stare at his eyes for hours and never get tired of looking at that unusual shade of blue. They made her think of a deep summer sky on a still afternoon. Brilliant, clear, and definitely warm.

"I'm fine, but I am going to need some parts. How do we go about getting those?" Ty asked, bracing himself as Baby spied him and came racing his direction. The dog slid to a stop before she plowed him over and raised her muddy paws to his chest, giving his chin a thorough licking before Swede and Lexi got her down and scolded her for her behavior.

"Baby, that is not okay. Don't jump on Ty. Naughty girl," Lexi said, holding the dog's big face in her hands and talking to her.

To Ty's amazement, the dog looked properly scolded and hung her head. Feeling bad for the dog, Ty reached over and pat her on the head, giving her ears a good scratch, perking her right up. She scooted over and leaned against him, whining.

Lexi looked at Swede with a raised eyebrow but didn't say anything. The dog was part of the reason they lost the last two mechanics she hired. In addition to not liking the isolated location of the ranch, they both were terrified of the dog. Neither of them lasted more than a few days before they packed up and left. It appeared Ty made more headway this morning than either of them had together because he was actually asking about parts. The other two never made it past inspecting the shop. True, it was hard to work with a hundred-pound dog growling at your every move, but she thought over the course of a few days they would have made some progress.

"You can give me a list and I'll run into town or you can go into Burns, whatever you prefer," Lexi said, waiting for Ty's response, trying to draw her gaze from his full lips and scruffy but solid jaw line. She put her hands in her coat pockets to keep from giving in to her sudden and completely irrational desire to run her fingers through the mechanic's thick, wavy hair.

"If you don't mind, I'd like to get the parts myself. That way I can meet the people there and if I need to phone in parts another time or have questions, they'll know who I am," Ty said, struggling to keep his attention on the conversation and not on his new employer's glowing green eyes or kissable lips. She had the most amazing cheek bones he'd ever seen up close and marveled at how beautiful she looked, even in an oversized chore coat and cowboy hat.

"Swede can give you directions. Now, if you boys will excuse me, I've got some paperwork I need to take care of," Lexi said, walking briskly toward the house, feeling six pairs of eyes watching her leave. One in particular made her neck feel hot as she went through the back gate of the yard and in the kitchen door.

"I guess I'll run in and get those parts, Swede, if you tell me where I need to go," Ty said, trying to bring his focus back to work after watching Lexi walk away. She had just enough sway in her walk to make him wish that coat didn't cover her quite so completely.

Ten months had passed since his last date. Being unemployed and homeless certainly dampened his interest in women. It was hard to think about having a good time when basic survival seemed much more important.

As his hand still tingled from Lexi's touch, he felt an attraction to his boss that he'd never felt for another woman. Ty needed this job too badly to mess it up, including getting any thoughts about Lex Jr. that were anything except professional. Sighing, he ran his hand through his hair.

"I'll jes go along with ya, Ty. We can grab some lunch in town and I'll show ya around. Ya might want to change before we go, though," Swede said, pointing to the two massive muddy paw prints down the front of his hooded sweatshirt.

Hurrying into the bunkhouse, Ty removed the dirty sweatshirt, washed his hands, combed his hair and put on his coat before hustling back outside. Swede was waiting in the pickup that had been hooked up to the horse trailer. The trailer was now parked in a big open shed near the barn. A large Rockin' R brand emblazoned the driver and front passenger doors of the truck.

Ty climbed in the passenger side and shook his head at Swede, making the foreman cackle.

"You could have warned me Lex Jr. wasn't a man," Ty said as they started down the gravel road. "I thought you said it was all guys out here on the ranch."

"I could have," Swede said between chuckles. "But thet would have spoilt half my fun. Sides, we all think of the boss as one of the guys."

"So what's the story with Lex Jr.?" Ty asked. He figured by the time they reached Burns, he wouldn't feel at such a disadvantage about his new employer. No one ever said Lex was a man, Ty just assumed. Last time he would make that mistake.

"The boss is named after her daddy. His mama was from Kentucky and named him Lexington, for her hometown. Lexington Joseph Ryan was his given name. Everyone called him Lex. When he up and married one of the prettiest lil' gals to ever be born, they wanted a baby somethin' fierce. They tried and tried, looked into adoptin' and finally jes gave up. That's when they found out Lex Jr. was on the way. Good-goshen, that was back a few years. Almost thirty years ago. Anyhow, Lex jes knew thet baby was going to be a boy and had the rest of his life all planned out. Little League, football games, college sports, then takin' over the ranch. Ol' Lex was left spitless when the doc told him it was a girl-baby."

Swede took a deep breath and went on. "They named thet baby gal Lexi Jo, and everyone called her Lex, jes like her daddy. When there weren't more babies, people added on the junior, knowin' she was as close to a boy as ol' Lex was gonna get. He taught her everythin' he knew about ranchin' while her mama tried to teach her how to be a lady. Her mama died when she was seventeen from kidney disease while waiting for a transplant. It was a sad, sad thing to see. Lex Jr. got it in her head she was done with ranchin'. Quick as she finished high school, she skedaddled off to Portland, put herself through college and managed investments for a bunch of snooty rich folks. When her daddy got sick last year with the brain cancer, she come home thinkin' he'd get well. But he didn't. Thet is not a good way to die, my friend. Not a good way at all."

"I'm so sorry," Ty said quietly. He couldn't imagine how awful it would be to have your brain slowly consumed by disease.

"Lex Jr. promised her daddy she'd keep the ranch runnin' so she went back to Portland, packed up her stuff, left her fancy job and come home to the Rockin' R permanently. She's been tryin' to git things straightened out since November. Her daddy's head was off longer than any of us realized and the ranch books are a mess, along with a lot of other things. She'd have the dealers work on the equipment, but she decided in the long run it would be less expensive fer us to hire a mechanic and have one on hand should somethin' break down instead of being at the mercy of the someone else's schedule. Her daddy was a fine, fine mechanic but never took the time to teach Lex or any of the rest of us. So we're mighty glad ya come when ya did. We got about six weeks before everythin' needs to be up and runnin'."

Ty absorbed this information. He admired Lexi for leaving her life in Portland to keep a promise to her father. It showed she was a person of honor and loyalty.

He also realized he was really going to have his work cut out for him if he had to get everything up and going in little more than a month's time. If he was familiar with the equipment, that would be one thing, but this was going to be trial and error as he went. Tractors, swathers, combines, balers and all the other farm equipment he'd discovered manuals for this morning were foreign to him.

"I'll do my best to make that happen," Ty said, wondering for the fiftieth time that day how he'd get all the work done. Maybe things weren't in that bad of shape. The tractor he was working on now looked to be a fairly simple fix. Maybe the rest of the equipment would be as easy to repair.

"I know ya will, son. I know ya will," Swede said. "Now, did Lex tell ya about yer other duties?"

"Other duties?" Ty asked. He was under the impression mechanic work was his full-time responsibility.

"Well, sure. When nothin's broke, she expects ya to help with whatever else needs done like ridin' herd or helpin' hay, thet kind of thing."

"Okay," Ty said, wondering what riding herd and haying entailed. He was fairly certain it was going to be way out of his comfort zone.

"Ya'll take to it like a duck to water. I'd bet on it," Swede said as he pulled in at the John Deere dealership in Burns. Going inside, Swede pointed out the parts counter, where he introduced Ty to the parts manager and let them know Ty could charge anything he needed to the Rockin' R account. After discussing the tractor and what he thought was wrong with it, the manager put together the necessary parts and gave them to Ty.

"You can always call and see if we're out that direction to save a trip into town," the manager said as Ty thanked him for his help.

"Thank you. Nice to meet you," Ty said as they turned to walk out the door. After loading the parts, they drove through town.

"How about we find some lunch?" Swede asked, pulling up at a building that appeared only marginally better than condemned.

Ty wisely kept that thought to himself and followed Swede inside. Although it looked somewhat less dilapidated inside than out, the food was delicious and Ty ate his fill, followed by a large piece of berry pie. Ready to pay for his share, Swede smiled and told him lunch was on the ranch.

Driving through town on their way home, Swede pointed out the store where they purchased clothes, tack, Baby's dog food, and an assortment of other things that Ty had never heard of.

As they left Burns and passed through Hines, heading back into the sagebrush covered landscape, Ty asked more questions about Lex, the ranch and his duties. He answered a few questions Swede asked. By the time they got back to the ranch, Ty was feeling more at ease with the foreman and more confident that he could handle the job.

"If ya need anything, jes come down to the barn. Me or one of the boys will be down there. We're headin' into calvin' season so we got to keep an eye on the lil' mamas," Swede said as he walked out the door.

Ty buried himself in his work and before he realized it, Swede was hollering in the door that it was nearly supper time.

Glancing at the big clock on the wall, Ty had been steady at work for several hours. With a few more, he hoped to have the tractor repairs complete. He planned to return to his work after dinner and see if he could finish up.

After a pleasant meal with Swede and the crew, he called Beth and gave her a brief run-down of the job and assured her everything was going fine. He made her laugh as he related meeting Lex and how it took him by surprise to realize his boss was actually a woman. Although everyone called her Lex or Lex Jr., Ty had no intention of calling her anything but Lexi. It was a shame to call a woman that beautiful by anything other than a name just as lovely.

Hanging up with Beth, he walked back toward the shop, noticing how much colder it was out now than it was when he came in for dinner. Carrying along the speakers for his phone, he gratefully returned to the shop where it was warm and peaceful.

Choosing Poison from his downloaded tunes, he turned the music loud enough to keep him revved up but not loud enough to blast anyone walking by.

He was washing up at the parts sink when the shop door opened and Lexi stuck her head inside.

"Oh, I didn't realize you were in here," she said, stepping in and closing the door. "I saw the light on and thought maybe someone forgot to turn it off. You don't have to put in such long hours, especially on your first day."

Ty was trying to remember how to speak. Lexi's hair was a rich, raven black and hung down her back in a long braid. Although she still wore the bulky coat, she literally took his breath away.

"I... uh, just wanted to finish what I was working on. I'm heading in now," Ty said, walking across the shop, turning off lights and taking his phone off the speakers as he went.

"You a big hair band fan?" Lexi asked as she turned off the overhead lights and closed the door behind her.

Ty looked down at her in the moonlight and the desire to kiss her swept over him. He was losing his mind out here in no-man's land. "Yeah, I grew up listening to eighties music. Makes me think of my mom."

Lexi laughed. "My dad listened to Aerosmith right along with George Jones."

"Sounds like you had an interesting musical upbringing." Ty smiled as he walked her to the house, not even realizing where they were going. She stopped when they got to the picket fence.

"Thanks again for coming out to the Rockin' R Ranch. Swede thinks you're the best thing since sliced bread," Lexi said with a grin before turning and walking up the steps and into the house.

Ty watched her go before strolling toward the bunkhouse. He really needed to get his head on straight before he found himself in trouble. Big trouble with beautiful green eyes, rosy red lips, and even white teeth that glowed in the moonlight.

Lexi leaned against the door as she closed it, trying to get her pounding heart to slow down and her breathing to return to some degree of normalcy.

Swede didn't warn her about the new mechanic, darn him. He seemed to think it was funny when she turned around and swallowed her gum to see Ty standing there looking all brooding, dark, and hunky.

Assuming he would be on the thin side from being homeless, Ty managed to have plenty of bulky muscle. Or at least she assumed it would be impressively bulging muscle that filled out his sweatshirt so well. Thinking how she had to tip back her head to look in his face, she decided he had to be around six-four or so, because she was nearly six-feet tall when she had her boots on.

His hair was a little too long, but it fell in finger-tempting waves of brown tipped with sun-bleached highlights. It looked too natural to be from a salon and a man who had been unemployed as long as he had, not to mention as virile as he appeared, wouldn't be getting his hair highlighted anyway.

His lips were full and tempting, his chin strong and solid, and those eyes, those beautiful blue eyes, seemed to bore right into her soul.

It had been way too long since she had a date. That had to be the reason her heart tripped at the sound of his deep voice and sparks shot up her arm when they shook hands this morning.

With a haircut and a shave, the man would be positively gorgeous. As it was, his longer hair and scruffy stubble made him look mysterious and dangerous.

Way more dangerous than a girl who obviously needed to get out more could handle. Thoughts of running her fingers through that wavy hair or seeing if those full lips would be as warm as they looked made Lexi shake her head at her wayward thoughts.

Walking into the kitchen, Lexi was greeted by Baby sitting near the fridge, wagging her tail. The dog somehow managed to open doors if they weren't locked and could be found just about anywhere on the place at any given time. Good thing she was well behaved or they could have a problem.

"Baby, what are you doing in here? You know the rules about being inside," Lexi said as she rubbed the dog's head, earning a slobbery lick to her hand. "I can't believe you like our new mechanic. Other than Swede and Dad, you just tolerate everyone else. What is up with that, Baby?"

The dog barked once then gave Lexi a look she was sure was a canine smile. She'd have to keep her eye on that dog.

Escorting Baby out the back door, she locked up the house and went to the office where she continued sorting through the mess her dad made of the ranch books during the year he was ill. Instead of focusing on the entries in the ranch journal, her mind wandered to a tall broad-shouldered mechanic who listened to rock music from the eighties.

Lesson Three
Learn the Native Tongue

*"If yer gonna buckaroo at this here spread,
ya got to learn the lingo."*

"I'm not kidding, sis," Ty said as his sister laughed from the other end of the phone line.

"You've got to be teasing, Ty, because nothing that ridiculous can be true," Beth said, trying to contain her laughter. She was thrilled Ty called on his day off so they could have a nice chat. Nate was trying to reconfigure their sparse furnishings to find room for a crib since the baby was due to arrive in just three weeks.

"I'm dead-honest serious, Beth," Ty said, feeling like he'd fallen down the rabbit hole into Wonderland. Except this one was full of foul smells, dirty animals, and a language he was trying very hard to understand. "I called Jimmy dude the other day and he threatened to punch me. I didn't know dude was a term they use to refer to people like me who grew up in civilization and prefer not to walk around with animal waste covering their clothes. You wouldn't believe all the odd ways they have of talking. I feel like I need one of those 'Idiot's Guidebooks' to figure out what they are saying."

"It can't be that bad," Beth said, trying to stop laughing. She could tell Ty was truly struggling to adjust to his new environment. "You're smart, you can figure this out."

"I could if there was any reason or rhyme to what they say. Like the other day I was at the gas station and someone said 'nice outfit,' so I looked down at my jeans and sweatshirt and said 'thanks.' The guy gave me a disgusted look and pointed to my pickup and said, 'no, your outfit.' Swede said they call pickups outfits. Apparently mine falls in the nice category."

Ty sighed when Beth launched into another round of giggles. "You wouldn't believe the way they blend words together either. Instead of 'you,' it's 'ya,' and 'you are' is 'yer.' Anything that ends in 'ing' automatically gets shortened by a letter like 'running' is 'runnin'.' You'll love this, too," Ty said, changing his voice to a twang. "I'm fixin' to learn ya up in how to speak our lingo, pard."

Beth was laughing so hard Ty could hear her gasping on the other end of the phone.

"Ty, you've got to stop. I can't breathe. Stop, stop, stop," she begged before he could further educate her on the language of his new home.

"Other than the language barrier, how is everything else going?" Beth asked, reading between the lines, knowing that Ty was homesick, but also enjoying his work.

"Good. I've learned a lot this week about big equipment repairs. The crew at the John Deere dealership has been really helpful when I've called with questions," Ty said, thinking about all he accomplished in the week and a half he had been at the ranch.

Since Sunday was his day off, he took a drive in his pickup and parked on the side of the road so he could talk to Beth without being interrupted by anyone or anything.

Baby, that overgrown lap dog, had adopted him as her own personal human and followed Ty everywhere. She decided the shop was her new domain and spent hours hanging out with him there. He wouldn't admit it to anyone, but he enjoyed her company, as long as she kept the slobbers to a minimum.

As Ty sat talking to Beth he watched Lexi drive by in a pickup Swede said was her dad's and waved. She wore her hair down and he almost didn't recognize her. He'd seen her drive the pickup before and since he was sitting at the end of the ranch road where it connected with the county road, he knew it was her. She smiled as she drove past him, heading toward the ranch.

Seeing all that hair around her face, he could hardly concentrate on what his sister was saying.

"Are you listening to me?" Beth finally asked with an indulgent smile in her voice.

"Yes, I am, but I better run. Call me if there is anything I can do for you," Ty said. As soon as he received his first paycheck next week, he would send a good portion of his wages to Beth.

"I will, Ty. Be safe and have fun learnin' the ropes," Beth teased before she hung up. "Love you."

"Love you, too." Ty disconnected and turned the pickup around, deciding to go back to the ranch. He really didn't have anything to do and the thought of driving around aimlessly wasting gas really didn't hold much appeal.

Going back to the ranch, he parked his truck and went into the bunkhouse. Everyone else was gone and the place seemed quiet, too quiet. He needed something to distract him from thoughts of his lovely boss and all that glorious black hair. Changing into work clothes, he went to the shop, turned up his music and worked on the engine he'd pulled out of a tractor on Friday.

Although the first tractor he fixed was simple, this one was proving to be a much bigger challenge. If he only had a computer in the shop, he could compare photos of parts, do some online diagnostics and make much better time in getting things repaired.

As it was, he kept referring to the owner's manual and when he got really stuck he called the dealership with questions. They referred him to a website that was helpful, but he either had to use his phone or the computer in the bunkhouse to pull up the info and neither was very conducive to quickly accessing the information he needed.

With all the great equipment and tools in the shop he was hesitant to ask for anything although Lexi had inquired a few times if there was anything he needed. The next time she asked, he might suggest a laptop or netbook. They were pretty inexpensive.

Baby opened the door and came inside, greeting Ty with a friendly yip. He walked over and closed the door, patting her on the head and getting a slobbery lick on his neck.

"Are you staying out of trouble today, Baby?" he asked the dog while he worked. His answer was a wag of her giant tail.

"Is everyone else gone?"

Another tail wag.

"Is Lexi home? Did you tell her hello when she came back?"

The dog barked and turned around in a circle before settling onto an old blanket in a corner on the shop floor.

Lexi was surprised to see Ty sitting in his pickup on the road talking on his phone. From the brief instant she saw him, he looked happy. He didn't smile much and she couldn't help but think how good it looked on him.

She wondered if it was a girlfriend. That thought made her grasp the steering wheel so tightly her knuckles turned white.

This was ridiculous. Why should she care if he had a girlfriend in Portland? Or in Burns. Or a dozen between here and there.

She shouldn't care, but she did. Lexi cared far more than she wanted to admit.

Since her fiancé called off their wedding a year ago, men had been the last thing on her mind. Lexi decided when James dumped her because he couldn't bear the thought of being married to someone who had a "questionable lineage," it was for the best. How she ever convinced herself she loved someone as shallow and pompous as him, she didn't know. She realized now he was much more interested in how much the ranch was worth than he was about her.

The girl she was a year ago was so different than the woman she was now.

At twenty-nine, she owned a large successful ranch that she was determined to keep running smoothly or die trying.

The only real problem was that her dad had withdrawn funds from several of his investment accounts and she couldn't trace any record of what he had done with the money. Exactly $500,000 was unaccounted for and she really needed to find it.

The ranch was in no means hurting financially, but that was a lot of money to just disappear into thin air.

She spent hours poring over bank statements, record books, and files. As a financial planner, she handled all of her dad's investments personally. Or so she thought.

It came as a shock after his funeral to discover a paper trail leading to a series of investments she knew nothing about only to then find he made odd withdrawals from each for the total of half a million dollars.

Finding no paperwork that he invested the money elsewhere or any record of the funds in any of the ranch books, she wondered what he had done with it. Donated it?

Gambled it? Purchased something she had yet to find? Buried it?

Thinking about the possibilities only gave her a headache.

Going upstairs to her bedroom, Lexi changed out of her church dress and into jeans. She put on a tank top and a flannel work shirt then braided her hair.

The pastor at her church and his wife invited her to stay for lunch today and not wanting to go back to the quiet house on the ranch, she joined them and their boisterous children for a lively lunch at a local restaurant. She spoke with them about her need for a new housekeeper and they promised to help find some candidates for the job.

Afterward, she ran by the grocery store and picked up a few supplies before coming home. She was thinking about her new mechanic and what a good job he was doing when she happened to look up and see him sitting in his truck, as handsome as ever. The bright blue of his eyes and his alluring smile still lingered in her thoughts.

Making herself a cup of tea, she took it into the office and sat staring at entries in a ledger book for an hour before she gave up, put on her boots and coat, and wandered outside. Walking toward the barn, she decided to check on the cows Swede had penned up waiting to calve. He was worried they might require help calving and brought them in from the herd.

They ran fifteen hundred head of Hereford cattle, many of them registered. Producing enough hay to feed their own livestock, they also sold a substantial amount to increase their profits, along with wheat and barley.

Lexi's passion, however, was horses. She loved to ride them and train them. Her dad never liked the idea of getting into breeding horses, so he kept just enough working horses on the ranch to get the job done.

Now that he was gone, Lexi fully intended to start a breeding program with quarter horses. Despite bad roads and Swede's repeated warnings about her not going, she drove down to Reno last week so she could pick up a new stud horse to get started on her dreams for the ranch. As soon as she finished the spring farm work, found the missing money, and got the ranch back on track, she was ready to move forward with her plans.

Opening the barn door, she went stall by stall checking on the five cows inside. One first-year heifer was having some difficulty so Lexi stepped into the stall and assessed the situation. It looked like the poor heifer had been laboring for quite a while and not making any progress. The calf needed to be pulled and Lexi knew she didn't have the strength to do it on her own. Usually one or two of the guys were around, but everyone just happened to be gone today.

She remembered seeing Ty's pickup parked by the bunkhouse. Running outside and across the ranch yard to the bunkhouse, she knocked before stepping in the door and calling his name. When he didn't answer, she decided to go to the shop. Stopping at the door to catch her breath, she could hear his rock music playing and smiled. If she remembered her big hair bands correctly, he was listening to Whitesnake today.

Opening the door, she wasn't surprised to see Baby curled up in the corner asleep or Ty laboring over a tractor part. He looked up when she came in and smiled.

"Hi," he said, wiping his hands on a rag as she stepped in and shut the door. Turning off the music, he wondered what Lexi needed because she generally avoided him unless she had a direct question for him.

"Would you mind coming to the barn to help me with a cow? She's in distress and I need a little assistance," Lexi asked holding her hands tightly together in front of her. She was afraid if she left them hanging by her sides they would somehow find their way into Ty's wavy hair. Lexi didn't know what it was, exactly, about his bad-boy looks that drew her interest, but the attraction was there, just the same.

"Sure. I don't know a thing about the cows except not to stand too close behind them," Ty said as he held open the shop door for her, closing it behind him. If Baby wanted out, she'd open the door herself.

"You'll be standing behind her, and things could get a little..." Lexi searched for the right word. "Messy."

"As in, scrubbing manure off my pants messy or worse?" Ty asked. He absolutely loathed trying to get cow poop out of his clothes. He thought mechanics got dirty but he usually wore coveralls when he was working in the shop to protect his clothes. A little motor oil was nothing compared to the stench and staining ability of manure. He learned that lesson in a hurry, thanks to Jimmy initiating him to cow pies his second day on the job.

Jimmy had a cow in the chute by the barn and asked Ty to step up behind her and catch her tail before she got it caught in the fencing. Instructed to hold it up high out of the way, the cow unloaded on him, covering his jeans and boots in manure. Ty didn't even flinch, just held the tail until the cow was done. Jimmy, expecting Ty to come unglued at the mess, looked at him in surprise, nodded his head, and offered a simple word of thanks. Ty casually walked off until he was out of sight, then made a beeline for the bunkhouse where he took a shower, changed his clothes and thought he might have to toss his jeans rather than try to get them clean.

Walking beside Lexi, he reflected on the crash course he received in both ranching and practical jokes in the past week. He sincerely hoped her request for his help wasn't some way of tormenting him. He didn't think he could handle teasing from her, too.

Instead of answering Ty's question about how dirty he was going to get, Lexi smiled at him, causing him to trip as they went in the barn door. Catching himself on the door frame, he tried to keep focused on anything except his disturbingly attractive boss.

She really shouldn't fling her smile around like that. It could be hazardous to her hired help, especially the one who was finding himself completely infatuated with her.

Lexi asked Ty to take off his coat. She took a look at his hooded sweatshirt and made him take it off along with the thermal long-sleeved shirt he had on under it.

"How many layers have you got on? You do realize this isn't Antarctica," Lexi teased as Ty removed his clothes and laid them on a bench near the door.

"Portland is quite a bit warmer than it is here. I just haven't gotten used to the cold yet," Ty said, pulling his long sleeved shirt over his head and fighting the urge to shiver.

Lexi fought a few shivers of her own as Ty's T-shirt slid up his well-toned abs while he was taking off the thermal shirt. She looked at the floor until he had his shirt tugged back in place.

When he was down to just a short-sleeved T-shirt, Lexi made him scrub his hands at the barn sink and put on plastic gloves that reached almost to his shoulders.

He was fairly certain the gloves were a good sign he was going to hate whatever it was they were about to do.

Peeling off her own coat and outer layers down to a tank top she was wearing under her flannel shirt for warmth, Lexi washed her hands, pulled on gloves, smeared lubricant on the gloves and directed Ty to the stall where the painful moans of the heifer echoed off the walls.

"I would normally let Swede take care of this, but since he and the rest of the hands are gone, this little lady needs some help now and can't wait," Lexi said, stepping beside the frightened heifer where she labored on a bed of straw. "I'm going to stick my hands inside and see if the calf is heading the right direction. Depending on what I find, I may need you to help pull it. For now, if you can try to hold her still, that would be great. The goal is to keep her down and not kicking, preferably. Okay?"

"Okay," Ty said, scared not of the cow, but of Lexi getting hurt. Although she was tall and looked strong, she had a smaller frame and he didn't think it would take much effort on the cow's part to knock her down. "Does she have a name?" he asked as Lexi examined the heifer.

"What's on her ear tag?" Lexi asked as she stuck her arm in up to the elbow and determined the calf was not breech, just too big for the poor little heifer to have on her own.

"A number," Ty said, looking at the ear tag.

"That would be her name, unless you'd like to give her one," Lexi said, removing her arm from the cow and stepping out of the stall. She came back with a set of chains that made Ty's eyes widen uncertainly.

"What are those?" he asked, rubbing the cow's head with a calm he was far from feeling.

"Calving chains," Lexi said as she slipped them around the feet of the calf. "This is where I need your muscle. Come back here and help me pull."

Lexi instructed Ty on how to position himself. On the count of three, she told him to pull for all he was worth.

If she hadn't been so intently focused on pulling the calf, Lexi might have sat transfixed, watching Ty's muscles bunch and strain against the soft fabric of his T-shirt. His physique was more than a little impressive and a lot disruptive to her normal ability to block out everything except what needed her attention at the moment.

Ty was worried about hurting the calf and the cow as well as Lexi hurting herself with the strenuous pulling. Giving another strong tug, the baby slipped out. Lexi quickly cleaned out its nose and mouth, laughing when it bawled pitifully. The cow moaned as she finished her work then turned to look at her offspring.

"You did a fine job number fourteen-seventy-three," Lexi said pushing the baby toward the heifer's nose. The mama sniffed her newborn then started licking it and mooing softly.

Ty was on his knees in the straw, observing both the cow and baby. He'd never before witnessed a birth and the miraculous experience left him feeling a rush of strange emotions.

"Wow! That was just… Wow!" he said, watching the calf as it tried to stand on wobbly legs while the cow licked and nuzzled it.

"I've seen hundreds of babies born, but it's special every single time," Lexi said, wiping her teary eye on her shoulder. Cleaning the chains and returning them to their proper spot, she stripped off her gloves and washed up. Ty washed as well but hesitated to put his outwear back on over his now filthy shirt and jeans.

Lexi wasn't any cleaner and wondered if she could make it to the house without freezing dressed in her tank top and jeans. Just thinking about it made her shiver with cold.

Struggling against his desire to intently ogle Lexi's womanly shape normally hidden beneath coats or baggy flannel shirts, Ty reached out to her toned arms and rubbed his hands up and down their length, trying to bring her warmth.

The contact of his hands to her skin made his blood zing through his veins and caused a nearly irresistible urge to pull her into his arms and kiss her passionately.

Going from freezing to a feverish state in mere seconds, Lexi made the mistake of glancing up at Ty as his hands seared her flesh with their touch. Hot blue mirrors reflected the intense longing in her own and she wanted more than anything to get lost in Ty's strong embrace.

Before she gave in to the unreasonable voice in her head telling her to kiss Ty, she took a step back and picked up her coat and shirt.

"As a thank you for helping, would you like to have dinner with me?" Lexi asked walking toward the barn door. "I think I owe you for your help on your day off."

"You don't owe me," Ty said, as they stood at the door. Part of him wanted to have dinner alone with Lexi. The other part, the part with some sense, told him it would be a huge mistake.

"Yes I do. Big time. And I'd welcome the company," Lexi said, wanting Ty to say yes for reasons she was unwilling to explore. "I'll take a quick shower and have something on the table in say, an hour?"

"I really don't..." Ty began but was cut off by Lexi holding a hand up in front of him with a warm smile.

"I insist. Just come in the back door in an hour. I'll have dinner ready," she said, opening the barn door and sprinting toward the house.

Ty stood watching her go. Taking a deep breath, he walked to the bunkhouse, hoping the frigid air would cool him down so he wouldn't have to stand in a cold shower.

Taking off his filthy clothes with a disgusted sigh, he sprayed them thoroughly with stain remover and left them soaking in the washer while he tried to wash the smell of barnyard from his skin and visions of Lexi from his mind.

Ready long before the hour was up, Ty paced through the still-empty bunkhouse. He turned the washer on the rinse cycle, straightened his already neat room and attempted to watch a few minutes of television.

He hadn't been this anxious when he was fourteen asking Kaitlin Shaw to go to the big school dance. Grown men with plenty of experience dating women should not be nervously chewing their non-existent thumb-nail or feel like they swallowed a bucket of lead for a simple dinner with a pretty girl.

Only there wasn't anything simple about Lexi Jo Ryan or the feelings she stirred in him. Ty had never felt this powerful all-consuming attraction for a female before and didn't quite know what to do about it. He'd never lacked for female companionship, but this was something entirely different.

Glancing in his bedroom mirror, he ran his hand through his hair again, buttoned and unbuttoned his Henley shirt twice, then shrugged into a zip-up sweatshirt as he hurried out the door.

Giving a brief knock at the kitchen door, Ty stuck his head inside, not seeing Lexi anywhere. Something smelled delicious, so he hung his sweatshirt on the coat rack by the door and inhaled deeply as he wiped his boots on the door mat.

"Hello?" he called, noticing two plates sitting on the counter along with a green salad and water glasses.

"Hey, Ty, I'll be right there," Lexi called from upstairs.

Settling on her menu as she ran back to the house from the barn, Lexi was glad she'd picked up the house the previous evening. While meat thawed in the microwave, she took the fastest shower of her life, washed her hair and left it wet while she ran back downstairs in her bathrobe and started assembling the meal. While the meat and sauce simmered, she ran back upstairs dressing in jeans and a soft sweater, quickly blow-drying her hair. She applied a little mascara and a spritz of perfume, thinking she didn't look too bad for a hurried rancher.

Racing back downstairs, she finished up meal preparations then decided she didn't want Ty to think she was trying too hard to impress him, so she ran back to her bathroom and pulled her hair into a ponytail, changing into a faded sweatshirt. She definitely looked casual now.

Despite her good intentions, she couldn't stop from pinching her cheeks when she heard Ty come in downstairs.

Lightly treading down the stairs, she breezed into the kitchen and had to forcibly keep herself from staring at Ty. He looked way better than any man had a right to, especially with a scruffy growth of stubble and hair that needed cut. Never mind the way his shirt clung to his arm and chest muscles or the way his jeans outlined his long legs or how his blue eyes glowed with warmth. Lexi decided she would definitely ignore all that.

What she couldn't ignore was the mega-watt smile he sent her direction when she came into the room. It made her momentarily unable to even form a cohesive thought.

"Sure smells good in here," Ty finally said, breaking the awkward silence, leaning against the counter with his hands in his jeans pockets. "Anything I can do to help?"

"I've got everything ready," Lexi said scooping the contents of a saucepan into a serving bowl and fishing slices of warm, buttered bread from the oven. "I'll dish up the food if you don't mind filling the water glasses."

Ty filled the glasses from the dispenser in the fridge door and returned them to the counter. Lexi motioned him to a barstool and he waited for her to sit down before taking his seat. His mother managed to instill in him a few good manners.

Surprised when Lexi took his hand in hers, she asked a blessing on the meal then gave him a warm smile as she passed him a steaming bowl of something that looked like cornmeal.

"Its polenta," she said, waiting for him to take a serving. "You put the sauce over the top. I promise it won't kill you or give you food poisoning."

Ty grinned and took the bowl, giving himself a healthy portion. Even if he hated it, he would eat every bite if it meant she might smile at him again.

She spooned sauce over her polenta and he followed her lead when she sprinkled freshly grated parmesan on top. A crisp green salad and the warm bread were the perfect complements to the delicious meal.

Unable to stop the moan of appreciation from escaping his lips as the flavors exploded on his tongue, Ty tried to keep from eating like a ravenous wolf.

Lexi grinned.

"I take it you like it?" she asked with a raised eyebrow, obviously pleased at her efforts and his response.

"What is it?" Ty asked as he took a bite of the bread before returning his attention to the entrée.

"Polenta Alla Romana. The sauce is made from chicken and sausage, chicken broth, herbs, and pasta sauce. Have you had polenta before?"

"Not that I know of," Ty said, taking another bite of the dish, savoring the taste. "But the texture reminds me of grits."

"Similar," Lexi said. She liked to cook when she had time and missed some of the 'fancier' foods she used to enjoy in Portland. Here on the ranch, she rarely took time to cook for herself. She relied mostly on salads, sandwiches, and bowls of cold cereal to stave off her hunger, unless she ate with the hands. She tried not to do that too often since they felt compelled to be on their best behavior and not relax when she ate with them.

"So it's Italian?" Ty asked, finishing his salad.

"Yes, it is."

"Do you have an Italian heritage?" Ty asked, wondering if an Italian ancestor was where Lexi inherited her dark hair and bronzed skin-tone.

"No. My Dad's family comes from good ol' English and Irish stock," Lexi said, hesitant to share the next piece of her family history. Although it was ridiculous, some people were still mired in their biased opinions and she didn't want to see a look of prejudice cross Ty's handsome face when he learned about her ancestry.

Taking a breath, she plunged bravely ahead. "My Mom was Indian, Paiute actually. My grandmother grew up on the reservation north of Burns. She took a waitressing job in town when she was nineteen. That's how my grandfather met her and declared it was love at first sight. They married two weeks later and had a happy life together."

"That's a great story," Ty said, studying Lexi so intently she felt like squirming although she sat perfectly still. "Do you look like your grandmother?"

"Some people say I do," she said, stirring the food around on her plate.

"That must be where you get that beautiful hair and amazing cheekbones," Ty said, wishing he could snatch the words back as soon as they left his mouth. There was something about Lexi that loosened his tongue and made him want to talk with her. He could see pink creeping into her cheeks and was pleased his words had her flustered.

Lexi snapped her head his direction and started to say something then closed her mouth quickly. She could see from the look on his face that he wasn't teasing, just saying what was on his mind.

"Thanks," she said quietly, trying to regain her composure after Ty's unexpected compliment. "If you'd like, I'll show you a painting of her after dinner."

"I'd like that," Ty said, taking another helping of the polenta. "Is she still alive?"

"Yeah, she is. She and Grandpa retired to Florida years ago and she decided to stay down there when he passed away. Grandma said the winters there are much more to her liking than the bitter cold of Harney County."

"Smart woman," Ty said with a teasing grin. He was still trying to adjust to the change in climate from Portland.

It was hard to think how much the landscape and temperature could vary in just a few hundred miles.

"She is at that," Lexi said with a smile as her appetite returned. She was quite pleased at Ty's reaction to her heritage. After James dumped her when he found out she was a part Paiute, she was hesitant to share that information with anyone. Ty seemed to accept it like he would if she said she was part German or French. In this day and age it shouldn't make any difference at all, but to some people it apparently still did. She was very glad Ty wasn't one of them.

Sitting next to him at the counter, heat seared her skin every time their arms brushed while they ate. She wondered what would happen if they kissed. Would he completely melt her lips?

Corralling her wayward thoughts, she finished her dinner, asking Ty questions about his life in Portland, discussing places they both had eaten and visited.

Ty helped her clean up the dishes while taking in the big, spacious kitchen that had obviously been updated recently. The dining area behind it was large and airy. He wondered what the rest of the house looked like. From what he could see, it was homey and inviting.

"That was a fantastic meal. Thank you for inviting me to dinner," he said, grateful for the good food and the chance to spend some time with Lexi.

"You're welcome. I don't cook much unless I have a reason to," Lexi said, wiping off the stove. "And I'm sorry you boys have to split cooking duties. My next project is to hire another housekeeper who can cook."

"You said another housekeeper. Did you used to have one?" Ty asked, curious.

"Yes, we did, but during his illness Dad ran off the last one," Lexi said, not wanting to think about all the crazy things her father did in his last few months before he was completely bed ridden. "It's hard to find someone who wants to live all the way out here and get up early to make sure you guys are fed at the crack of dawn."

"That could be a problem."

Drying the last dish, Ty handed it to Lexi to put away. She looked at him thoughtfully.

"Are you adjusting okay? Do the wide open spaces bother you too much? Or the lack of civilization?"

"Honestly, I like the quiet peacefulness of being out here. As far as civilization, I think the cattle and Baby are much better behaved than a lot of supposedly civilized people I know. I can't say that I miss the noise and traffic, although I'm still getting used to the smells."

Lexi laughed. "It does take some getting used to. I'll grant you that," she said.

Hanging the dish towel up to dry, she swept her hand toward the hall. "Want to see the rest of the house?"

"Sure," Ty said, following her down a hall past what she called the sitting room and the music room to a formal living room filled with antique furniture.

"No one ever uses this room. Although it's nice to look at, the furniture was made for much smaller bodies that weren't used to overstuffed chairs," Lexi said, directing him to follow her up an impressive mahogany staircase in the front foyer to the second floor. He lingered back just far enough to get an appreciative eyeful of her jean-clad posterior as it went up the stairs.

So intently focused on the vision before him, he almost missed the last step and grasped the banister to keep from falling. She turned and grinned at him further distracting him.

"There used to be six bedrooms up here and another sitting area. Can you imagine? Anyway, Mom and Dad converted all that into four bedrooms, each with a private bath."

"Very nice," Ty said, admiring the large master suite with its balcony and high ceilings, along with the beautifully carved four-poster king-sized bed. A vision of Lexi in that bed with her silky raven hair fanning across the pillow forced him to step out of the room and wander down the hall, trying to keep focused on the architecture of the house and not his tour guide.

She took him down a narrow set of stairs at the back of the hallway. When they reached the bottom, she turned down a short hall into the room she referred to as the office. One wall was filled with a bookcase holding books, memorabilia, and family photos. A big rock fireplace, when lit, would no doubt fill the room with warmth. A massive desk with two chairs in front of it took up space across from the fireplace while wooden filing cabinets sat against the wall behind the desk.

Ty stepped into the room and admired the woodwork. He noticed the outside entrance to the room. That was handy for ranching purposes. Two big windows allowed Lexi to see across the ranch yard toward the barn and keep an eye on things while she worked at the desk.

Retracing their steps down the hallway, past the back stairs, they entered a room that was fully modernized with a big screen television, leather couches and comfy chairs. A fire crackled merrily in the gas fireplace and Ty went to stand in front of it, warming his hands. It was then he noticed the painting hanging above the mantle. It looked exactly like Lexi; only instead of green eyes the woman had big brown eyes.

"This must be your grandmother," he said, turning to smile at Lexi. She stepped beside him and grinned.

"How did you guess?"

"There's just the slightest family resemblance," he said, amazed at how much she looked like the woman in the painting. "What's her name?"

"Sunny," Lexi said, thinking how well the name suited her grandmother. She was a bubbly, happy person who never let anything get her down for long.

"I can see in her eyes and smile that the name suits her," Ty observed, surprised to hear himself voice his thoughts. He generally wasn't one to share what he was thinking, but Lexi seemed to have that effect on him.

Lexi, who was thrilled by Ty's reaction to her grandmother, couldn't stop smiling at him. "It does suit her. She's a beautiful person."

"Rather like her granddaughter," Ty said, again surprised his thoughts tumbled out his lips. Keeping his focus on the painting, Ty tried to think of a tactful way to run off to the bunkhouse before he said anything else he shouldn't.

Searching for an excuse to leave, Lexi took his hand and pulled him over to a couch before he could come up with a good reason. Sinking down onto the soft leather, she sat on one end while he occupied the other. She asked him questions about his family, growing up in Portland, and how he was adjusting to living out in the wilds of Harney County.

"Are you sure you have everything you need at the shop? If there is something that would help you do your work better or easier, just let me know," Lexi offered again. Her Dad had just about every tool known to man, but things upgraded and changed so quickly, she wanted to be sure Ty had what he needed to do his job efficiently.

"If I'm way out of line, just say so, but it would sure help to have a computer in the shop. The owner's manuals work okay, but I could move the repairs along a lot faster if I had access to some websites that list parts and have updated information. I've been trying to either use my phone or the computer in the bunkhouse, but it has been a little cumbersome. I just thought I'd mention it, since you asked."

"Why didn't you say something sooner?" Lexi asked, thinking she should have thought of that herself. Goodness only knew how much time she spent doing research online and never even thought that Ty might need to be looking up information, especially on some of the older equipment pieces. "I've seen you running back and forth to the bunkhouse with parts and wondered what you were doing. If you think of something that will help you get your work done faster and better, don't be afraid to speak up. Deal?"

"Deal," Ty said. "I just don't want you to get the idea I'm not grateful. I appreciate you giving me this opportunity more than you can know. I never dreamed the shop would be so well-equipped or I'd have such a nice place to live. Thank you for giving me a chance."

"You're very welcome and I appreciate you being willing to move out here and give the Rockin' R a chance. Are the guys treating you okay?" Lexi asked, knowing Jimmy was bad about playing jokes.

"Yeah, they made me feel right at home," Ty said, thinking how even the few pranks they'd played were meant in fun and ended up making him feel like part of the crew. "I'm having a tough time picking up the language, though."

"The language?" Lexi asked, with an idea of what was challenging Ty. Swede could lay on the cowboy lingo so thick she sometimes had to think hard to know what he was saying.

"You know, the way a lot of people talk out here," Ty said, not wanting to elaborate and offend Lexi, although she spoke without a hint of the twang he'd noticed all the guys on the ranch having as well as a few of the people he'd encountered in town.

"They use a different language?" Lexi asked. Keeping a straight face, she decided to have a little fun at Ty's expense.

"Sure. Like instead of washing anything, they worsh it. There is no running or talking, it is runnin' and talkin'," Ty explained. "You mean you don't notice it?"

"Notice what?" Lexi asked, playing dumb. "What else do you notice?"

"That a rig is not my truck, an outfit has nothing to do with what you are wearing and you only call someone dude around here if you want to get your nose busted," Ty said with an exasperated look.

"The guys are 'learnin' ya up' are they?" Lexi teased in her best imitation of Swede and burst out laughing.

Ty gave her a narrowed glare which made her laugh harder. When she could talk without giggling, she released a sigh.

"I know what you mean. When I moved back from Portland, every time I heard someone drop the 'g' from the end of a word it made me cringe. I guess I got used to it again. When I first moved away, the kids at college made fun of me and wanted to know what part of the south I came from with my funny twang. It didn't take long for me to never say the word wash and to learn to speak so people wouldn't think I was a redneck."

Ty looked at her, realizing how hard it would be for a girl who grew up in such a tiny little community to move to Portland on her own. He bet learning to overcome some language issues was the least of her worries.

"I'll let you in on a little secret, though," Lexi said, leaning near him and dropping her voice.

"What's that?" Ty asked, leaning close enough he could see golden flecks swimming in her mossy green eyes.

"As much as I tried to get it to go away, my neck is always going to be just a little bit red," Lexi said with a grin.

"Are you sure?" Ty asked, scooting closer to her, keeping a serious look on his face. "Maybe I better look and see."

Lexi turned around and held her ponytail up, exposing the flawless expanse of her long neck. "Look close, I'll bet you see some red."

"Nope, I don't see a thing," Ty said, edging closer. He could smell Lexi's enticing scent and breathed deeply. "Oh, wait, right there it is."

Refusing to think about what he was doing, Ty leaned over and pressed a warm kiss to her skin, watching red flush up her neck.

Lexi dropped her ponytail and spun around, unable to think let alone speak. Shivers of pure delight raced through her and she shoved her hands under her legs to keep from burying them into the tempting waves of Ty's hair.

"You, Mr. Lewis, are a tease," she finally said, trying to keep the conversation light.

"Guilty as charged," Ty said, deciding he better leave before he did something to get himself fired.

After all, he'd not even been on the ranch two full weeks and here he was flirting shamelessly with the boss. What was wrong with him? Getting to his feet, he held out a hand to Lexi. She took it reluctantly and walked him through a doorway back to the kitchen, stopping at the door.

"Thank you for the meal," Ty said, not wanting to leave. "It was one of the best I've had in a very long time."

"You're welcome. Thanks for keeping me company. The house gets kind of quiet sometimes," Lexi said, staring at the floor, not sure she could keep from kissing Ty if she looked into those gorgeous blue eyes again. "And thanks again for helping pull the calf. I'm really glad you were here."

"Me, too," Ty said honestly. He could witness the miracle of birth a hundred more times and still be in awe. "If I can ever help, just let me know."

"I will. Goodnight," Lexi said, raising her face to look into his as he opened the door. Despite the cold air seeping in, Lexi felt thoroughly warmed by his intense gaze.

"Night, Lexi," he said, stepping outside and closing the door behind him.

Lexi sighed as she sank down on a kitchen chair. He called her Lexi. Not Lex Jr. not Lex, not boss. Lexi.

Here on the ranch, it helped keep the guys focused on her being the person in charge and not a young single female to have them call her Lex or boss. But for reasons she didn't want to examine, her heart fluttered in response to Ty calling her Lexi.

As she went to turn off the gas fireplace in the family room, she could still feel the light brush of his lips heating the skin of her neck.

Mercy, she didn't know what she'd do when he got caught up on the mechanic work and it was time to teach him about ranching. As good as he looked in his grease monkey attire Ty would be positively lethal to her system in boots and Wranglers.

Lesson Four
Good Manners Aren't Optional

*"Thet's yes ma'am, no sir, please and thank ya.
There's jes no excusin' bad manners."*

Settled into his routine on the ranch, Ty was getting ready to work on a plow. He only knew it was a plow because that is what Swede told him it was. There was a whole shed full of farm equipment he was slowly learning the names of one piece at a time.

Three days after his dinner with Lexi, he came back from a trip to the parts store in Burns to find a computer in the shop. In an empty spot between the work bench and fridge a new high desk with a bar stool now took up residence. A hard drive sat in an enclosed cupboard at the bottom of the desk along with a printer, to keep it away from dust and grime. A sliding drawer held the keyboard and the monitor was a huge thirty-inch LCD screen that was nicer than anything Ty had ever seen.

Thanking Lexi profusely that evening as she walked by on her way to the house from the barn, she accepted his gratitude with a smile and told him if he needed anything else to let her know.

Now, three weeks later, he was making great progress with his repair projects thanks to the time the computer saved him.

Backing his pickup into the second bay of the shop, he flagged down Cal and Keith as they walked by the open doors.

"Hey, can you guys help me a minute?" Ty asked as they walked over.

"Sure, dude," Cal teased, using the name they all called Ty. "What'd you need?"

Ty opened his truck bed cover to reveal his collection of tools. He was ready to put them in the shop and get them out of his pickup. Making a place for them along one wall, he wanted to keep them separate from the ranch tools. From his days as a mechanic at the repair shop, all his tools had his initials etched onto them anyway, so they were easy to identify.

Keith whistled as he looked over the side of the pickup at the impressive array of tools. Ty had two big rolling tool boxes that he laid down in the bed to make transporting them easier. Rather than take the time to empty all the drawers and move them, he figured with some help he could lift them out and onto their rollers and be ready to go.

Cal climbed into the pickup with Ty while Keith stayed on the floor and between the three of them they soon had all the tools unloaded.

"Thanks. I appreciate the help," Ty said as they finished. He went to the fridge and handed them each a cold pop from his stash. They accepted the beverages gratefully and tipped the bottles toward him as they headed out the door.

"Anytime, dude," Cal called over his shoulder.

Ty left the doors open to catch the morning breeze. The snow had melted, now that it was mid-March, and today was warmer with a hint of spring in the air. Swede said the weather was fickle this time of year, but to enjoy each day of sunshine that came along until spring finally arrived.

Intending to do just that, Ty looked out at blue sky and the shoots of green struggling to push up through the brown dead grass of winter. Taking a deep breath, he filled his lungs and grinned. One thing he didn't miss about Portland was the smog and pollution. Out here, the air was crisp and fresh and clean. You could take deep gulps of it and feel renewed - as long as you weren't standing too close to any fresh cow pies.

Admittedly, Ty also liked the way you could see the sunrise and sunset, hear the birds and the cattle without the disrupting sounds of traffic and harried crowds. There was a certain peace and tranquility that hovered around the ranch he had never experienced but was quickly coming to appreciate.

Lost in his musings about his new home, Ty didn't notice Baby come in the shop until she jumped against him, throwing him off balance. He had to take a quick side step to keep from falling over.

"Baby, what are you doing?" Ty said, ruffling the dog's ears and making her smile. He had no idea animals could have such expressive facial features, but Baby certainly did. He was giving her back a good rub when his phone rang. Since he had been listening to music, he left his phone attached to the speaker and heard his sister's voice fill the shop when she said hello.

"Hey, Beth, how are you?" he asked, surprised she would call in the middle of a work day.

"I'm really good, Ty. We just left the doctor's office and she said the baby could come any time," Beth said.

When she heard the word baby, the dog perked up her ears and looked around to see who was saying her name. Ty smiled and continued rubbing her back.

"That's exciting news," Ty said, anxious and excited about the upcoming arrival of his niece or nephew. "Is everything else going okay?"

"Yes, it is, thanks to you. The money you sent was a huge help. But you need to keep more of your paycheck for you," Beth said, grateful for the extra funds but worried about Ty just scraping by. "The office threw a huge baby shower for me last week and you wouldn't believe all the wonderful things we received. This baby should have enough diapers to last at least the first two months."

"I bet the apartment is wall-to-wall baby stuff," Ty said, laughing as the dog frantically looked around each time she heard the word baby.

"What's so funny?" Beth asked, hearing Ty's chuckles.

"Every time we say the word b-a-b-y the dog looks around to see who is talking to her. She's getting pretty worked up."

"Who names a dog Baby, especially when she is the size of a pony?" Beth asked. Ty could hear the humor in her voice.

"I don't know, but it suits her," Ty said, scratching the dog behind her ears as she settled back down. "So when my nephew decides to make his arrival, Nate is totally going to Skype me, right?"

"We'll see about that. I really don't think it is the best plan the two of you have ever hatched," Beth said. "You have no idea what you are asking for, do you?"

"I have a better idea now than I did before I left Portland," Ty said, having helped pull several calves during the course of the last few weeks. For some reason, the hands decided his brute strength could be beneficial to them in several ways, not just as the mechanic.

"Be that as it may, please remember I'm not a cow," Beth said. He could hear a car engine start and knew Beth and Nate were back in their vehicle.

"Yes, ma'am, I'll remember," Ty said.

"You turning into a cowboy on me?" Beth teased "What's with that ma'am business?"

"I've been informed multiple times that it is good manners to address any female as ma'am and any man older than me as sir. There is a whole list of manners that I am trying to memorize because believe me, it is not just a code, but a way of life that these people are determined to ingrain into my head," Ty explained as Baby went to her blanket in the corner and flopped down.

"Let's hear some of the things on the list," Beth said. Ty could picture her smiling as she and Nate drove through the horrific traffic from the doctor's office toward their apartment.

"I've been given a printed copy. I'll send it to you later," Ty said. "I'm glad you're doing well. Promise you two will let me know the minute my nephew arrives?"

"We promise," Beth said. "Love you, Ty."

"Love you, too."

Ty was in a good mood after talking to his sister and his thoughts chased around the upcoming arrival of her baby. He wanted to find a special gift, but had no idea what to buy. If he had time after dinner, maybe he'd do some looking online and see what he could find.

The morning passed quickly. When Ty stopped at noon to eat a sandwich, he emailed his sister the "guide to upright living" Swede gave him a couple of weeks ago. It was part of the foreman's efforts in "learnin' ya up to how things are done."

Smiling, Ty read through them again:

1. Once you give your word and a handshake, it's as binding as signing a contract.
2. Never betray a trust.
3. Never lie, cheat or steal.
4. Treat all children, animals, and old folks like you want to be treated.

5. Call your elders sir and ma'am.
6. Treat women with respect and care.
7. Always tip your hat to a lady and take it off at the dinner table and in church.
8. Work hard and give your boss an honest day for your pay.
9. If someone needs a hand, lend yours to the task.
10. Respect the flag and our nation.
11. Be clean - both on the outside and inside of your person.
12. Never stop learning.
13. Never make fun of someone who gave it their best.
14. Never wear your spurs or dirty boots in the house.
15. Fight fair, be brave, and stand up for what's right.

Ty had always followed rules number one through four. He also tried to follow rule six as well as eight through thirteen. He was learning to apply "sir" and "ma'am" and since he had not yet been coerced into purchasing a cowboy hat, he wasn't worried about rule number seven. The same went for rule number fourteen since he had neither spurs nor cowboy boots. As for rule fifteen, that was part of the unwritten code he'd set for his life. He tried to live peacefully with everyone, but if he had to, he would stand up for himself and do it honorably.

Grinning, he thought of teaching his nephew how to throw a right hook when he was old enough. It was going to be hard to not be there when he made his big entrance into the world. Despite Beth's protests, he and Nate had a plan all worked out so he could virtually be there to hear the baby's first cries.

Returning to work, Ty finished the plow and hooked it up to a tractor, dragging it out of the shop so he could get started working on a harrow.

He was digging in a drawer that housed an assortment of nuts and bolts, organized by size, when he couldn't quite reach into the back to the size he needed. Tugging on the drawer, it seemed to be stuck so he worked it around until he carefully got it out. Bending down to peer into the space, he noticed a crumpled envelope in the back of the cabinet.

Setting down the drawer full of parts, he fingered the envelope and smoothed it out. He noticed a scrawling hand had written "Lexi Jo" across the front. Unfastening his coveralls, he stuffed the envelope into his jean's pocket, refastened the coveralls and got back to work, wondering if the letter was from Lexi's dad.

Hours later he glanced at the clock and jerked off his coveralls, running to the bunkhouse with Baby hot on his heels. It was his turn to make dinner and he forgot about it. He had less than an hour until everyone showed up, ready to eat.

Lexi had hired two housekeepers in the past few weeks. One lasted almost a week while the other one only made it until noon her second day. She might have lasted longer except Baby scared her half to death when she opened the kitchen door and ran in barking.

For now, they were back to cooking and cleaning for themselves.

Washing his hands, Ty grabbed steaks out of the freezer and stuck them in the microwave. While they were thawing, he ran outside and fired up the gas barbecue, then hustled back in, washing a bunch of potatoes. Cutting them into chunks, he dropped them in a bowl with a little olive oil and some spices and put them in the microwave when he took the steaks out. Preheating the oven, he opened cans of green beans and dumped them into a skillet with some crumbled pieces of bacon left over from breakfast.

Popping open a couple cans of biscuits, Ty put them in a greased pan and stuck them in the oven.

Seasoning the meat, he took the steaks outside to the grill, put them on low and ran back inside. Searching the pantry, he found some instant pudding and a few leftover butter cookies. He made the pudding, pouring it in individual bowls then sprinkled crushed cookies on top.

Taking the potatoes out of the microwave, he found a potato masher and smashed them, stirring in grated cheese, sour cream, bacon bits and a little ranch dressing before dumping the mixture onto a foil-lined cookie sheet. He stuck it in the oven with the biscuits, hurried to set the table and mixed up a gallon of lemonade.

While he frantically pulled dinner together, Baby sat by the door watching him run in and out. When he talked to her, asking her why she didn't remind him it was his turn to cook she lifted her head at him and barked once, as if to say it wasn't her fault he forgot.

As the sounds of boots thudded outside, Ty placed golden biscuits hot from the oven into a bread basket.

"Whooee! Thet meat sure does smell good," Swede said as he came in and went to the closest bathroom to wash up.

The rest of the crew ambled in, hanging up their hats and washing their hands.

Ty was outside with a platter taking the steaks off the barbecue when Lexi came down the walk.

"Hey, Ty. Mind if I join you for dinner? Those steaks smelled so good, they were tempting me when I came in from the field," she said, taking the platter from him as he put the steaks on it and turned off the grill.

"It would be our pleasure to have you join us, ma'am," Ty said with a wink that made Lexi nearly drop the platter as heat flooded her insides and her arms and legs morphed into a weak, rubbery substance.

Taking the steaks from her, Ty hurried to hold the door open with his other hand.

"Look who's joining us for dinner, boys," Ty called as she walked up the steps, hoping his message would warn the rest of the men inside to not come to the table half dressed or otherwise indecent.

Lexi was warmly greeted by her men and given a place to sit at the end of the table opposite Swede. She was surprised, and secretly pleased, to find Ty sitting beside her. When everyone was seated, Swede asked the blessing and the food was passed around the table.

Despite the teasing, it was obvious everyone was enjoying the meal Ty prepared. Bringing out the bowls of pudding for dessert, he was afraid he might get cooking duty every night from the compliments thrown his direction.

Ty tried to pry his eyes away from Lexi's lips as she sat licking pudding off her spoon. Staring at their rosy fullness, he wondered if they would taste as warm and sweet as they looked.

When her leg accidentally bumped his under the table, it was all he could do not to jerk away from the connection that felt like an electrical jolt.

"For a city dude, you sure know how to grill a good steak," Cal said, slapping him on the back. Ty finally learned Keith had the mole on his cheek and Cal was the more talkative of the two. It was the only way to tell the twins apart.

"Thanks," Ty said, drawing his gaze away from Lexi and to his own half-eaten bowl of pudding. "My Mom worked at a steakhouse for a while when I was a kid. I learned a lot about cooking meat when I hung out there after school."

"It was one of the best steaks I've ever had, Ty. No kidding," Lexi said, nursing her glass of lemonade. "Thanks for letting me eat with you."

"It's your steak, you can eat wherever you like," Jimmy teased.

"True," Lexi said with cheeky grin that caused Ty's temperature to spike.

Needing some form of distraction, he got up and started doing the dishes. He turned to finish clearing the table only to run right into Lexi as she carried dirty dishes to the counter. Grabbing her arms to keep from knocking her down, his hands gentled their grip, but he didn't want to let go.

What he wanted was to pull her into his arms and kiss her with a depth and intensity he'd never before shared with a woman.

Lexi felt her arms go limp at Ty's touch and quickly moved to set the plates down before she dropped them. How could a simple touch from him set her nerve endings on fire and make her wish for things she'd long ago given up dreaming were possible? Needing to put some space between her and the good-looking mechanic, she offered a hasty word of thanks for dinner and turned toward the door.

Before she could escape, Ty grabbed her arm and placed a crumpled envelope in her hand.

"I found that in the shop today," he said quietly as Lexi looked at the writing and tears formed in her eyes.

Nodding her head, she hurried from the bunkhouse, running back to the security of her home. Going into the family room, she sank onto the comfy couch, wishing she had someone she could talk to about her feelings for Ty, about the things her father had done.

Deciding it was crazy to entertain the idea that she could be falling in love with Ty, she told herself to forget about him. To ignore the way being near him made her heart pound and her palms grow clammy. To block out the dreams of his big, strong arms holding her tight and those tempting lips caressing her own.

Sitting up, she pushed thoughts of Ty from her head and looked at the envelope in her hand. After months of searching and wondering, would this finally give her some idea of where her dad hid the money, what he'd been thinking?

Carefully slitting the envelope with her fingernail, she pulled out thick folded sheets of paper.

Sniffing it, she could smell her dad's aftershave and the scent made her heart catch. She missed him so much.

Unfolding the letter, she took a deep breath and read:

My darling Lexi Jo,

If you are reading this then I'm either dead or nearly so. I know I should have told you much sooner about the cancer, but I didn't want you to worry. I didn't want you to feel obligated to come home.

You've built a great life for yourself in Portland and I'm so proud of you. I've always been proud of you, even if we didn't always see eye to eye.

You are every bit as beautiful as your beloved mother and I'm so glad all her lessons in how to be a lady weren't wasted. She would be so pleased to see the wonderful woman you've become. Although you look so much like her and your Grandma Sunny, I know you inherited your ol' dad's stubbornness, sense of humor and love of cars if that sporty little thing you drove home last time is any indication.

I feel confident leaving the ranch in your very capable hands, Lexi. You know and love every inch of this place. If, at some point, you decide you'd rather sell it than live here, do it with my blessing. I only want for you to be happy.

From what the doc tells me, my mind won't be my own when this thing ends so in the event I do something completely crazy before anyone can stop me, I'm leaving you some money that won't be in a bank account.

I could draw you a treasure map and turn you loose, but I want you to work for it a little. My pop always said the harder we work for something, the more we appreciate it.

You've always appreciated all your many blessings. Lex. Always be that sweet girl and know I love you.
Dad
P.S. Your first clue... The Raven

Lexi stared at the letter in her hand, swiping at her tears before they dripped on the page and smeared her father's precious words. She needed so badly to have his approval, to feel his love, and tonight it was there, wrapping around her as comfortingly as the blanket draped across the back of the couch.

She'd worry about the money and clue tomorrow. Tonight she just wanted to remember all the wonderful things she loved about her dad.

Saturday was a bright and beautiful day with unusually warm temperatures in the mid-60s.

As Ty walked toward the shop that morning he could hear cattle mooing, horses whinnying, birds chirping and stopped a moment just to absorb the sounds.

He could really get used to this country living. Although he was so busy he sometimes felt like his eyes might close with weariness before he finally dragged himself to bed, life seemed to move at a slower, less hectic pace. For the first time in his life, Ty was taking time to notice the smells, sounds, sights and tastes that encompassed his days. He loved this new life.

The other thing he loved, all too much, was watching Lexi. She could ride the hands into the ground, wrestle animals into submission, and still look lovelier than any other woman he'd ever seen.

Ty had yet to see her dressed in anything but boots, jeans and work shirts, other than the night he saw her in a tank top when he helped pull the calf. Lexi made whatever she wore look good.

Way too good.

Glancing at the big ranch house, he was surprised to see what appeared to be Lexi's posterior sticking out of Baby's doghouse. Although the dog rarely used it, she did have a nice doghouse in the corner of the backyard.

Knowing he should keep walking to the shop, Ty instead made a beeline for the doghouse and absorbed the view as Lexi's fanny wiggled back and forth while she dug around in Baby's domain.

"Have a craving for a well-chewed bone?" Ty finally asked. He grimaced when Lexi smacked her head on the top of the doghouse. She scooted out and sat on her heels, rubbing her head.

"Hey," she said, giving him a narrowed glare. "You startled me."

"Sorry about that," he said, offering her his hand so she could get to her feet. "Did you lose something in there?"

"Not exactly," Lexi said, still rubbing her head. She wasn't sure if she should tell Ty the truth, but decided he'd more than proven himself trustworthy. The clue about the raven her dad left behind led her to his collection of literature where another clue was stuck in a book of Edgar Allen Poe's poems.

My Baby

Assuming her dad was referring to the dog, Lexi decided to look through the doghouse first. The doghouse, unlike many slapped together projects, had siding painted the same buttery shade of yellow as the house with green and white trim. It also boasted a wood floor. Baby had a big cedar-filled pillow on top of an old blanket to lie on when she randomly chose to stay in her abode.

"Need any help?" Ty asked, holding on to Lexi's hand that wasn't rubbing her head.

"Maybe," she said, releasing a deep breath and Ty's hand. "Here's the thing, Ty. My dad, he …um… well, he wasn't himself for a while before he died and he hid some money somewhere on the ranch. That letter you gave me the other day confirmed my suspicions that that was exactly what he'd done and instead of telling me where it is, he made a series of clues I'm supposed to find and decipher. No one else knows about this, even Swede, and I'd really like to keep it that way."

"Sure, Lexi, I understand," Ty said, and he did. The thought of finding buried treasure could bring out the worst in some of the hands if they got wind of it. "So one of the clues brought you out to Baby's house?"

"Yeah. The first one was 'The Raven,' which led me to dad's book of Poe's poetry. The clue I found there said 'My Baby.' I'm assuming he's referring to the dog," Lexi said, hoping she hadn't made a mistake in trusting Ty.

He squatted down and removed everything from the dog's house including chewed up toys, bones and things he didn't want to know what were. There wasn't any place inside Lex could have hidden a clue. Realizing the dog house was moveable, Ty tipped it up while Lexi looked beneath it, but didn't find anything. He ran his hands under the edges of the frame and still found nothing.

Standing up, lost in thought, he finally turned to Lexi with a smile.

"Did your dad have a favorite photo of you?"

"Yes, he did," Lexi said, walking toward the house as Ty followed along behind her. "He kept it on his desk. I shoved it in a drawer when I took over the ranch."

Lexi went into the office and sat down at the desk. Rummaging in one of the drawers, she pulled out a framed photo of her sitting on her dad's lap in his car, looking into his face with adoration.

Running her fingers across the frame of the photo, she stared at it a moment before turning it over and removing the back. Taped to the back of the photo was another clue.

1969

"Is that a significant year?" Ty asked, glad they found the next clue.

"My dad graduated from high school that year. He's got a box with year-books somewhere around here. Guess I'll have to find it before I can discover the next clue," Lexi said, putting the back of the frame on the photo and placing it carefully on a corner of the desk.

"If you need any help, just let me know," Ty said, walking to the office door, followed by Lexi.

"Thanks, Ty. I really appreciate it," Lexi said. She placed a warm hand on his arm that made them both jump when heat snapped between them.

"You're welcome. And don't worry. I won't say anything to anyone. Knowing Cal and Jimmy, they'd start digging holes all over the ranch looking for a treasure."

"That they would," Lexi said with a grin as Ty walked out the door. He stopped in the yard long enough to put all of Baby's stuff back in her house before returning to the shop.

An hour later, he was still focused on Lexi and the vision of her digging around in Baby's house. Shaking his head to clear his thoughts, Ty turned his attention to the part in his hand just as Gus popped his head in the door.

"The boss is making lunch for us today. Said to be at the house at noon, dude," Gus said as he hurried on his way to the barn.

"Thanks," Ty called after him. The day was getting better and better. Knowing Lexi's culinary talents, he looked forward to the meal.

At a quarter of twelve, he took off his coveralls and washed up. Looking in the bathroom mirror, he combed his hair, which was too long again. He stopped at barber shop in Burns last week to have it trimmed, but the guy that cut it assured him women went wild over hair like his and didn't cut it as short as Ty wanted. Ty didn't feel like arguing with him, so he resigned himself to getting it trimmed again in a few weeks.

Making sure he didn't have any grease on his face, Ty decided he looked presentable. Calling to Baby, who was lounging on her bed in the corner, the dog followed him to the house where she plopped down on the back porch.

Lexi was outside grilling burgers. A big picnic table was covered with a checkered cloth and held an assortment of chips, dip, a fruit salad, buns and all the fixings needed for a great hamburger.

As the rest of the crew ambled into the yard with clean hands and faces, they all tipped their hats at Lexi and thanked her for inviting them for lunch.

"It's too nice a day not to barbecue something," Lexi said with a laugh. "I'm not quite as handy with the grill as Ty, but I think I can make an edible burger."

"I'm sure it will be dandy," Swede said, fishing a bottle of pop out of a cooler Lexi placed near the table. "Ya didn't need to go to extra work for us."

"It's my pleasure," Lexi said, flipping burgers. "You have all worked so hard, let's just call this a little thank you."

As they sat down to eat, the conversation was lively. Ty thought he might actually give in to his desire to kiss Lexi when she brought out a huge chocolate cake with ice cream. None of the guys were good at baking so his sweet tooth had really been feeling deprived lately.

"This is so good," Ty said as Lexi offered him a second piece and he gladly accepted it.

After helping clean up the dishes and leftovers, the hands sat around the yard resting in the sunshine and enjoying a rare break mid-day. Lexi told them to relax as long as they wanted when she disappeared into the house.

Teasing Jimmy about something he'd done the previous day, Ty opened another bottle of pop. Following Jimmy's stare toward the back door of the house, he looked up, missed his mouth and slowly poured the sticky drink down his shirt front before he realized what he was doing.

Lexi came out the back door looking like she stepped out of a photo shoot for a fashion designer. Her long black hair floated around her in glossy waves, her lips were ruby red and trendy sunglasses covered her eyes. She wore a black sequined cocktail dress that hugged her curves to perfection and hit her a few inches above her knees. Her legs, her crazy long legs, carried her toward Ty one swaying step at a time on a pair of heels that made his thoughts spin in directions they really shouldn't go. All the while, ZZ Top's song *Legs* played loudly in his head.

Realizing pop was soaking into his shirt, Ty set the bottle down next to his chair and jumped to his feet, along with the rest of the crew.

"Land sakes, boss, where in tarnation are ya' headed?" Swede asked as Lexi stopped by him.

"Portland. I promised a friend I'd attend a fundraiser tonight, so I need to get on the road if I'm going to be there in time. You guys just enjoy your afternoon. I'll be back tomorrow before dark," Lexi said, adjusting the overnight bag on her arm as she addressed the group, although her attention was centered on Ty. "Mind helping me with the garage doors?"

"Sure thang," Swede said, following her out the back gate. Looking at the bunch of guys staring at their boss like she'd grown a second head, he called to Ty. "Dude, come help me with this door."

Ty managed to engage his brain long enough to run over and help Swede pull the two big garage doors open. Lexi backed out in a cute little sports car, waved her hand and zipped down the driveway.

Watching her go, Swede slapped him on the back and cackled. "Whooee! She plumb threw ya for a loop, didn't she?"

Ty didn't pay any attention to Swede. He was watching Lexi drive away in her Nissan Nismo 370Z – a sexy car for a very sexy woman.

"If ya like that car, I bet ya'll love the one in the garage," Swede said and tugged on Ty's arm.

Turning around and walking into the building that Swede said was originally a place Lexi's ancestors stored their carriage and sleigh, Ty looked at the cloth covered vehicle still parked inside.

Swede pulled off the cover to reveal a machine that made Ty grin from ear to ear. Although in need of a paint job and no doubt a complete restoration, Ty couldn't stop from running his hand along the fender and over the hood of a black 1969 Mustang Boss 429.

Letting out a whistle, he opened the door and allowed the musty air to escape before sitting in the seat. The interior needed some work, but nothing that wasn't manageable.

"Is this her car?" Ty asked, putting his hands on the wheel and imagining driving the car down an open road.

"Nah," Swede said, leaning on the door frame. "This was her daddy's car. Lex bought this brand-spankin' new back when he was a young feller. He was always going to restore it but jes never got around to it. Lex Jr., says it reminds her of her daddy and plans to get the car fixed one of these days."

Ty climbed out and popped the hood. He suddenly wanted to fix this car. Not just for the challenge of fixing it, which was plenty of motivation for him, but because it would make Lexi smile.

"Ya know anything about this kind of car," Swede asked, watching Ty look over the car.

"A little. They only made 859 of these cars in 1969. Ford wanted to develop a Hemi engine that could compete with Chrysler in a NASCAR race so that's how this car came to be. They contracted an outside company to create the Boss 429 by making extensive modifications to the Ford Mustang," Ty said, warming to the subject. Cars that looked good and went fast were among his most favored hobbies. "They rated the cars at 375 horsepower with 450 pounds of torque but the actual output was well over 500 horsepower. Just imagine how this baby could rip up the road."

"Don't have to imagine," Swede said, giving Ty a grin. "Lex let me ride in it a few times and I even drove it to Bend once."

"No way," Ty said, looking at the weathered foreman.

"Yep. And yer correct, she rips right on down the road," Swede said with another cackle. "Thet's more words than I've heard ya string together since ya been here. If I ain't careful, I'd get the idea ya have a things for sports cars and purty girls."

Ty snapped his head up at Swede's observation. He could deny it, but that would be lying and directly violated rule number three on the cowboy code Swede gave him. Instead, he offered the older man a grin.

"Guess that might be true," Ty said, looking only mildly guilty. "I may be out in the sticks but I'm not blind or dumb."

Swede laughed and slapped Ty on the back as they closed the garage doors. "Didn't think ya would be where the boss is concerned. Ya just don't go gettin' any ideas about lovin' and leavin' her. She ain't that kind of gal."

"I never thought for a moment she was," Ty said, narrowing his gaze and glaring at Swede. "She's a lady and my boss. I haven't forgotten that."

Swede nodded his head and finished closing the door. "Good. Glad we are ridin' the same direction on thet subject. Jes so ya know, I don't think a little lookin' can cause any harm."

"Right," Ty said, thinking a little looking had already caused him a great deal of harm. He was in complete danger of losing his heart to the alluring and enchanting Lexi.

In the midst of making a chocolate cake after inviting the guys for lunch, Lexi was surprised when a friend called to remind her about the fundraiser she promised to attend that evening. With all the farm work, it completely slipped Lexi's mind. The last thing she wanted was to make the long drive to Portland, spend the evening with a bunch of snobby, stuffy people nibbling on food that wasn't all that tasty, spend money on something she didn't really want, and act like she was enjoying the entire experience.

Months ago she told her friend to count on her being there to offer support and she wouldn't go back on her word now. She didn't want to disappoint the guys either, so she decided a quick barbecue lunch would still give her time to get ready and on the road.

She had her bag packed, clothes laid out, and everything ready to go as soon as she finished playing host to the hands for lunch. Her car was gassed up and waiting in the garage.

While the men lingered, eating more cake and swapping stories, she cleaned up the food, curled her hair, and did her makeup. By the time she came down the stairs wearing the black dress with a smattering of sequins and made sure everything in the house was turned off, she was warming to the idea of being dressed up and feeling like a woman instead of one more hand on the ranch.

The opportunities for her to wear cocktail attire were extremely limited in Harney County and she decided it could be fun to pretend she was a trendy urbanite for an evening.

Hiding her smile, she watched Ty spill his soda down his shirt front and his eyes nearly pop out of his head as she walked toward him. She had never been so openly ogled before. It gave her a heady feeling as she engaged her feminine powers, which had been in hibernation for months. She could feel his gaze roving over her as she talked with Swede and then went into the garage.

If she'd had time to think about it, she might have worked up the nerve to ask him to go along with her this evening. Waltzing in on Ty's arm would have set her old group of friends into a gossiping frenzy. Picturing Ty in a suit, all cleaned up, made her breath catch in her throat. He was dangerous enough in a T-shirt and jeans. She didn't think her mental and emotional well-being could handle him in a suit or tux.

Backing out of the garage, she wasn't sure if the look of blatant desire on Ty's face was for her, the car she was driving, or both.

As she revved the engine of the car and sped toward Portland, Lexi hoped it was more for her than her wheels.

Lesson Five
Family Is Everything

*"No matter where ya go or what ya do,
nothin' is more important than family."*

With his head buried under the hood of a two-ton dump truck that had seen better days, Ty didn't hear his phone buzzing. It rang twice more and still he didn't hear it. The fourth time it buzzed, Baby ran over to Ty and grabbed a mouthful of his coveralls, tugging on his leg.

"Baby, what do you think you're doing?" he asked as she pulled so hard, he had to step down from the truck's bumper onto the shop floor to keep from being yanked over backward. "That is not okay, Baby."

Just as he was about to scold the dog, his phone rang again and he hurried to answer it.

"Bro, where have you been? We've been trying to call for an hour," Nate said, sounding both nervous and excited.

"Hey, man, what's up?" Ty asked, wiping his hands as he held the phone with his shoulder to his ear.

"The baby, that's what," Nate said.

"What?" Ty said, losing his hold on the phone, barely catching it in his hand before it hit the concrete floor of the shop. "What did you say?"

"The baby. Beth went into labor this morning. We've been here at the hospital for about an hour. The doctor said it could be a while before things get moving along, but I wanted to let you know we are going to have a baby today."

"Oh, man, this is awesome," Ty said, feeling both elation and fear for his sister and brother-and-law. He hoped the delivery would go smoothly and both Beth and the baby would be fine. After getting first-hand experience in the arrival of babies, albeit with livestock, he had a new appreciation for what women suffered through during the trials of childbirth. "How's Beth?"

"She's doing really well," Nate said. "She said she'd talk to you the next go round, assuming we'll be checking in periodically until the baby arrives."

"Sounds good," Ty said, leaning against the workbench. "Are all systems go with your phone?"

"Yep. I'll Skype you in as soon as things get exciting. Beth made me promise that neither I nor the phone will have a view of anything south of the equator."

"Too much info, man," Ty said. He just wanted to be able to hear the baby's first cry and see the look on Beth's face when she held it in her arms. Anything beyond that, he had no interest in being a part of and certainly didn't want to see it live via Nate's phone.

"Sorry. I'll call you in an hour or so. Make sure you've got the computer ready to connect."

"I will. Give Beth a hug for me," Ty said as he hung up the phone. It was going to be hard to keep his head in his work when he really wanted to be at the hospital in Portland, waiting outside Beth's door. If he asked, Lexi would more than likely let him have the time off, but they were so busy on the ranch, he hated to even think about requesting a few days away. He'd been there a just a little more than a month and didn't feel like he'd earned the right to ask.

An hour slipped by without a call from Nate, so Ty kept working for another thirty minutes before he had to know what was going on. Calling his brother-in-law, Nate answered on the second ring.

"Hey," Ty said as Nate answered. "Any exciting news?"

"Not yet, but she is progressing right on schedule," Nate said. "The doctor said it will be another hour or so before anything really starts to happen. I won't give you any details, but just be glad you are there, man. Giving birth seems to make women pretty cranky."

Ty laughed.

"I've been witness to several births here on the ranch and I can agree to that statement. Only imagine having a mama who can kick you through a wall and weighs several hundred pounds."

"No thanks, bro. I'll stick with my lovely little wife," Nate said. "I'm putting her on the phone right now."

"Hello," Beth said, sounding out of breath.

"Hey, Bethie, how are you?" Ty asked.

"As good as I can be under the circumstances," Beth said. "I'm not sure this baby won't be an only child after this experience, but the doctor assures me everyone says that their first time."

"I'll be a proud uncle to however many you decide to have," Ty teased. "Nate said you're doing great and it shouldn't be much longer. I'm anxious to find out if I'm right and it's a boy."

"You and Nate just won't quit, will you? He's convinced this baby is going to be the next star quarterback at Oregon State."

"You know it," Ty said.

"Ty, I want you to know how much I…" Beth stopped and gasped as another contraction ripped through her.

"You okay, sis?" Ty asked, concern filling his voice.

"Just a contraction," Beth said between pants for breath. "Gotta go."

Ty stared at the phone after Beth hung up, worried about her. He busied himself with repairs on the old truck. After thirty minutes he gave up trying to concentrate.

Calling for an update, Nate said the doctor didn't think it would be much longer before Beth hit the final stages of labor and he'd call back when he had something to report.

Losing the ability to focus on his work, Ty instead found himself mindlessly browsing online, trying to find a baby gift. When that didn't work as a distraction, he started pacing back and forth, waiting for Nate to call.

Baby had gone from resting in the corner on her blanket to pacing along with Ty. The more worried he got about Nate calling, the more anxious Baby became. She finally let out a howl that made Ty cringe from the noise and stop his pacing. Patting his leg, the dog ran over and leaned against him.

"Have I got you all upset, Baby?" Ty said, scratching behind her ears. "I'm sorry, girl."

"What's the ruckus all about?" Swede asked as he hurried in the shop out of breath. Lexi and Jimmy weren't far behind, running into the shop thinking some tragedy had befallen Baby for her ear-piercing howl.

Ty gave them a chagrined look. "Sorry. I got a little anxious and Baby seemed to pick up on it more than I thought she would."

Lexi took a step forward and studied Ty. His normally calm and aloof demeanor had been replaced with one of concern and worry.

"Is everything okay?" she asked, placing a warm hand on his arm, ignoring the burst of heat that raced through her hand to her shoulder at the contact.

"Everything is fine. It's just, um…" Ty hesitated to share too much. He certainly didn't want the guys thinking he was mushy and emotional, even though he wasn't. This was his only sibling, though. Raking his hand through his hair he let out a sigh. "My sister is having a baby today… now… and I'm waiting for my brother-in-law to call. He's going to try to Skype it, so I can feel like I'm there."

"Well, don't thet beat all?" Swede said, slapping him on the back with a big grin. "What's Skype?"

"It's a way of calling someone but instead of just talking on the phone, you can actually see who you're talking to," Lexi explained. "It's basically like a live video feed."

"Ya tuggin' my rope?" Swede asked, looking at Lexi doubtfully.

"Nope. That's the honest truth," Lexi said, holding up her hand like she was making a vow. Turning to Ty she put her hands on her hips and gave him a narrow glare. "Why didn't you tell me your sister was expecting any day. I would have given you time off."

"I figured you would, but there is a lot of work that needs done," Ty said, waving his hand at the dismantled truck engine for emphasis.

"Don't you know nothing, and I mean nothing, is more important than family?" Lexi asked in a huff.

She herself didn't understand that until it was far too late. If she had, she might not have run off to Portland right after high school. At the very least, she would have come home to be with her dad before the cancer took his mind and then his life. She'd give anything to have a few hours to spend visiting with him.

"Yes, ma'am, I do," Ty said, wondering what he'd done to make Lexi mad. "But being the new guy on the job, I didn't feel right about asking for time off already."

"Well, that is just the most as…" Whatever Lexi was going to say was cut off by the ringing of Ty's phone.

"Hey, Nate. Yep, I'm ready," Ty said, turning to the computer. "Let's see if it works."

He held his breath and waited a moment before he found himself right in Beth's delivery room, looking Nate in the face."

"Hey, bro! Good to see you," Nate said, seeing Ty and a group of people standing behind him. "Looks like you are turning this into a regular party."

Ty turned to the three people and dog behind him, grinning. He motioned them forward and they gathered closer to the computer.

"This is Lexi Ryan, my boss," Ty said, introducing Lexi first. She waved at the computer and smiled. He introduced Swede next, who took off his hat and grinned, followed by Jimmy. Usually full of teasing and jokes, Jimmy was oddly quiet, soaking in both the technology and the experience. Not to be left out, Baby barked twice and nuzzled next to Ty. "And this is Baby."

"Hi Baby and crew," Nate said with a laugh. Baby barked again and wagged her enormous tail, beating it against Ty's leg. "The doc says it won't be long now, so I'm going to be standing up here by Beth's head. Here's Beth. Wave to your brother, honey."

"Hey, Ty," Beth said, forcing herself not to take the phone from her husband and throw it against the wall. The last thing she wanted was to be made a spectacle in front of anyone, especially half of the ranch where Ty worked.

Ty forced himself to keep smiling as he looked at Beth's pale, sweat-glazed face and saw her grimace in pain.

"Are you doing okay, Beth?" Ty asked, concerned.

"Just great," she said, panting through another contraction. "I'd be even better if you two could just talk on the phone like normal people without involving me up close and personal."

"Too late for that," Ty said as Nate took the camera off Beth's face.

"She's getting a little testy," Nate whispered with a wink into the camera. A slap was heard and his hand jerked. "And violent. She's also getting violent."

Ty and Swede chuckled while Lexi smiled. Ty turned to the three people standing behind him. "Are you all staying?"

At their nods, he pulled over two more stools and the rolling mechanics seat, so they could sit down. Baby put her head on his lap and whined.

Nate held his phone with the camera turned toward the window in one hand and had Beth's hand in the other. They could hear Beth's pants, gasps, and muffled cries, along with instructions from the doctor to push, and Nate's encouraging dialogue as she labored to deliver the baby.

When the doctor said "here we go," all four of the adults in the shop leaned forward, anxious to see or hear something.

The cry of a baby filled the space just as Nate turned the phone to show the doctor lifting the baby up and handing him to a nurse.

"It's a boy! It's a boy!" Nate said, clearly excited. "Bro, you were right on."

A sound behind them caused Swede, Ty and Lexi to turn just in time to watch Jimmy pass out and fall to the floor. Swede and Lexi rushed to his aid, while Ty kept one eye on Jimmy and one on the computer screen.

It was just a few moments that seemed like hours until Beth smiled as a nurse placed the baby in her arms.

"He's beautiful, Beth. Just like you," Ty said, wishing he could be there in person. Virtually was almost as good. "Congrats, Nate, you've got a fine son."

"Thanks, man," Nate said, holding back the camera so Ty could see the three of them - Nate, Beth and the baby.

"Did you ever decide on a name?"

"Yes, Ty, we did," Beth said, sounding exhausted but happy. "We're going to name him Jaxton Nathaniel Jarvis. After Nate and you."

"Aw, Beth," Ty said, feeling his throat close with emotion. Taking a deep breath, he swallowed twice. "That's a great name. Thank you."

"Thank you, Ty, for all your help. We couldn't have made it the last month without you," Nate said. Remembering the audience, he held the camera out further and smiled. "Nice to meet all of you at the Rockin' R Ranch. Thanks for taking care of Ty for us."

"Nice to meet you, Nate, and congratulations on your beautiful baby boy," Lexi said with a wave. Jimmy had come around and turned the shade of an overripe tomato at fainting. Getting to his feet, Swede patted him on the back and told him not to worry about it.

Nate and Ty said goodbye and then the screen went blank.

"Well, I never in all my born days would have imagined somethin' like thet," Swede said, slapping Ty on the shoulder. "Congratulations, uncle."

Ty was grinning from ear to ear and unable to stop. "Thanks. And thanks for making it possible for me to share that with them. It meant a lot to us."

"Is Beth your only sister?" Jimmy finally asked, as his color returned to normal.

"Yep. She's the only family I have left in this world, and she's pretty special to me," Ty said, opening the door to his heart a little more than he intended.

While it was cracked open, Lexi took advantage of a peek inside and liked what she saw.

"Really, Ty, congratulations. That was just amazing," Lexi said, giving him an impulsive hug then quickly pulling back. Although brief, she knew in that moment she could spend the rest of her life wrapped up in Ty's arms.

Ty cleared his throat and ran his hand through his disheveled hair. Lexi wanted to follow his fingers through the thick, wavy locks but instead clasped her hands in front of her.

"Thanks again. After all this excitement, I think I'm ready for some lunch. Anyone want a sandwich?" Ty asked, opening the shop fridge.

Working long into the evening, Ty was rubbing his tired eyes when Lexi came in the shop. He didn't need to turn and see her standing inside the door to know she was there. He could smell her scent as it floated in around him, engulfing his senses and setting his nerve endings at attention.

She smelled fresh and sweet, with just a hint of something floral. He found the aroma more enticing than his overloaded senses could process at the moment. Taking a deep breath and inhaling a good whiff of cleaning solvent helped him focus.

"What are you doing out this late?" Ty asked, trying to sound casual as he looked up from the parts manual he was studying.

"Just wanted to check on the new uncle and see how he's doing," Lexi said with such warmth in her smile and eyes, Ty fought the urge to pull her into his arms and kiss her.

"I'm doing fine," Ty said. Deciding to lighten the tension that seemed to hang between them, he asked if she wanted to see the baby gifts he picked out. She readily agreed.

Going to the computer, he opened up his email account and clicked on an order confirmation, showing photos of several onesies all bearing some sort of tool with funny sayings like "Future Mechanic in Training," "My

Uncle is the Best Mechanic in the World," and "Don't Mess with My Drill."

He also ordered a few funny bibs. The one that made Lexi laugh out loud said, "These Fools Put My Cape on Backward."

"Oh, Ty, those are awesome," Lexi said, grinning at the fun things Ty ordered and had shipped directly to Nate and Beth. It gave her a glimpse into his sense of humor.

"I've got some other things I'll send later," Ty said, trying not to show his excitement about the baby, but failing.

"I appreciate you sharing that very special moment with all of us today," Lexi said, putting her hand on his arm as they sat together in front of the computer. Her fingers tingled and butterflies swarmed her stomach, but she couldn't seem to move or take her gaze away from the glowing heat in Ty's blue eyes. "I know it was something very personal, but it meant so much to us to be a part of it."

"No problem," Ty said, trying to stay aloof but finding it difficult to form coherent words with Lexi's hand on his arm. Even through his shirt-sleeve, he could feel heat spreading from her fingers through his arm and right to his heart. "I'm not so sure Jimmy enjoyed the experience. For someone who can get in there and pull a calf with the best of them, I was kind of surprised when he bit it."

Lexi laughed. "I think Jimmy had an eye-opening adventure, even if he didn't really see anything. He's young and hasn't had a lot of experience out in the world. He asked quite a few questions about women being pregnant. I'm not sure he'll ever have kids after his experience today."

"I wondered about that by his reaction," Ty said with a chuckle. "Give him a few years and he'll forget all about it."

"Doubtful, but possible," Lexi said as she slid off the stool and walked to the door. "Thanks again for letting us stay."

"It's your ranch. You can go anywhere you like," Ty said, only half-teasing.

"Oh, I don't know. I see this shop as your domain. Well, yours and Baby's."

Ty laughed at the thought of the dog. She seemed to think he came to the ranch just to be her pet human. She usually stayed with him as long as he was in the shop, but she'd wandered outside an hour or so ago.

"Baby allows me to hang out here with her. If I ever get on her bad side, I'm done for," Ty said with a twinkle in his blue eyes that made it hard for Lexi to keep walking instead of throwing herself into Ty's arms and kissing him until she was lightheaded.

As Ty turned off the lights and picked up his phone, Lexi waited at the door. Stepping outside into the cool of the evening, he walked her toward the house.

"So your middle name is Jaxton?" Lexi asked as they strolled along, in no hurry to reach her back gate.

"Yeah. I don't know where Mom came up with it, but there it is, just the same." Ty said. He had never been overly fond of his odd middle name. He didn't know why his mother couldn't have called him something simple like David or Andrew.

"I like it," Lexi said, with a saucy grin. "Tyler Jaxton Lewis. Has a nice ring to it, for a bad-boy grease monkey, anyway."

"Is that so?" Ty asked, giving a Lexi a look that let her know he was sizing her up. "Bad-boy grease monkey, huh? What makes you think I'm a bad-boy? Haven't I been on good behavior since I got here?"

Lexi stopped at the gate and realized she had started something she wasn't sure she could finish. Teasing Ty wasn't like joking with one of the other guys. There was too much attraction and tension snapping between them.

"You've been on very good behavior," she said honestly. "I couldn't ask for a better employee. But that bad-boy image isn't about what you do or how you act."

"It's not?" Ty asked, wondering if she had seen through his aloof façade.

"Nope," she said, twirling a strand of hair around her finger nervously.

"Then what *is* it about?" Tyler asked, curiously waiting for her response with his hands in his pockets. The desire to touch her was about to get the best of him.

"Stuff," she said, unable to admit her thoughts.

"That's not an answer," Ty said, taking a step closer. So close, in fact, she could see the moon reflected in his eyes and smell his wonderful manly scent while the warmth of his presence permeated her being.

"Sure it is," she said, turning toward the house with plans of escape. When she spun around, Ty grabbed her around the waist and started tickling her. She nearly doubled over giggling as he relentlessly ran his fingers along her sides, easily holding her captive with one muscled arm.

"Still not going to tell me?" he asked, his breath warm and minty by her ear. His nearness was making her limbs sluggish while her heart raced.

"Nope," she said, struggling to get away. He tightened his arm around her and went back to tickling. Gasping for breath, she slapped at the hand making her giggle. "I give! Stop tickling me! Please!"

"Okay, but only if you tell me why you think I'm a bad-boy," he said with a smile in his voice and his eyes. He didn't release his hold, but rested his hands on her waist instead of tormenting her sides with tickles.

"Because…"

"Because why?" Ty asked, running a teasing finger down Lexi's side, making a shiver race through her involuntarily.

"Because you…" Lexi took a deep breath. Before she could stop herself, words exploded out of her mouth. "Because you look like one with that square jaw all covered with stubble and sexy hair and bedroom eyes not to mention that hard body carved out of granite," she said, feeling heat flood her cheeks as she pushed him away and ran in the door.

Slamming the door and locking it behind her for good measure, Lexi buried her face in her hands, mortified at what she'd just said. How did her thoughts find their way past her lips? She meant to tell him it was his sweatshirts and work boots and rock music that gave him away as a bad-boy.

Sighing she twisted her hair around her finger again. It was going to be extremely difficult running the ranch while hiding in the house to avoid seeing Ty. She couldn't possibly face him again.

Watching Lexi retreat into the house, Ty was stunned by her words. She thought he had sexy hair and a granite body? And bedroom eyes?

He'd been told many times he was good looking. Women had said he was handsome. A few had even commented on his physique. But none, not one, had ever made him feel like Lexi did with her unexpected appraisal. He knew it was honest by the way it made her face flame red and sent her running into the house in embarrassment.

Grinning into the darkness, he whistled as he went back to the bunkhouse. It had been a great day. First, the arrival of his nephew and then Lexi basically admitting she was attracted to him. He was marking this day on his calendar. It was one he didn't want to forget.

Lesson Six
A Horse of a Different Color

"Ya can't live on this ranch and not learn how to ride.
It's jes a matter of keepin' the horse between
yerself and the ground."

Dreaming something was holding him down, paralyzing his legs, Ty struggled to move. Coming awake, he sighed, realizing it wasn't real until he tried to move his legs and couldn't. He felt weighted and fought to wiggle his feet.

Stretching his arm out, he reached for the bedside lamp and flicked it on.

Baby was stretched across both his legs, sleeping soundly.

"I should have known it would be you," Ty said, jostling the dog. She twitched and whined, moving only slightly as she settled back into sleep.

"Baby, you get off this bed right now," Ty said firmly. Moving around until he worked one leg loose from beneath her weight. "I mean it. Get up."

Raising her head, Baby glanced at him to see if he was serious. Deciding he was, she yawned and slowly got off the bed, standing at the bedroom door.

"Who let you in here? You know you aren't supposed to be in the bunkhouse." Ty scolded as Baby continued to stare at him. "Did you let yourself in?"

Ty got up and took the dog by her collar, marching her down the hall and out the front door. "Be good, Baby." He wondered how she found his room, but then decided Baby seemed to have an innate sense about where he was and what he was doing.

Going back to bed, he looked at the clock that read four in the morning and tried to fall asleep. Tossing and turning for a few minutes, he gave up and got ready for the day. It was his turn to cook breakfast, so he didn't mind having some extra time to get the meal on the table.

By the time everyone else was up, Ty had breakfast ready and his bedding in the wash. Baby left her white hair all over his comforter. As soon as he finished up with breakfast, he planned to clean the floor, noticing the white trail the dog left behind. He wondered if she was okay with all the hair she was shedding.

"Did I hear you talking to someone this morning? Calling someone Baby?" Jimmy teased as he sat down at the table. "You got a girl coming out here we don't know about?"

"That's right, Jimmy," Ty said, not ready for a round of teasing this early in the day. "I've got a girl that sneaks in after you all turn in for the night. She's sweet and funny with big eyes and white hair and questionable breath."

Swede cackled and slapped Jimmy on the back. "Sounds like your kind of girl."

Jimmy's ears turned red as he glared at first Swede then Ty.

"So the dog was in the house?" Gus asked, helping himself to another muffin. Ty was pretty handy in the kitchen as long as it was simple food or something he could mix from a box or a can.

"I woke up with her on my legs and couldn't move," Ty said, realizing it was now kind of funny. "I still can't figure out how she knew which room was mine."

"She's got yer scent. Someone forgot to lock the front door last night and she probably jes marched right in and made a beeline to yer room," Swede said.

"I'd much rather wake up to a girl on my bed than that beast," Cal said with a wicked grin.

"Wouldn't we all," Keith said, elbowing his brother as he waggled his eyebrows. "Wouldn't you, dude? Someone tall with dark hair and green eyes maybe?"

Ty ignored their comments and tried not to brood on Keith's observation as he spent the next few days buried in his work. The only time he'd caught a glimpse of Lexi was when she hurried past the shop door or windows. He had the idea she was trying to avoid him and so far her plans were working.

The third morning after their interlude by the gate, Ty needed to run into town and get some parts. He generally checked with everyone before he went to make sure no one else needed anything. He walked toward the barn and found a pile of Baby's fur outside the side entrance.

Startled, he looked around, expecting to see Baby lying wounded somewhere for the amount of fur left behind. He couldn't see any blood, but worried about the dog all the same. Calling her name, she didn't come loping out to meet him.

Looking in the barn and the outbuildings, Ty couldn't find her in any of her usual hiding places. He checked the bunkhouse and even stuck his head in the main house, calling for the dog and getting no response.

No one else seemed to be around either. It wasn't unusual for Ty to be the only one on the main place as the rest of them did spring farm work or rode out to check on fences and the cattle.

What was unusual was for Baby to be gone. Since he'd arrived, she stuck to him like a shadow.

Calling Swede, he let the foreman know he was heading to town and asked if he needed anything.

"Nope. I'm all set. Ya might check with the boss, though," Swede said in his gravelly voice.

"Have you seen Baby?" Ty asked, wondering if the dog had gone off with one of the other guys.

"Nope. But don't worry about her. She wanders all over this ranch and half of creation and hasn't forgotten to come home for dinner yet."

"Okay. I just… nevermind. Thanks, Swede."

Ty disconnected and took a deep breath. Calling Lexi, he tried to sound calm and uninterested when she answered.

"Hey, I'm going to town for parts. Do you need anything?" Ty asked, enjoying the sound of her voice. It made him think of something smooth and silky.

"Nothing today, but thanks for checking," Lexi said. She managed to avoid running into Ty since she completely embarrassed herself the other evening. Even talking to him on the phone, she could feel heat creeping up her neck. She knew she needed to say something about it, but was dreading it worse than a trip to the dentist.

"Ty, about the other night, I'm sorry. I shouldn't…" Lexi said, struggling to find the right words to express how much she regretted blurting out what was on her mind. Before she could continue, Ty cut her off.

"Don't, Lexi. It's fine. I shouldn't have tickled you like that. We can pretend it never happened," Ty said, remembering every second of how Lexi felt in his arms and wanting, more than anything, to feel her there again. Hoping to ease her discomfort, he changed the subject. "Have you seen Baby? She disappeared and there is a huge pile of her fur out here by the barn."

"I guess we forgot to tell you that Baby molts twice a year," Lexi said with a laugh in her voice. She could just picture the look on Ty's face when he came across the pile of Baby's shed hair.

"Molts?" Ty asked, trying to understand what Lexi was saying. "You mean she sheds like that twice a year?"

"That's right. She needs brushed every few days when she's shedding. I brushed her this morning and forgot to throw the fur away. Sorry if it startled you," Lexi said, realizing the pile of fur could be a little disturbing.

"I'm just glad she's okay," Ty said, relieved the dog was fine. He didn't want to admit it, but he'd become quite attached to the behemoth canine. "Do you know where she is?"

"The last time I saw her, she was in the barn pouting. She gets a little upset when she sheds. I think it damages her pride," Lexi said, understanding the dog all too well. She'd been hiding from Ty herself and now it looked like the dog was, too. So much for the Rockin' R females. Ty had them all shame-faced and hiding out.

"Okay. I'll just head into town, then. Sure there isn't anything you need?" Ty asked, walking into the bunkhouse to change his shirt before heading into town.

"I'm fine, but thanks. Talk to you later," Lexi said, hanging up the phone. What she really wanted to do was go along with Ty. A couple hours locked in a vehicle with him sounded both terrifying and wonderful.

Returning from town a few hours later, Ty worked right through dinner. Swede offered to bring him a plate, but Ty brushed him off, intent on finishing his project. The last streaks of sunlight were fading into the twilight when he slid out from beneath the truck he was working on to have his face washed in licks from Baby.

"Well, hello to you, too," he said, sitting up on the mechanic's creeper and rubbing the dog's head. Baby was grinning at him as he got to his feet and turned toward the bathroom. Ty was surprised to find Lexi watching him, holding a plate in her hand.

"Swede said you missed dinner. Figured you'd be hungry by now," Lexi said, holding the plate out in his direction. "Baby was ready to come out of hiding, so we came to see you together."

"I'm glad you both came," Ty said, ducking into the bathroom to wash his face and hands. If only Lexi had greeted him half as eagerly as the dog. The image that stirred in his mind made him grin in the bathroom mirror. Running his hands through his tousled hair, he was going to attempt to subdue it then decided maybe it was better left alone. After all, Lexi had called it sexy.

Lexi set the plate on a clean corner of the work bench and sat down on the stool next to Ty's. He lifted the foil covering to find slices of baked chicken, rice pilaf, steamed mixed vegetables and two dinner rolls slathered with berry jam. His stomach grumbled in anticipation and he smiled at Lexi.

"I know this didn't come from the bunkhouse," he said, taking a bite of the moist, tender chicken.

"I had leftovers," she said, not wanting to admit that when Swede mentioned Ty skipped dinner, she hurried into the house and made a special one. She needed to eat something anyway, so it wasn't like she was making an extra meal. At least that was what she told herself as she seasoned the chicken, made the rice and cooked the vegetables. The rolls were out of the freezer, as was the jam. Although she had a dozen things she needed to be doing this evening, somehow making dinner for Ty seemed like the highest priority. When she found Baby hiding on the back porch, she cajoled the dog into coming with her to see Ty.

She and Baby were both pathetic when it came to the handsome mechanic.

Finishing up the excellent meal, Ty thanked Lexi for dinner and offered to walk her back to the house. Turning off the lights and tools in the shop, Ty carried the plate and followed Lexi back to the house in the semi-darkness. Going down the walk, they discussed what was happening on the ranch and the fact that Lexi hadn't discovered any more clues. She found her dad's box of yearbooks, but the one from his senior year was missing.

Reaching the back door, Lexi wasn't quite ready to say goodnight to Ty as she turned and looked at him imploringly.

"I should probably turn in and let you get your rest," Ty said, handing her the plate and scratching Baby on the head, trying to ignore his longing to follow Lexi inside.

"That's too bad," Lexi said, stepping inside, but leaving the door wide open. "I've got an apple crisp in the oven and was hoping I could find someone to help me eat it."

"I wouldn't want you to be forced to eat alone," Ty said with a teasing grin as he followed her into the kitchen. Baby trailed him in and sat down by the door. The smell of apples and cinnamon filled the space, making Ty's mouth water even after the big, delicious meal he just consumed.

Washing her hands at the kitchen sink, Lexi took the crisp from the oven and set it on a hot pad to cool. Getting out plates and vanilla ice cream, she and Ty chatted for a few minutes while the crisp cooled and she made coffee. She put large servings on two plates then scooped vanilla ice cream on top. A drizzle of caramel sauce completed the dessert and she slid a plate across to Ty.

Rolling his eyes in pleasure, he savored the first warm, heavenly bite.

"Like it?" Lexi asked, grinning at him.

"Yes, ma'am, I do," Ty said, taking another big bite. It was quite possibly the best apple crisp he'd ever had. Hot from the oven with ice cream melting in a creamy pool with just a hint of caramel, it was sweet perfection. The hot coffee was good, too. Some of the boys in the bunkhouse were not skilled in the art of making coffee and Ty really missed a good cup of morning java.

"I'm glad I could twist your arm into having some," Lexi said with a teasing light warming her green eyes.

Ty suddenly felt everything go into slow motion as he watched Lexi take a bite of her dessert, a tiny drip of caramel on her lip. When she ran the tip of her tongue out and licked it away, he felt his pulse pick up tempo while his hands grew clammy. Her cheeks were a rosy shade of pink and her beautiful eyes, highlighted by her lush, black lashes, sparkled with golden flecks.

More than anything, Ty wanted to lean forward and kiss her. The part of his head telling him that was a very bad idea won out over the part telling him to sweep her into his arms and show her how he was coming to feel about her.

Lexi glanced at Ty and tumbled into the warm liquid orbs of blue that stared back at her. She watched a muscle work in Ty's jaw as he studied her. The longing that radiated from him fed her heart and reflected what was in her own.

If she wasn't terrified of his reaction, of being rebuffed, she would lean closer and bridge the chasm keeping them apart. Instead, she held his gaze, feeling caressed by Ty although he didn't touch her.

Swallowing back a sigh, Ty broke the intimate moment and carried his dirty plate and cup to the sink. He had no business entertaining any thoughts about Lexi. She was his boss and a lady. He had absolutely nothing to offer her beyond himself and he didn't think that was quite good enough.

Ty was a homeless mechanic who could fit everything he owned in this world in the back of his pickup with room to spare. She deserved much better than him.

Walking to the door without making eye contact, he finally settled his gaze on her face and saw the look of hurt and confusion in her eyes. Leaning against the door, Ty crossed his arms in front of his chest, studying his boss. She was feeling the powerful tug between them every bit as much as he was.

As a gentleman, it was his place to maintain the distance and their current level of professionalism. There could be no more dinners together, no more time spent alone in her house. It was just too hard for him to ignore the temptation of wanting his alluring boss.

Lexi wondered if Ty had any idea how entirely unsettling that enticing pose was to females in general, and to her in particular. As he leaned there, muscles flexing, tousled hair begging to be touched, and devil-may-care attitude projecting from the set of his jaw, she wanted to take that scruffy face in her hands and kiss those full lips until she was breathless.

Instead, she started twirling a strand of her hair around her finger, wishing Ty would show some interest in kissing her. All he had to do was meet her halfway.

"Thank you for the wonderful meal and that amazing crisp. It was really good," Ty said, not making any move toward leaving.

"You're welcome. Thanks for coming in and keeping me company. The house gets too quiet sometimes," Lexi said, hoping he believed her. It was true. The big house sometimes echoed with its emptiness and made her lonely. Like now.

"I'm sure Baby can keep things lively around here," Ty said, rubbing the dog's head again.

"She does. I just don't let her in very often," Lexi said, taking a step closer to both man and dog. "I can't stand having her hair all over."

"Baby does leave behind a well-marked trail," Ty said with a chuckle as he thought of all the fur he'd seen earlier that morning.

"Thanks again, Ty," Lexi said, watching Ty's eyes grow darker and his jaw set tightly.

"Anytime, Lexi," he said quietly, reaching out and taking the lock of hair she'd been twirling into his own hand. He ran his fingers along the silky strands as a sigh escaped Lexi's rosy lips.

What could one kiss hurt? He'd kiss her and neither of them would feel anything then all this awful tension between them would disappear.

Ty took a step closer, dropping her hair as his hands settled on her waist, drawing her closer to him. He gave Lexi a heated look that let her know exactly what he was intending if she wanted to pull away.

Anticipating her resistance, he let out the breath he was holding when she slid her hands up his arms, around his neck, and slowly lowered her lashes. He was so close, he could almost feel the softness of her lips, taste the sweetness of them. Her wonderful, warm floral scent flooded his senses as he lowered his head. When just a breath of space was all that separated his lips from hers, Baby barked and shoved her way between them, effectively killing the moment.

"I guess that's my signal to leave," Ty said with a nervous laugh. Sending Baby a reproving glare, he opened the door and stepped outside. "Thanks again, Lexi. I appreciated the good food and company.

"You're welcome," she whispered as Ty went down the steps and out the back gate. Turning to Baby, Lexi took the dog's face in her hands and frowned at her. "That was naughty, Baby. Very naughty."

Baby licked her hand and wagged her tail, obviously pleased with herself. If Lexi didn't know better, she'd think the dog wedged between them intentionally.

"Out you go, then," Lexi said, opening the door and shooing the dog outside. If it wasn't for that crazy dog, she would have finally felt the touch of Ty's lips on her own. She could still smell his scent and her skin tingled at her waist where his hands lingered.

How would she ever get any sleep when all she wanted was for Ty to come back and pick up where Baby interrupted?

Going upstairs, she went into the guest room her dad claimed as his own after her mother died and he could no longer stand to be in the master suite. His scent still drifted through the air and she ran her hand along the desk where he kept his personal things. Opening drawers, she didn't find anything that sparked her interest.

Going through the books piled on the night stand, she happened to discover his yearbook. A tiny scrap of paper marked a page with a photo of her dad in his football uniform.

The Power of a Horse

Lexi had no idea what that clue meant.

Deciding to think about it for a day or two, she tried to go to sleep only to have Ty's bright blue eyes and heartbreaker smile haunt her dreams.

The next morning, Ty was trying to decide if he should be mad or grateful to the dog. While he was mulling over the two options, he heard Swede and Lexi at the shop door, talking quietly. They seemed to be arguing about something.

Opening the door, he caught them both by surprise as they turned to look at him with wide eyes.

"Hey," he said, with a jaunty smile. "What evil are you two plotting?"

"No evil," Swede said, shifting his weight from one bowed leg to the other. "We're jes discussin' who was gonna break some news to ya that ya might not like to hear."

Panic coursed through Ty as he wondered if his behavior last night was about to get him fired. He had to get his head on straight and treat his boss like a boss instead of the woman who had invaded his dreams at night and thoughts during the day.

"Ty, don't worry, it's nothing major," Lexi said, placing a gloved hand on his arm. Even through the leather, he felt the heat of her touch. "Today we are giving you your first riding lesson. Swede and I were just discussing the best way to go about it."

"Riding lesson? What riding lesson?" Ty asked. Swede mentioned when he hired him that he would sometimes be required to help with the farming and ranching, but Ty hoped his mechanic skills would be in such demand he wouldn't actually have to learn the other stuff. He didn't mind helping pull calves or the occasional work they had him do driving a tractor or the feed truck. But riding? He wasn't sure he liked the sound of that at all.

"You knew we would eventually need you to help in other areas on the ranch. Now that you've gotten most of the equipment repaired, we need to train you to take on some other responsibilities," Lexi explained as they stood in the early morning sunshine.

Although the day promised to be warm and beautiful, Ty suddenly felt a chill crawling up his spine.

"What type of responsibilities?" Ty asked, not exactly sure what any of them did when they saddled up and rode off for the day. Sitting around the bunkhouse table, they threw around phrases like "ride the line" and "wrangling doggies" that made no sense to him.

"Ridin' fence, chasin' cows, thet sort of thing," Swede said, taking Ty's arm in his gnarled hand and leading him toward the corral where three horses stood saddled and ready to ride.

"I'm sure you'll pick it up in no-time," Lexi said, encouragingly as they neared the horses. "Piece of cake."

Instead of arguing or agreeing, Ty remained silent. He would do whatever they asked of him, but it didn't mean he had to like it.

Lexi could tell from the change in Ty's body language that he had resigned himself to the task ahead. She was proud of him for willingly going along with their plans. In a few weeks, it would be time for spring branding and they would need every extra set of hands they could find. Ty was going to have to help gather the cattle. She also intended for him to help ride herd throughout the summer months in addition to assisting with the farm work.

It was just part of life on the Rockin' R Ranch. Everyone was expected to help out wherever they were needed.

It was Swede and Lexi's job to make sure everyone was cross-trained and able to do it.

None of the other hands could take over Ty's duties as a mechanic, though. Not a single one of them had any skill in that area and Lexi didn't have time for Ty to teach anybody. Being a mechanic was still his number one focus, even if they were forcing him into the role of farmer and cowboy.

"Have you ever ridden a horse before?" Lexi asked Ty as they leaned against the pole fence of the corral and watched the horses.

"No, ma'am," Ty said, mentally gearing up for the adventure ahead. Shoving his hands in his pockets, he took a deep breath. He could do this.

"Do you know anything about horses?" Lexi asked as she rubbed her hand along the closest horse's neck.

"Only that the good guy always rides away with the girl on one in the old westerns," Ty said with a teasing grin.

Swede cackled and slapped Ty on the back. "I'm gonna let Lex learn ya about horses while I take care of a few things then we'll go for a ride." Ambling off into the recesses of the barn, Ty was left standing alone with Lexi and the three horses.

"Here are some basics, Ty," Lexi said, motioning him to step closer to the horse. "Never walk behind a horse unless you want kicked. Mount and dismount on the left side. Stay calm because they can sense your feelings. Don't startle them. Let them know right off you are in charge."

"Okay, sounds simple enough," Ty said, listening more to the sound of Lexi's voice than to what she was saying. He loved hearing her talk and thought she could easily use her voice on the radio or in commercials. Men would definitely sit up and pay attention to hear her smooth, honeyed tones.

"There are three pieces of equipment you need to remember when you are going to ride: saddle blanket, saddle, bridle," Lexi said, taking the saddle off the horse followed by the blanket. She demonstrated how to place the blanket and the saddle on the horse's back, giving Ty step-by-step instructions in how to properly put on a saddle. She'd get into the parts of the saddle another day. Right now, he just needed to learn how to put the saddle on and cinch it so it would stay on the horse.

She then showed him the bridle and talked about the headstall, chin strap, bit and reins. Removing the horse's bridle, she held the horse by a lead rope while verbally walking Ty through putting on the bridle.

Lexi stressed how important it was to be sure everything was smooth and placed properly on the horse or it would get sores.

"You are wonderful with animals, so I know you'll be gentle with your horse, but I'm giving you my 'This is a Horse 101 Class.' Bear with me," Lexi said with a smile that would have made Ty agree to anything she said.

Lexi, who loved being around horses, was happy to share her passion for them with Ty. He eagerly absorbed what she was telling him and on the second attempt saddled the horse perfectly without her assistance.

"Are you ready to give riding a try?" Lexi asked as she eyed Ty's clothes. His jeans were a little baggy and his work boots weren't exactly made for riding, but they would work for his lesson today.

"Sure," Ty said, deciding learning to ride couldn't be all bad. Lexi certainly seemed to enjoy it.

She showed him how to mount and dismount, how to hold the reins, and discussed pointing his toes, clamping his knees and the finer points of balance.

"I'm not quite sure I've got that," Ty said, watching her mount again. It put her backside level with his range of vision and he was greatly enjoying the view. "Can you show me again?"

"No problem," Lexi said, swinging her leg over the saddle and dismounting. "You put your foot here and swing your leg over, just like this."

"Maybe I need to watch you a few more times," Ty said, trying to sound serious. When Lexi looked at him, she noticed his mischievous grin and shook her head.

"No more demonstrations, buckaroo," Lexi said, stepping out of the saddle and holding the horse still while Ty got into position. Lexi made it look so simple and easy when she slid into the saddle. With one foot stuck in the stirrup, Ty struggled to pull himself up and swing his leg over. The motion felt so foreign to him, as did sitting on the saddle. When the horse shifted beneath him, he felt a moment of panic, but remembered he needed to relax.

Lexi beamed at him with a smile that went right to his heart. If she asked him to tap dance on a bed of nails with his bare feet, he'd pull off his boots and socks and get to it.

"Good job. I'll adjust the stirrups and you can try again," Lexi said, lengthening the stirrups to fit Ty's long legs. At six-four, he needed some extra length from where Lexi had them set.

Ty did as she said and was able to mount with more confidence the third time she made him go through the motions.

"We're ready to go for a ride. Swede and I will stay right beside you, so don't worry about a thing," Lexi said, giving Ty a pat on the arm. "Just wait here and I'll get Swede."

Lexi ran over to the barn and quickly returned with the foreman.

"Well, look at ya sittin' up there," Swede said as he easily swung into the saddle. "Ya seem to hit it off just fine with ol' Delilah."

"My horse is named Delilah?" Ty asked Lexi as she mounted her horse.

"Yep. My horse is Rowdy and Swede's is Kitty," Lexi said, reining in next to Ty. "Delilah is the gentlest mare on the place. She used to be my mom's horse."

"Nice to meet you, Delilah," Ty said, patting the horse on the neck the way Lexi had done earlier. The horse whickered and bobbed her head, as if in greeting.

"She's saying hello to you," Lexi said with a grin. Ty seemed to be relaxing and didn't act afraid of the horse, which was a very good sign. He looked good in the saddle and she had to forcibly shift her thoughts into teacher mode, away from her handsome pupil.

"Ready to give this a whirl?" Swede asked, riding up on the other side of Ty as they slowly walked the horses away from the corral.

"Sure," Ty said, hoping he didn't fall off and embarrass himself. He wished it was just Swede with him because if something did happen, at least Lexi wouldn't be there to witness it first-hand.

As they walked along, Lexi gave him instructions about turning and stopping the horse, using his knees and core to stay seated, and keeping his weight balanced.

Heading away from the buildings, they followed a narrow dirt road Ty knew led out to the fields. He'd gone running on it a few times. Keeping in shape, he occasionally added running before or after his day's work ended. Sometimes he ran down the driveway to the paved road, other times he followed the various dirt and gravel roads around the ranch.

Getting used to the feel of the horse moving beneath him and the smell of leather from the saddle and bridle, Ty relaxed and enjoyed the beautiful morning. He watched Swede and Lexi with his peripheral vision and copied the way they sat and held their hands.

Turning his head, he noticed movement in the sagebrush and pointed.

"What's that?" he asked as he eyed some horned animal he hadn't seen before. Half a dozen of them stared intently at the three riders on horseback.

"Antelope," Swede said, following the direction of Ty's pointing finger. "Ain't ya ever seen one before?"

"No, I haven't," Ty said, studying the animals.

Spooked, they turned and raced through the brushy ground.

"They move fast, don't they?" Ty observed, turning to Lexi with a grin that made the butterflies in her stomach take flight. She suddenly had a vision of what he must have looked like as an adorable little boy. That picture in her head was rapidly melting her heart as she studied the man absorbing some of nature's wonder.

Topping a rise where the road widened, Lexi informed Ty they were going to speed up a little.

"Horses have four basic speeds," Lexi explained. "Walk, trot, canter and gallop. You did really well with walking. We're going to skip trotting because it can be hard to hold your seat until you get used to the movement. Cantering will feel really strange at first and if you are worried about falling off, you can hang onto the saddle horn until you get comfortable."

"Lex, don't tell him thet. Ya know only a wuss grabs the horn," Swede said with a twinkling glint of mirth in his eye.

"Swede, you just hush up," Lexi said, not wanting Ty to think he couldn't hold onto the saddle horn if he needed to. Turning back to Ty, she gave him some pointers and assured him he would do fine.

Urging their horses forward in a canter, Delilah followed the other horses without Ty having to encourage her. As he jounced along, he tried to keep his seat like Swede and Lexi instructed him, but he slid all over the saddle. He was determined to only grab the saddle horn if he was going to fall off.

"Why are we doing this?" he asked, convinced his stomach was jiggling between his chin and toes.

"Because ya got to learn how to ride at all speeds," Swede said. "If it was a car, ya wouldn't jes drive it in first gear, would ya?"

"No," Ty said, knowing he looked like an idiot as he bounced all over the saddle.

"Let your hips move with the horse, not your whole body," Lexi said, trying not to laugh at him. Although she prevented a giggle from escaping, she couldn't control her smile. Ty looked miserable, but at least he was trying.

Riding close to him, she put her hand on his leg and felt tight, tense, muscles. She also felt electricity spark up her arm and jolt down her spine at the contact with his well-muscled thigh. Blinking her eyes to regain her focus, she pulled back her hand.

"You've got to relax your thighs. Hang on with your knees and let your thighs relax," Lexi said, moving her hand to his back. "Straighten your back and picture your spine straight up and down. Your whole body doesn't move. Let your hips do the work. Let your seat roll forward with Delilah."

Trying to pay attention to what Lexi was telling him was extremely difficult when her touch on his thigh nearly made him fall off the opposite side of the horse. Her warm, delicate hand on his back seared through his shirt and melted into his skin.

Swede cackled and drew near on Ty's other side.

"What she's tryin' to say is keep yer butt on the saddle. Pretend your back is a broom handle and your rear is the broom, sweepin' back and forth," Swede said, enjoying the lesson and the resulting look of discomfort and annoyance on Ty's face. "Ya look like one of them bobble-head toy things, bouncin' all over creation."

"Yes, sir," Ty said, under his breath as Lexi drew her hand away. She gave him a warm smile and an encouraging nod. Visualizing a broom, Ty tried hard to follow their direction and soon found himself moving with the horse instead of fighting against it.

"That's awesome, Ty. You've got it," Lexi said with a triumphant grin. "Look at him, Swede."

"Yer doin' just fine, dude," Swede assured him.

They cantered for a few more minutes then Lexi told him they were going to try a gallop. She explained that it was like cantering, only faster and smoother.

"Instead of three beats, you'll hear four," Lexi said, still riding close to Ty.

"Beats?" Ty asked, trying to maintain his successful movements with Delilah.

"Hoof beats," Lexi said with an indulgent look on her face. "When a horse canters, you hear three hoof beats hitting the ground. Galloping you'll hear four. You like music and drums, listen and see if you can hear it."

Lexi and Swede urged their horses ahead and Delilah picked up speed, following their lead. As they hit full gallop, Ty realized Lexi was right. The gait was smoother and listening he could hear four beats that sounded drum-like. The world was zooming by and Ty almost felt like he was flying as the horses raced along an open pasture. He could get used to this.

As Lexi and Swede reined in their horses and gave Ty instruction in doing the same, he couldn't wipe the grin off his face.

"This is cool," he said as they slowed the horses back to a walk.

"You're doing very well for your first lesson," Lexi said, looking at Swede for confirmation.

"If I didn't know better, I'd say yer a natural at this, son," Swede said with a wink.

"Thanks, sir. That means a lot, coming from you."

They rode back to the house a different direction. Lexi alternated between cantering, galloping and walking all the way back and Ty was really enjoying the experience. In fact, he was looking forward to his next lesson. Not just for the opportunity to spend time with Lexi, but because he had fun riding.

"I can't wait to tell Beth about this," Ty said as they stopped at the barn and dismounted.

"What will she say?" Lexi asked as they took off the saddles.

"That she can't believe I not only rode a horse but liked it," Ty said, following Lexi into the barn carrying his saddle. They stored them and Lexi showed him how to brush down the horses before turning them loose in the fenced pasture by the barn.

Lexi walked with him back to the shop, stopping at the door before he went inside.

"I'm really proud of you, Ty. You were a wonderful student and Swede's correct, you took to that like you were born to it. I look forward to another lesson with you soon," Lexi said. She pressed a quick kiss to Ty's scruffy cheek before hurrying toward the house.

Ty watched her go and had the fleeting thought that he might need to start shaving a little more frequently.

Lesson Seven
Clothes Make the Man

*"Ya got to walk the walk, talk the talk,
and wear the boots, pard."*

Although Ty was a little sore as the day wore on from the ride, he didn't give it another thought, until he woke up the next morning in agony.

Muscles he didn't even know existed burned and cried out in protest of being forced into use. From the neck down, he was a hot, aching mass of sore muscles. After multiple efforts, he finally managed to sit up in bed. Taking an inventory of his pain, Ty decided the worst of it was between his waist and his knees.

Getting dressed, he had to sit on the bed and gingerly pull on one jean leg, then the other. When that was done, he rested before attempting to put on his socks and boots. Not only were his muscles aching, his baggy jeans had rubbed sore spots on his inner thighs and backside.

Groaning as he stood and zipped up his pants, he certainly hoped Lexi didn't have plans for a lesson today. He didn't think he could get in the saddle, let alone sit on it.

Doing his best to walk normally, he sauntered out to the breakfast table and joined in the good-natured teasing. Mustering every ounce of bravado he possessed, he walked to the shop and collapsed onto his padded stool. It was going to be a very long day.

Mid-morning, Lexi poked her head in the door and watched him shuffling around the shop. Hearing movement, Ty thought it was Baby and didn't even look up to see what the dog was doing.

"Hey, Baby, come give me some love," Ty said when he didn't feel the dog lean against his leg like she usually did when she came in.

"What did you have in mind?" Lexi teased as she walked over to him.

Ty's neck turned a bright shade of red and his face felt hot.

"My apologies, ma'am," Ty said, embarrassed. He should have picked up on Lexi's scent floating across the shop, but it was so ingrained into his brain he randomly smelled it when she was nowhere around. "I thought you were the dog."

"Is that your customary greeting for Baby?" Lexi asked, finding it amusing to see Ty flustered. He was usually so calm and aloof, she didn't know he could get so rattled.

"Yeah, I guess it is," Ty admitted. He had a soft spot the size of Texas for that darn dog and now everyone would know about it.

"I think it's sweet," Lexi said, leaning against the counter next to where he worked on some small part that looked like a foreign mass of metal to her. "No wonder Baby thinks you're the best thing to come along since the invention of dog food."

Ty laughed and turned to look at Lexi. She was so beautiful. With her leaning against the counter and him sitting on the stool, their eyes and lips were at the same level. He could see the warm flecks of gold shining from her deep green eyes and noticed for the first time a little mole at the corner of her left eye. He had the most intense desire to kiss the mole then work his way around to her rosy lips.

As her warm, floral scent floated around him, he swallowed twice just to keep his thoughts from spiraling out of control.

Lexi should have stayed at the door instead of getting close to Ty. Every time she did, she seemed to lose her ability to think with any degree of sense. All she wanted to do was feel Ty's arms around her and his lips on hers. Just once. That's all she needed.

When he thought he was talking to the dog, Lexi wanted nothing more than to comply with his order and give him some love. She wouldn't mind having him call her baby, either. The sound of that deep voice saying her name made her toes tingle every single time.

Instead of giving in to her desire to sit on Ty's lap and kiss him senseless, she got down to the matter at hand that brought her to the shop in the first place.

"I was wondering how you were feeling today. You did so well with the riding yesterday, I realized too late we probably over-did it," Lexi said, looking at Ty and trying to decide if he would admit he was in pain. Her guess was probably not.

"I'm fine," he said, giving her what he hoped was a convincing smile.

"Good. I wouldn't want you to be sore or anything," Lexi said, realizing Ty was in fact not telling her the truth as he moved uncomfortably on the stool. "Because if you were, then I'd tell you to rub some liniment into the muscles and put some antibiotic cream on any open sores you might have. But I'm glad to hear you're fine. I don't have time for a lesson today, so we'll plan on resuming tomorrow. Okay?"

"Yep, that's fine," Ty said, trying to keep his tone even, wondering how Lexi could possibly know he was hurting. "Thanks for letting me know."

"Anytime, buckaroo," Lexi teased as she walked to the door, noticing Ty didn't get up and walk with her like he always did. "Maybe we can discuss giving you some love another time."

Ty watched her retreating form, wondering if she was teasing or serious. Before he had time to get worked up about it, his sister called.

"Hi Beth, how's my favorite nephew and his mama?" Ty asked, hoping Beth had more photos she would send him. Nate had kept up a steady stream of pictures, but he didn't get any yesterday.

"We couldn't be better, unless you were here," Beth said, sounding excited.

"What's up? You sound like you've got good news," Ty said, attuned to his sister's tone of voice.

"Nate got a job!" Beth said enthusiastically. "He'll be able to mostly work from home, so he can take care of Jax and we won't have to leave him with a sitter very often. Isn't that great?"

"It's better than great. It's fantastic," Ty said, joining in her excitement. "When does he start? Who's he working for? What will he be doing?"

Beth filled him in on the details. They chatted for a few minutes, before the baby began to cry, ready for a feeding.

"Take care of Jax and give him a kiss for me, Beth," Ty said, wishing he could see the baby in person. "Tell Nate congratulations. I'm so happy for both of you."

"I will," Beth said. "Oh, and Ty?"

"Yeah?"

"You need to stop sending us your money. Now that Nate is employed, we'll be fine. You need to start building your nest egg back up. You never know when you're going to need it."

"But Beth, I've already told you..." Ty said, exasperated at his sister's stubbornness. She and Nate helped him out when he lost his job as much as they could. It was his turn to help them.

"I don't care what you've told me. Nate and I both appreciated all your help, but we truly are going to be fine now. You hang onto your money. If we get in a tight spot, I promise to tell you to hand it over," Beth said, trying to joke with Ty.

"Just be sure you do," he said, deciding to bank his money and save it for whenever Nate and Beth might need help. "Love you, sis."

"Love you, too. Bye."

Hanging up with Beth, he got lost in his thoughts. The growling of his stomach a couple of hours later alerted him that it was nearly noon. Washing up, he made a sandwich and took a cold bottle of pop from the fridge, moving slowly back toward the stool. If anything, he felt worse instead of better. How could he sit there the rest of the day, in misery? Contemplating what to do, he was yanked out of his musings when Swede bustled in the door with a grin.

"Ya about done with yer lunch?" Swede asked as Ty took the last bite of his sandwich.

"Yep. What can I do for you?" Ty asked, throwing the paper plate into the trash and his empty soda bottle into a box he kept for recycling.

"Lex told me to get ya properly outfitted before yer next riding lesson. So let's get goin'." Swede stood in the shop door, waiting for Ty to put some hustle in it and come outside.

"Right now?" Ty asked, getting off the stool and attempting to take off his coveralls. Apparently he didn't hide his grimace as well as he thought when Swede let out a cackle.

"Yer as stove-up as a three-legged mule in a mud hole. Let's get ya to town and we'll pick up something to help 'em sore muscles while we're at it."

"Yes, sir," Ty said, shuffling out the door and following Swede to the ranch truck.

An hour later, he was in the big feed store staring at row after row of cowboy boots. Swede made him try on half a dozen pairs before Ty started getting a feel for what he wanted. Trying on a dozen more, he finally narrowed down his selection to a pair of brown boots that would serve him well on the ranch. Should the occasion warrant, he could clean them up and give them a bit of polish to wear to mandatory cowboy functions. The boots were sturdy, yet comfortable, and affordable.

"Ya made a good choice, son," Swede said, leading him to the men's clothing department. "Now we need to get ya some jeans. Those baggy butt things you been wearin' are fine in the shop, but ya can't ride in them. Bet ya got some friction sores from ridin' yesterday, don't ya?"

"A few," Ty said, trying to hide his discomfort, both from the sores and the conversation. Looking at the stacks of blue jeans, he tipped his head toward Swede. "Why don't you show me what I need and I'll try them on?"

Swede pointed to a table full of Wranglers, helped Ty find his size and waited while he tried them on. Ty thought they felt strange and way too tight, but when he came out wearing them, Swede nodded his head.

"Are you sure they're supposed to fit like this?" Ty asked, making sure he could bend over in the jeans.

Getting the attention of a nearby, salesgirl, Swede asked for her opinion. When she turned around and saw Ty, who was squatting down to make sure the jeans would move with him, her eyes grew wide and her cheeks turned pink, but she smiled broadly.

"I think those are the perfect size," she said, unable to take her eyes off the handsome newcomer or the way the Wranglers fit him like a smooth leather glove. He was someone she'd not seen in the store before, but if he was with Swede, that must mean he'd be out at the Rockin' R

Ranch. That Lex Ryan was one lucky girl. "Absolutely perfect."

Ty felt heat climbing up his neck at her obvious perusal and approval. He was now convinced the jeans were too tight, but supposed Swede knew more than he did.

"Good. He'll take three pairs," Swede said, holding on to Ty's boot box and pointing to Ty's size. The salesgirl took the jeans and boots up to the counter, but looked back their direction several times.

"Is that it?" Ty asked as he came out of the dressing room with the third pair of jeans in his hand.

"Nope. Ya need a hat. Ya can't be out in the sun without one and yer ball cap just ain't gonna cut it," Swede said, going to a display of straw cowboy hats.

"Should I get one like yours?" Ty said, pointing to a display of felt hats. He wasn't sure about the straw hats and if he was going to have to wear one, he'd rather get one he liked.

"Ya can," Swede said, looking at Ty. "Git a felt hat now and when summer hits, ya can git a straw hat. The felts git a might warm in the summer, but they'll serve ya well the rest of the year. If ya git a good one, it should last ya a long, long time."

"Well, let's get a good one then," Ty said with a grin. He tried on a variety of styles, finally settling on a black cattleman style hat with a wide brim. He felt completely stupid standing there with the hat on but decided he would look at the new cowboy clothes as part of a costume required for his job.

"Thet's a dandy!" Swede said with a cackle as Ty adjusted the hat on his head. "A real dandy."

"All right. I've got boots, jeans and a hat. I suppose shirts are next on the list?" Ty said, wondering how much this shopping trip was going to cost him.

"Yeah, we better git ya a few. Ya'll be glad for these in another month or so when it's hot enough to fry a lizard on the sidewalk," Swede said, looking through a rack of cotton shirts with snaps. Ty choose four, all in shades of blue or gray.

"Are we done now?" Ty asked as they neared the front of the store. He never thought he'd see the day when he'd be dressing like a cowboy. Or trying to become a cowboy, however reluctantly.

"Almost. Ya need a good pair of leather gloves and ya better grab a couple pairs of boot socks. I'll git yer socks, while ya try on some gloves. One of these will work fine," Swede said, pointing to a display.

Ty tried on several, selecting a pair that was smooth and soft. They made him think of the way Lexi's skin felt beneath his hands the few times he'd touched her. Thinking of her made him smile. He wondered what she'd say when she saw him in his new clothes.

"You should do that more often," the salesgirl said from beside him.

Ty looked down at her, confused. She was a pretty girl, dressed in western wear with a canvas apron emblazoned with the store name across the front. She looked up at him with a smile that was more invitation than friendly gesture.

"Pardon?"

"You should smile more often. It makes you look not quite so dangerous," she said, stepping around him to the cash register. "You ready to check out?"

"Not quite, but thanks," he said, looking around for Swede. He finally spied the foreman deep in conversation with another rancher who appeared to be Swede's age. Walking that direction, Swede waved him over and introduced him.

"Ty, this is Jim Gardner. He's one of our neighbors. His place borders ours on the west," Swede said as the men shook hands. "Ty is our new mechanic."

"Mechanic you say? What can you fix?" Jim asked.

Before Ty could answer, Swede grabbed his arm and hustled him toward the cash registers. "Sorry, Jim, didn't realize how late it was gittin' to be. Talk to ya soon."

"What was that all about?" Ty asked as they got in line and Swede handed him several pairs of socks.

"Jim finds out how good ya are, he'll try to steal ya away from Lex," Swede said, looking over his shoulder to make sure no one was listening.

"He could only steal me away if I was willing to go, and I'm not," Ty said, somewhat annoyed that Swede thought he'd jump ship that easily. "I came to work for the Rockin' R Ranch and until you or the boss tells me otherwise, that's where I plan to stay."

Swede looked at him a moment then gave him a broad smile along with a slap on his shoulder. "I knew ya were a keeper. Jes knew it."

Ty anxiously watched the salesgirl ring up his purchases. He'd been sending most of his paychecks to Nate and Beth, only holding back a little to live on. He hoped he had enough in his account to cover the expenses of the clothes and still pay his few bills. If he didn't, he'd have to put it on his credit card and pay it off with his next paycheck.

When she gave him the total, he pulled out his credit card, but before he could pay, Swede whipped out a handful of cash and peeled off what was needed.

"What are you doing?" Ty asked, caught off guard.

"Payin' for these ranch supplies," Swede said as the salesgirl took the cash and gave him change.

"These aren't ranch supplies, they're my clothes. I'm paying for them," Ty said, angry that Swede was ignoring his protests as he gathered up the bags and motioned Ty out the door.

"Accordin' to the boss, these are beyond what is required in yer job description and therefore, the ranch is payin' for them."

Swede opened the pickup's back door and set the bags he carried inside.

Ty was livid as he set down the boot box and the rest of the bags. The fact that he couldn't afford to pay for all these purchases and Lexi knew it grated on his nerves and pride. He was not a charity case.

"Quit standin' there like ya sucked a bad lemon. I've got a hankerin' for a piece of pie and a cup of good coffee. Then we'll run by the drug store and git ya somethin' for yer other problems," Swede said, starting the pickup.

Ty got in but didn't say a word all the way to the restaurant. He and Swede talked about what he could expect in the next couple weeks as they rounded up the cows and went through branding, but Ty had a hard time focusing on the conversation. The more he thought about being a charity case to Lexi, the angrier he became.

Running by the grocery store's pharmacy, Swede showed Ty what to get for his sore muscles and Ty picked up a few other things, including a large tube of antibiotic cream. Swede had a grocery list from Lexi he filled and Ty helped him load everything in the pickup before they headed home. To pass the time, Swede gave Ty a lesson in taking care of his boots and hat as well as proper hat wearing etiquette. He mentioned multiple times to "tip yer hat to a lady comin' or goin' and never wear it in a church, in someone's home or any public place ya might block someone's view."

"Got it," Ty said, still feeling sullen and resentful of Lexi telling Swede to buy his western wear.

"Look, son," Swede said, giving him a narrowed glance as they drove down the ranch's driveway. "I know ya got somethin' stuck in yer craw, so ya might as well spit it out before it chokes ya. If yer mad at Lex about buying yer stuff, go talk to her. She'll listen and the two of ya can work somethin' out."

Ty looked at Swede, but nodded his head.

Stopping at the main house, Swede knocked on the back door as he opened it, carrying groceries inside. Lexi came down the hallway and greeted them both warmly. She helped them carry in the rest of the bags and couldn't help but notice the dark cloud of thunder that had settled on Ty's face.

"Ty, you mind coming back in once you help Swede with the rest of the supplies?" she asked, wondering what happened to make him so mad that his brow was puckered and his jaw muscle twitched angrily.

"Sure, just give me a minute," he said quietly, closing the kitchen door behind him.

He and Swede carried groceries into the bunkhouse then Ty took his new purchases to his room. While Swede parked the ranch truck back in its designated spot, he walked to the house, fury pounding out of every step.

Knocking curtly on the back door and studying the toes of his work boots, he glanced up when Lexi opened it with a smile.

"Want a glass of iced tea?" she asked in a friendly tone, motioning him inside.

"No, thank you," he said, staring at the floor.

"Let's go sit in the office," Lexi said, leading the way down the hall to the big, open room. Instead of sitting behind the desk, she took one of the two chairs in front of it. Ty sat in the other.

If possible, he looked even madder than he had when he and Swede first came back from town.

"Okay, buckaroo. Out with it. What's the problem?"

Ty was surprised she cut right to the chase, but Lexi didn't exactly seem like the kind of girl to waste time beating around the bush.

"I pay my own way," Ty ground out, clenching his hands as he leaned forward on his knees. "I don't need your charity."

"My charity?" Lexi asked, confused. "What are you talking about?"

"The stuff you told Swede to pay for today. I don't… I can pay for it myself. I'm not a charity case," Ty said, eyeing Lexi cautiously. He suddenly felt like he was seven once again, being taken to get a few school clothes by some well-meaning woman at their church. Ty hated every single thing he came home with because the woman made sure to let him and Beth know they were her personal charity case. From that day on, he would rather have worn rags than feel that small and insignificant again.

"Oh, that," Lexi said, waving her hand his direction. "That's not charity, Ty. That's business. You would never in a million years buy, or need, any of that stuff if I wasn't making you learn how to be a cowboy. It isn't your primary job so I look at it as additional equipment. You shouldn't be forced to pay for something that isn't part of your basic job description."

"I don't care how you see it. I'm still paying for it. So how would you like me to pay you back?" Ty sat up so stiff he thought his back might actually spasm.

"Ty, this is ridiculous," Lexi said, but stopped herself when she saw the look of humiliation and anger in Ty's eyes. Realizing she damaged his pride, she felt remorse and regret. The last thing she wanted to do was hurt him. "Look, if it's that important to you, why don't I split the total between your next two paychecks. Will that work for you?"

"Yes, ma'am," Ty said, releasing his breath and running his hand through his hair as he relaxed against the chair. "I'd appreciate that very much."

"I'm glad that's settled, although I better get something in writing. Here, sit still a minute while I type something up."

Lexi walked around the desk to the computer. She quickly typed a document, printed it and slid it across the desk for Ty to date and sign. When he read it, he raised an eyebrow her direction.

I, Tyler Jaxton Lewis, being of sound mind, mulish attitude, and an abundance of stubborn pride, agree to have my employer, Lexi Ryan of the Rockin' R Ranch, deduct from my paychecks, for the next two pay periods, the following amount...

"Think you're funny, don't you?" Ty asked, trying to keep from smiling, although a corner of his traitorous mouth kept tipping upward. He filled in the amount, signed the paper and slid it back to her.

"No. I know I am," Lexi said with a broad smile and a wink that zinged across the desk and tickled his heart where it landed.

"Maybe a little," Ty said, getting up from the desk and walking to the outside entrance of the office. "Thanks, Lexi. I really do appreciate it."

"You're welcome, Ty, and I'm sorry," Lexi said, looking contrite.

"For what?" he asked as he held the door knob in his hand.

"For hurting your pride."

Ty nodded his head her direction and walked outside. That had gone much better than he expected. Now that he wasn't feeling quite so worthless, his mood lightened considerably. His muscle soreness had loosened up during the course of the day and he hoped by tomorrow the friction sores would feel better as well.

Whether they did or not, according to Swede, he was going to be riding again tomorrow and quite likely for the next several weeks.

Lesson Eight
Earn Your Spurs

"Hard work never killed nobody. At least nobody I know."

Sitting on the back porch sipping a cup of hot coffee, Lexi was enjoying the peaceful beginning to her morning as she watched the sunrise fill the spring sky with gold and orange hues. It looked like it was going to be a beautiful day. Although chilly at that moment, the temperature was supposed be in the mid-sixties by afternoon.

Normally it didn't get that warm this early in the year, but Lexi would take any nice days Mother Nature decided to share with them.

Watching the guys file out of the bunkhouse, she knew Swede would have given them all their work details for the day. Cal and Keith teased Jimmy while Gus and Swede walked together, talking about something related to the good old days, no doubt.

Taking a sip of the rich brew in her cup, she nearly spewed it out when one fine-looking cowboy swaggered his way across the ranch yard to the shop. From the top of his new Stetson to the tips of his shiny brown boots, Ty looked like he stepped out of an advertisement for some western apparel company.

She wished she had binoculars so she could get an up-close view. Even from her seat on the big wicker chair she could tell those Wranglers fit him like a second skin, highlighting muscles and long legs that were definitely going to make it hard for her to keep a professional distance from the man. His blue plaid shirt accented the breadth of his shoulders and the way his chest tapered down to a narrow waist.

Had she known those Wranglers would fit him so perfectly, she might have thought twice about teaching him riding and ranching. She had a hard enough time keeping her head on straight where he was concerned. Looking like he did this morning, Lexi knew it was going to be even more of a challenge.

When Ty turned and waved at her, she almost dropped her coffee cup, hoping he couldn't see the heat flaming into her cheeks at her wayward thoughts.

Ty was convinced that his pants were too tight. He'd grown up wearing relaxed fit jeans and couldn't think that he'd ever owned a pair that fit so… snug. Trying to look at the rest of the guys without appearing to be studying their jeans, he decided theirs weren't any tighter or looser than his.

Swede warned him that his boots would take a few days to fit just right and might cause a few blisters in the mean time. With that thought in his mind, he was glad he bought a huge tube of antibiotic cream and a big bottle of ibuprofen. Until he and his new clothes were broken in, he was fairly certain some pain would be involved.

Seeing Lexi on the porch, he waved, hoping she couldn't sense his thoughts. Ty felt like he was wearing some costume that was not quite his size. The hat felt strange, although not uncomfortable, and the shirt fit well. The boots, so far, were comfortable. He supposed, given time, he'd get used to the jeans.

Taking off his hat and hanging it on a peg by the door, Ty rolled up his shirt sleeves and worked on putting together the pieces he'd disassembled from the riding lawnmower. The grass would need mowed soon and Lexi couldn't get the mower to run. It didn't take long for him to find the problem last night and would be simple enough to finish the repairs today.

He was tightening the last bolt when Swede came in the shop.

"Hey, dude, ready for yer next ridin' lesson?" Swede asked, bending down and watching him finish the repair job.

"Sure," Ty said, going to the sink to wash the grease off his hands. When they were dry, he rolled his shirt sleeves down and snapped them, picked up his new gloves from the work bench and grabbed his hat as they went out the door.

"Boss said to git ya saddled up and have ya go out with her to the north herd. She wants ya to git used to bein' around the cattle. Shouldn't have much runnin' today, jes workin' around the herd. We'll start bringin' them in next week."

"Okay," Ty said as they walked to the barn. Swede had Kitty saddled and ready to go, but Delilah stood patiently waiting with her lead rope tied to the fence. Ty got the saddle blanket and saddle from the barn, putting them on like Lexi taught him.

He smoothed out the blanket and made sure it was precisely placed before settling the saddle on top. Adjusting the position, he pulled up the cinch, waiting a minute for Delilah to let out the breath she was holding then finished pulling it tight. Dropping the stirrup into place, he put on her bridle and removed the lead rope.

Swede made sure the saddle was cinched tight, checked the bridle and gave an approving nod.

"Good job, son. Yer a fast learner, fer sure," Swede said, beaming with pride at Ty. From the first time he spoke with him on the phone, Swede took a special interest in the young mechanic. Deciding to make him his special project, the foreman wanted him to succeed. "Let's head out."

Ty mounted and followed Swede to one of the pastures he hadn't been in before. It took almost an hour to get there, although they never urged the horses above a walk. Still a little sore, Ty appreciated not bouncing on the saddle. It was hard enough to keep his seat without showing his discomfort as it was.

When they arrived, Swede waved at Lexi before veering off to the west, leaving Ty to ride toward her alone.

"Hey, buckaroo," Lexi teased as he rode beside her. "Looking good. How do those new clothes feel?"

"Odd, strange, uncomfortable," Ty said honestly, although he added a grin that made Lexi's heart skip a beat or two.

"You'll get used to them. Maybe even like them," she said, knowing how different everything had to feel to him. This entire lifestyle had to feel odd and strange to him, although he was fitting in remarkably well. So well, in fact, she often forgot he was a city boy who had no rural experience. When Swede talked her into hiring him, she was sure they'd have a mess on their hands with a city guy unwilling or unable to adjust to the country.

Ty continually surprised her with his ability to not only adapt but thrive in his new environment. He faced whatever they threw at him head-on and was proving to be a very valuable employee.

Trying to keep him in her thoughts as a student instead of a gorgeous, virile man, she talked to him about the cattle, their behaviors, and how to move them. She went over the reasons they would bring them in for branding and what she expected him to do during the next few weeks.

Working together to move the herd to a pasture closer to the main portion of the ranch, Ty quickly picked up what she taught him.

"Are you sure you haven't ridden before?" Lexi asked, watching him ride Delilah with growing confidence and ease. He was a natural and looked entirely too appealing on the back of a horse.

"I'm positive," Ty said, thinking if he got off the horse, the odds were high he wouldn't be able to lift his leg high enough to get it back in the stirrup to remount. He hoped Lexi couldn't tell how much pain his posterior was feeling. He supposed after a few days, the unaccustomed position he was in wouldn't seem so different or painful.

"You're doing a great job," Lexi called as she trailed after the cattle. Ty was working the other side of the herd. He urged Delilah forward to keep one ornery cow from escaping into the brush. When he did, the horse lunged forward, bucked a few times, and sent Ty flying over her shoulder as she came to an abrupt halt.

Lexi wheeled Rowdy around and hurried to Ty. Jumping off her horse, she bent near his head.

"Ty, are you okay? Are you hurt anywhere?" Lexi asked, concern and something else, something Ty couldn't define, filling her voice.

Embarrassed, he sat up and shook his head.

"I'm fine," he said. He could wiggle his toes and fingers. Looking down, nothing appeared to be bleeding or broken and he could take a deep breath without anything hurting. Getting to his feet, Lexi looked intently into his eyes before placing a warm hand on his arm.

"You're sure?" she asked, trying to gauge if he was hurt and hiding it or telling the truth.

"I'm sure," he said, attempting to walk normally to where Delilah and Rowdy stood waiting. He wondered what he'd done to upset the horse. "What did I do to make her throw a fit?"

Lexi laughed and the sound of it made Ty smile.

"She didn't throw a fit, she was just feeling her oats and having fun," Lexi said, patting Delilah on the neck.

"She only bucked a few times. You would have stayed on if she hadn't stopped so quickly. I haven't seen her do that in years, so I wouldn't worry about her doing it again anytime soon."

"I think I'll keep my guard up just the same," Ty said, looking at the stirrup like it was ten feet above his head instead of a couple feet off the ground.

"It's okay if you're a little afraid. Everyone gets bucked off now and then," Lexi said, taking his hesitance to remount for fear rather than his inability to move his stiff muscles.

Ty wasn't sure what was worse, having her think he was afraid of the horse or letting her know he couldn't lift his sore leg off the ground. His pride told him fear was worse than soreness, so instead of admitting to either he took a deep breath and forced himself to put his foot in the stirrup, remounting Delilah.

When he was settled in the saddle, Lexi placed a hand on his thigh and squeezed. "I'm so proud of you, Ty."

Lexi realized the danger of touching Ty's leg as soon as her hand made contact. She could feel the tight muscles and strength. Even through her gloved fingers, scorching heat blazed a trail up her arm and settled in her mid-section. Hurrying to Rowdy, she mounted and turned back toward the herd. She had no business entertaining thoughts about her mechanic. None at all.

Ty tried to focus on moving the herd but it was difficult when he could still feel Lexi's touch on his leg. He was sure when he took off his jeans her handprint would be embedded on his skin. He had to quit thinking about her as a woman, an incredibly desirable woman, and focus on the fact she was his boss.

Throughout the rest of the morning, Ty didn't have any problems and managed to stay on Delilah. Other than being saddle sore, he was thoroughly enjoying himself. It was a perfect spring day, he was out in the fresh air learning something new, and a pretty girl kept flashing him a beautiful smile.

Life was pretty darn good.

Just before noon, Ty found himself trying to herd a stubborn cow and her calf out of the sagebrush. The cow went willingly, but the calf got himself high-centered in the middle of a big bunch of sagebrush. Ty got off Delilah and begged her not to run off while he picked up the calf and carried it safely out of the sagebrush. When he set it down, the calf bawled loudly, bringing his mama on the run. Ty hurriedly got back on Delilah before the cow got any ideas about running him over. Lexi and Swede had both warned him the only thing worse than tangling with a mad mama cow was a mad mama bear. A smart man avoided them both.

His stomach was growling and he tried to resign himself to missing lunch when Lexi rode over and handed him a bag of jerky, a candy bar and a bottle of water that was closer to warm than cold.

"Not much of a feast, but better than nothing," Lexi said, taking a bite of jerky.

"Thanks," Ty said, accepting her offerings. "I'm so hungry, I'd eat just about anything."

"Anything?" Lexi asked with an impish grin.

"Almost anything," Ty corrected, wondering what hideous thing Lexi thought she could feed him.

"I'll keep that in mind for the next time I make you dinner," Lexi said, teasing Ty. As she sat on Rowdy watching Ty eat, she couldn't believe how much at home he looked not only in the saddle, but on the ranch. Like he was always meant to be there.

Shaking her head to dislodge her ridiculous thoughts, she took another bite of jerky.

"You're a great cook, so I'm not too worried," Ty said, finishing his jerky and candy bar. Changing the subject, he asked how her treasure hunt was going.

"I found the yearbook in dad's room with another clue. It said 'the power of the horse.' I haven't quite figured out what that one means. I think I need to dig through his tack but I haven't had time."

"Does anyone use his tack?"

"No. At some point during his illness he moved all his stuff into a little storage room off the main part of the barn and locked it. I've got a key and gone in a few times, but I haven't cleaned it out like I probably should."

"I can help you look sometime, if you like," Ty offered.

"Thanks. I might have to take you up on that offer."

Finishing their lunch, the two of them went back to trailing behind the cattle. In another hour the cattle were moved to the pasture where Lexi wanted them.

Shifting in his saddle, Ty thought he might be crippled for life. He wasn't convinced his sore legs would hold him when he finally did get off Delilah.

Riding toward the house, they were almost to the barn when Baby came running out to greet them. She barked once and ran over close to Delilah, gazing at Ty adoringly.

"Well, I guess we know who her favorite is," Lexi said as the dog ignored her.

"I wouldn't take it personally," Ty said, digging a piece of jerky out of his shirt pocket and tossing it to Baby, who devoured it without even chewing. "She knows I come bearing treats."

Lexi laughed and Ty felt his heart warm at the sound. He could listen to her honeyed voice for the next sixty years and never tire of it.

Dismounting at the barn, Ty managed to get Delilah's saddle off, brush her down, and turn her out to pasture before hobbling toward the shop.

Putting the final touches on the lawn mower, he started it up and drove it over to the ranch house. Testing it out, it worked fine, so Ty went ahead and mowed the lawn, cleaned up the clippings and the lawnmower, leaving it full of gas, and put it in the shed behind the garage where Lexi kept the garden tools and equipment.

Going back to the shop, he started working on the post-hole digger that hooked on to the tractor. Cal and Keith were installing a new section of fence and giving the auger a demanding workout. The machine needed serviced and the blades sharpened before being put back to work tomorrow.

Finishing up just in time for dinner, Ty removed his dirty coveralls and washed up before putting his cowboy hat on and heading to the bunkhouse. It looked like Gus was cooking which meant they'd be eating either meatloaf with mashed potatoes or hamburgers, the two things he seemed to be able to make that were somewhat edible. Considering the fact he didn't have much lunch, Ty was hoping for the meatloaf.

Leaving his hat on a peg by the door, Ty joked with the rest of the guys, gave Cal and Keith a bad time about the post-hole digger, and teased Jimmy when he leaned back too far in his chair and tipped it over.

After dinner, Ty went back out to the shop and worked until it was nearly dark before coming in and taking a long, hot shower. He was drying off when he glanced in the mirror and saw something on his shoulder that made his eyes go wide. Trying to get a better look in the mirror, whatever it was appeared to be some kind of insect. Brushing at it, he discovered it was firmly attached.

Trying not to panic, Ty had no idea what it was or how to get it off. Hating to ask any of the guys, he didn't know what else to do. Wrapping a towel around his waist, he dashed across the hall to his bedroom, pulled on clean underwear and a pair of running shorts, and slid his feet into slippers. Going into the big main room of the bunkhouse, Cal and Keith were the only two around, watching a rodeo on TV.

"Hey, do you guys know what this thing is?" Ty asked, bending over close to Cal. Keith leaned over and whistled.

"Looks like you get one whopper of a tick," Keith said, getting up off the couch so he could see it better. "He's a hungry sucker, too."

"Yep, that's a tick," Cal said, offering his expert opinion. "No doubt about it."

"How do I get rid of it?" Ty asked, trying to remain calm while a case of the heebie-jeebies raced through him. He wracked his brain trying to remember anything he'd ever heard about ticks. They sucked blood, obviously. He recalled something about them carrying diseases.

"We could burn it off," Cal said with a grin. Ty wasn't sure if he was teasing or serious.

"Best way is to pull it out with a pair of tweezers. Swede has a pair," Keith said, resuming his seat on the couch.

"Swede's still gone, isn't he?" Ty asked, looking out the window at Swede's darkened house. He went into town for a meeting and said he'd be back late.

"Yeah, you could ask the boss. She might be able to help," Cal said, no-longer interested in Ty's tick as he turned his attention back to the TV.

"Thanks," Ty said with a hint of sarcasm as he walked out the door and hurried toward the ranch house. Baby met him at the gate, licking his hand as he walked up the porch steps and knocked at the front door.

He could hear noise in the house and waited a minute before knocking again. Lexi finally came to the door wearing a bathrobe with her hair wrapped turban-style in a towel. The scent of flowers floated around Ty as she opened the door.

"Ty, what's up?" she asked through the screen door. She had just stepped out of the shower when she heard what sounded like a knock at the door. The guys didn't

147

come to the house unless there was some emergency Swede wasn't around to handle. Pulling on her robe and wrapping her hair in a towel, she ran down the stairs.

When she looked out the window and saw Ty standing on her porch, shirtless, of all things, she thought twice about opening the door. As hard as it was for her to resist him fully dressed, seeing him without his shirt was making her pulse race while her insides bubbled into a molten mess.

"I seem to have picked up a tick today and Cal thought you might be able to get it out. Swede's gone or I'd ask him," Ty said, not adding the only two humans awake at the bunkhouse weren't particularly interested in providing assistance. He'd remember their lack of helpfulness the next time they asked him for a favor.

"Certainly, come in," Lexi said, stepping back as he came in the door. "Go on into the kitchen and I'll get my tweezers."

Ty walked down the hall toward the kitchen while Lexi went upstairs to the bathroom collecting tweezers, a couple of cotton balls, and a bottle of rubbing alcohol. She hated bugs, spiders and anything that could be considered creepy-crawly, but growing up on the ranch, she had removed plenty of ticks.

Hurrying down the back stairs to the kitchen, she found Ty seated at the bar, waiting for her. Good gracious, but his shoulders looked massive as he sat with his elbows propped on the counter. Muscles bulged in his arms, rippling along his back and tapering down to the waist of his shorts. She wouldn't allow herself to look at his legs. Emotionally and physically, she just couldn't handle any more of the buff, good-looking man at the moment.

"Have you ever had a tick before?" she asked as she set down her supplies and got out a tiny dish. Pouring in rubbing alcohol, she set it aside then took her tweezers to the sink and poured a liberal amount of alcohol over them.

"No, ma'am," Ty said, fighting to keep control of his urge to shudder in revulsion. He imagined he could feel it sucking his blood as he sat waiting for Lexi. Even though he knew it was impossible, the thought kept entering his head. It was important to him to maintain his calm façade although inside he was shouting in protest at having the disgusting thing attached to his shoulder. "I don't know any more about ticks than I do ranching or farming."

"Then you'll be happy to know this particular kind of tick doesn't carry diseases like deer ticks. We're supposed to have a bad year of them since the winter was mild. Hard winters tend to kill off a lot of bugs and spiders. We didn't have that many days of bitter cold this year so we'll have more than our share of insects," Lexi said as she moved a bar stool closer to the bright light by the kitchen sink and motioned Ty to sit down.

"So we'll have problems all summer?" Ty asked, not liking the idea of being a traveling buffet for ticks until the weather cooled off again.

"Probably," Lexi said as she worked the tweezers under the tick, trying to get as close to its head as possible. "Ticks feed off warm bodies, be it cattle, dogs, horses, sometimes humans. I'm guessing you picked up this freeloader out in the sagebrush this morning. From now on, when you come in from the range, you might want to do a full body check. Just get a hand mirror and hold it in front of the bathroom mirror. That way you can easily spot if you've got one attached somewhere. You should throw your clothes in the dryer to make sure you kill any that might still be searching for something to eat."

"Good to know," Ty said, sitting so still he was afraid to even breathe.

"If any of the guys offer to burn one out or smother it in Vaseline, ignore them. The best way to remove them is to yank them out by the head with tweezers," Lexi said, pulling out the tick and dumping it in the dish with the alcohol, effectively killing it. She poured alcohol on a cotton ball and swabbed the spot on Ty's shoulder, rubbing it gently. "All done. You can smoosh the tick if you like, but I warn you it makes an awful mess."

Ty shuddered, not from the tick, but from the nearness of Lexi and her warm softness pressed against his back. Before he could think about what he was doing, he spun around on the stool and pulled her against his chest. The towel on her head fell to the floor and he buried his face into the fragrant, damp locks.

It had been almost a year since Ty held a woman in his arms. His girlfriend dumped him as soon as he lost his job. A homeless man has no worthwhile dating prospects. Although he'd nearly forgotten how wonderful it felt to hold a woman close, he knew none had ever felt as good or made his blood thrum like Lexi.

"Thanks," Ty said, drawing her tighter in his arms. Waiting for her to pull back, to offer some resistance, she instead melted against him.

"Anytime," Lexi whispered against his neck, her lips hot and moist against his skin. She was surprised when Ty put his arms around her and held her close. If she had any sense at all, she would pull away, walk him to the door, and bid him goodnight. But her need to be close to him was winning over common sense.

The reality of being held in Ty's powerful arms against his hard muscled chest was ten times better than any of the multiple dreams involving him she'd played out in her head. This close to him, her ability to think and reason completely vanished.

Sliding her hands up his arms, she savored every touch of her fingers to his body, memorizing the feel of his muscles, the smell of his scent, the warmth of his skin. Giving in to the temptation, she ran her hands through his thick, brown hair, twining her fingers at the back of his head in the wavy strands.

"Lexi," Ty growled in her ear, making her lift her head. He slipped into the deep green depths of her eyes as he lowered his lips to hers. An explosion of fire jolted through him as he tasted and tested her sweet, soft lips. Getting to his feet, he drew her tighter against his chest, while his hands gently rubbed up and down her back.

The only thought Lexi could process was that she wanted to be closer to Ty and took a step forward, leaving only a breath of space between them. Standing on tip-toe, she returned his passion kiss for kiss. Engulfed in his arms, surrounded by his presence, Lexi felt herself falling into a place she'd never before been. A place where only she and Ty existed.

When Ty started to draw away, Lexi tugged him back to her lips. "Not yet, Ty, don't stop."

He moaned as he kissed her long and deep, until they both were gasping for breath. Resting his forehead against hers, Ty ran his hands over her arms, down her back and circled her waist, realizing her robe was all that stood between him and discovering if his dreams of Lexi were half as good as he imagined. Grasping at the last bit of control keeping him on the right side of doing something wrong, he released a sigh.

"I'm sorry. I shouldn't have done that. My apologies," Ty said, feeling contrite, but not quite remorseful enough to let go of her and walk out the door. She was so warm, so real, so beautiful. Ty knew no woman had ever fit so perfectly in his arms and he had the fleeting thought that none ever would.

"It's okay, Ty. I shouldn't have enjoyed it quite as much as I did," Lexi admitted as much to herself as Ty. Staring at his sculpted chest, his stubbly cheek rubbed against her temple. "It's as much my fault as yours."

"You mean you planted the tick on me, made sure no one who could be of assistance was around so I'd have to come seek your help, and then planned to seduce me while you took it out?" Ty asked with a teasing grin tipping the corners of his full lips.

"Of course not! Don't be ridiculous!" Lexi said indignantly as she stepped back from Ty. When she saw the playful look he was wearing, she smiled. "You're wicked and ornery."

"Yes, ma'am," Ty said, kissing her again, just to make sure he hadn't dreamed the past several fantastic moments of holding her in his arms.

Unable to resist him, Lexi gave herself to the kiss and felt her knees growing as weak as her resolve to stay away from Ty.

"I think it's time for you to go," Lexi whispered when he drew back, smiling at her with such warmth, she could feel heat radiating throughout her entire being. Yanking the ties on her robe tighter, she walked him to the door.

"Thanks for removing the tick," Ty said, as he lingered at the door. "And for kissing me all better."

"Get out of my kitchen, buckaroo," she said, shooing him out, but giving him a wink that let him know she enjoyed their kisses every bit as much as he had.

Lexi watched him stride down the walk and back to the bunkhouse before she closed the door. She held her robe closed at the neck, feeling the need to mentally hold herself together much the same way. So much for her theory that after one kiss, they'd realize they weren't really attracted to one another. Thinking one kiss from Ty would quench her thirst for him was like expecting an eyedropper full of water to put out a rampaging wildfire.

If she thought she had a problem keeping her mind off Ty before, Lexi had no idea how she'd keep from being consumed with him now. She had never in her life been kissed like that, never had her emotions explode like that, and wanted more than anything to continue exploring the wonder of it all.

◇◇◇

Ty could feel the heat of Lexi's gaze boring into his back as he walked to the bunkhouse. It took no small amount of effort to leave her when what he really wanted was to go on holding and kissing her the rest of the night.

He knew it was wrong, knew he shouldn't even think about it, but Lexi reached places in his heart that he hadn't known existed until their lips met in a fiery burst of heat and passion.

Going up the steps to the bunkhouse, Cal and Keith looked at him as he came in the door.

"Get the tick out?" Cal asked as Ty stopped in the kitchen to get a glass of water.

"Yep," he said, drinking the glass in one long swallow.

"You okay?" Keith asked, watching him down the water.

"Yep. Goodnight," Ty said, giving them a nod as he went down the hall to his bedroom. Collapsing on the bed, the smell of Lexi's sweet floral scent still filled his nose and clung to his skin. Closing his eyes, he could feel her warm body pressed against him. How was he going to keep thinking of her as his boss when he knew, without a doubt, that she was the one woman on the planet meant to fill his arms and his heart?

The next morning, Swede asked him if he was feeling fine as they left the bunkhouse after breakfast.

"Heard ya had yer first tick encounter," Swede said as they walked toward the shop. "Creepy lil' boogers, ain't they?"

"Yeah, they are," Ty agreed. If Lexi would remove them like she did last night, including the kissing session, he might go see if he could find another one today.

"Boss said she took one off for ya. Said ya didn't even flinch," Swede said, slapping Ty on the back. "I think ya jes may have earned yer spurs, my friend."

Ty wasn't sure what that meant, exactly, but from the pleased look on Swede's face, he assumed it was something good.

Later that afternoon, he came into the shop to find a set of used spurs and a pair of worn chaps on the workbench along with a note.

Ty,

Swede thinks you've more than earned your spurs and chaps. I agree. Wear these proudly, they belonged to my dad.

Lexi

Lesson Nine
Treat Women with Respect

*"Treat a woman like she's made of glass,
even tho' she's made of steel."*

Ty was cleaning off the workbench and washing out the big sink he used to clean parts when Lexi stuck her head in the door of the shop. Baby wagged her tail in greeting, beating Ty on the leg. Looking up, he swallowed twice before he could speak, remembering the impassioned kisses he shared with his employer a few nights ago.

"Hi, Lexi. What are you doing out so late?" Ty said, drying his hands on a paper towel and tossing it in the garbage. Outwardly he attempted to appear calm and cool although just the sight of Lexi made his heart start to pound and his insides heat.

"I could ask you the same thing. I saw the shop light on and figured you were burning the midnight oil," Lexi said, stepping in the door but keeping a safe distance away from Ty. If she got too close, she was afraid she might kiss him. Or let him kiss her. Either way, she couldn't allow it to happen. "I had a question to ask you."

"Okay," Ty said, leaning against the counter and shoving his hands in his pockets. If he didn't, he was afraid he would reach out to Lexi and pull her to him. A hug would lead to a kiss and he couldn't think beyond that.

"I'm going to Portland tomorrow to meet with a client and I wondered if you'd like to go along to see Beth and the baby. I'll be leaving bright and early and get back after dark, but I'd be happy to have company on the drive if you'd care to go," Lexi said, knowing it was going to be torture trapped in the car with Ty for hours on end. She really did want some company and she wanted him to get to see his nephew. The baby was three-weeks old now and, according to what Ty shared, Beth would be returning to her job full-time the following week.

"Are you kidding me?" Ty asked, not sure he heard her correctly. "You want me to go to Portland with you, I can see my family, and then we'll be back tomorrow night?"

"That's what I said, buckaroo," Lexi said with a flirty smile as she nervously twirled a strand of hair around her finger. "Unless you're afraid of my driving?"

"No, ma'am. I'd like to go. Are you sure it's okay for me to be gone? I mean, everyone is busy getting ready for branding and the spring farm work isn't finished," Ty said, not wanting the guys to think he was getting special treatment.

"I already mentioned it to Swede and he thought you've more than earned a day off, especially since you seem to work on Sundays instead of getting away from here. So, if you want to go, just be at the house at five in the morning. I've got a client meeting at ten-thirty. If you wouldn't mind, maybe I could have lunch with you, Beth, and Nate, so I could meet little Jax, too."

"That would be awesome," Ty said, warming to the idea. "I'd really like for them to meet you."

"Great, it's settled then. I'll see you in the morning," Lexi said, walking toward the door. She stopped when she felt Ty's warm hands on her shoulders.

"Thanks, Lexi. You have no idea how much this means to me," Ty said, pressing a kiss to her cheek before taking a step back. Momentarily forgetting his plans to remain strictly professional with the boss, he held her hand in his. "Thanks for the spurs and chaps, too. Are you sure you want me to use them? They've got to be special to you since they belonged to your dad."

"They are, but I know you'll take good care of them," Lexi said, squeezing his fingers. "Dad had multiple pairs of each, so don't give it another thought. You really have earned the right to wear them."

"Thanks."

"You're welcome," she whispered before hurrying outside. Lexi hoped the evening air would cool down her hot cheeks.

Deciding she had finally lost her mind, Lexi knew there was no way she could spend all day with Ty tomorrow and come away unchanged by the experience.

Hearing footsteps on the porch a few minutes before five the next morning, she opened the door to find Ty standing there wearing a big grin along with his western attire. From the black hat in his hands to the polished boots on his feet, he definitely looked like a cowboy. A very dangerous cowboy if the effect he had on her system was any indication.

The blue striped shirt he wore made his eyes even bluer and accented the breadth of his shoulders and chest. His cheeks were smooth and clean shaven and he smelled better than any man should at five in the morning. Lexi pulled her gaze away. Her insides were already churning and she felt overheated despite the cool morning air.

"Aren't you going with me?" she asked as he stepped inside while she gathered up her things.

"Yes, ma'am," he said, still grinning. He knew she would be dressed in something besides her work shirts and jeans, but Ty wasn't expecting to see her in a soft green suit that complimented her eyes while highlighting her tall figure. High heels, the same tone as her skin, made her legs look a mile long. She was absolutely beautiful, especially with her hair hanging down her back in thick black waves. Lexi's scent enveloped him as soon as she opened the door and Ty shoved his hands in his pockets in an effort to behave himself.

"Then why are you dressed like that?" Lexi asked, picking up her purse and briefcase. She was going to try and balance two travel coffee mugs, along with everything else she had in her hands until Ty took the coffee from her and held the door as she walked outside onto the porch.

"I thought Beth and Nate would get a kick out of seeing me this way," Ty said, following her to the garage. He was really excited about getting to ride in her sports car. He'd worked on one at the garage once and took it for a test drive. It was definitely a fun ride.

Opening the side door of the garage, Lexi put her things in the car and retrieved the coffee from Ty while he opened the big doors. She drove the car out then he closed the doors and slid into the passenger seat of the Nismo. Laying his hat behind the front seat, he buckled up and admired the inside of the car.

"Nice wheels," he said, moving the seat back to accommodate his long legs.

"Thanks. I kind of like it myself," Lexi said with a grin as she shifted the car and started down the driveway.

"What made you choose a Nismo?" Ty asked, sinking into the soft leather seat and inhaling Lexi's scent that floated enticingly through the car.

"I wanted a sports car, something fun to drive. I looked at everything from a Mustang to a Porsche. This one wasn't so ridiculously priced," Lexi said, leaning toward Ty with a conspiratorial look. "And if you really want the truth, I loved the color and none of the others could match it."

Ty laughed. Now, that was something he would expect a female to do – choose a car based on the color scheme. Admittedly, it was a pretty burgundy shade called black cherry.

"Don't you laugh at me," Lexi said, giggling. "It was a major influence on my decision."

"Anything besides the color, of course, that made you decide to buy this particular car?" Ty asked, picking up the coffee closest to him.

Sitting at the stop sign that intersected the highway, Lexi waited for him to take a drink and return his cup to the holder before she pulled out on the road.

"Yep. The V6 engine with 350 horsepower and 276 pounds of torque may have helped me with my decision. But the fact it will go from zero to sixty in just about five seconds was the clincher on the deal," Lexi said, accelerating so quickly Ty wasn't sure it took a full five seconds to hit sixty. By the time a minute passed, they were roaring down the road doing eighty.

Unsure what to think, he wisely refrained from commenting on her speeding and hoped nothing like a cow or deer decided to cross the road in front of them.

"You like to drive fast?" he finally asked, taking his eyes off the road long enough to study Lexi's profile. The sight of her flawless skin in the early morning light, highlighted by her crown of dark hair, warmed his insides far more than the coffee he'd been drinking.

"Sometimes," Lexi said, expertly handling the car on the stretch of road before them. There wasn't much of anything to see except sagebrush and more sagebrush for the next hundred miles. "I enjoy driving and this empty stretch of road is a great place to see what a car can do."

"I noticed your dad's old mustang in the garage. Is that where you got your love of fast cars?" Ty asked, wanting to know more about Lexi, who she was, and what made her so unique.

"Dad loved that car," Lexi said, her voice quieting as a wistful expression filled her face. "I can remember him taking me for rides. Sometimes Mom would go along, too. He had big plans to restore it, but never seemed to have the time. He ordered the parts he needed to do the work, he just didn't get it done. I know I should do something with that old car, but too many memories of my dad are attached to it. Someday I'll look into having it restored."

"How long was your dad sick," Ty asked knowing her father died of brain cancer. From what he heard, it was a horrible way to die.

"A lot longer than he let anyone know," Lexi said, staring at the road. "He was diagnosed about eight months before he finally told anyone the news. By then, there was no denying the fact. As soon as he let us know what was going on, I came home, but that wasn't until the end of August. He tried to keep going, but we lost a little part of him every day those last few months. Three weeks before he died, he didn't recognize any of us and Swede and I agreed he needed more care than we could provide so we placed him in a nursing home. Dad would have hated the way it ended."

"I'm sorry," Ty said, feeling sorry for the man who had been such a strong influence in Lexi's life.

"I should have known something was wrong long before he admitted it," Lexi said, thinking back to all the odd things her father had done last year. He forgot things, was easily upset, and then he started hiding tools and parts and tack, acting like someone was trying to steal his things.

She shouldn't have been surprised to find all that money missing. Now she just needed to figure out where her dad hid it. Lexi was sure it was somewhere on the ranch.

"You can't blame yourself. I'm sure your dad needed time to adjust to the idea before he let everyone know," Ty said insightfully. He certainly would need some time to come to terms with news like that. "Have you found any more clues?"

"Yes, I found one in his farrier kit. I haven't been able to decipher it, though."

"What did it say?" Ty asked, genuinely interested, not because of the money, but because it was something Lexi needed to find to have some closure with her father's passing.

"Girls Demand Excitement," Lexi said with a shake of her head.

"Sounds right to me," Ty said with a wicked grin.

They drove along in silence for a few miles before Lexi started asking Ty about his history.

"What made you decide to become a mechanic?" Lexi asked, honestly interested in Ty's story. She wanted to know everything about him.

"My mom," Ty said, with a smile, remembering his childhood. "I loved to take things apart but I wasn't always very good about putting them back together. Mom worked two, sometimes three jobs, to keep us fed and a roof over our heads. Money was pretty tight so what we had needed to last. She'd just bought a new toaster and I wanted to find out what made the toast pop up when it was done. I dismantled the entire thing and was studying the pieces when Mom came home from work. She didn't yell at me or read me the riot act for what I'd done. Instead, she sat down at the table and cried."

Ty ran his hand through his hair. That was the first time he realized he couldn't deal with women's tears. Each salty drop ripped at his heart and made him want to promise anything to get them to stop.

"Then what happened?" Lexi asked, interested in the story.

"She wiped her face, took a deep breath and looked me in the eye. She told me we couldn't afford another new toaster or anything else for a while. If I wanted to take things apart, she said I had to learn how to put them back together and make sure they worked. If I didn't, I couldn't ever take anything else apart. So I learned. The older I got, the bigger the things were I took apart. I finally started playing with wrecked cars. When I was fourteen, we moved into a place that was just down the road from a junkyard. The owner was a friendly old guy who let me take apart anything I wanted to work on. My first and second cars both came from the junkyard. He never charged me a thing for them and helped me get them running."

"That's great you've always had that curiosity to learn and delve into things to see how they work," Lexi said, wishing her dad had taught her even some basic mechanic skills. "I know you received certification. That must have made your mom very proud."

"Yeah, she was pretty excited when I graduated from tech school. I was part of a competitive mechanics team in high school. The year I was a senior, we won the state level and got to compete in the nationals in Washington D.C. We took second place and I received a few job offers along with two scholarships. I took one of the scholarships, got my certification, and never looked back," Ty said, thinking of all the years he worked for the garage before they let him go and turned his life upside down. Right now, it didn't seem so bad since he ended up at the Rockin' R Ranch with Lexi.

"What about your dad?" Lexi asked. Ty was such a good man she assumed there had been some positive male role model in his life somewhere along the line.

"My mom married a loser, thinking she could change him. The only thing that changed in the three years they were married was my mother's idea that he would grow up and be responsible. He couldn't hold down a job, drank up what little money my mom earned, and spent most of his time running around with other women. When Mom had

Beth, she thought he'd settle down, but things got worse. When she announced she was expecting me, he ran off and we never heard from him again."

"Ty, that's terrible," Lexi said, taking his calloused, grease-stained hand in her soft, delicate one.

Squeezing her fingers, he absently wondered how a hard-working rancher had such lovely hands.

"I don't know. My mom loved us both, gave us what she could, and taught us how to work hard and live right," Ty said, turning a warm blue gaze her direction. "When they were alive, Beth and I spent summers with our grandparents. They lived in Eugene. It always seemed so green and fresh there. My grandpa was killed in a boating accident and my grandma just gave up the will to live. Beth and I were on our own during the summers after that."

"How old were you?"

"I was eleven, so Beth would have been thirteen. Old enough to get into all kinds of trouble, but we tried to walk the straight and narrow. We didn't want to upset Mom when she already had so much to worry about."

"What happened to your mother?"

"She passed away a few years back. One winter she got pneumonia and just couldn't shake it. She refused to take care of herself and ended up in the hospital. She never came home. The doctor said her heart was completely worn out," Ty said, watching the sagebrush whiz by in the early morning light.

"I'm so sorry. I know how hard it is to lose a parent," Lexi said, trying to not get emotional. Losing first her mom and then her dad had been really hard. But she'd had them both during her growing up years. She never wanted for anything and always felt surrounded by their love.

"I know you do. I'm sorry for your losses as well," Ty said, rubbing his thumb gently across the back of her hand.

"Well, aren't we a sorry pair of maudlin orphans this morning," Lexi asked, trying to lighten the mood.

Ty chuckled and turned a smile her direction that caused her to swerve into the other lane before he said, "Car, Lexi. Oncoming car!" and she swerved back.

"Sorry," she said, refusing to admit he had her so befuddled it would be a miracle if they arrived in Portland in one piece.

"You need me to drive?" he asked, smug in his ability to distract Lexi.

"No, I'm fine," Lexi said. Giving him a quick glance, she offered a cheeky grin. "You're looking for any excuse to get behind the wheel, aren't you?"

"Yes, ma'am," Ty said with a grin that warmed his eyes and her heart.

They talked about everything from their favorite books to their favorite movies on the way to Portland. Lexi stopped in Bend long enough for them to grab a bite of breakfast and fill the gas tank before getting back on the road.

"So before you moved back to the ranch, you were a financial planner?" Ty asked as they drove out of the forest and into the rolling hills of farmland southeast of Portland.

"Yes. I absolutely loved it. I started as a peon with a firm downtown and worked my way up to a great office with a wonderful client list. When I returned to the ranch, a few of my elderly clients refused to let anyone else handle their accounts, so I maintain them from home. Once in a great while, I meet with them in person. The client I'm meeting today is ninety-three and as sassy as they come. She refuses to learn how to use a computer, which is why I need to meet with her in person. My former boss allows me to use one of the meeting rooms at the office, which works really well for both me and the clients."

"That's great. So what do you do for them?" Ty asked, not entirely sure he understood what financial planning entailed.

"Some clients need advice on what types of mortgages or insurance they should have, how much they should keep in an emergency fund, or what changes could improve their tax situation. Others need assistance deciding what they want their financial future to look like. I mostly work with those who need retirement plans and make investments on their behalf as well as managing those investments. My job is to make sure the client's financial goals will be met over a given period of time," Lexi explained, warming to the subject.

"Sounds very important," Ty said, realizing he needed to be more mindful of making some plans and investments for his future now that he was once again employed. Nearly thirty, he didn't want to be one of those people who waited until they were fifty to start putting away money for retirement.

"I like to think it is. After all, if you don't plan for your future, what kind of mess will you be in when you're sixty or seventy?" Lexi said, whipping through the morning traffic with practiced ease. Ty was as impressed with her driving as he was everything else about the fascinating woman.

Arriving in downtown Portland, Lexi stopped the car in front of a large office building. Turning to the backseat, she picked up her purse and briefcase, then handed Ty her car keys.

He looked from the keys to her, confused.

"This is my old office building where I'm meeting my client. Why don't you take the car, go see Beth or do whatever, then pick me up at noon? We can have lunch with your family and then hit the road," Lexi said, looking in the mirror and waiting for traffic to clear before opening her door.

Ty continued to stare at her, unmoving.

"What's wrong, Ty?" Lexi asked, looking at him in concern. His face seemed a little pale and he hadn't moved since she dropped the keys in his hand.

"I just… seriously? You're just going to hand me your car keys and turn me loose like that?" Ty asked, unable to digest Lexi's trust and faith in him. "You really trust me that much?"

"Yes," Lexi said with a grin. "You do promise to come back and get me, don't you?"

"Of course!" Ty said, closing his fingers around the keys as he warmed to the idea of having the car to drive around for the next couple of hours.

"Great. Then what's the problem?" Lexi said, studying Ty. She decided he should have worn his relaxed-fit jeans and hooded sweatshirt with a scruffy face. Dressed like a cowboy he was going to draw a lot of attention, particularly from girls who liked seeing a rugged, good-looking man in snug-fitting jeans and boots.

"No problem. None at all," Ty said with a grin as he got out of the car, ran around and held her door open for her. Lexi was afraid he'd get hit in the traffic, but he didn't seem concerned about it. He walked her to the sidewalk, tipped his hat, and ran back to the driver's side of the car. "I'll be waiting right here at noon."

"Just see that you are, buckaroo," Lexi teased, giving him a jaunty wave as he pulled into traffic.

Taking a deep breath, Lexi turned and looked at the office building. It was large and held a variety of businesses in addition to the financial planning firm where she worked. There were business offices, a few attorney offices, and other professional suites. Her former fiancé, James, worked in one of the posh corner offices on the top floor. If her luck held, she'd be in and out of the building without running into him.

Ty still couldn't believe Lexi would hand him her car keys and walk off, but he wasn't going to argue with her.

He drove out of downtown to a mall where he picked up a few things for Jax and gifts for Beth and Nate before driving to their apartment. Wanting to surprise them, he didn't mention to Beth he was going to be in town today when he spoke with her the previous night.

Hurrying upstairs and down the hall, he rang the doorbell and waited for Beth to answer. He was surprised when the door didn't immediately swing open. Knocking on the door, he hoped Beth was home. When all remained quiet, he felt an overwhelming sense of disappointment. Where was Beth? Or Nate for that matter? Beth said he worked from home. Trying to remember what she'd said last night, he didn't recall any mention of what she was doing today.

Turning, he was sulking back down the hallway when the elevator door opened and Beth and Nate got off. Nate carried the baby's car seat while Beth dug in her purse for her keys.

"Hey," Ty said as they walked up to him.

Nate glared at him while Beth eyed him warily. "May we help you?" she asked, holding her keys in her hand like a weapon.

"I'd like to think so, Bethie," Ty said, realizing they might not recognize him in western clothes, with a shaved face and trimmed hair. He admittedly looked pretty rough when he left Portland a couple of months ago.

Hearing the name only Ty called her, Beth looked at him in surprise, then a happy cry escaped her lips before she threw herself into his arms.

"Ty, my goodness. Is it really you? Look at you! You've gone all cowboy on us. You look amazing, Oh,

I'm so happy to see you," Beth gushed, hanging onto his neck and sobbing against his shirt.

"I'm happy to see all of you," Ty said, a big smile lighting his face as he hugged his sister and patted her back. "If I ask real nice, can we go inside the apartment so I can hold this nephew of mine?"

"Oh, absolutely," Beth said, beaming at Nate, and swiping at her tears. "It's Ty, Nate. It's Ty!"

"Yes, honey, I'm aware of that," Nate said, indulgently, nudging Ty with his elbow as Beth hurried to unlock the apartment door. "Sorry we didn't recognize you at first. Didn't expect to see you in the hall and definitely not dressed as the Marlboro Man. What are you doing in town?"

"The boss had to come to Portland for a business meeting today and asked if I wanted to come along. She thought I'd waited long enough to meet Jax," Ty said, following Beth and Nate into the apartment. Setting his gifts on the floor by the table and taking off his hat, he impatiently waited while Nate put down the baby carrier and Beth quickly undid the fasteners, lifting out the sleeping baby.

"Here he is," Beth said, handing the baby to Ty as he sat down on the couch. Never having held a baby before, Beth gave him instruction on how to properly hold an infant. Ty felt a warming in his heart that was wonderful, scary and exciting as love for Jax instantly sprang to life.

Bending down, he breathed in the heavenly scent of the baby's head and smiled.

"He's wonderful," Ty said. He knew even less about babies than he did about ranching, but he knew this baby was special. From the top of his head, covered in dark hair, to his round little face and long fingers, he was amazing.

"Thanks, Ty," Beth said, swiping at her tears, while holding Nate's hand in hers. She was thrilled to see Ty looking so healthy and happy. She was over the moon to have him here, holding her beloved son. "We think he's pretty terrific."

"I can see why. Just look at those fingers," Ty said, touching the baby's tiny hand with his forefinger. "Perfect for catching a football, don't you think, Nate?"

"That's what I keep telling her," Nate said with a chuckle. "I've already got his career all planned out."

"Right on," Ty said, staring at the baby, absorbing the wonder of the miracle in his arms. Remembering Lexi's request, he looked at Nate. "Do you guys have plans for lunch?"

"Nope, we're free as birds the rest of the day," Nate said, looking to Beth for agreement. She nodded her head. "Why?"

"The boss wants to meet you both and she said she would really like to see the baby. Would you mind having lunch together?" Ty asked, not looking up from his nephew's face. The baby was yawning and squishing his eyes, making Ty grin.

"I'd love to meet Ms. Ryan," Beth said. "What time and where?"

"I'm supposed to pick her up downtown at noon. What about the restaurant you guys used to go to all the time when you were dating. It's nice with good affordable food, isn't it?" Ty asked, as the baby opened his eyes and started to fuss.

"Yes. Sounds like a great plan. We can meet you there," Beth said, waiting for Ty to hand the baby back to her. Instead, he just watched Jax squirm and fuss. When the baby let out a full-fledged cry while his face turned red, Ty looked to her and shrugged.

"Guess he told me what he thinks of me," Ty said, as Beth took the baby and turned her back to the guys.

"He's just hungry," she said, covering both herself and Jax with a light blanket and nursing the baby while sitting on the edge of the bed across the room.

While Jax ate, Ty got out the gifts he purchased. He bought Jax a stuffed pony and a couple of storybooks that were farm themed. For Beth he had a large basket of bath products he knew she loved and for Nate he purchased a box of his favorite chocolates.

"It isn't Christmas. What's with all the gifts?" Nate asked as he opened the box and took out a piece of chocolate before offering one to Ty. Ty shook his head, knowing Nate would enjoy every single piece of candy in the box.

"I just wanted to say thank you," Ty said, thinking how lovely motherhood looked on his sister.

"For what," Beth asked, shifting the baby beneath the blanket.

"For always being here for me. For being my family, no matter what," Ty said somberly with a humbleness Beth and Nate hadn't seen before. Being on the ranch had definitely changed Ty, even in the short time he'd been there.

"Ty, you're going to make what's left of my mascara run," Beth said through her tears, making both Nate and Ty chuckle.

"I don't think there's any left, honey," Nate teased as Ty got to his feet.

"If I'm going to pick up the boss on time, I better get a move on," Ty said, kissing Beth on the cheek and shaking Nate's hand. "I'll see you at the restaurant at twelve-thirty."

"We're looking forward to it," Nate said, walking him to the door.

Ty made it back to Lexi's office building with five minutes to spare. Finding a parking space out front, he waited for her to come out. At five after twelve she still hadn't appeared and he began to worry. Ty decided to go wait at the door of the building for her. Getting out of the car, he was nearly across the expansive forecourt area when Lexi came out the door followed by a handsome man in an expensive suit who appeared to be arguing with her.

Anger oozed from her, evident not just in the grim set of her mouth and the flash of fire in her eyes, but from the way she walked and rigidly held herself. She was close enough now Ty could hear the conversation.

"Lex, you are a foolish, stubborn girl. Why can't you listen to reason?" the man said, stepping in front of her so she had to stop walking. She glared at him with a look of loathing before stepping around him and continuing her march toward the street.

"I could listen to reason if something reasonable was being said. Considering the words are coming out of your mouth, there's not a thing worth listening to," Lexi said, her tone belying her barely contained hostility. "I've asked you twice and I'm not asking again. Leave me alone, James. Let it go and leave me alone."

"This is ridiculous. For once in your life, make a smart decision," James said grabbing Lexi around the arm with enough force it made her stumble forward. "You know you want to be with me."

Lexi caught herself but before she could jerk her arm free, James was pushed aside and Ty stepped between the two of them.

"I believe the lady asked you to leave her alone," Ty said, feeling his own irritation rise. No one manhandled a woman in his presence. No one. The fact that some jerk was treating this particular woman so disrespectfully lit the fuse of his temper.

"And who might you be, Bubba?" James asked with a sneer, looking at Ty like he was something stuck to his shoe, although Ty towered over him. James was actually shorter than Lexi, although he was definitely stronger.

"No one you want to mess with," Ty responded in a tone that would have been a warning to most men to back off.

James laughed and quickly stepped around Ty, grabbing Lexi by the other arm.

"I'm not finished with you, Lex. I insist you come with me right now," he said, tightening his clamp on her arm and trying to pull her back toward the building. "We can work this out if you'll stop acting so stupidly."

Instead of Lexi following him, James instead felt his arm twisted behind his back and he yelped in pain.

"Let go of me, you cavedweller," James gasped, trying not to cry out in pain.

"Leave the lady alone," Ty warned, letting go of James' arm. When he did, James turned around and swung at Ty, missing him entirely. Ty swept out his leg, catching James behind the knees while pushing him over onto the pavement. "If I ever see or hear of you bothering Miss Ryan again, I might not be so inclined to behave like a gentleman."

Ty half expected the guy to get up and swing at him again, but he sat on the ground looking at Ty with fear in his eyes.

Lexi gave James a curt nod as Ty took her elbow and escorted her to the car. He could feel her shaking like a leaf as they walked down the steps and across the sidewalk to the street.

"Are you going to be okay?" he whispered as he held the passenger door for her.

"Yes," she said, biting the inside of her cheek to keep from crying.

Ty climbed behind the wheel, started the car and pulled into traffic. When they were out of sight of the building, Lexi buried her face in her hands and gave in to her emotions.

"Lexi, don't cry," Ty said, feeling his heart break at her tears. Driving out of downtown, he pulled into the parking lot of an office supply store and stopped the car. Reaching across the seat, he put a warm hand on her back. "Lexi?"

"I'm so glad you showed up when you did," Lexi said, turning to him with tear-streaked cheeks. "I don't know what would have happened if you hadn't been there."

Despite the bucket seats, Ty pulled Lexi closer and gave her a comforting hug.

"Who was that guy?" he asked, gently rubbing his hand across her back and shoulders.

"James. I... um... was engaged to him for a while," Lexi said, taking a deep breath.

Ty leaned back so he could look in her face. He gave her a disbelieving stare along with a raised eyebrow in question of her former taste in men.

"You're kidding me."

"Unfortunately, I'm not," Lexi said, leaning back in her seat. "He called things off when he found out about my mom's heritage. I won't even repeat what he said then, but needless to say, I haven't spoken to him since. He happened to catch me in the elevator on my way out and suggested that we 'reconsider out relationship strategy,' as he put it. He had the nerve to suggest that even though I'm not suitable wife material, I could be his mistress. That's when I slapped his face and tried to leave."

"I should have punched him," Ty said, livid that anyone would treat Lexi the way James treated her.

"No, you shouldn't have. I was very proud of you for only pushing him down when you could have easily cleaned his clock," Lexi said, mad now that the threat of James hurting her had past. "He's such a jerk."

"You'll get no argument from me," Ty said, using his thumbs to wipe away the last of Lexi's tears. "Did he always treat you so disrespectfully?"

"I guess he did, I just didn't notice," Lexi said, thinking what an idiot she'd been and how grateful she was to no longer be involved with James.

"Did he hurt you?" Ty asked, looking at her with heat in his eyes.

"I'll be fine," Lexi said, ignoring the spots on her arms where she was sure bruises would soon show. At least with the three-quarter length sleeves on her jacket, no one would know anything happened today.

Picking up her purse, she flipped down the visor mirror and touched up her makeup while Ty pulled back into traffic and drove to the restaurant.

"Are you sure you feel up to having lunch with Beth and Nate?" Ty asked, finding a parking space. "They'd understand if you want to go home."

"No. I want to meet them and I can't wait to see the baby. Is he as adorable in person as he looks in his pictures?" Lexi asked as Ty held open the car door and escorted her into the restaurant.

"He's even cuter," Ty said with a grin as he waved at Beth and Nate, already seated at a table with Jax.

Several hours later, Lexi and Ty left behind the traffic of Portland, heading back to the ranch. Most of the conversation centered on Jax and what a wonderful, sweet baby he was.

When they stopped in Bend for dinner, Lexi asked Ty to drive the rest of the way home. She was exhausted and the run-in with James had been completely draining.

The next thing she knew, she was in Ty's arms as he carried her out of the garage, across the yard and up the steps to the back door. She hadn't been picked up and carried since she was a little girl.

The feeling of being held close to Ty's chest, gently cradled in his arms was amazing and she didn't want it to end too soon, so she pretended to still be asleep.

Ty carefully bent down and opened the door, carrying her inside the house. He glanced at the stairs then at the light on in the kitchen. Deciding it was best to leave Lexi at the door, he held her for another moment before saying goodnight.

"Lexi, this is the end of the ride," Ty said, his breath warm by her ear. "Wake up, babe."

Slowly opening her eyes, Lexi wrapped his endearment around her heart. Looking into his face, she offered him a smile that made his insides hot and his knees weak.

"Hi," she whispered as Ty slowly set her on her feet.

"Hi," he whispered back, placing a hand on her cheek. "Thanks for taking me along today. It meant more than you can know to see Jax."

"I'm glad we both got to see him and I appreciated meeting Beth and Nate. They're great, Ty. I can see why you care so much about them," Lexi said, squeezing his hand. "Thank you for rescuing me today. You really are my hero."

Ty grinned shyly, but looked pleased. It wasn't every day he got to come to a lady's rescue and it made him feel needed and strong.

"I'm glad I was there. You let me know if he bothers you and I'll take care of it," Ty said, with a steely edge to his voice Lexi hadn't heard before. His concern made her feel cherished and safe.

"Thanks, Ty, for everything. I hope you didn't strain your back carrying me in from the car. You could have just given me a shake to wake me when you pulled into the garage," Lexi said, glad he hadn't.

"I know, but I kind of liked the idea of holding you close," Ty's eyes glinted with mischief and the smile riding his full lips made him nearly irresistible. "Besides, if you were really worried about it, you would have spoken up before I started across the yard, when you first realized you were getting a free ride to the door."

"You knew I was awake and carried me anyway?" Lexi asked, showing both surprise and guilt at being caught in her little deception.

"Yes, ma'am. I think my efforts need some sort of reward," Ty said, pulling her against him, not wanting to say goodnight yet.

"What kind of reward?" she asked, leaning into him, absorbing his warmth and strength.

"A kiss would be a good start," he said, leaning down and touching her lips with his as electricity jolted through him. He would have continued exploring the possibilities of a suitable reward except he was hit from behind by Baby, knocking them both off balance. Ty grasped Lexi to him with one arm while throwing the other out and catching the stair post, trying to keep from toppling to the floor.

"Baby! That is so not okay. Naughty, naughty girl," Lexi said, as she and Ty caught their balance and looked at the dog.

Baby was so excited Ty was home, she leaned against his leg and whined, keeping herself between him and Lexi. She appeared to be smiling as she looked up at Ty, eyes big and bright.

"Guess this is goodnight then," Ty said, tipping his hat to Lexi and going outside, taking the dog with him.

As he walked to the bunkhouse, he scolded the dog.

"Baby, I'm not sure how you could have any worse timing. Are you trying to keep me and Lexi apart? Don't you want me to get to know her better?" Ty asked, scratching the dog on her back as he stood on the bunkhouse porch. At this late hour it looked like everyone was already in bed. Opening the door, he blocked Baby from following him inside. "Scoot, Baby. See if you can behave the rest of the night."

Going to his room, the sweet scent of Lexi clung to his clothes and he inhaled deeply, knowing she would invade his dreams all night.

Lesson Ten
Go with the Flow

*"If ya ever feel like a fish out 'a water,
jes watch what everyone else is doin'
and follow their lead."*

"Are ya ready for this?" Swede asked Ty as they stood watching pickups pulling horse trailers flood into the ranch yard bright and early that morning.

"Ready or not, here they come," Ty said with a grin. Although Swede had tried to give him an idea of what would happen during branding, Ty knew he was going to be on a big learning curve the next three days.

The cattle had been gathered and sorted into three herds of five hundred each. The plan was to work through one herd a day. Swede explained to Ty that although they could do the branding and work the cattle with less help if they used a calf table and a working chute, it wouldn't necessarily speed up the process. That was why they liked to do things the old fashioned way with a bunch of ropers and wrestlers and a lot of fun.

Neighbors and friends would help them get the work done and then they would spend the next couple of weeks traveling to neighboring ranches to return the favor.

While a few of the women would join the men out with the cattle, the rest would put together a big lunch as well as morning and afternoon snacks and a light dinner. Lexi would have hired a caterer, but the women working together to make the food was as much a part of the tradition as the men swapping stories while they burned brands.

Lexi came out the door of the main house and was soon lost among new arrivals, sharing hugs with the women and smiles with the men. Some she hadn't seen since her father's funeral and it was nice to reconnect with people she had known all her life.

So busy getting ready for branding and finishing up spring farm work, Ty and Lexi had hardly seen each other. He kept an eye on her now, watching the way she was accepted among the crowd. She appeared to be a favorite with young and old alike. He couldn't blame anyone for having good taste.

Dressed in jeans, boots, and a long-sleeved cotton work shirt with a hat on her head, Lexi blended in with the rest of the cowboys and cowgirls. Her raven hair fell in a thick braid down her back and Ty noticed the roses in her cheeks and the pink of her lips as she worked through the crowd.

She was nearly to the bunkhouse when a rig stopped nearby and a woman barreled out of the passenger door of the pickup, sweeping Lexi up in a tight hug.

"Oh, my sweet girl, I haven't seen you forever," said a woman who looked like an older version of Lexi as she hugged her tightly.

"Aunt Bertie! I didn't think you guys could come," Lexi said, beaming as she hugged her aunt.

Bertie let go of Lexi, only to pass her off to a man that appeared to Ty to be at least three inches taller than him, although he was slim and lean.

"Uncle Linc," Lexi said as he swung her off her feet and spun her around. "It's so good to see you. Thank you for coming."

"Well, you didn't think we'd miss out on branding, did you?" Linc asked, leaving his arm around Lexi as they walked toward the bunkhouse.

Linc shook hands with Swede while Bertie gave him a hug.

"Aunt Bertie, I want you to meet my new mechanic and good friend, Ty Lewis," Lexi said, taking Ty's hand and pulling him toward her aunt and uncle.

Ty tipped his hat, as Swede had taught him, and shook her aunt's hand before extending a hand to her uncle. These two were perfect strangers to him, but Bertie looked so much like Lexi, he would have pegged her as a relative if they'd met on the street in downtown Portland.

"Ma'am, it's a pleasure to meet you," Ty said, drawing on his best manners. "I thought for a minute Lexi had a sister she forgot to mention."

"Oh, go on with you," Bertie said, slapping his arm, clearly pleased with his comment. "Her mama was my older sister and this little gal has been my baby since she was born."

Hearing her name, the dog came skittering around the corner and plowed into Ty. He braced himself for the impact and only had to take a couple of side steps to maintain his balance.

"Looks like you won over the dog," Linc said with interest. "The only man she cottoned to was Lex."

"So I've heard," Ty said, patting Baby while she happily wagged her tail at the attention. "For whatever reason, she has adopted me."

Linc and Bertie exchanged a glance with Swede who imperceptibly nodded his head. The three of them had known each other since before Lexi was born and they all watched out for her best interest. The dog had run off more people than they could count so to see Baby completely taken with Lexi's new mechanic made him more than a little noteworthy.

"Shall we get this show on the road?" Linc asked as the last of the trailers pulled into the yard and unloaded their horses.

"Yep," Lexi said, linking her arm through her aunt's as they walked back toward the house. Lexi had been trying to figure out how to be two places at once: out with the cattle where she wanted to be and in the house helping the women prepare the food where she felt like she should be. Now that Aunt Bertie was here, she could work with the men and not worry about what was happening in the house. Her step lightened as she kissed her aunt on the cheek and hurried to the barn to saddle Rowdy.

Those on horseback rode out to the pen where the first bunch of cattle was ready to be worked. Sorting out the cows from the calves, Ty mentally went through the process as Swede had explained it to him. It seemed simple enough.

Branding irons grew hot using portable propane tanks while syringes were being filled with vaccine. At Lexi's signal, a group of ropers went into the calves and roped the first five. As the horses drew the ropes taut, they pulled the calves back to where the brands heated. The wrestlers took over, throwing the calves on their sides and removing the rope. The rest of the ground crew converged, branding, vaccinating, tagging and dehorning. The bull calves were castrated. Watching the first one go under the knife, Ty inwardly shuddered and prepared himself for a long day ahead.

He watched the first group be worked then stepped up to do his part as one of the wrestlers.

Mid-morning, women arrived with a multitude of doughnuts, hot coffee and coolers of beverages. After a quick break, the women returned to the house to finish getting lunch ready while the rest of them went back to their work.

Breaking at noon for lunch, Ty stretched his muscles, knowing he'd be sore before the day was out. The crew returned to the big ranch yard for lunch where make-shift tables were set up and piled high with food. Ty wasn't sure he had ever seen that much food in one place before in his life and took a moment to look it all over.

Much to his surprise, he found himself sitting next to Lexi. After she asked her Uncle Linc, who was sitting on her other side, to bless the food, they all dug in. Ty bit into crispy fried chicken, savored bites of fall-off-the-bone ribs and inhaled the yeasty scent of fresh rolls, still warm from the oven. Dessert was a buffet of delectable temptations including brownies, pie and slices of cake.

Taking a rest to let their food settle, good natured joking and visiting went on around the tables until Swede and Linc stood, along with Lexi, signaling it was time to get back to work.

The afternoon passed in a blur of dust, ropes, bawling calves and burning hide for Ty. He'd gotten used to the smell when the brands burned into the sides of the calves and resigned himself to being coated from head to toe in manure and blood due to the nature of his job for the day.

Wrestling the calves to the ground and holding them there, he was right in the line of fire of anything and everything, but he tried to take it all in stride and act like he'd done it hundreds of times before. He was glad Swede had warned him to wear his oldest clothes, ones he didn't mind getting completely filthy. He was wearing a ratty old T-shirt and a pair of jeans that had definitely seen better days, along with his steel-toed shop boots. Although they weren't considered cowboy attire in the least, he managed to get the job done as well as the next guy. He was grateful more than once for the boots protecting his feet from stomping, kicking hooves.

He looked up and caught Lexi watching him with a proprietary look in her eyes a few times throughout the day, which made him feel a little smug. He was intently watching her instead of paying attention to the large calf he was holding when the calf yanked its leg back and delivered a kick to his inner thigh that made him suck in a huge gulp of air. Sharp needles of pain raced up his leg and he bit his lip to keep from saying words he shouldn't.

Closing his eyes against the throbbing in his thigh, he held the calf, hoping the ground crew was about finished so he could go walk off the pain. He was grateful the calf hadn't kicked a little higher or he'd have a hard time keeping his cool.

Smelling Lexi's unique floral scent, he felt her presence about the time her hand settled on his back.

"Ty, are you okay?" she asked, bending down by him. "Are you hurt?"

"I'll be fine," he said, clenching his jaw as the calf attempted to deliver another kick but missed.

"It looked like he nailed you pretty hard," Lexi said, still close. She knew most men would have hollered and cussed and pitched a fit if they'd received the kick the calf delivered to Ty. Instead, he barely flinched, continued doing his job and acted like nothing had happened.

Watching him throughout the day, she could hardly believe how well he fit in with everyone. Even dressed in his "city-dude" clothes, as Swede called them, everyone accepted him and he more than proved he could do the work, better than many of them.

It hadn't exactly been a hardship for her to watch him wrestle calves all day. In the form-fitting holey T-shirt he wore, every muscle was outlined and accented. From the bulging biceps of his arms to the thick muscles of his chest, Lexi couldn't think when she'd enjoyed a branding more.

"I'm fine, but thanks for asking," Ty said, wishing Lexi would step back. He didn't want her to get hurt and he really didn't want her watching too closely when he stood up and limped off until it was his turn to wrestle another calf. Deciding to man-up, as Swede often said, he put on his best poker face, released the calf and walked away like he was on top of the world.

When the last calf was branded and turned out with its mama, Ty joined the rest of the crew in their pilgrimage back to the ranch yard. The women had dinner prepared and Ty sat down to eat with the rest of the crew. What he really wanted was a hot shower and a soft bed, but for now he passed bowls and platters around the table, heaping up his own plate.

Swede passed him a platter of some unidentified deep-fried meat that looked golden brown and tasty. He took several pieces and passed it on. Trying a few bites, he still couldn't identify the mystery meat. Not impressed with the flavor, he focused his attention on the other tempting treats on his plate.

Turning to ask him a question, Swede looked at Ty's plate and slapped him on the back.

"Whooee! You've crossed the line to official cowboy territory, dude!" Swede cackled. Others joined in Swede's laughter although Ty was clueless as to what was so funny.

"What?"

Pointing a finger at the uneaten fried lumps on Ty's plate, Linc leaned around Swede and laughed. "Rocky Mountain oysters, my friend, are a cowboy delicacy."

"Oysters?" Ty asked, confused. The fried lumps he had eaten were certainly not oysters.

"Sure, dude. Cowboy caviar," Swede said, waggling his bushy eyebrows at Ty. "Calf fries."

"Calf fries?" Ty asked, his eyes growing wide as he suddenly realized what he had eaten. "You fry up the…"

Unable to finish his sentence, Ty clamped his jaw shut to keep from losing what dinner he had eaten.

Sitting there, covered in blood and manure, with his thigh throbbing painfully, he thought he'd been a pretty good sport throughout the day. He ignored the teasing that morning for his "city-dude" attire and put his back and muscle into wrestling more calves than any two of the other guys. After all that, he was not going to sit here and eat… animal parts that should never see the inside of a kitchen, while the guys around the table made fun of him.

Mumbling excuses, he got up from the table and retreated to the shop where he knew he could have some peace and quiet. Hoots of laughter followed him across the ranch yard.

Turning on his music, Baby came in and looked at him mournfully, sensing his mood as she settled down on her blanket in the corner.

"That is just disgusting, Baby. Absolutely disgusting," Ty said, picking up a part he'd been working on before he got called into cowboy duty a few days ago.

Baby barked and wagged her tail, showing her agreement.

Losing track of the time, Ty looked up when Lexi came in the shop door carrying a plate with a big piece of berry pie and a scoop of vanilla ice cream.

"I come in peace," Lexi said, sliding the plate onto the clean end of the workbench where Ty often sat to eat his lunch.

Ty raised an eyebrow at her, but went into the bathroom and washed his hands. Coming out, he pulled another stool to the end of the bench, waited for Lexi to have a seat, then sat down.

"Since you didn't get much dinner, I thought you might need a snack," Lexi said as he took a bite of the pie. She'd warmed it up and the ice cream was slowly melting into a rich creamy lake around the flaky crust and sweet berries.

"Thanks. It's good," Ty said, realizing he was hungry and the pie was quite tasty.

"I'm really sorry, Ty. I heard what happened and I should have warned you about Rocky Mountain oysters," Lexi said, placing a warm hand on his him.

Her touch sent fiery jolts racing up both their arms. Despite the electricity snapping between them, Lexi left her hand in place and Ty looked in her eyes. Although she sounded sincere in her apology the mischievous sparkle dancing in the green depths, along with the twitching corners of her mouth, gave away her humor over the matter.

"Not a biggie," Ty said. Not yet at the point he was ready to see any humor in the situation, he was slightly annoyed that she could. "I'll survive."

"I know you will," Lexi said, trying without success to hide a grin. "But I am truly sorry we caught you by surprise. You fit in so well with everyone, I just keep forgetting you've never done this before and all these experiences are new for you."

"You really think I fit in?" Ty asked, uncertain if she was offering flattery to soothe his wounded pride or if she really meant it.

"Absolutely. You worked as hard as anyone out there today, picked up on what needed done without anyone telling you what to do, and I think you probably wrestled more calves than the three Johnson boys together."

Ty hid his pleasure at her praise behind the last bite of pie.

"I mean it, Ty, you did a great job today and I'm really proud of you. You've taken to life here on the ranch so well it's easy to forget you haven't always been here. You're definitely learning the ropes very quickly."

"Thanks, Lexi," Ty said, rubbing his hand on her arm. Wanting to pull her into a hug and steal a kiss or two, Ty decided that would have to wait for another day. Preferably one when he wasn't coated in cow poop and gore. Getting off the stool, Ty put his phone in his pocket, picked up the empty plate and walked Lexi to the door.

"Come on, Baby," Ty called to the dog. She lumbered to her feet and preceded them out the door.

"Oh, you were talking to the dog," Lexi teased as Ty turned off the shop lights and shut the door.

Taking her hand in his, he walked her toward the house. As he leaned down, she could feel his breath warm by her ear. "You're far too beautiful to be called the same thing as that ridiculous dog, Lexi Jo."

Lexi blushed but held tight to Ty's hand as they approached the house. Walking through the gate, Ty could see Swede and Linc visiting on one side of the porch while Bertie sat on the porch swing.

"Girlie, come sit down by me," Bertie said, patting the seat next to her.

Ty offered greetings then took the dirty plate into the kitchen before coming back out. He visited a few minutes with the guys, nodded to the women and bid them all goodnight.

When he was out of earshot, Bertie smacked Lexi playfully on the leg. "Girlie, he has got one fine caboose, even in those baggy jeans. And muscles! My gracious, honey-pie! How do you get anything done around here? I'd spend all day watching him."

"Aunt Bertie! You aren't supposed to notice those things," Lexi said in feigned shock.

"I may be old, Lexi girl, but my eyesight works just fine."

Lesson Eleven
Don't Tempt Mother Nature

"A little rain can't hurt ya,
but only an idiot stays out in a storm."

By the third day of branding, everything ran like a well-functioning machine with everyone doing their part to keep things moving smoothly.

The morning flew by and they only had seventy-five head of cattle left to work when the crew stopped for lunch.

Following the meal, most of the neighbors decided to head for home. While the women helped clean up the dishes and set the kitchen to rights, the men loaded horses, swapped stories and made plans for their own brandings.

Ty was flattered to receive several invitations to work as wrestler at various brandings and assumed he'd be working them all since Swede said they went to help anyone that helped them.

Lexi gave warm hugs to Bertie and Linc as they prepared to leave. Living just south of the little community of Pilot Rock in northeastern Oregon, they spent the last couple of days with Lexi and were anxious to get back to their own place.

"Come visit us for a few days, girlie," Bertie said, giving Lexi another motherly hug. "Bring that gorgeous mechanic of yours along, too. It's no hardship to have to look at him. Not at all."

"Aunt Bertie!" Lexi giggled as they said goodbye. "I might take you up on that when things settle down a bit."

"See that you do," Bertie said as she climbed in the pickup. "And get yourself a housekeeper. You don't have time to run a ranch and scrub toilets. Get your priorities straightened out!"

"Yes, ma'am," Lexi said with a wave as Linc pulled into the line of vehicles heading down the driveway. "Love you guys!"

"Love you, baby!"

With that, the dog barked and wagged her tail, thinking Bertie was talking to her.

Heading back out with a small crew to finish the work, Swede kept looking to the sky.

"What's wrong, Swede?" Ty finally asked, noticing the foreman's preoccupation with the clouds overhead.

"I think there's a storm rollin' in," Swede said, rubbing his knee.

"Are you kidding?" Ty asked, wiping sweat off his brow and staring up at the sunny, blue sky. "It practically feels like summer."

"Yeah, well, practically ain't the same as the real deal. Ya mark my words. Rain will hit the ground before the day is over."

Deciding maybe Swede knew something he didn't Ty refrained from making any further comment as he wrestled another calf.

About two dozen calves were left to work when the air dropped in temperature and the sky suddenly turned dark.

As the working crew took stock of the upcoming storm, Swede yelled to the neighbors who stayed behind to finish up branding.

"Go on and get home while you can," he said, waving his hat as they hurried back toward the house. Turning to the ranch hands, Swede cackled. "Let's see if we can beat the storm, boys."

Ty thought they'd been working fast and furious the last two days but it was nothing compared to what they were doing now. Despite the sense of urgency to work quickly and finish before the rain hit, they made little progress when the first drops of water hit.

"Lex, you head on up to the house. No need for us all to get soaked," Swede called to Lexi where she sat waiting to rope the next calf.

"I'm fine. I won't melt!" she said with a laugh, turning her attention back to the cattle.

Thunder boomed and lightening crackled making the hair on the back of Ty's neck stand on end. He'd never witnessed anything quite like a spring rain storm in wide-open country.

The lightening seemed to crack open the sky and rain began falling in torrential sheets. They were soon soaked and chilled.

As Lexi dragged a calf over for Ty to wrestle, he saw her shivering from the rain and the chill in the wind.

"Lexi, go on back to the house. You don't need to stay out in this," Ty said as he held the calf while Cal and Keith put on the brand and Jimmy vaccinated it.

"It's my ranch, my cattle, and I'm staying," she said with a determined lift of her chin, riding off to get the next calf.

"Stubborn woman," Ty muttered under his breath. If he had the option of getting out of this mess, he'd gladly take it.

Not only was he covered in manure and blood, but now the churned up mud made it nearly impossible to hold onto the calves. Slipping and sliding in the muck, the work that should have taken them just a few minutes to finish stretched into more than a miserable hour.

Turning the last of the calves back in with their mamas, they cleaned up the mess and headed back to the house. Lexi was shivering so hard Ty thought she might fall off Rowdy.

Beating the rest of them back to the barn on the four-wheeler, Ty was waiting when she rode Rowdy inside. He could hear her teeth chattering and noticed a bluish tinge to her lips.

"Are you crazy, Lexi?" Ty asked as Rowdy stopped beside him.

Lexi's eyes were closed and her body racked with shivers. Putting a hand to her thigh, he wasn't even sure she heard him. Giving her a gentle shake, she started to slide off the saddle on the opposite side.

"Lexi!" Ty had gone past concern to fearful as he put a hand around her waist and pulled her off the saddle to his chest. Scooping one arm beneath her knees and securing a hand behind her back, he turned to see Swede hurrying their direction as he ordered the other boys to take care of the horses.

"I think she passed out," Ty said, walking toward the door of the barn.

"Let's get her to the house and warm her up. Can you carry her that far?" Swede asked, walking beside Ty.

"Yeah. Can you go ahead and maybe light the fire in the family room and get something hot ready for her to drink?" Ty said as he walked as fast as he could across the mud-slicked ranch yard. Coming through the back gate, he was glad Swede left the door open, making it easier for him to carry Lexi inside.

He hesitated for a moment as he dripped mud and manure on the sparkling kitchen floor.

"Don't worry about the mess, now. Gettin' her warmed up is more important," Swede said as he hustled back into the kitchen from the family room with a big fleece blanket in his hand. "We probably better get the wet stuff off and then see if she'll wake up."

While Ty held Lexi, Swede took off her sodden hat, and boots, removed her soggy socks and untied the silk scarf around her neck. Unwilling to remove anything else, Swede draped the blanket around her and instructed Ty to carry her into the family room where the gas fireplace was throwing out welcome warmth.

Carrying her into the room, Ty was grateful for the heat and stood close to the fireplace hoping Lexi would soon warm up and wake up.

Swede hurried in carrying three cups of hot tea and set them down on the coffee table.

Lexi's shaking was getting worse instead of better and Ty could tell she wasn't warming up like she should.

"Swede, are there any women around who could come help?" Ty asked, already knowing the answer.

"None thet could get here anytime soon. Besides with this rain, ya'll be hard pressed to find anyone able to get far in the storm," Swede said, realizing why Ty was asking.

"Well, do you think we should... I mean she isn't going to get warm in these wet clothes and she isn't exactly able to get them off herself. What should we do?" Ty asked, not wanting to do anything improper, but fearful for Lexi's well-being.

"Let's try to wake her up," Swede said as Ty gently placed Lexi on the couch.

Tapping her cheeks and calling her name elicited no response. Swede even tried pinching her arm but got no reaction.

"She's out cold," Swede said, standing next to Ty and watching Lexi shiver. "We got to do somethin'. She was always quick to take a chill as a kid. Guess she never outgrew it."

"We've got to get her out of those wet clothes. How about we take off her shirt and jeans, wrap her in the blanket, and hope for the best," Ty suggested.

"Okay, but don't enjoy this none and don't look any more than ya' hafta," Swede instructed, turning his back to Lexi.

"Me? Aren't you going to help?" Ty asked as he bent over Lexi's still form trying to decide the easiest way to take off her clothes without seeing anything he shouldn't.

"Nope. I ain't gonna do it. She's like a daughter to me and I ain't turnin' around til she's wrapped up in thet blanket. So ya just do what has to be done and do it fast."

Releasing a sigh, Ty was glad Lexi wore a western shirt with snaps. One strong tug and it was undone. Quickly removing it, he wasn't surprised she wore a tank top beneath it.

He would have left it on her, but it was as soaked as her shirt. Holding her up with one hand, he pulled it over her head and averted his gaze to her jeans as he laid her back down on the couch.

Taking a deep breath, he unhooked the buckle of her belt, fumbled to unfasten the button at the top of her jeans and pulled down the zipper. He'd dreamed of doing something similar, but in his dreams Lexi was wide awake and a willing participant.

Shutting his mind on that train of thought, he grasped her sodden jeans in both hands and worked them down over her hips, pulling them off as quickly as he could. Grabbing the big blanket, he wrapped it around her, trying not to look at her nearly naked body and stood back up.

"Done," he said as Swede spun around.

"Good job, Ty," Swede said, handing him a steaming mug of tea. "You're the only man I'd trust to do thet, jes so ya know."

"Why's that?" Ty asked, standing by the fire, absorbing some of the heat.

"Cause ya care about her and yer an honorable man. I know we can trust ya to do what's right."

Ty was caught off guard by Swede's words and felt his throat swell shut. Instead of speaking, he nodded his head and took a drink of the hot tea.

"I'm afraid if we pour the tea down her now, she might choke. Why don't ya run to the bunkhouse and get cleaned up right quick, then come back. I'm thinkin' this lil' gal is gonna need some doctorin' and attention this evenin'."

"Okay. Do I need to go to Burns and get a doctor or anything?" Ty asked setting his half-empty mug of tea on the coffee table.

"Nah, let's jes see if we can get her warmed up and awake. Go on and get yerself clean, then I'll take a turn."

Ty waited until he was out of the house to sprint across the ranch yard, ignoring the driving, cold rain as he ran. Bursting in the bunkhouse door, the guys were in various stages of getting clean or already changed as he ran inside. Thankfully, no one was in the bathroom he used.

Taking a fast shower, he hurriedly dried off and put on clean clothes. He was pulling on a pair of old sneakers when Jimmy poked his head in Ty's bedroom door.

"Is she okay, dude?"

"Not yet. We can't get her warmed up, but Swede and I'll stay with her," Ty said, pulling on a hooded sweatshirt and hurrying toward the front room. Ty gently squeezed Jimmy's shoulder as he opened the door. "If we need some help, I'll let you know."

Running back to the house, Ty hurried in the kitchen door, removing his now wet sweatshirt and muddy shoes.

Returning to the family room, Swede sat in a kitchen chair he'd placed by the couch, talking to Lexi, who still shivered, although her lips didn't look quite so blue.

"Is she awake?" Ty asked as Swede stood up.

"Nah. I jes thought it might help to talk to her, ya know?"

"Yeah, I know," Ty said, remembering the hours of one-sided conversations he had with his mom when she was in the hospital. What if Lexi got pneumonia? What if he lost her, too?

He couldn't stand the thought of it.

"You go get cleaned up and I'll see what I can do," Ty said, carrying the cold mugs of tea to the kitchen to reheat.

Swede scurried off to his little house as fast as his bowed legs would carry him. While the tea warmed, Ty called Beth and told her what happened.

"You need to get her body temperature back up as quickly as possible," Beth said, stating what Ty already knew. "Do you have anything you can warm and place around her, like hot packs? Have you tried getting her to drink something hot?"

"No. We didn't want to choke her since she doesn't seem awake," Ty said, taking the tea out of the microwave.

"Hold her head up and see if you can get her to take a little sip. If you can get her to drink a little, it might help her wake up, too. I'll stay on the phone while you try," Beth said, racking her brain for ideas that could help.

"Okay," Ty said, carrying a mug of hot, but not scalding tea, back to Lexi. Getting down on his knees by the couch, he put the phone on speaker so Beth could hear him and placed his hand behind Lexi's neck. Lifting her head up, he held the mug to her lips and tried to coax her to take a sip.

"Come on, Lexi, you need to drink this hot tea. It will warm you up and you'll feel better in no time," Ty said, tipping the mug just enough the liquid touched her lips. Forcing the mug between her lips, he poured a little in her mouth and waited to see what she would do. When she appeared to swallow, he repeated the process and got her to take several sips.

"Ty, what's going on?" Beth asked, listening to the quiet.

"She took a few sips, I think," Ty said, holding the mug again as Lexi accepted the warm liquid. "Her lips aren't blue anymore and the shivering seems to be less violent."

"That's great," Beth said brightly, hoping Lexi would be fine. She genuinely liked the woman and got the idea Ty had more than a passing interest in his lovely employer. "Keep trying to get something hot inside her. That will help as well as anything."

"I know. I'll keep trying," Ty said. Hearing baby Jax fuss in the background, Ty smiled. "I think Jax is making his demands known. I won't keep you, sis, but thanks."

"Anytime, Ty. Call if there is anything we can do to help. Love you," Beth said, disconnecting.

Patiently working with Lexi, Ty got most of the tea down her before Swede returned.

"Well, look at that," Swede said, noticing Lexi's color was better and she wasn't shivering like she was when he left. "Ya done good, dude."

"My sister offered some pointers," Ty said, as he and Swede watched Lexi, uncertain as to what they should do next.

"Sisters are good thet way, ain't they?" Swede said. A look came over his face like a light bulb had burst to life and he smacked his leg with a cackle. "Now why didn't I think of that before!"

"Think of what?" Ty asked, curious as to what had Swede looking like he'd just won the lottery.

"A grand idea," Swede said, vaguely. "I'm gonna play this hand close to the chest until I see if it will pan out and strike gold."

"Okay," Ty said, not exactly certain what had Swede all excited. He didn't feel like investing the effort into deciphering Swede's statement at the moment. "So what do we do now?"

"I don't know," Swede said, not any more accustomed to being a care giver than Ty, especially not to a young woman. "Why don't you sit here with her while I clean up the mess we made bringin' her in. Maybe if you sat on the couch with her, shared some of your warmth, it would help her warm up faster."

Ty was willing to try anything. While Swede went to find a mop and something to get the mud out of the carpet, Ty picked up Lexi. Making sure the blanket stayed tucked around her, he sat down on the couch with Lexi on his lap. Holding her close to his chest, he hummed and stared into the fire.

Lexi couldn't remember ever being so miserably cold and wet. She should have paid more attention to what Swede was saying about a storm rolling in and just finished the branding tomorrow instead of trying to beat the rain.

It also wouldn't have hurt for her to have listened when he told her to head back to the house before she got drenched or even when her teeth first began to chatter. But it was her ranch, her responsibility, and she didn't want to appear weak in front of her men, so she stuck it out.

As they finished up, her fingers were so cold, they felt numb and she couldn't hold the rope well enough to even cast a loop. Gus roped the last four calves by himself while she sat watching and freezing.

On the way back to the barn, she remembered feeling like she was being sucked down into a dark, cold tunnel where nothing seemed real. Lexi recalled Ty's voice asking her a question, but she didn't know if she responded. Her body felt strangely detached from her brain as it shook from the cold.

Voices penetrated the fog in her head, but she couldn't hear what they were saying. She recognized Ty's presence, felt someone holding her, but the chills that rampaged through her forced away any coherent thoughts.

Shaking and trembling, she felt warm liquid trickle down her throat, and could smell something that made her think of Ty. She thought she recognized his voice again, felt his gentle hand touching her.

Trying to push her way past the shroud of confusion in her mind, she felt warmth seeping into her cold body, felt herself being held tenderly against something solid and strong, could hear a pleasant rumbling that almost sounded like a song. As clarity returned to her thoughts, she recognized the song as Whitesnake's *Is This Love*.

A smile touched her lips as she opened her eyes and found herself staring into Ty's warm blue orbs.

"Hey, babe," Ty whispered, smiling at her as she came fully awake, realizing she was wrapped in a warm cocoon and held in his strong arms. "I'm really glad to see those beautiful green eyes of yours."

"Hi," she said, still disoriented and not quite sure how she'd gotten from the back of her horse to the couch in her family room. "Were you singing *Is This Love*?"

"Me? You must have been dreaming," Ty said with a teasing smile. Of all the songs he could have picked, he knew the lyrics of that one really fit what he was coming to feel for the woman in his arms. He just wasn't ready for her to know it yet.

Shifting so she was in more of an upright position, Lexi realized she was wrapped up in the big fleece blanket she kept on the back of the couch.

She still felt chilled, but not freezing like she'd been out in the rain.

"Would you like some more tea?" Ty asked and she nodded her head. Raising his voice, he yelled in the direction of the hall, "Swede, the lady would like more tea."

Swede hurried into the front room, mop still in his hand, with a big grin on his face.

"Well, Lex, you jes about had me scared half to death," Swede said as he picked up her empty mug. "I'll be right back with more tea."

"Thanks," she called after her foreman as he retreated to the kitchen. Looking around, Lexi noticed wet, dirty clothes in a pile on the floor at the end of the couch. Clothes that looked exactly like the ones she had been wearing earlier. Moving her hand, she touched bare skin where her shirt should have been. Upon further investigation, she was grateful to find her underclothes still in place, even if they were damp.

Her face flushed red as she thought about Swede and Ty removing her cold, soggy clothes. She would die of mortification.

"What happened?" she asked, going stiff in Ty's arms. He felt the change in her and rubbed his hand reassuringly along her back.

"You sort of passed out in the barn so I carried you in here and Swede and I tried to warm you up. We finally decided you needed out of the wet clothes, so…"

"So the two of you took them off?" Lexi asked, completely horrified at the thought.

"Well, not exactly," Ty said, knowing this was bound to be embarrassing for them all, but not fully realizing how much until right this moment. "Swede turned his back and made me do it."

"Oh," she said, not wanting to examine why the knowledge that it was just Ty made her feel better.

"I promise I didn't look at anything," Ty said, with a wicked grin. "At least not much."

"You are insufferable," Lexi said, trying to act offended. She would have slapped him on the arm if she hadn't been wrapped in the blanket so securely or suddenly felt as weak as a newborn colt.

"Honest, Lexi, I just did what needed done and wrapped you in the blanket as fast as I could. There was no unnecessary peeking."

Before she could respond, Swede returned with a steaming cup of tea. Lexi wiggled one hand free of the blanket and took the mug from Ty. It felt like a lead weight in her hand and Ty must have sensed she was about to drop it as he placed his hand around hers on the mug.

"Need some help?" he asked, guiding the mug up to her lips. She took a sip, enjoying the feel of the hot liquid along with the taste. Swede wasn't much of a cook, but he could make a fine cup of tea.

She finished the cup, with Ty's help, while Swede cleaned up the muddy mess from the floor and took her wet clothes into the laundry room off the kitchen.

"What now?" Ty asked as she sank back into the warmth and strength he offered.

"I'd like to take a hot shower and then maybe have a little something to eat before going to bed," Lexi said. How she was going to make it up the stairs, take a shower, fix herself dinner and then get herself back up the stairs to bed was beyond her ability to comprehend at the moment. She could hardly hold up her head.

"Yes, ma'am," Ty said. Getting to his feet with her still in his arms, he walked toward the staircase in the back hall. Pulling the tail of the blanket off the floor so he wouldn't trip on it, he started up the stairs.

"What are you doing?" she asked. Not only was he carrying her like she weighed no more than a sack of potatoes, he seemed to have read her mind about her inability to navigate the stairs.

"Taking you upstairs so you can get that shower you wanted," he said, trying not to huff as he reached the top of the narrow staircase. He should have gone up the main stairs in the front entry. They had a wider tread and weren't quite as steep as the steps in the back hall. "Which room?"

Lexi pointed him to a door on his right and he carried her inside the spacious room painted in a soothing sage green with cream trim. He gently set her down on the big bed and grinned.

"Can you manage that shower by yourself or do you need my assistance?" he teased, giving her a wink fit for a rascal.

She glowered at him and pointed a finger toward the door.

"I think I can manage by myself, thank you very much."

Ty chuckled as he stepped in the hall. "If you need me, just yell."

As he disappeared downstairs, Lexi gave herself a mental pep talk, convincing herself she could make it to the shower.

Walking on wobbly legs, she turned on the steaming water and took the fastest shower of her life. Warmth was returning to her blood, but she also felt light-headed and dizzy. Quickly drying off, she pulled a warm flannel gown over her head and was reaching for her robe when everything went dark.

Cleaning up the last of the mess they'd made on the floor, Ty and Swede were warming up some soup and digging leftovers out of the fridge when they hear a loud thump overhead.

Ty ran down the hall and took the stairs two at a time, racing into Lexi's room to find her passed out on the floor by her dresser. Lifting her into his arms, he cradled her close and tapped her cheeks.

"Ty?" she asked groggily.

"Yeah, babe, I'm here," he whispered, glad she had come to. His heart was still racing and he was pretty sure he'd just lost a few years off his lifespan.

"I guess I needed some help after all," she said, making him grin.

"You've got help now," he said, carrying her to the bed.

Swede came panting in the door, and folded back the covers so Ty could lay Lexi on the smooth sheets. Tugging the blankets and comforter up around her, she sank back into the pillows looking pale and wan.

"Thanks, guys. I guess I owe you overtime pay for this," she said, before her eyes drifted shut again.

"Leave her be for a bit," Swede said, taking Ty by the arm and walking him back to the hall. "I think the lil' gal is plumb tuckered out. Let's eat some grub and see how she feels then."

Warming up plates of food, Ty half-listened to Swede while keeping one ear tuned to any noise from upstairs as they ate.

"She'll be fine, son. She comes from tough stock, even if she has a tendency to catch cold faster than ya can blink," Swede said, noticing Ty's anxious looks toward the hallway. "Did I ever tell you about the first time I met her granddaddy?"

"No, I don't think you did," Ty said, glad for the distraction of Swede's story-telling. He knew Swede had been employed on the ranch since he was a young man, but it was interesting to hear more details.

As Ty cleaned up the dishes, Swede talked about the family, sharing amusing stories about Lex and Lexi. Ty even found himself chuckling a few times. Wiping off the counter, Ty looked around the clean kitchen and wondered what they should do. He hated to leave Lexi alone, but wasn't exactly sure she'd welcome their presence in her room.

"Should we sit up with her tonight?" Ty asked as they walked down the hall and started up the stairs to check on Lexi.

"Let's see how she feels and then decide," Swede said, puffing up the last few steps. "I tell ya, these stairs get steeper ever time I climb them."

Ty was grinning as they walked into Lexi's room. She was still asleep but her face looked flushed. Touching her forehead, it felt hot.

"Do you think she's got a fever?" Ty asked, looking at Swede.

Swede touched her head and felt the heat radiating from her. "I'd say so. Ya know anythin' about doctorin' sick women?"

"Nope, but Beth might," Ty said, calling his sister. Beth told them to pull off some of the blankets, to keep Lexi hydrated, and to see if they could find a thermometer. She warned them if Lexi's temperature got too high, they should take her to the hospital.

While Swede adjusted blankets, Ty ran downstairs and poured a big glass of juice for Lexi and hurried back upstairs, getting her to take a few sips. Going into her bathroom, he found a washcloth and ran tepid water over it, wringing out the excess. Taking it to Lexi, he placed it on her forehead and she seemed to calm down a little.

"Where would she keep a thermometer?" Ty asked, not willing to go through her things in the bathroom.

"I'm sure I don't know," Swede said, nodding his head toward the bathroom door. "Somewhere in there, I'm guessin'."

With a resigned sigh, Ty returned to the bathroom and looked in the medicine cabinet. Luckily, the first shelf he searched had a thermometer that could be placed on the forehead to take a temperature. Returning again to Lexi's bedside, he ran it across her forehead and got a reading of 101.

"Thet's high, ain't it?" Swede said looking at the digital reading.

"Yeah," Ty said, getting more worried as the evening wore on. "Are you sure we shouldn't take her to the hospital? Isn't there one in Burns? Are there any doctors who make house calls out here?"

"If her temperature gets any higher, then I think we better haul her in," Swede said, staring at Lexi. "There's a hospital in Burns and only one doctor makes house calls and he can't see to drive at night. So let's jes do the best we can and go from there."

Ty got Lexi to take a little of the cold juice then rinsed out the washrag and replaced it on her forehead. Swede disappeared and came back holding a book. Pulling up a chair by the bed, he sank into it and started reading. Ty was surprised by Swede's choice of *The Virginian* and soon got lost in the story as he continued trying to help Lexi.

Another hour passed when they heard voices downstairs. Ty peeked over the banister to see Jimmy and Keith standing on the rug by the front door in the foyer.

"Hey guys," he said as they looked up toward the landing.

"How's she doing?" Jimmy asked.

"Not great. She's got a fever and passed out on us a couple times," Ty said, glad to see the hands showing some interest in the welfare of their employer.

"Anything we can do to help?" Keith asked, shifting from one foot to the other, clearly uncomfortable being in the boss' house.

"Not right now. Swede and I are trying to get her fever down. We may be here a while. Any of you guys have any medical training?"

"Nope. Not unless cows count," Jimmy said with a lopsided grin.

"I'll be sure to tell the boss you said that," Ty teased. "We'll let you know if there is anything you can do. Thanks for checking in."

They waved before going back out the door.

Ty returned to the room to find Swede involved with his reading. Ty took Lexi's temperature again and it was still at 101.

Putting another cool cloth on her head, he got her to sip more juice then sank down on the floor by her bed.

He'd spent the last three days doing some of the hardest, most physical labor he'd ever done in his life. His body felt battered and abused from wrestling calves, chasing cows, and dodging flying hooves. Spending the last several hours worried about Lexi, Ty felt exhaustion dragging him down.

"You look done in, son," Swede said, setting aside the book and giving him a thoughtful glance. "Why don't ya take a lil' siesta and I'll keep an eye on the boss. Then we can trade."

"Are you sure?" Ty asked, thinking he could stretch out on the floor and be asleep in a few seconds flat.

"Haul yerself into one of the other bedrooms and get some shut-eye."

Ty hated to leave Lexi but knew he needed some rest if he was going to be any help to her at all. Opening the door to one of the guest rooms, he collapsed on the bed and was soon asleep.

"Wake up, son," Swede said, giving Ty a shake.

Ty opened his eyes, confused, finally remembering where he was.

"Is it Lexi?" Ty asked sitting up on the bed.

"Yep, she's been mumblin' in her sleep and keeps sayin' yer name. I thought maybe ya could try to calm her down. She's been mighty restless."

Swede didn't stop to wonder why Lex was talking to Ty in her dreams. He knew she was quite taken with the mechanic and for now he didn't see any need to ask questions.

Ty hurried back to Lexi's room to find her tossing and turning. Not knowing what else to do, he sank onto the bed beside her and pulled her into his arms, holding her against his chest.

"It's all right, Lexi. I'm here," Ty whispered, brushing the hair off her forehead and planting a soft kiss to her temple. "Everything's fine. I'm right here with you, babe."

Lexi relaxed and Ty held her for a while. He could tell her breathing evened out and deepened. A hand to her forehead confirmed her fever was dropping.

When Swede came back, he settled himself in the chair he'd occupied most of evening and was soon emitting soft snores.

Drifting off to sleep, Ty awoke to Lexi pushing against his chest.

"Ty? What's going on? What are you doing?" Lexi asked in a raspy voice.

"You've been pretty sick. Swede and I stayed to take care of you," Ty said, pointing to Swede asleep in the chair. In the muted light from the hall, Lexi could see her foreman snoring away in a chair by her bed.

"You guys have been here all night?"

"Yeah. We couldn't just leave you," Ty said, gently rubbing Lexi's back.

Rolling back her head to better look at Ty, she couldn't believe he would step in and take care of her, especially as tired and sore as he had to be.

"Thank you," she said, feeling tears roll down her cheeks. Being sick always made her weepy.

"You're welcome," Ty said, brushing away her tears and feeling the tug at his heartstrings as he watched more fall from her eyes. "Don't cry. Everything's just fine."

Lexi sniffled and nodded her head.

Ty got her a glass of cold water and made her drink the whole thing before he took her temperature again. It was down to ninety-nine.

"Much better," he said, rubbing his fingers gently across her forehead and down her jaw line. "Do you need anything?"

Lexi shook her head as she sank back into her pillows. She remembered taking a shower and pulling on her nightgown. After that, she only remembered cool fingers on her forehead and quiet voices. For some reason, a western story was playing around in her head and Ty kept appearing in her dream as the hero. She was the heroine and he rescued her from the bad guy.

"I'll wake up Swede and we'll let you get back to sleep," Ty said, taking a step toward the foreman.

"No, don't go," Lexi said, holding out her hand to Ty. She knew what she was asking was way above and beyond the call of duty, but it's what she wanted all the same. "Will you hold me again, until I go to sleep?"

"I'll hold you as long as you like," Ty said, sliding back onto the bed next to her and wrapping his arms around her. Lexi turned her head so it rested on his chest and Ty felt her relax against him. Sinking down against the pillows, Ty let out a contented sigh and closed his eyes.

It wouldn't take much for him to get used to holding Lexi this way every night.

Lesson Twelve
Maintain Control at All Times

"If ya start to lose yer grip, grab onto it with both hands and hang on fer all yer worth."

"Are you joking, girlie?" Bertie asked so loudly Lexi had to hold the phone away from her ear. "You've got to be kidding me."

"Nope, that is the honest truth," Lexi said, smiling as she sat at the kitchen counter, sipping tea.

Tired of the confinement of spending the last three days in bed, Lexi was ready to be up and about although she figured one more day spent in the house probably wouldn't hurt. She dressed in jeans and a T-shirt, thought about going outside, but changed her mind. It was still cool and rainy out and the last thing Lexi wanted to do was to make herself sick again. So she called Aunt Bertie to see what was going on in her world and told her aunt about being sick.

"I can't believe that ol' goat and that handsome mechanic of yours would take such good care of you," Bertie said.

"Believe it or not, it's true," Lexi said, dropping bread in the toaster. "I'm not sure I've ever had better nursing care when I've been sick."

"Then quit messing around and put your brand on Ty. Mark my words, baby, he's a keeper."

"Aunt Bertie…"

"Don't 'Aunt Bertie' me, honey-pie. I know what I'm talking about and so do you. Think about what I said. You won't find too many men like him in a lifetime, especially ones who are quite so fine to look at."

"Aunt Bertie!"

Bertie laughed.

"I've got to run, but you call if you need anything. Love you, girlie."

"Thanks, Bertie. Love you, too."

Buttering her toast and eating it, Lexi mused over her aunt's words. The woman was crazy if she thought Lexi could just walk up to Ty and tell him she was branding him as hers. She liked Ty and was attracted to him with an intensity that sometimes frightened her. She knew he was a hard worker and a good, solid man.

Every day she found herself falling more in love with him. She just wasn't sure if she could trust her feelings. After all, she thought she was in love with James.

Ty and Swede had hovered around her like two fussy old women since she'd taken ill the last day of branding. They brought her tea and toast, fluffed her pillows and made sure she had plenty of tissues. Swede finished reading her dad's copy of *The Virginian* to her and Ty carried her down to the family room to watch movies.

It was while he was digging in the entertainment center where her dad had an assortment of movies that Ty discovered an old John Wayne movie called *Girls Demand Excitement*.

Opening the case, a slip of paper fell out with yet another clue.

Best Bucket

He and Lexi spent quite a bit of time speculating on what that meant before deciding to watch the movie.

While she loved Swede like an uncle, her feelings for Ty were something else entirely. She finally recovered from her initial humiliation of him undressing her, then seeing her with a red, runny nose and watery eyes.

It never crossed her mind that someone as big, strong, and as much of a loner as he was could be so tender and gentle in caring for a pathetically sick woman. If she hadn't been half in love with him before she got sick, she was completely smitten with the man now. The problem was she didn't know what to do about that infatuation.

Lost in her thoughts, Lexi didn't hear the kitchen door open and jumped when Baby pressed against her leg.

"Hey, Baby! I haven't seen you forever," Lexi said, rubbing the dog's damp head. "Let's get you dried off and you can hang out with me awhile."

Lexi grabbed a couple of towels from the laundry room and dried off the dog then mopped the floor where the canine tracked in water and mud. Lexi put an old sheet on the floor by the counter and Baby plopped down, watching Lexi intently.

"Did you miss me, too, Baby?"

The dog barked and wagged her tail.

"I didn't think you liked any human but Ty these days," Lexi said to the dog as she finished her cup of tea.

Wanting to do something, she decided to make Swede and Ty some cookies as a thank you for taking care of her. They both seemed to have a sweet tooth and she knew the treat would be appreciated.

Creaming together butter and sugar, she began stirring up a batch of sugar cookies. Turning up the music she was listening to, she quickly mixed the dough and enjoyed another cup of tea while it chilled, flipping through a new clothing catalog.

Taking the dough from the fridge, she rolled it out, using a glass to cut rounds before sprinkling the tops with sugar and popping the buttery circles in the oven.

Waiting for the cookies to bake, Lexi cranked up the volume when Luke Bryan's *Country Girl (Shake It For Me)* started to play. Dancing around the kitchen with abandon, Lexi was unaware she had an audience.

Not expecting Lexi to be up out of bed, Ty could hear music blaring when he stepped onto the porch. Knocking on the door, he waited for Lexi to invite him in. He and Swede had been in and out of the house multiple times the last few days without knocking as they took care of Lexi, but if she was up and about he didn't think it seemed right to just barge in. He took the music playing as a good sign that she was feeling better.

As he waited for her to come to the door, he listened to the lyrics and found himself entertained by the song. Maybe Lexi's country music had some merit. When he knocked again and got no response he decided Lexi must not be in the kitchen.

Sticking his head in the door, he noticed Baby on the floor before he spied Lexi dancing around the kitchen, shaking a posterior that should be registered as some sort of assault weapon on the male senses, especially in the jeans she was wearing.

Ty leaned against the counter and watched her move, quickly losing his ability to think rationally. The more she danced, the hotter his blood ran and the tighter his insides twisted.

The only thought registering in his head involved wrapping his arms around that beautiful body and kissing her until they both forgot everything but each other. And if she wanted to wiggle around the kitchen a little more, he wouldn't object to that either.

Doubting Lexi would be quite so uninhibited if she knew she had an audience, he was soon proven right.

Seeing Ty, Baby let out a bark which made Lexi spin around and stop mid-shake in her dance. Lexi looked at him, her cheeks and neck red from her furious blushing, while Ty silently wished Baby would have kept quiet for just a little longer.

"Don't stop on my account," Ty said, sticking his finger in the cookie dough and snitching a bite, acting like he didn't have a care in the world although he was surprised he could form coherent words with the way his senses were on Lexi overload.

"I… it was… you… Oh!" Lexi said, embarrassed and flustered. How long had he been standing there, anyway?

"Feeling better today?" Ty asked, stealing another bite of dough, desperately wanting to feel Lexi in his arms.

"Yes, I am," Lexi said, busying herself with the pan of cookies that needed to come out of the oven. Placing the cookies on a rack to cool, she put in another pan before looking at Ty, who continued to grin at her.

"I might have to start listening to country music if the songs all make you move like that," Ty commented, taking a step toward Lexi. She took a step back as he took another forward, until she bumped into the fridge. Putting his muscled arms on either side of her, blocking her in, he melded his hot blue eyes to her green ones. His voice dropped as he leaned close to her ear and asked, "You want to shake it for me again, Lexi Jo?"

"No, I don't. I didn't shake anything for you to start with," Lexi said, unable to pull her eyes from Ty's as heat, tension, and desire pulsed between them. "I don't make it a habit of dancing around the kitchen, just so you know."

"Maybe you should," Ty growled. His sweet sugar-laced breath was warm on her face.

"I was just…" Lexi stammered, unsettled by the intense light glowing in Ty's bright blue eyes and the warmth of his body so close to hers.

"Making it really, really hard for me to not do this," Ty said, dropping his arms to her waist. While his lips trailed hot kisses along her neck, his hands slid down her hips and landed on her firm backside, pulling her flush against him.

Lost in the wonder of being held so closely to Ty with his kisses branding her skin, Lexi ran her hands up his arms and around his neck. As his lips tempted hers, Lexi momentarily forgot everything except Ty, except for the glorious sensations he was stirring in her. When his hands slid up her sides beneath her shirt, she gasped and shoved against his solid chest.

"Ty! You can't..."

"Lexi, I'm sorry," Ty interrupted, feeling genuinely remorseful now that common sense had flooded back into his head. "I didn't mean to get so carried away. My apologies."

Before she could say anything further, Ty ran his hands through his hair and let out his breath. The spell they both were under was broken and he was out of line. Way out of line. Taking a big step back, he released a sigh.

Still breathing hard, Lexi scrambled to find her mental footing. She felt chilled now that she was no longer surrounded by Ty's warmth. "I shouldn't have encouraged you. It's okay."

"No, it isn't. I'm sorry," Ty said, genuinely concerned of how she would react to him now. He honestly didn't come to the house planning to get quite so close to her. He only thought to see if she was feeling better and offer to make her breakfast.

Seeing Lexi do her fanny-shaking dance that would, quite likely, be emblazoned in his brain for the remainder of his life on earth, wasn't exactly anything he planned on this morning. It caught him by surprise. How else was a red-blooded man supposed to react? Despite his best intentions, Ty couldn't keep from touching the body that constantly tempted him.

Knowing men generally fell into like, lust, or love with a woman, Ty decided what he felt was quite likely a lethal cocktail of all three. The problem was that the more he tasted, the more he wanted to drink of it deeply and intently.

"I don't want you to be afraid of me," he said with sincerity. It would kill him if she was.

"I'm not," Lexi looked at him warmly and placed a hand on his arm. "I'm a little afraid of this...um... thing between us, but not of you."

Ty wasn't exactly reassured by that statement, but at least she hadn't told him to get out. Gently placing his hand over hers, he rubbed soft circles on the back of her hand with his thumb.

"I'm a little afraid of this thing too, Lexi. I've never..." Ty realized he was about to say more than he probably should but plunged ahead. "I've never felt like this before."

"Me either," she whispered, staring at his chest, not quite able to meet his eyes. "Despite that, we can't keep getting carried away. What are we going to do?"

"Take it slow and easy," Ty said with one of the grins that made Lexi's knees feel wobbly. "I'm not going anywhere, you aren't going anywhere, so we have all the time in the world to explore whatever this is."

"Okay. Slow and easy," she repeated as the smell of burning cookies reached her nose. "Oh! The cookies!"

Grabbing a pot holder she pulled a pan of overly browned cookies from the oven and dropped it on the counter.

Baby, who sat quietly watching the proceedings between her two favorite people, suddenly grew excited and jumped between them, barking and wagging her tail, nearly knocking Lexi off balance as she put another pan of cookies in the oven.

"Guess you better not shake and bake anymore," Ty teased with a wicked glint in his eye, picking up a handful of not-burned cookies from the cooling rack.

Lexi threw her potholder at him with a grin. "Get out of my kitchen, Ty Lewis! And take that blasted dog with you."

"Yes, ma'am," Ty said, running for the door as Lexi snapped a damp dish towel at him, Baby hot on his heels.

Waking up the next day with a sore throat and pounding headache, Ty realized he probably shouldn't have gotten quite so cozy with Lexi while she had a cold. He rarely got sick and didn't think much of it until later in the day when his head felt like it was stuffed with cotton. He could barely swallow and he felt feverish.

Swede came in the shop to ask him a question only to take in his glazed eyes and flushed skin with a shake of his head.

"Son, ya done got what the boss had, don't ya?" Swede asked, pulling off his glove and putting a calloused hand to Ty's forehead. "Whooee! Ya could fry an egg on yer head, dude."

"I'm fine," Ty tried to say around his thick tongue and sore throat.

"Sure ya are, and I'm a monkey's uncle. Let's git ya to bed, pard," Swede said, putting a hand on Ty's shoulder and giving him a gentle nudge off the stool where he was sitting.

"I don't think…" Ty said, fighting off the dizziness that was making the shop spin.

"Now, dude, don't ya go passin' out on me. Yer too big fer me to wrangle. Lean on me and I'll have ya in the bunkhouse in no-time."

Ty closed his eyes and shuffled his feet, following where Swede led. He felt sunlight on his face as they made it out the door, but the world picked up the pace in its spinning.

"Jimmy!" Swede bellowed in the direction of the barn.

Jimmy stuck his head out the door of the tack room and saw Swede trying to keep Ty upright. Sprinting to them, Jimmy got there just in time to keep Ty from falling to the ground.

Between the two of them, they dragged Ty across the ranch yard, up the bunkhouse steps and to his room. Unlacing his boots and pulling off his coveralls, they let him flop back on the bed.

"Jes leave him be for a while. I'll go tell the boss he's sick. She'll want to know," Swede said as Jimmy backed out of the room, not wanting to get whatever Ty had. "Thanks for coming to help. Thought he was gonna eat dirt for a minute."

"He almost did," Jimmy said with a grin as he returned to the tack room.

When Swede told Lexi Ty was sick, she insisted on having him moved to the house so she could take care of him. Swede told her it wouldn't be proper, so she marched to the bunkhouse and into his room. Ty was right where Swede had left him, fully clothed on his bed, heat radiating from his fevered skin.

"Get him undressed while I get a cool washcloth," Lexi ordered Swede, sweeping out of the room.

Dressed in his usual T-shirt and baggy jeans, Swede managed to strip Ty down to his underwear and pull a sheet over him before Lexi came back with a couple of washcloths and a bowl of tepid water.

Sitting on the edge of the bed, Lexi placed a cloth on Ty's head then began sponging down his arms and chest. Swede brought a glass of cold juice and helped Lexi coax Ty into drinking some before he drifted off to sleep.

The rest of the ranch hands were surprised to find Ty sick and Lexi taking care of him when they came in for dinner. Swede shooed Lexi out before bedtime, assuring her he could take care of Ty.

Before midnight Ty's fever broke, so Swede went back to his house to rest.

They were all supposed to leave the next morning to go to a two-day branding for one of the neighbors. Ty stumbled out to the table and slumped in his chair, trying to muster up the energy to take a drink from the mug of coffee Gus sat in front of him.

"Ya ain't gonna go nowhere today, son," Swede said as he came in the door. "Jes haul yer tough ol' hide right back to bed."

"I promised Mr. Anders I'd help," Ty rasped around his sore throat.

"I know thet, but ya couldn't wrestle a sleepy kitten today let alone a half-grown calf. I'm tellin' ya, yer stayin' home. Rest up and ya can go with us to the next one. Ya don't want to miss it," Swede said, pointing down the hall toward Ty's room.

"Fine," Ty said, not moving from the table. Right now it seemed like more effort than he could muster to get that far.

"Cal, Keith, git him up," Swede said, instructing the twins to help Ty. They flanked him, while Ty draped his arms over their shoulders.

"Thanks, guys," Ty said, embarrassed by his inability to move without assistance.

"No problem, dude. Maybe next time the boss is sick, you'll keep a little distance," Cal teased.

"Yeah. I wonder how come Swede didn't get sick?" Keith asked, trying to sound innocent.

"Maybe 'cause he and the boss aren't on as friendly terms as she is with this one," Cal commented as they dumped Ty on his bed.

"I don't see her wanting to cozy up to Swede the way she does ol' dude," Keith said, joining in the teasing.

If he could have thought of a snappy comeback or stirred up enough strength to punch either of them, he would have.

"Thet's enough, both of ya," Swede said, from the hallway. Cal and Keith left snickering, but not before Cal made several kissy-face motions Ty's direction.

"Thanks," Ty said, closing his eyes and going back to sleep. He'd have plenty of time to plot some payback for the twins.

Waking up hours later to a quiet house, Ty felt much better. Wandering to the kitchen, he made himself some toast and drank a cup of hot water, since he couldn't find any tea bags. A note on the table from Swede said they'd be back after dark and not to worry about anything.

Ty went back to bed and slept for a while, called Beth and caught up on her news before going in search of something to interrupt his boredom.

He tried watching one of the talk shows on TV but found it ridiculous, so he picked up a book to read and made it through the first chapter before he fell asleep on the couch. He was still sleeping there when the crew returned.

Lexi's scent, mingled with that of horses and cattle, drifted around him and he felt her cool hand on his head. He decided feigning sleep would be to his advantage and kept his eyes closed.

"His fever's gone," Lexi commented as she touched his cheeks and pulled the blanket from the back of the couch over him. "I feel bad he got sick taking care of me."

"Don't worry about it too much, boss," Swede said. "I don't think ya could've made him stay away from ya if ya wanted to. He does a right smart job of nursing, too. Where ya 'spose he learned how?"

"His mom," Lexi whispered, not wanting to share anything personal in front of the rest of the hands. If Ty wanted them to know, he'd tell them himself. "I think he took care of his mother when she was sick."

"I knew he was a good egg," Swede said, walking toward the kitchen and the slap-dash meal the hands were throwing together from leftovers.

"I'll run up to the house and make him some soup," Lexi said, turning toward the door. Looking at Swede she studied him a moment. "You feel okay?"

"Fit as a fiddle," Swede said with a knowing smile. "I think dude got a little more exposure to your germs than I did."

"Oh," Lexi said, blushing as she hurried out the door. That was the last time she'd kiss anyone when she was sick. Well, technically Ty did the kissing, but she let him. Taking herself to task, she knew they couldn't lose control like that again.

Ty was definitely missed at the branding and some of the single women were extremely disappointed to find out he wouldn't be coming. Their interest in him made Lexi unreasonably annoyed and a little jealous.

Maybe she should give a little more thought to what Aunt Bertie said about putting her brand on him.

Lesson Thirteen
The Desert Blooms as Paradise

*"Sometimes ya gotta throw on the brakes
and take a minute to enjoy creation."*

"Sure you feel up to going?" Lexi asked Ty for the third time that morning.

Instead of reassuring her again that he was fine after two days of bed rest and another day of recuperating, he rolled his eyes.

Everyone, with the exception of Gus, was planning to drive to her uncle's spread in Fields for branding. His ranch was a good two-hour drive south of Burns on Highway 205, also known as the High Desert Discovery Scenic Byway.

Swede, Jimmy, Keith and Cal were taking the big dually truck and pulling the six-horse trailer. Ty and Lexi would come with the overnight bags and gear in the ranch pickup.

Giving the other guys a head start, Lexi and Ty helped Gus finish the morning chores. Someone needed to stay behind and keep an eye on the ranch and Gus volunteered for the job. Ty was glad he felt well enough to go. He didn't mind taking responsibility of the ranch while everyone was gone for a few days, but if one of the animals needed assistance and the vet couldn't come, he had no idea what to do. Gus could handle whatever emergency arose, if any did.

Finally ready to leave, Ty gave Baby a loving pat on the head and told her to mind her manners with Gus. The dog barked and whined as he got in the pickup.

"You spoil her," Lexi commented, knowing she was every bit as guilty of babying Baby.

"Maybe," Ty said, giving Lexi a sideways glance and a warm smile. "She's not the only female I'd like to spoil."

"She's not? You planning on making a brat out of Delilah next?"

"Nope. I had a girl with two very long, lovely legs in mind, not four."

Lexi grinned at him. "When have you had time to find a girlfriend out here in the sticks?"

"I haven't had time to find one, she found me," Ty said, sliding his hand across the seat and capturing Lexi's in his. He pressed a hot kiss to her palm before she jerked her hand away.

"Ty," she said a little breathlessly. His touch made it hard for her to think and his kiss threatened to alter her ability to breathe normally. "We need to maintain a level of professionalism the next few days. If we don't, I can't guarantee I'll get you there and back again in one piece. If you keep kissing my hand like that, I'll run off the road before we ever get to Burns."

Ty laughed, patted her leg and retreated to his side of the pickup.

"I'll behave, for now," Ty said, flashing a smile filled with white teeth. "Unless you want to pull over and let me do more than kiss your hand?"

"I'm warning you, buckaroo, to back down," Lexi said sternly although the sparkle in her eyes gave away her pleasure at his teasing.

"It's gonna be a long drive if I can't touch you at all, so you better think up some good stories to keep me entertained."

Lexi smiled and started talking about past brandings, her uncle's ranch, and things she remembered about her dad. Ty asked more questions about her father's cancer and what he was like before he got sick.

"That must have been hard to come back to, Lexi," Ty said, sympathizing with her giving up her life in Portland and coming back to the ranch only to find a tangled mess in the fallout of her father's disease.

"Well, I've got the accounts straightened out and most everything back to rights except for the money," Lexi said.

"Have you found any more clues?"

"No. I still haven't figured out the last one. 'Best Bucket.' What does that mean?"

"We'll figure it out," Ty said, taking her hand in his.

"I appreciate your help. It was hard not to have anyone to talk to about it. It's not every day someone hides half a million dollars on the ranch."

"What?" Ty said, his face registering his surprise. He assumed when Lexi said her dad hid some money it was a few thousand dollars. It wasn't his place to ask her specifics. All he knew was that money was missing and she needed to find it.

"My dad withdrew $500,000 from invested funds I didn't even know he had and that's what I'm searching for."

"You mean he didn't let you handle his money? But that's what you did for a living," Ty said, trying to process this information.

"I did invest money for him. I thought it was all the money he invested, but I found several other accounts he opened and he withdrew odd amounts from each of them not too long before he got really sick. The withdrawals totaled $500,000."

"That's interesting," Ty was trying to imagine how Lexi would ever find the money. There were thousands of acres with a dozen buildings. It could be anywhere: hidden in a wall, buried under a tree, beneath a clump of sagebrush. "Have you told anyone else about it?"

"No. Not even Swede," Lexi said, hoping Ty understood that he was the only person she felt comfortable confiding in.

"Lexi, I... thank you for sharing this with me," Ty said, humbled by her trust. It meant the world to know she put enough faith in him to keep a $500,000 secret, especially considering just a few months ago he was unemployed, homeless, and desperate.

"I know I can trust you," Lexi said, squeezing his hand. "Besides, if I find you rifling through the house looking for treasure, I'll fill that fine caboose of yours full of buckshot."

"You think I've got a fine caboose?" Ty asked with a grin, gently squeezing her fingers. When she blushed, he let her off the hook. "I've got no doubt that you would. We just need to figure out the next clue."

"I know but I've got absolutely no idea..."

"Stop, Lexi! Stop the truck!" Ty yelled and Lexi slammed on the brakes.

Out his window he looked across the open expanse to see a herd of magnificent wild horses grazing.

"Those are the Kigers," Lexi said, unbuckling her seat belt and leaning across the seat so she could see out his window.

"Kigers?"

"Kiger Mustangs. They run wild here. The BLM manages the herd and does occasional adoptions, but they've been here forever. Aren't they beautiful?"

"They're awesome," Ty said, rolling down his window and snapping some photos with his phone. He had to send some to Beth. Looking around, he realized the landscape around them was amazing, like something he'd see on the Discovery Channel. "They have some unique coloring."

"The majority of them are duns. A lot of them have the striping you see on that one right there," Lexi said, leaning across Ty and pointing out the window. Ty put his arm around her and pulled her closer so they both could look out the window. "The herd supposedly goes back to the Spanish horses brought to the Americas in the seventeenth century."

Ty had never seen anything quite like the Kiger Mustangs, so free and wild. A deep appreciation settled over him for the wonders he had the opportunity to see because of this job.

Lexi knew Ty would see some things on the drive to her uncle's ranch he probably hadn't seen before. That was one reason she wanted him to ride with her. That way they could take their time and stop if he wanted to. Swede and the other boys would have laughed if they asked to pull over to watch the horses and look at wildflowers, which was next on her list to show Ty.

They watched the horses for a few more minutes before Lexi slid back across the truck seat and buckled her seat belt.

"I've got a few more things I want to show you before we get to Uncle Rob's."

"Like what?" Ty asked, continuing to watch the horses as they drove on.

"You'll have to wait and see," Lexi teased, giving Ty a flirty smile that made him grin right back at her.

During the rest of the drive, she showed him the Steens Mountain, took a side trip to see Peter French's Round Barn, and fields filled with wildflowers that looked like a master artist had dropped bright blooms of color against a brilliant blue background of sky. They were nearing the turn-off to her uncle's ranch when Ty spied a herd of big horn sheep.

"I can't believe what I'm seeing," Ty said, as Lexi stopped so he could get a better look at the animals he had previously only seen in the Portland Zoo. There were adult males and females as well as the spring batch of babies. "This is so cool."

"I'm glad you're enjoying the drive," Lexi said, smiling. "And here you thought you were going to be bored to death."

Ty looked at her with heat in his eyes. "I could never be bored with you, Lexi Jo."

As heat fluttered into a burning flame in her middle, Lexi tried to return her attention to the road. Every time Ty called her Lexi Jo it made her absolutely melt. She loved hearing him say her name.

"I'm glad," she said, giving one last glance at the sheep before heading on down the road. "I kind of like having you around."

Lexi's Uncle Rob was nothing like her Aunt Bertie. Where Bertie was boisterous and fun, Rob was serious and all-business.

Arriving at the ranch, Ty joined the rest of the hands bunking down in spare beds in the bunkhouse while Lexi stayed at the ranch house with her family.

Riding Delilah beside Lexi the next morning as they rounded up cattle, Ty asked about her mother's family.

"There were five kids. My mama was second oldest," Lexi said, keeping an eye on the terrain as they followed the group out to bring in the herd. Her uncle had about 600 head of cattle and the plan was to work them all tomorrow.

"How many boys and girls?" Ty asked, interested in Lexi's family tree. Having no aunts or uncles, he was fascinated by her seemingly large family.

"Slade was the oldest. He died when he was in high school. He got bucked off a horse he thought he could break and died of head trauma two days later. Next came my Mama, Rose, then Uncle Rob, Uncle Dean and Aunt Bertie. Her name is really Roberta, but everyone calls her Bertie."

"I'm sorry about your uncle," Ty said, thinking how hard it would be for parents to lose a child.

"Mama always spoke of him fondly. He was just a year older than her and I think they were close. Uncle Dean and his family live in Arizona, so we don't see them very often," Lexi said, smiling to see some desert phlox blooming. Stopping her horse, she got off to look at it.

"What's that?" Ty asked, dismounting and standing beside her.

"Phlox. Isn't it pretty?" Lexi said, admiring the pale pink blooms.

"Sure, if weeds can be pretty," Ty said, not sure why they were standing looking at the scraggly blossoms.

"It isn't a weed," Lexi huffed, remounting Rowdy. "It's a desert wildflower. I used to pick them for my mama, but they wilt faster than you can blink. I tried digging some up one time, but they won't grow in a flower bed at all. They are meant to bloom wild and free."

"Rather like another sassy little blossom I know," Ty said, giving Lexi a warm look. "She seems to bloom when she can be wild and free. Shaking things up."

Lexi blushed and slapped at Ty with her hat, making him laugh.

"The two of ya gonna quit messin' around and help us round up these doggies?" Swede asked with a fatherly scowl as he rode up next to them.

"Yes, sir," Ty said, urging Delilah forward. When he flashed his white-toothed grin at Lexi, she felt her heart pick up tempo. How was she going to keep that good looking man at a distance?

Lexi didn't need to worry since the crew rounding up the cattle split into groups and went to work. She found herself riding with some of her cousins and a couple of Uncle Rob's neighbors. A few of the single females asked her about Ty, which made her feel uptight and irritated.

She and Ty didn't have an understanding, hadn't even said anything other than acknowledging there was something going on between them. She hoped his plans to take things slow and easy didn't mean he'd move at a snail's pace. With all the interested females looking his direction, she was starting to wish she'd taken Bertie's advice and burned her brand on him.

Ty stuck close to Swede, knowing the foreman would give him direction as needed. Other than riding on the Rockin' R, Ty had never ridden anywhere else and hoped he'd do fine on Delilah.

"I ought to warn ya right now, dude, if ya hear somethin' rattling, back off real slow like and git as far from it as you can. Rob's got more than his share of rattlers in the brush, so be careful. As warm as it's been, he said he's already killed a few," Swede said, looking Ty's direction.

"Rattlers?" Ty asked, trying to understand what Swede was saying.

"Rattlesnakes," Swede said. "Ever seen one?"

"Nope. Just on TV," Ty said, sending up a silent plea that he wouldn't see any today either.

"Well, shoot, dude. Jes be real careful today. If ya hear somethin' that sounds like a rattle, stay away from it. They like to be warm and sun themselves on rocks and such, so never stick yer hand somewhere ya can't see what is on the surface. Try to stay on yer horse and if Delilah shies away from somethin', don't fight her," Swede instructed, hoping he covered all the basics.

Ty was not encouraged by this information and decided he was not getting off the horse unless absolutely necessary.

That necessity came sooner than Ty expected when he found himself trying to herd a cow and her calf out of the brush. The cow went on ahead, but the calf seemed to have its hoof caught between the branches of a scraggly sagebrush.

Ty reluctantly climbed off the horse and walked up to the calf. He couldn't believe how pretty the high desert, as everyone referred to this part of Oregon, could be. There were several different types of flowers blooming in profusion and with the spring rains, everything looked fresh and green. In the calf's attempts to get free, it had broken off some pieces of sagebrush and the pungent scent filled the air.

It was a stark contrast to the manicured lawns and rows of rhododendrons Ty was used to seeing in Portland.

If not for his fear of coming across a rattlesnake, he would have enjoyed walking around to look at the landscape. He never had much time or desire to learn about plants and flowers, but since moving to the Rockin' R, he had a growing interest in the nature surrounding him. It all looked so wild and rugged and unrestrained.

Although a city boy born and raised, Ty was quickly coming to think of this untamed country as his own paradise.

Reaching the calf, Ty talked softly to it like Swede had taught him, running a gentle hand across its back while it struggled to get free. Moving slowly, he grasped its leg and tugged it loose from the brush at the same time he heard a buzzing noise.

The calf lunged forward, startling a snake that had been sunning itself nearby. The snake struck before Ty had a chance to react. Fangs sank into the leather chaps covering his shin and he yelled in surprise.

Ty wondered how long it would take to die of a snake bite. He knew people rarely did these days because immediate medical care gave you good odds of living. Only they were hours away from the nearest hospital and he seriously doubted anyone had any antivenom in their saddlebags.

Seeing the snake struggle to free itself from where it's fangs where caught in his chaps, Ty watched the writhing body twist and turn. Unfastening the buckles holding on his chaps, he quickly removed them, making sure the snake was still caught, then stomped it to death.

Looking down, Ty could see a fang hole in his jeans, but realized it didn't make it through the leather of his boots.

He was suddenly grateful for the clothes Swede and Lexi insisted he have for riding. If he hadn't been wearing his chaps, he would have been full of snake venom instead of relief.

Between his initial yell of surprise and killing the snake, Delilah spooked and ran off toward the herd.

Swede caught her and looked around, noticing Ty standing at the edge of the brush by the pasture.

"Dude, ya get bucked off?" Swede asked as he rode over leading Delilah.

"No sir," Ty said, still trying to gather his composure. Adrenalin was pumping through him and his knees felt a little wobbly.

"Where's yer chaps? You don't want to git caught without 'em on out here," Swede said, thinking Ty needed a few more lessons about why they wore the clothes they did.

"Over there," Ty said, pointing to where his chaps covered the snake.

"Well, why in tarnation did ya take 'em off?"

"To kill the snake."

"Snake? What snake?" Swede asked, getting off Kitten and handing Ty the reins to both horses.

Carefully lifting up the chaps, Swede whistled when he saw the dead body of the snake, fangs still embedded in Ty's chaps.

"Whooee! Yer one lucky son of a gun, my friend!" Swede said, taking a good look at the snake and carrying it in the chaps back to Ty. "I'll get out my knife and cut the buttons off for ya."

"No thanks," Ty said, not wanting any sort of reminder of the experience. His legs were just now starting to feel like a substance other than rubber.

"Mind if I keep it?" Swede asked, finding a stout piece of brush and prying the snake's fangs out of the chaps before handing them back to Ty.

"Knock yourself out," Ty said, buckling his chaps back on and thinking if he never encountered another rattler, it would be too soon.

Jimmy noticed Swede and Ty on the ground and rode over to see what was going on. Swede showed him the snake and the two of them admired its size.

"Well, son, ya win the award for good luck today," Swede said with a cackle, slapping Ty on the back as he took Kitten's reins. "At least ya know what a rattler sounds and looks like now."

"That I do," Ty said, still unsettled by the encounter with the snake. "Here I was thinking this desert of yours looked a little like paradise."

"Even the Garden of Eden had a serpent," Swede said with a wink as Ty mounted Delilah and they returned to gathering the herd.

That afternoon when they were finished rounding up the cattle, Lexi heard about Ty's encounter with the snake. She'd been helping her aunt and cousins get food ready for a big barbecue dinner, but dropped the head of lettuce she'd been rinsing and ran outside when her cousin repeated the story. Hurrying to where the men were lounging around in the backyard, Ty jumped to his feet as he took in her white face and the look of fear in her eyes, meeting her half-way across the yard.

"Are you okay? I just heard," she said, standing so close, Ty could see the golden flecks floating in the green depths of her eyes.

"I'm fine, Lexi," Ty said quietly. "No biggie."

"Yes it is," Lexi said, taking a step closer, needing the reassurance that Ty was, in fact, no worse for wear.

"It was just a snake," Ty said, pulling Lexi into his arms, not caring who was watching. They both needed the comfort only the other one could offer.

"Just a snake full of poison that had its fangs caught in your chaps," Lexi said, shuddering. She'd killed plenty of snakes before, but never had one that up close and personal. What if the snake had bitten Ty? What if he'd died before they could get medical treatment? What would she do without him? "Please be careful, Ty. I can't lose you, too."

"You won't lose me, Lexi Jo. I've got too much to stick around for," Ty said, rubbing his hand along her back. "I can't wait to tell Beth and Nate about this. She was convinced I'd get eaten by a bear, not bitten by a snake."

"A bear?" Lexi said, relaxing in Ty's arms, ignoring the stares being sent their direction from both her hands and her uncle's family. "Not likely."

"I think I better let you go now because your uncle is heading this direction with a protective father look on his face," Ty whispered, dropping his hands. "Maybe we can take this up again later?"

"I'll count on it," Lexi said with a wink at Ty as he stepped back and walked off in the direction of the other Rockin' R hands who were admiring the rattler's buttons Swede was passing around.

"Lex, what are you doing?" Rob asked as he stood glaring at her.

"Getting ready to wash up for dinner," Lexi said with a smile at her uncle, knowing that was not what he meant.

"That's not what I was talking about. What's up between you and him," Rob said, tipping his head Ty's direction. "You know better than to chase after the hired help."

"I'm not chasing anyone," Lexi said, dropping her voice and straightening her spine. "He's not just a hired hand, he's a good friend."

"Yeah, I saw how friendly, all right," Rob said with a sneer. "You better watch yourself, girl. Your daddy left you sitting pretty and any money-grubber with half a lick of sense will be after it any way he can get it."

"Ty's not like that," Lexi said, growing angry at her uncle. "He's a good, honest man who works hard, cares about others, and never talks bad about anyone. If you don't believe me, ask Swede. He thinks the world of him."

"I'll talk to Swede later," Rob said, seeming to calm down a little. "Just what are his intentions toward you? He is your hired hand, isn't he?"

"Yes, he's my mechanic."

"Mechanic? I thought he was another wrangler."

"We're teaching him how to cowboy, but I hired him to be our mechanic. He's a professional and our equipment has never run so well," Lexi said, staring down her uncle. None of this was really his business, anyway, but since her father passed away, both Uncle Linc and Uncle Rob thought it was their responsibility to watch over her.

"Did he have prior ranching experience?" Rob asked, more than curious about his niece's newest hired hand.

Lexi laughed. "No. He'd never been out of Portland, never ridden a horse, never seen a cow up close, and never even owned a pair of Wranglers."

Rob whistled.

"He must be a quick learner, cause he rides like it's something he's always done," Rob said with admiration.

"Ty is a quick learner and he's been willing to do whatever we ask of him without complaint. He's cool-headed and not easily riled, which is more than I can say for a lot of guys," Lexi said, looking pointedly at her uncle, who was known to have a hot temper.

"Swede said he was cool as a cucumber when he killed that snake, so I'll give him credit for that. But honestly, Lex, where do you think a relationship with your mechanic can go?"

"I don't know," Lexi said, not wanting to discuss the affairs of her heart with her hot-headed uncle. "It's not like we're dating or anything. We're friends."

Rob snorted and shook his head.

"Girl, men don't look at women like he was looking at you unless they are a lot more than friends. I'd bet my best horse that boy is in love with you and judging from the look on your face, the feeling is mutual."

"Uncle Rob, you don't…"

"Don't understand?" Rob asked, cutting her off. He looped an arm around her shoulders and turned her toward the back yard where his wife and daughters were setting out the big barbecue dinner. "I understand all too well, Lex. You forget I have three daughters of my own and two of them are already married. I intend to have a talk with your young man before you leave."

"That won't be necessary," Lex said, inwardly cringing at the thought of her uncle raking Ty over the coals.

"Oh, but it will be," Rob said with a grin. "And I might even enjoy it a little."

As the Rockin' R crew was packing up to leave after the branding was finished, Rob took Ty aside and talked with him for a few minutes while Lexi nervously watched.

Ty kept any emotion from showing on his face and gave Rob a firm handshake as they parted.

Walking up to Lexi, Ty held the driver's door for her as she climbed in before going to the passenger side.

"Well?" Lexi asked, as she started the pickup and fastened her seat belt.

"That's a deep subject," Ty teased, removing his hat and settling in for the long drive ahead.

"Aren't you going to tell me what Uncle Rob said to you?"

"Maybe. Sometime," Ty said, giving her a teasing grin.

Lexi huffed and muttered something about men under her breath, waving at Rob as they pulled out of the driveway. He gave her a broad wink as she drove by and she wondered exactly what that meant.

"Are you really not going to tell me?"

"He told me he was impressed with my cool head and quick thinking in regard to thinning the rattlesnake population."

"And?" Lexi asked, impatient for Ty to get down to what she really wanted to know – if Rob mentioned her.

"He said if you ever lose your mind and fire me, I can work for him anytime," Ty said, staring out the window.

"That's quite a complement from Uncle Rob," Lexi said, not surprised her uncle would try to steal Ty out from under her. He recognized a good hand when he saw one. "What else did he say?"

"He asked me what my intentions are toward his favorite niece. Do you know who that might be? I'd like to meet this girl before I decide what my intentions are."

"Could you please stop kidding around?" Lexi said, annoyed by Ty's inability to just tell her everything she wanted to know as quickly as possible.

"I could, but it would suck up so much of my fun," Ty said, taking Lexi's hand in his and giving it a squeeze.

She jerked it away and slapped at his arm.

"Just tell me what he said!" Lexi said, glaring at him so intently, she started to weave across the road.

"Road, Lexi, focus on the road," Ty said with humor filling his voice. No doubt, Swede would think they were doing something they shouldn't as he followed behind them in the dually truck.

She pulled the pickup back on to the right side of the road, but gave Ty a scowl.

"What is it you think I'm not telling you?" Ty asked, knowing exactly what she wanted to hear.

"What did you really tell him about your intentions?"

"That I have some," Ty said evasively.

Lexi glared at him again.

"Lexi Jo, let's talk about this later," Ty said, giving Lexi a look that let her know he wasn't willing to talk about the conversation he had with her uncle. "For now, let's enjoy this beautiful desert of yours."

Lexi nodded, wondering what Rob said and irritated Ty wouldn't discuss it with her. She hoped her well-meaning uncle hadn't scared off the best thing that had ever happened to her.

If he had, she was going to have a hard time forgiving him.

Lesson Fourteen
Say What You Mean and Mean What You Say

*"No good comes from beating around the bush.
Ya got somethin' to say, just spit it out."*

Sunday afternoon found Ty hanging around the shop, cleaning up a few projects. Baby was sleeping on her blanket in the corner and the rest of the hands had left for the day.

Ty saw Lexi come back from church right after lunch and thought about going to the house to see her, but fought back the urge.

Since they returned from her uncle's house nearly a week ago, they'd barely spoken or seen each other. He tried to convince himself it was just the fact that they had been incredibly busy with work on the ranch. The only time he'd spent in the shop had been making repairs to the baler. The rest of the time, he was either on a piece of equipment in the fields or on Delilah riding fence. Ty didn't want to admit it was because he was trying to decipher his feelings for the intriguing woman and figure out what he wanted out of a relationship.

Rob had grilled Ty heavily about his plans regarding Lexi. Ty told him he honestly didn't know. He loved her, of that he was certain, but he wasn't sure how she felt and he absolutely had no business chasing after his boss. He couldn't tell Rob all that, of course, and instead told him he was interested in Lexi and promised not to do anything to hurt her.

Taking pity on him, Rob told him he approved of whatever intentions he had, shook his hand and told him not to wait too long to give in to the inevitable, whatever that meant.

Deciding to go for a walk, Ty stepped out into the warm sunlit afternoon and headed past the barn. Following a path he used to run when he first arrived at the Rockin' R, he noticed Lexi on a blanket beneath a big cottonwood tree.

He stood for a while with his hands in his pockets, watching her, before climbing over the fence and quietly walking to where she rested on a quilt beneath the shade of the tree.

Lying on her stomach, she wore cut off shorts and a soft T-shirt with her hair loose and flowing down her back in a wild tumble.

Ty thought she was the most beautiful girl he'd ever seen. Her cheeks were flushed from the warmth of the afternoon and her lips were slightly parted as she breathed evenly, taking a much-deserved nap.

Not wanting to disturb her but unable to stay away, he sank down on the blanket and waited for her to awaken. He watched the clouds drift across the blue sky and breathed deep of the fresh spring air.

Unable to stop himself from touching Lexi any longer, he bent down and trailed kisses from her ankles up her exposed tan legs to her knees. Ty pressed a heated kiss to the back of each knee, continuing on toward the hem of her cutoffs. Before he reached it, Lexi opened her eyes and looked over her shoulder at him with a smile that made his insides churn with heat and his heart pound.

"Hey," he said, trying not to let the desire he was feeling for this lovely woman override all rational thought.

"Hi," she said rolling over. She looked soft and warm and so enticing, Ty was sure he'd never seen, let alone dreamed, of a woman looking as alluring as she did at that moment. "I thought I was having quite a dream but it was you all along."

"Yeah," he said, scooting down beside her on his side. Picking up a silky strand of her hair, he rubbed it between his fingers as he raised himself up on one elbow. "I went for a walk and saw you out here. I couldn't stay away."

"I'm glad," Lexi said, pulling his head down to hers. Their kiss was hot and urgent, filled with the longings they'd banked as they went through the daily tasks of ranch work.

Ty rolled onto his back, pulling her on top of him. "I missed you. Missed this," he rumbled, kissing her with such a growing intensity, Lexi thought she might completely melt right there in the pasture. She had been dreaming of Ty, the feel of his arms around her, his lips possessing hers, when she sensed his presence and smelled his unique scent. She thought it was all part of a wonderful dream until she woke up to feel his lips teasing the backs of her legs. It was the most exciting, tantalizing sensation she'd ever experienced.

"I missed you, too," she whispered against his lips. "So much."

Burying his hands in her hair, Ty continued kissing her, tasting her, teasing her, until they both were breathless.

"Ty," Lexi said, leaning back so she could look in his face, fall into those bright blue pools of his eyes. "What are we doing?"

"I thought that was obvious," Ty said, giving her another searing kiss. He felt Lexi smile against his lips.

"Not right this second," she said, sounding slightly exasperated. "I meant us, what are the two of us doing? Where is this going?"

Ty gently moved her off him and sat up. She sat beside him as he sighed and ran his hands through his hair. It needed another trim and Lexi fought the urge to bury her hands in the rich brown waves.

"Your Uncle Rob asked me the same thing," Ty said, holding Lexi's hand in his and rubbing gently with his thumb on her palm.

"And what did you tell him?" Lexi asked. Ty had been distant since they came home from Rob's and she wasn't sure if it was the workload, or if he was avoiding her.

"I told him I couldn't speak for you, what you are feeling, or what your plans are," Ty said, giving Lexi a quick glance. Only it wasn't quick because one look in her eyes pulled him into the green depths. "He didn't take that for an answer any more than you will."

Lexi nodded.

"I'm not good at talking about feelings, Lexi, but I'm also not very good at talking around a subject. I told your uncle I care for you a great deal, that my intentions are honorable."

"Oh," Lexi said, not sure what to think as she looked away. She already knew he cared for her a great deal. He cared for Baby a great deal, too. Did she mean any more to him than the dog?

Ty gently grasped her chin in his hand and turned her to face him.

"That isn't all I told him, Lexi Jo. He was quite persistent in getting the answer he wanted."

"What answer was that?"

"If I plan on sticking around."

"What did you tell him?" Lexi asked, afraid of the answer.

"That I'm staying here as long as you'll let me" Ty said, sliding his arms around Lexi, picking her up and settling her across his lap. She looped her hands around his neck and looked at him intently.

Ty wanted to tell Lexi what he was really feeling, that he was in love with her, but he just wasn't quite ready to voice that exciting and somewhat frightening news.

"Then you can stay forever," Lexi said, kissing him on his chin, his jaw, and his neck.

"Lexi, I honestly have good intentions. I want to be the best mechanic you'll ever know, to be a valuable employee, and to be a friend you can count on and trust," Ty said, watching Lexi nod her head. "All my good intentions fly right out the window when I look at you. You are so beautiful, I have a hard time remembering my name, let alone anything else when we're together. Just like now. You feel so good in my arms, you taste like the most wonderful nectar ever created, and your scent fills my senses."

"Ty," Lexi whispered, enchanted by his honest words. No one had ever said anything that sounded so romantic and wonderful to her before and she was completely wrapped up in the strong, dangerously handsome man holding her close in his arms. She didn't want to think about anything except how right it felt to be this close to him.

"I'd really like to take you on a date, Lexi. I think that would be a good first step in seeing where this would go. Doing something normal couples would do. So, will you go out with me Friday night?" Ty asked before common sense got the better of him and he kept his mouth shut.

"You mean a real leave-the-ranch kind of date?" Lexi asked, suddenly wanting more than anything to go on a date with Ty.

"Yeah," Ty said, pulling Lexi just a little closer, hoping he wouldn't have to work hard to convince her. If she turned him down, he didn't know what he'd do.

"I'd love to go on a date with you," Lexi said, giving him a tight hug and kiss on his cheek. "What time should I be ready?"

"Well, if my slave-driving boss will let me off a little early Friday, we could leave at five," Ty said, giving Lexi an ornery grin.

"I think she might be persuaded to let you off early, but don't tell anyone," Lexi said, lowering her lashes as her lips melded against Ty's. "She wouldn't want the rest of the crew to think she was playing favorites."

"How much persuading does she need?" Ty whispered against her mouth.

"A lot more than that, buckaroo," Lexi said, pushing at Ty until he fell back on the quilt. Moving so she was flush against him, she kissed his jaw, working her way up to his lips.

"Like this?" Ty asked, flipping over so he was on top of Lexi as he pressed fiery kisses to her neck, nibbled on her ear and ended with a barely restrained kiss that completely blew Lexi's mind. She had never, in her twenty-nine years, been kissed quite so deeply, passionately or thoroughly.

"Just like that," she rasped when she could once again speak. "You can definitely leave early Friday, if you promise another kiss like that is involved."

"If that's the boss' orders, then I have no choice but to oblige her do I?"

"Nope," Lexi said with a wink. "I think we better head back in, though."

Burying his face in her hair, she heard Ty groan, could feel his struggle to do what was right. Finally, he lightly kissed her lips, got to his feet and pulled her up with him.

"I think we've let things go far enough for the afternoon," Ty said with a wicked grin. He bent down and picked up the quilt and Lexi helped him fold it. He carried it in one hand while he held her hand in the other.

They strolled across the pasture, enjoying the beautiful day and each other. Half way to the fence, they felt the ground tremble and heard pounding and huffing. Turning, they both looked with wide eyes to see one of the bulls racing full tilt toward them.

Lexi tightened her grip on Ty's hand as they started to run toward the fence.

"What did you do?" Lexi asked as they ran.

"Me? I didn't do anything except come out to see you," Ty said, starting to wonder if they'd make it to the fence before the bull reached them. The crazed bovine was moving a lot faster than Ty would have thought possible.

"How did the bull get in here?" Lexi asked, running as fast as she could, keeping stride with Ty's long legs.

"Didn't Swede say something yesterday about moving the bulls around?" Ty asked, recalling a conversation from breakfast the previous day.

"I completely forgot," Lexi said, realizing her thoughts were so muddled with Ty, she was forgetting important details. Like dangerous bulls. "I'm sorry."

"No biggie," Ty said, pouring on a burst of speed as they neared the fence. Before Lexi could climb over, Ty swept her up and over the pole fence along with the quilt. Placing his hand on the top pole, he vaulted over a second before the bull slammed on the brakes and slid into the fence, making it rock.

Keeping their momentum, they continued running for several yards before Ty bent over with his hands on his knees and drew in huge gulps of air. Lexi dropped the quilt and sat on it, trying to catch her breath.

"Whew, that was close," she finally said, grinning up at Ty.

"You think?" he said, a teasing glint in his bright blue eyes. "That was a little too close, babe."

"Where's your sense of adventure?" Lexi teased from her seat on the quilt, squinting up at Ty.

"Right here," Ty said, pulling her up into his arms and kissing her with a ruthless intensity that she easily matched. Both of them could feel their hearts pounding as adrenaline and longing coursed through them.

Hanging on to his last little speck of sense, Ty finally set Lexi back, picked up the quilt and tugged her toward the house.

"I think after all that, you need to feed me dinner," Ty informed Lexi.

"Is that so?" Lexi asked with a smile.

"That is so," Ty said, giving her a swat on the bottom. "Let's call it hazard pay."

Lexi laughed. "We'll both cook. You grill the steaks and I'll do the rest."

"Deal," Ty said, kissing her cheek as they walked to the house. He was grateful for that section of fence Cal and Keith recently finished rebuilding. At the time, he wondered why it needed to be so tall or stout. Now he knew.

Ty was helping Lexi finish cleaning up their dinner dishes when a knock came at the back door followed by a "hallo in the house," from Swede.

"Come on in, Swede," Lexi called, putting away the last clean dish while Ty hung the dish towel on a rack to dry.

Ty and Lexi both turned to watch Swede come in, escorting a tall, attractive woman with white hair, sparkling brown eyes and a warm smile.

"Howdy," Swede said, grinning from ear to ear.

"Hey, Swede. Did you enjoy your day off?" Lexi asked as Swede dragged the woman further into the kitchen.

"I sure did. Made a trip to Boise today," Swede said, sweeping off his hat. "This here is my sister, Janice. Everyone calls her Jan. Sis this is Lex Ryan, the boss, and thet feller with the dishpan hands is Ty, the best mechanic I've ever met."

"Hello, Jan," Lexi said, extending her hand to the friendly-looking woman. While Ty was shaking her hand, Lexi took a moment to study the older woman. She could see a faint family resemblance between Jan and Swede. "Welcome to the Rockin' R Ranch. Are you going to be visiting Swede for a while?"

"Well, I'm not…"

"Actually, Jan ain't here to visit me," Swede said, nervously twisting the brim of his hat in his hand.

Ty watched the ranch foreman with interest. This was one of the few times he'd seen the man nervous.

"Oh, well…" Lexi started to say, but Swede interrupted.

"I fetched her to be yer housekeeper. She can do the job with her eyes closed and ya got to have some help before we hit high tide with summer comin'. The boys ain't got time to mess with cookin' and cleanin' and ya said yerself ya didn't have time to keep chasin' down help thet won't stay. Jan'll stay with me in my house and it'll be dandy."

Lexi wasn't sure what to think or say. It wasn't like Swede to just spring things - employees - on her, but she was tired of searching for a housekeeper and they did need the help.

"So, Jan, you have experience housekeeping and cooking?" Lexi asked, wanting to at least know a little background.

"I wed at 18 and had five babies by the time I was 25, so I know a bit about keeping a house orderly. I had to with my brood. My husband and I opened a restaurant and ran it successfully for twenty-seven years. His illness forced the sale of the business and when he passed away last year, it left me with too much time on my hands," Jan said, looking fondly at Swede. "So when this rascal said you needed my services, I decided to jump into a new adventure. I've never lived on a ranch before but Swede tells me I'll adjust just fine."

"You aren't the only one getting used to living on a ranch," Lexi said, pointing at Ty. "This one had never even seen a cow up close until he moved here in February."

"It appears I'm in good company, then," Jan said with a warm smile Ty's direction. "Growing up in Seattle, Francis knew from the time he was old enough to talk that he wanted to be a cowboy. While other little boys got paper routes and played baseball, this one practiced learning to walk, talk and live like a cowboy. He left home the day after he graduated from high school and has been living his dream since."

"Francis?" Ty mouthed, shooting Swede a devilish look.

Swede glared at him and shook his head.

"So there's hope for me yet," Ty commented with a broad grin, tucking away Swede's real name for later tormenting purposes.

"You already knew that," Lexi said, giving Ty's arm a squeeze. She turned her attention back to Jan. "Is there anything I can do to help you settle in?"

"No, Swede helped me move my few things into his spare room already. I was staying with my daughter in Boise and didn't have a lot to bring along. I would be happy to start in the morning if that sounds satisfactory."

"If you feel up to it, that would be great," Lexi said, relaying the times she'd like to see breakfast and dinner served. "After breakfast, we can go over the job details, if that sounds good to you."

"That would be fine," Jan said, as she looked around the beautiful ranch house kitchen. "So I'll be serving meals here?"

"Oh, no," Lexi said with a laugh, imagining the discomfort that would bring the hands. They all acted like they were treading on sacred ground anytime they needed to come in the house. Swede and Ty were the only two that acted normal when they were there. "Meals will be served in the bunkhouse. It has a full kitchen and we can work on a grocery list tomorrow."

"Very well," Jan said, glancing at Ty. "Do all the hands join you for Sunday dinner here?"

"No. The hands have Sundays off, so that would include you as well," Lexi said, taking Ty's hand in hers and giving it a squeeze. "This guy thinks he gets special privileges."

"I see," Jan said, although she didn't at all. Although the tall mechanic, as Swede referred to him, looked like any other wickedly handsome cowboy, she wondered what the relationship was between him and the boss.

"Well, let's head back to the house, sis," Swede said, escorting his sister to the door and slapping his hat back on his head. "Thanks, boss, for givin' this a try."

"Sure, Swede. You haven't steered me wrong yet," Lexi said then looked pointedly at Ty, giving him a wink.

"I'll walk with you," Ty said, knowing he needed to say goodnight before he and Lexi got involved in more kissing that would lead to places they really shouldn't go.

"Night," Lexi said, waving at Swede and Jan before kissing Ty's cheek.

"Night, babe. Thanks for dinner and a great afternoon," Ty whispered, following Swede and Jan out the door.

"Well, Ty, you are the mechanic and also are learning to be a cowboy?" Jan asked as they walked across the yard, enjoying the pleasant evening weather.

"That's right, ma'am," Ty said.

"And you've only been at this since February?"

"Yes, ma'am."

"Well, you seem to be a very fast learner," Jan said with a smile.

Ty nodded his head in thanks and bid both Swede and Jan a pleasant evening as he went on to the bunkhouse. Doing his laundry, he called Beth and caught her up on what had happened in the last few days, including getting chased by the bull.

"What were you two doing in the pasture, anyway? I would think you would have noticed him before he got that close," Beth said.

"We were... um... a little... um," Ty stammered.

"You were what? Tyler Jaxton Lewis, what have you done?" Beth asked, using the tone that always let him know he was in trouble.

"I haven't done anything, exactly," Ty said, running his hand through his hair and releasing a sigh. "We were just kissing."

"Kissing!" Beth laughed. "And why would you be kissing your boss?"

"Because I can't seem to help myself," Ty answered honestly. "I've got it bad, Beth."

"How bad?"

"Really bad," Ty answered. "I've never felt this way before about anyone. She's all I can think about, and yes, I know it is crazy and about the dumbest thing I've done."

"I don't think it is crazy or dumb," Beth said. Ty could hear the smile in her voice. "Does she kiss you back?"

"Of course," Ty snorted, somewhat offended Beth would even ask.

"Hmm…" Beth said, thinking about Ty and Lexi. "That's interesting."

"You might as well just spit it out," Ty said, folding the clothes he'd dumped on his bed. "You know I'm not good at deciphering your hidden messages."

"I think it's about time you fell in love, really fell in love, and Nate and I both think Lexi is wonderful. If she isn't opposed to being close enough to kiss you, I think you should see where this goes," Beth said, smugly satisfied Ty finally admitted what she already knew. She could tell he was infatuated with Lexi when they'd visited right after Jax was born.

"What if it goes to the unemployment line?" Ty asked, knowing that was a very real possibility. "What if we end up breaking things off and she tells me to find a new job?"

"Worry about that when it happens. Don't borrow trouble or obsess over the what-ifs. The opportunity to find real love is worth risking everything for, isn't it?" Beth asked.

"Yeah, I think it is," Ty said, deciding he was truly crazy. He had absolutely nothing to offer Lexi except himself and right now that didn't seem like much. "I asked her on a date so we are officially going out Friday."

"Make sure you take her somewhere nice for dinner and buy her flowers and wear something besides one of your hooded sweatshirts," Beth said with maternal authority.

"Yes, mother," Ty teased. "Thanks, Beth. I'll let you know how it goes."

"Be sure you do," Beth said. "And make sure you behave like a gentleman."

"Right," Ty said with a sigh. That was the very last thing he wanted to do.

Lesson Fifteen
Lighten Up

"The only person takin' ya that seriously is the one lookin' back at ya when ya shaved this mornin'."

"Boss, yer strung as tight as a fresh-tuned fiddle," Swede commented as he rode next to Lexi early Friday afternoon. "What's got ya as jumpy as the lone cat at a dog fight?"

"Nothing," Lexi said, looking anywhere but at Swede.

"Nothin'?" Swede said with a glint shining in his eyes. "Thet must be the same nothin' thet's got dude's rope in a twist today."

Lexi looked at Swede and he offered her a knowing grin.

"What time are ya supposed to be ready for yer date?"

"He's picking me up at five," Lexi said on a sigh. She wanted so badly for the evening to go well, she was more nervous than she'd ever been before. The reasons behind that she refused to delve into, but the feeling was there nonetheless. "Do you think I'm making a mistake?"

"In goin' out with Ty?"

"Yeah. Since he's an employee and I... well, you know."

"Little late to worry about thet now ain't it?" Swede cackled. "He took care of ya while ya was sick, he's a hard worker and a good man. From what all the girls in town say, he's more than a little handsome. Seems to me ya'd be makin' a mistake not to go out with him, especially when ya like him as much as ya do."

Lexi stared at Swede and watched a grin spread across his face. "If'n I were in yer boots, boss, I'd have me a fine time and not worry so much about what others might think. Yer daddy would have approved of Ty and I certainly do."

"But what about the other hands? Won't they give him a bad time? Think he's getting special treatment?" Lexi asked, not wanting Ty to suffer on her account. "I don't want them harassing him."

"He can hold his own with that bunch," Swede said, reaching over and patting Lexi on the knee. "They ain't gonna say a thing about the two of ya and if they do, it'll be a mighty short conversation. Jes forget about the ranch and the crew and everythin' but being a young woman with a hot date."

Lexi laughed. "If you insist."

"I surely do," Swede said, cackling again. "Now, how is Jan workin' out?"

"Oh, Swede, she's the best. I'm so glad you talked her into coming to the ranch," Lexi said, her eyes bright with gratitude. "She can run circles around me. I don't know when the house has been so clean and I can't tell you how nice it is not to have to worry about cooking and housekeeping or what you guys are eating. She's so sweet to leave me dinner up at the house so I can relax and you guys can talk about how awful the boss is without her in the room."

"Now, Lex, ya know no one would say a thing about ya," Swede said, getting defensive until he saw Lexi grin. "But it's nice not havin' to worry about cookin'. That sister of mine always was purty handy in the kitchen."

Lexi and Swede continued visiting as they rode the fence line. They finished up a lengthy repair when Swede looked at his watch and whistled.

"Ya better hustle it up, boss, or yer gonna be late and that is one man ya don't want to keep waitin," Swede said, showing her the time.

"Good grief! How'd it get so late?" Lexi asked, jumping on Rowdy and taking off toward the house. "Thanks, Swede," she called over her shoulder as she nudged the horse into a full gallop.

Reining in at the barn, she stripped the saddle from Rowdy and asked Gus, who was working on some tack repairs, to cool down the horse before he put him away.

Taking a minute to remove her chaps, hat and boots by the back door, Lexi raced up the stairs to her room, stripping off her shirt and undoing her belt buckle as she went. In record time, she took a shower, washed, dried and curled her hair, put on mascara and lip gloss, and stood staring uncertainly into her closet.

All Ty said was that he'd pick her up at five. He didn't say where they were going. If it was into Burns, jeans would be fine to wear anywhere they might go. If it was to Bend, she wanted to dress up a bit.

Deciding to go for dressed up, she selected a figure-skimming slim black dress highlighted by a swirl of moss green foliage and bright pink flowers along with a pair of black heels.

Spritzing on perfume, she grabbed a sleek black handbag and tossed in the essentials she might need for the evening before snapping on a watch and fastening a dainty black necklace around her throat. Picking up a black cardigan sweater, she hurried downstairs, reaching the bottom step just as Ty knocked on the front door.

Lexi smiled as she opened it and welcomed him inside. For a moment she thought he was going to refuse to come in as he stood staring at her.

Ty spent a good part of the day giving himself a mental pep talk about all the reasons he should find Lexi and tell her they couldn't go out tonight. He was her hired hand, he had no business dating someone like her, and it was an overall bad idea. But every time he started to call her cell phone, he thought about how perfectly she fit into his arms, how good her lips tasted, how much he wanted to kiss her again, and lost his resolve.

Hurrying back to the bunkhouse at half-past four, he had to hustle to take a shower, shave and get dressed before five. He'd washed and polished his pickup the night before, cleaning out the inside as well. Swede must have said something to the rest of the crew, because so far none of them had given him a bad time about his date with the boss. Then again, it wasn't like it was general knowledge.

He took a deep, fortifying breath as he strode up the steps to the house after driving the pickup to the end of the walk. Giving Baby a lecture about staying down, she sulked around a corner of the house and looked back at him with what appeared to be a pout. Trying to hold in his laughter, it was hard not to find humor in a huge dog with her bottom lip stuck out and her big eyes all sad.

All thoughts of laughing at the dog flew right out of his head when Lexi opened the door. Her dress hugged each and every curve and fit her to perfection. The green in the floral print accented the deep mossy shade of her eyes, which were glowing and bright. Her high heels showcased her long, long legs and she smelled so tantalizing Ty wondered how he'd manage not to devour her.

Gathering his composure, he smiled at her and stepped into the foyer.

"Lexi, you look beautiful," he said, kissing her cheek and inhaling deeply of her warm, floral scent. She always looked beautiful to him, but he particularly enjoyed seeing her look so soft and feminine. His hands itched to bury themselves in the thick black curls cascading down her back so he shoved them in his pockets.

"Thanks," she said with a slight blush under his intense perusal. "You don't look so bad yourself."

In fact, Ty looked so good, Lexi was afraid some woman might try to steal him away from her at dinner. Dressed in his Wranglers with polished boots, he wore a light blue shirt that accented the color of his eyes along with a dark gray sports coat. As nice as he looked, he could have been any one of the ranch owners in the area, only better looking and definitely more dangerous to her ability to think with any degree of clarity.

"Beth told me I couldn't wear a sweatshirt," Ty said with a grin as he opened the door and followed Lexi outside.

"Well, I'm glad she did," Lexi said, thinking it was going to tax every bit of her self-restraint to keep Ty an arm's length away all evening. "That jacket is really nice."

"A left-over from a wedding I was in. You just never know what kind of costume you'll need out here in the sticks," Ty teased as he held Lexi's door and helped her in his truck.

"You seem to have pulled your costume together quite well," she commented, feeling her temperature rise as Ty's unique, manly scent filled the truck. "I'm guessing we aren't going to Burns or Hines for dinner."

"No, ma'am. I thought we'd run into Bend. You've got some time to decide if you'd rather have Italian, Mexican, Chinese or barbecue," Ty said, giving Lexi a heated glance. "Although looking as nice as you do, I think we better take barbecue off the list."

Pleased with his compliment and glance, Lexi smiled. "I know just the place." She fiddled with his GPS system and sat back. Adjusting her seat belt, she put on sunglasses and began to allow herself to enjoy the idea of being with Ty. Alone. On a date.

"Are you going to tell me where we're going?" he asked, as he turned onto the road leading to the highway.

"It will be a surprise," she said with saucy smile. "You like surprises, don't you?"

"Depends on what kind of surprises. Snakes-burying-their-fangs-in-my-chaps kind of surprises, not so much. Being-with-you kind of surprises, maybe."

"Maybe," Lexi huffed in feigned irritation. "You better just turn this truck around and take me back home, buckaroo."

Ty captured her hand and pressed a hot kiss to the palm, which quieted her down immediately.

"I can't do that, Lexi Jo. I've been looking forward to spending this evening with you all week and it would be cruel and unusual punishment to deprive me of the experience now that I've seen you looking like that," Ty said, rubbing lazy circles on her arm.

Lexi shivered, despite the heat coming in the window from the sun.

"I wouldn't want you to be deprived," she said, mentally grasping for any topic to relieve the tension that was building between them. At this rate, she might implode before they ever reached Bend. "How are Beth, Nate and Jax? I haven't seen any baby photos for a while."

Glad for a safe topic, Ty talked about his family and she mentioned a phone call she'd had from Bertie inviting them to come for a weekend when they were caught up on work.

Lexi let Ty know she found the next clue in her dad's ongoing treasure hunt for the lost money. This one was in an old wooden bucket that was stored in the barn loft. A small storage area held antique farm and ranch equipment that had been in their family for ages. Lexi finally remembered her dad talking about the old wooden bucket his grandma used to carry around. Although it had seen better days, it was preserved in the storage area. Lex taped a clue to the bottom of the bucket.

Don't Hem Me In

With no time to go searching for that clue, Lexi did have a few ideas on where to look. Discussing where it might be hidden, time flew and they were soon on the outskirts of Bend.

"Are you really not going to tell me where we're going?" Ty asked, half amused by Lexi's secrecy. "What if the GPS malfunctions?"

"Then I'll tell you where to turn. Just follow the directions," Lexi said, looking out the window.

With the directions ending in a section of downtown near the river, Ty found a parking space, ran around the truck and held the door while Lexi climbed out. Offering her his arm, she pointed to a neat looking brick building just down the block. The tempting smells of food mingled with a warm color scheme for a pleasing atmosphere as they stood in the entry.

"Do you have room on the deck?" Lexi asked as the hostess greeted them. They were escorted outside to a cozy little table for two that overlooked the river. The homes on the other side were massive and sprawling. Ty tried not to gawk and instead held Lexi's chair while she took her seat.

"This is amazing," he said, looking out at the lazy moving water. Surrounded by trees and a profusion of flowers, the deck was a very romantic place to sit and spend a warm spring evening. "I'm glad you surprised me."

"Me, too. I haven't eaten here for a couple of years, but the last time Dad and I came, I thought how nice it would be to see in the spring," Lexi said dreamily. What she'd really thought was how much she'd like to come here on a date, but didn't want to voice that opinion, particularly with a date as undeniably breath-taking as Ty.

Studying the menus, they made their selections then sat back, continuing their friendly conversation talking about nothing and everything.

When their meals arrived, they ate with pleasure. Both were too full to indulge in dessert, but Lexi ordered a cup of hot tea. The evening was starting to cool down and she left her sweater in the pickup.

Noticing her discomfort, Ty removed his jacket and draped it around her shoulders.

"Chilly?" he asked, rubbing his hands up and down her arms.

"I am, thanks," Lexi whispered, engulfed by Ty's scent and warmth as she pulled his jacket more firmly around her shoulders. His touch on her arms was sending goose bumps racing across her skin and she shivered again.

"You must be freezing. Do you want to leave?" Ty asked, starting to rise from his chair.

"No, I'm fine. Really," Lexi said, looking gratefully to the waitress when she appeared with the tea. Lexi sipped it while she and Ty looked across the water, making up imaginary stories of the people who lived in the homes across the river. As Ty added a funny accent to one of the characters they made up, she laughed so hard, she thought the restaurant owner might ask them to leave. Instead, a few of the older couples sitting nearby smiled at them indulgently.

When the waitress brought the bill, Lexi tried to take it but Ty grabbed it and shook his head.

"Ms. Ryan, being an old-fashioned kind of guy means I'm buying," Ty said, paying the bill and leaving a generous tip. He gave Lexi his hand as she got to her feet and smiled.

So used to picking up the tab it never occurred to Lexi that Ty would want to pay. Smiling, she squeezed his hand. "Thank you, then, for buying me dinner."

"You're welcome," Ty said, holding open the door as she walked out of the restaurant. "Thank you for agreeing to come with me. I could have just taken you to the Dairy Queen in Burns, but coming to Bend seemed like a better idea. Can I talk you into a movie?"

"You won't have to talk too hard as long as you promise to get a super-huge bucket of popcorn with extra butter," Lexi said, placing both hands on Ty's arm and squeezing gently.

"Deal," he said, patting her fingers where they circled his bicep. Ty walked her back to the pickup, helping her inside. Her hands were nearly searing his skin, but he tried to maintain his unaffected demeanor. He wasn't sure he could trust himself to spend two hours in a dark theater cozied up to her, but he was willing to try.

Lexi gave him directions to a movie theater and as they took in the options, Ty resigned himself to watching a chick flick. He was surprised when she pointed to a movie that would start in a few minutes.

"What do you think of that one?" she asked.

"I think you're taking pity on me and suggesting that one so I won't have to suffer through a girlie movie," Ty said with a smile that made Lexi's knees feel weak.

"No, I'm not. I'm completely selfish when it comes to movies I like, so I wouldn't offer to go to something I didn't want to see. My dad was a big comic book fan and I heard that one is supposed to be good," Lexi said, tugging Ty toward the ticket window.

Not only was Lexi beautiful, she'd rather watch an action-movie based on comic book characters than a romantic comedy. He thought she couldn't get any more perfect.

Lexi started to dig in her purse, but Ty purchased the tickets and hurried her inside where she ordered a huge bucket of popcorn and he got a large Dr. Pepper. When he asked what she wanted to drink she told him she'd rather share.

No doubt about it. She was beyond perfect.

Ty was glad the movie was exciting and moved along quickly, otherwise he might have acted on one or two of the ideas that kept flitting through his head as he watched the young couples sneaking kisses under the dark cover of the theater.

As it was, Lexi was leaning against him with her hand on his thigh, rubbing tantalizing circles that were about to drive him wild. In an effort to keep from embarrassing them both, Ty finally took her hand in his and kissed her palm before lacing their fingers together.

When the movie ended, Lexi suggested they go for a walk in the Old Mill District that sat on the banks of the river. Ty readily agreed. Although it was getting late, he wasn't in any hurry for their evening to end.

Strolling along the walkway, they first looked in shop windows before changing direction and walking along the river bank. The moon was full and bright, allowing Ty the opportunity to watch Lexi as they wandered along.

Sighing contentedly, she curved against him and he put his arm around her, drawing her close to his side.

"What was that sigh for?" he asked, kissing her temple.

"It was a happy sigh," she said quietly, turning to look at him. In all her years of dating, she couldn't remember enjoying a first date more than she had this one. She'd been on all sorts of exciting dates, but none that spoke to her heart the way Ty had tonight. Walking in the moonlight along the river was a fitting finish to the wonderful experience.

Lexi hadn't missed the admiring glances women continued casting Ty's direction. She had sent him several herself during the course of the evening. How could you not admire the tall, fit man with the finger-tempting waves of brown hair that practically begged female hands to run through it? Coupled with his bright blue eyes, strong jaw, and that somewhat dangerous look he always seemed to have, he was more appealing than any man Lexi could ever remember seeing. Lexi appreciated the fact that he was wearing his boots and snug Wranglers tonight.

"So you have a sigh for every occasion?" Ty asked with a mischievous glint in his eyes.

"No," Lexi said, grinning. "What about you? You look pretty pleased with yourself."

"I am."

"About what?" Lexi stopped walking so she could look intently in Ty's eyes. They seemed to be glowing, lit by an inner fire, and threatened to suck her into a place she wasn't sure she'd ever be able to leave.

"You," Ty said, taking her hand and pulling her along the walk as they circled back toward the parking lot.

"What about me?" she asked, curious as to what he was thinking.

"It's just…" Ty said, not comfortable sharing his feelings, but feeling somewhat intoxicated by Lexi's warmth and presence at his side. "I never imagined being here with you, never dreamed you'd actually go out on a date with a homeless mechanic who doesn't have a thing to offer the world."

"I wouldn't go out with someone like that," Lexi said, tightening her hold on Ty's hand reassuringly. "But I would go out with someone who is a hard-working man, who is compassionate and caring and always tries to do what's right. Someone funny and exciting. The one man on the planet my dog actually likes. Then there's that whole good-looking bad-boy factor."

"Is that right?" Ty asked, deciding to lighten the mood as he moved his fingers around Lexi's side and began tickling her.

As she giggled, he led her toward his truck. Opening the door, she pressed against him, still laughing. The sound wound its way from his ears past his heart right down into Ty's soul.

"Lexi Jo, what am I going to do with you?" he asked, pulling her into a warm embrace.

"What do you want to do?" she whispered, sliding her hands around Ty's neck.

"Lexi," he growled before giving her a kiss that would have caused heads to turn their direction had anyone else been in the parking lot at the moment.

Ty wanted more than anything to find some dark, secluded place to park his truck and ravish Lexi with kisses. Instead, he gave her one more searing kiss, gently picked her up and sat her on the pickup seat, and shut her door.

"We've got a long drive home, babe, and if we keep kissing like that, I can't promise I'll get you there in one piece," he said as he started the truck and headed out of the parking lot. Lexi gave him directions back to the highway and they were soon leaving civilization behind.

They chatted for a while, but fatigue got the best of Lexi and she soon found it impossible to keep her eyes open. Leaning her head back, she could feel Ty's hand holding hers as they drove through the miles of sagebrush.

Past midnight when they arrived back at the ranch, Ty pulled the truck up by the front gate of the house and parked. Turning off the engine and the lights, he unfastened his seat belt and stared at Lexi for a few moments before releasing a sigh and walking around to her door. She was still sleeping, so he carefully unbuckled her seat belt and scooped her into his arms. Smiling, he remembered the last time they did this she pretended she was asleep just so he'd hold her longer.

From her deep, even breathing, he knew this time she was definitely not pretending.

Going up the porch steps he somehow managed to open the door and step inside. Baby sat in the foyer, looking at them like a parent who'd sat waiting up for a child out past curfew.

"Sorry, Baby, we didn't mean to be out so late," Ty whispered, trying to decide if he should carry Lexi upstairs or leave her in the foyer. The dog glared at him and sank down to the floor, letting him know she was maintaining her role as chaperone. Deciding to take Lexi to her room, he started up the stairs only to have Baby grab his pant leg. Looking down at the dog, he frowned at her. "Baby, stop that. I promise to behave."

Baby turned loose of his jeans and sat wagging her tail.

Ty carried Lexi up to her room and gently laid her on the bed. Turning on the bedside lamp, he softly tapped her cheeks, but got no response. Deciding to give her a quick kiss goodnight, he pressed his lips to hers. Just when he was ready to move away, Lexi's hands slid around his neck and pulled him into a deeper kiss.

Melding their lips, their bodies pressed close together, Ty frantically grabbed at the last few threads of rational thought before he completely unraveled. Resting his forehead against Lexi's, he let out a ragged breath.

"Lexi, thank you for the best date I've ever had. You are amazing and I don't know how you could look any more beautiful than you do tonight," Ty whispered, kissing her eyelids, her cheeks and her nose.

"Thank you for asking me, Ty. I had a wonderful time and I hope we can do it again. I don't know when I've enjoyed an evening more," Lexi said, tugging Ty into another tight embrace.

After a quick hug, Ty got up quite suddenly and crossed the space to the door in a few long strides. The blue in Ty's eyes looked molten as he turned his heated gaze to Lexi, making her limbs feel languid and weak.

"Night, Lexi," Ty said, forcing himself to keep moving away from her instead of going back to the bed and staying there all night. "Sweet dreams."

"Thanks, Ty. You, too," Lexi whispered, wanting Ty to take her back into his arms, but knowing he was doing the right thing.

Hurrying down the stairs, Baby greeted him with a smile and leaned approvingly against his leg.

"Come on, mother hen," Ty said, motioning the dog out the door as he locked it behind them. "You can turn in your chaperone hat for the evening."

Lesson Sixteen
Stand Up for What's Right

"If yer gonna bring the hammer down,
make sure ya hit the nail square on the head."

"We're going where?" Ty asked, not quite sure he heard Swede correctly.

"To the Big Loop Rodeo in Jordan Valley," Swede said at breakfast Friday morning. "It runs for two days, but we're jes gonna go fer the day tomorra."

"Why do I need to go?" Ty asked as Jimmy passed him the plate of fluffy biscuits Jan made that morning. After serving breakfast, she ran a plate of food over to Lexi at the main house and hadn't yet returned.

"Boss said," Swede said, giving Ty a look that dared him to argue with that. "We're all going except for Gus."

"If you'd rather go, Gus, I can stay home and keep an eye on things," Ty volunteered, not exactly sure why the idea of going to a rodeo was putting him into a tailspin. He could ride well enough no one casually watching wouldn't know he hadn't been doing it for a long time. He had adjusted to dressing like a cowboy and was secretly quite pleased with the way the clothes looked on him, although he'd never admit it. Everyone on the ranch and the neighbors had gotten used to him and didn't think anything of his background, but he was sure at a rodeo he would stick out as a city boy.

"Thanks for the offer, dude, but I'd much rather stay home. I can't hardly stand to sit in the truck for that long and resting my bones on those hard bleachers all afternoon don't appeal to me at all. You go on and have fun," Gus said, taking a bite of crispy bacon.

"Have you ever been to a rodeo, dude?" Jimmy asked.

"Nope."

"Well, maybe you'll learn something new," Jimmy said with a mischievous smile.

Ty could only hope Jimmy wouldn't get it into his head to pull one of his pranks while they were there.

"I think the best way for you to learn all about rodeos is to participate," Jimmy commented, kicking Cal under the table.

"For sure, we better sign you up for something," Cal said, following Jimmy's lead.

Cal and Keith were entering the team roping event while Jimmy was participating in the ranch-style saddle bronc riding.

"I don't think so," Ty said, envisioning them signing him up to do something crazy like ride a bull. He knew enough about rodeos to know he didn't want to try that.

"Aw, come on, it'll be fun," Jimmy said, not giving up on his quest to involve Ty. "You can barrel race or ride a cow."

Ty glared at Jimmy.

"He's on to you man," Keith said, slapping Jimmy on the back. "He may be green, but he ain't stupid."

"Let him be. He can jes take this one in and decide what event he'll master after that," Swede said slurping his coffee.

The next morning, Cal, Keith, Jimmy and Swede all left bright and early after hurrying through the chores, pulling a horse-trailer with their horses. Swede wasn't competing, but he often volunteered to help where he could and liked to have Kitty handy.

Jan decided riding to Jordan Valley a couple of hours away, sitting on the bleacher seats, and then riding home didn't sound like the most fun way for her to spend a Saturday and chose to stay at the ranch instead.

Lexi told her to take the day off and enjoy doing something fun, so Jan thought she might run into Burns and browse through some of the shops.

Finishing up a few additional chores, Lexi and Ty were the last to leave for the rodeo. She considered taking her car, but didn't want it to get scratched or dented in the rodeo crowds, so she drove her dad's pickup, even though Ty offered to drive his truck.

On the drive to the rodeo, Lexi gave Ty a run-down on the various rodeo events, the history of this particular rodeo and what he could expect from the day.

By the time they arrived at the arena, Ty was looking forward to the afternoon.

"So, do you want to consider this a well-chaperoned second date?" Lexi asked as they stood in line to buy tickets.

"Only if I get to buy the tickets and hold your hand," Ty said with a devilish smile. "And there has to be kissing involved for it to count as a date."

"What kind of girl do you take me for, Mr. Lewis? You seem to assume I'd be willing to kiss you and hold your hand on our second date. Isn't that a little presumptuous on your part?" Lexi teased with a saucy grin.

Ty leaned down and placed his lips close to her ear. Lexi could smell his fruity gum, as his unique scent flooded her senses.

"I take you for the most wonderful kind of girl, Ms. Ryan. One I like very much. One I enjoy holding and kissing. One I plan to kiss repeatedly before the day is through, if this is, in fact, a date."

Lexi felt warmth flood through her and her knees suddenly felt like they might turn to gel. Ty's teasing promise made butterflies explode in her stomach while she grew lightheaded.

Sensing her feelings, Ty pressed a quick kiss to her neck and put his arm around her slender shoulders, drawing her into his warmth and strength.

"Date or not?" Ty asked as they stepped up to the ticket counter. The heat in his blue eyes challenged her ability to think, let alone speak.

"Date," she finally whispered.

Ty dug out his wallet and bought two tickets. He returned his wallet to his pocket and was handing Lexi a ticket when Jimmy snatched it from his hand.

"If you're buying, you can get mine, too," Jimmy teased before handing Lexi the ticket.

"You're on your own, man," Ty said, giving Jimmy a slap on the back then taking Lexi's elbow as they started toward the stands.

"Save us a good seat," Jimmy called after them.

"Lead the way," Ty said, feeling completely out of his element. At least he looked like he fit in with the crowd dressed in his pressed Wranglers, polished boots, a blue striped western shirt and his Stetson.

Walking behind Lexi, he admired the way her jeans fit just right. Rather than her standard work shirts, she wore a soft blouse and left her hair down instead of in a braid. She smelled fresh and warm, like a springtime afternoon, and he found the scent of her to be intoxicating. He was going to have to work hard to keep focused on what was going on around him instead of the woman who would be sitting beside him.

It took a while to work their way through the crowd since Lexi seemed to know a good portion of those attending. Several people offered condolences over the passing of her father while others teased and laughed with her. Although Ty tried to stay out of the way while she was visiting, she kept looking back for him, reaching for his hand, and introducing him to more people than he'd ever be able to keep straight. Ty appreciated that she didn't introduce him as a hired hand, but as her "good friend."

Finally, they reached the section of bleachers closest to the chutes and Lexi looked up, waving to her Uncle Rob and his family where they had saved several seats. Going up the steps, Lexi pulled Ty along behind her across the top row.

Hugging her aunt and cousins, she motioned Ty to take the seat at the end of the row while she settled in next to him.

"You mean you didn't get talked into riding or chasing something today?" Rob asked Ty.

"No, sir. It wasn't for lack of trying," Ty said with a grin, pushing his hat back on his head so he could better visit with those sitting close by. The action came so naturally, Lexi smiled as she watched him. She recalled seeing her dad do the same thing thousands of times over the years.

Ty might have been born and raised a city boy, but something in his spirit was all cowboy. One outrageously handsome cowboy who was drawing a lot of attention from the single female attendees in the crowd, much to Lexi's annoyance.

Rob laughed and reached around Lexi to slap Ty on the leg.

"If you change your mind, let me know. I'm sure we can get in a last minute entry."

"I think I'll just sit back and watch the action today," Ty said, leaning against the back railing and draping his arm around Lexi's shoulders. It was a possessive and bold move on his part with all her family watching, but her uncle only grinned when Lexi slid a little closer to him.

They didn't have long to wait before the rodeo began. Lexi quietly explained each event to Ty and much to his surprise, he found himself enjoying the rodeo.

When Jimmy came busting out of the chute on a bucking bronc, they all clapped and cheered. He stayed on for the full ride and Ty could see Swede standing on the fence by the chutes waving his hat with pride.

Lexi and a couple of her cousins disappeared and returned with hamburgers and icy cold pop for everyone in their group. Ty didn't realize just how hungry he was until Lexi handed him the hamburger.

"I'm buying the meal on this date, buckaroo," she whispered as she sat back down beside him.

"Whatever you say," Ty said, too involved in the big, juicy hamburger to argue. Although juice threatened to run down his arm, it was one of the best burgers he'd ever had. Maybe the company and the warm spring day had something to do with how good it tasted.

They were wiping the last of the grease from their fingers when Cal and Keith rode into the arena, competing in team roping. They did an excellent job and Lexi commented to Ty she was sure they would place. He was intently watching how the competitors performed in each event.

Finally it was time for the bull riding. Ty thought every single one of the guys riding either had to be brave or crazy or some bizarre combination of both.

Even though he'd never do it, he did find it extremely fascinating to watch.

As the last event wound down, Lexi squeezed his hand and grinned. "What did you think of your very first rodeo?"

SHANNA HATFIELD

"I liked it," Ty said, nodding his head. "I really never thought about the amount of strength and agility it takes to compete in these events. I'm impressed."

"I'm glad," Lexi said, standing up and waiting for the crowd to thin so they could get out of the bleachers. "We'll probably have the opportunity to attend a few more this summer and you have to go with me to Pendleton to the Round-Up in September. If you thought this was fun, you have to see it. We always stay at Bertie and Linc's place."

"Sounds great," Ty said, holding her hand as they trailed behind her uncle's family.

They were barely on the ground when Swede and Jimmy hustled over, both talking a mile a minute. Jimmy placed third in the bronc riding while Cal and Keith took first in team roping for the day. All of them wanted to stay for the rodeo the next day, so Lexi told them to have fun and she'd see them all Monday morning.

"Looks like the two of us will have some extra chores to do in the morning," Lexi said as they strolled toward the parking area.

"Lucky us," Ty said dryly as their group wandered through the booths selling everything from silver jewelry to hand-tooled tack and home décor.

"Hey, you two want to join us for dinner?" Rob asked looking back at them as they walked through the crowds.

"If you're buying," Lexi teased.

Rob gave Ty a once over and shook his head.

"I don't know if I can afford to feed that one, but I'm willing to try," Rob said with a smile. "We'll meet you at the café."

The café was a dining establishment in Rome, on the way back to the highway that would take Rob's family home to the south while Lexi and Ty headed north. The food was generally good and filling and there wouldn't be

270

such a big crowd there since it was a few miles out of Jordan Valley.

When Lexi parked the truck, Ty raised his eyebrow at the outside of the building but said nothing.

Going inside, the place was busy, but the waitress managed to push three tables together to accommodate their group. They laughed and teased, enjoying the good food and companionship.

Lexi told her aunt and cousins about Ty's nephew, Jax, and they wanted to see photos. Remembering he left his phone in the truck he hurried out to get it. On his way back in, he stood waiting for a family to come out the door and overhead two guys nearby talking.

"It's too bad about ol' Lex Ryan."

"Yep, but I hear his girl does a good job of runnin' the ranch. She's one hot little squaw," the shorter and older of the two men said.

Ty knew he shouldn't be eavesdropping as his hand clenched into a fist.

"I hear she's got a city boy who's keeping her teepee warm these days, if ya catch my meanin'."

"Must be nice to be a kept man, livin' off ol' Lex's hard work. That is one lucky dog. Wonder how long it took him to worm his way into the house. Shame that girl didn't at least have sense enough to pick a nice country boy. He must be a slick talker to win her over so easy. Somebody said he showed up out there a couple months ago. Poor ol' Lex is probably…"

Ty knew the smart thing to do would be to go back inside the restaurant and pretend he'd never heard what these two said. But doing what was smart wasn't always aligned to doing what was right. At least with Ty.

"I think you two better stop talking about Ms. Ryan like that," Ty said shoving his phone in his pocket and stepping next to the duo, stretching up to his full, intimidating height. "She's a lady and she's done nothing to deserve your filthy-minded speculation."

"And you would be?" the shorter guy asked, taking a step back away from Ty, toward the parking lot. He might like to run his mouth, but he sure wasn't looking for a fight, especially not with someone who looked like he could take down the both of them without even working up a sweat.

"The city boy," Ty growled, taking a step forward. "I prefer to not let my fists do the talking, gentleman, but if I ever hear either of you saying anything derogatory about Ms. Ryan again, I can guarantee it won't be to your advantage."

"No, sir. I mean yes, sir. Come on, Kel, let's go," the shorter guy said, walking backward toward his truck with his friend at his side.

Ty watched them leave before returning to Lexi and her family. Sitting down beside her at the table, he was still unsettled by the conversation and encounter outside.

The warmth of Lexi's hand on his arm made him turn toward her. When she smiled up at him, he felt the corners of his mouth lift in return.

"Find your phone?" she asked.

"Yes, ma'am," Ty said, taking it out and pulling up the latest photos of Jax. The women all offered the appropriate comments on what a sweet baby he was while Ty's thoughts ran a hundred different directions.

Was his relationship with Lexi damaging her reputation? What right did he have, after all, to be involved with her? He was a nobody. He grew up a poor kid from the wrong side of the tracks and deep inside, he still felt like that. He didn't deserve to be with someone like Lexi.

Withdrawing mentally from the group, Ty's sudden quietness didn't go unnoticed by Lexi. She placed a hand on his thigh and patted gently. Even though her touch seared into his leg, Ty refused to acknowledge the sensation or the comfort her presence brought.

The right thing to do was to distance himself from Lexi before he caused her any more grief. Before he lost any more of his heart to the only woman he would ever truly love.

Lesson Seventeen
Believe in Yourself

*"What others think or say about ya
ain't none of yer business. Not one lick."*

Lexi had no idea what had gotten into Ty, but since the day of the rodeo, he had kept their relationship strictly professional.

Almost a month had passed and she was completely bewildered by his behavior. He was still kind and courteous, but he didn't ask her for another date, he didn't seek her out Sunday afternoons, and he certainly didn't make any excuses to come to the house looking to steal a kiss or two.

It was the longest month of Lexi's entire existence.

She missed his warmth and laughter, the way he would tease her and tickle her before kissing her senseless. She missed the feel of his arms around her and resting her head on his strong chest. She missed his scent filling her senses and the sound of his deep, rumbling voice. She missed the comfort of his presence and the airless feeling that settled in her stomach when he focused his brilliant blue eyes on her.

Head over heels in love with the man, she was convinced he didn't feel the same. After their first date, she half-expected him to say the words, to say that he loved her, but he didn't need to. She knew it from the look in his eyes, from the gentleness in his touch.

Now, after a month of cordial, yet respectful conversation, she had no idea what happened to drive him away. She still saw the heat and longing in his eyes, even if he held himself away from her.

Sitting at her kitchen table, distractedly stirring a cup of hot tea before she began her day of hard labor, she didn't even glance up when Jan came in with a plate of food.

Although Lexi never made a habit of eating at the bunkhouse, she refused to set foot in the door as long as Ty was pushing her away. It was just too hard to be around him.

"You look like you lost your best friend already this morning and it isn't even a quarter past six," Jan commented as she set a plate of biscuits, eggs and bacon in front of Lexi.

A sigh was Lexi's response. She said a silent word of thanks for the meal, but pushed it around on her plate instead of eating anything.

"Honey, I know I haven't been here that long, but I can't help but notice that whatever is bothering you seems to be bothering that nice, handsome mechanic of yours. I'm here to listen if you ever want to talk." Jan sat at the table across from Lexi, sipping a cup of coffee.

"Thanks, Jan. I… I thought… Ty and I were…" Lexi couldn't continue talking through the tears that clogged her throat and filled her eyes. Taking a sip of tea and a couple of deep breaths, she swiped at her cheeks. "I thought we had something really special, but since the day of the rodeo, he backed away and won't talk to me about it. I don't know if I did something, if someone said something, if he found someone he likes better. I don't have a clue."

"I can tell you right now there isn't someone else. His heart is in his eyes every time he looks at you. He's as tormented and hurting as you. Only he can tell you what made him change his mind, but if you keep waiting for him to come forward and share his feelings, you'll spend a long time waiting, honey. That's just not the way of men, especially not men like Ty. That's one bull you are going to have to grab by the horns."

A smile tipped the corners of Lexi's mouth at Jan's words. She reached across the table to the older woman and squeezed her hand.

"Thank you, Jan. I appreciate your concern and your advice. I should have listened to Aunt Bertie a couple of months ago," Lexi said, taking a bite of her biscuit.

"What did she tell you?"

"To slap my brand on Ty and not let him out of my sight," Lexi said with a grin.

"Smart woman, your aunt," Jan said with a wink.

Ty felt sick. He had for weeks, since the day of the rodeo when he decided to let Lexi go. It was the single hardest thing he'd ever done.

He wanted her in ways that defied logic and sense, but more than that, he wanted her to be happy. In his mind, he just knew some day she would realize he was nobody, a nothing, and be sorry about hooking up with him. He decided by breaking things off with her now he'd save them both a lot of heartache later.

Only he wasn't sure how much more his heart could hurt as he watched her from afar.

He was more than happy to be spending time out riding fence and checking the cattle because he generally did that alone. Out there he didn't have to see Lexi, hear her voice, smell her enticing scent, although her scent was ensnared somewhere in his brain and the vision of her lovely face filled his mind every time he closed his eyes.

The depth and intensity of his feelings for her, his sense of loss at not being near her, were beyond his ability to comprehend. All Ty knew was that the idea of a life without her in it, without her by his side, was too painful to consider.

It wasn't just that he wanted her. He needed her. The very core of his being craved her presence and Ty didn't think he would ever get past that desperate longing.

If he had some way of working to better himself, to provide something better for her than what she had, he might hold out a hope for their future. But there wasn't a single thing in the world he could offer her that she didn't already have or couldn't buy if she wanted. The only thing he had to offer her was himself and in his sight that was nothing.

He knew he shouldn't let it get to him, but the guys at the café talking about him being a kept city boy really bothered him. Ty didn't want Lexi to go through life making excuses for him or having people speak badly about her because of her relationship with him. And, if he cared to admit it, he didn't want anyone thinking he was like one more of Lexi's pets. He had no plans of being "kept" by anybody.

Ty refused to acknowledge stubborn pride factored into his decision to step away from Lexi's love. He kept telling himself he was doing it all for her benefit. Even when he saw the look of hurt in her eyes and could feel the pain he caused her. He recognized the pain since he was feeling it himself.

Riding past one of the ponds on the ranch used for watering the cattle, Ty stopped Delilah under a tree and sat looking at the water. The heat was nearly unbearable for June and Swede assured him it was nothing compared to how hot it would be in July and August. As Swede would phrase it, Ty was panting like a lizard on a hot rock.

Deciding to take a quick swim to cool off, Ty set his new straw hat on the saddle horn, walked to the edge of the pond, stripped off his clothes and dove into the water. It was tepid, but cooler than the air around him. The water wasn't exactly sparkling clean, but right now he didn't care. Anything felt better than the sticky heat of being in the saddle.

Breaking the surface, he heard a dog bark and turned to see Baby sitting on the bank.

"Hey, Baby, what are you doing out here?" Ty asked as he continued to tread water. "Want to swim?"

The dog backed up a few steps and barked again.

"Not a fan of the pond, huh?" Ty asked with a chuckle, diving back into the water. He swam for a few more minutes then decided he better get back to work. Swimming to the bank, he didn't see Baby anywhere. He also didn't see his clothes. That obnoxious dog had taken his clothes! All she left behind were his boots.

Running out of the water, he grabbed the boots and looked around trying to see where the dog and his clothes had gone. Attempting to dry off his feet on the grass, he yanked on the boots and started walking toward the horse.

"Baby," Ty shouted. "Baby, get back here right now. So help me…"

"You definitely look like you need some help," Lexi commented as she rode toward him.

Flushing red from the top of his head to his feet, Ty ran to Delilah and used her as a shield from Lexi.

"What are you doing out here?" Ty ground out, looking over the saddle at Lexi where she had reined in Rowdy a few feet away.

"I could ask you the same thing, buckaroo," Lexi said with a teasing smile. She could see Ty's well-muscled calves and part of his thighs below Delilah's belly and the tops of his shoulders above the saddle. "You do know the pond has leeches, don't you?"

"Leeches?" Ty asked, trying to think what he knew about leeches. Were they as bad as ticks?

"Yes, leeches. They attach themselves to warm bodies and suck blood. They are slimy and gross, which is why I stay out of this pond," Lexi said, removing her hat and wiping her forehead on her shirt sleeve. "You want some help checking to see if you have any?"

"No!" Ty said, afraid she might make good on her offer. He needed her to turn around and leave.

"Since you can't run away from me, how about you tell me why you've spent the last month acting like nothing was happening between us," Lexi asked, riding a little closer and staring at Ty with narrowed eyes.

He glared back, setting his hat on his head.

Lexi grinned, knowing there was a whole lot of very attractive man exposed between his hat and boots, hidden behind the horse.

"Well?"

"I don't want to talk about it," Ty said, breaking their eye contact and looking away.

"That's obvious," Lexi said, urging Rowdy closer. "Tell me something I don't know."

"No," Ty said. He wasn't about to share what those men said at the café. He certainly wasn't going to spell out all the reasons he was completely wrong for her.

"No? That's not the right answer, buckaroo. Try again," Lexi said, leaning out of her saddle toward Delilah.

"I said no, boss, and I mean it," Ty said.

He rarely called her boss, and that fact wasn't lost on Lexi. She sat back in the saddle and stared at him.

"Guess I'll have to get off Rowdy and come over there to talk some sense into you," Lexi said, starting to swing a leg over the saddle. Only she couldn't because Baby grabbed hold of her foot on the other side of Rowdy.

"Baby! You let go this instant," Lexi demanded, regaining her seat in the saddle and shaking her leg, trying to dislodge the dog.

Ty laughed. "Looks like Baby knows as well as I do you have no business getting out of that saddle. Now, scoot. I've got clothes to find and a fence to finish riding if you don't mind."

"I do mind. Besides, I consider this payback for when I was sick and you undressed me," Lexi said, turning Rowdy back toward the home place. "I'll leave, but don't think this is over, Tyler Lewis. It's a long way from over."

Lexi urged Rowdy off into a gallop and Ty waited until he was sure she couldn't see him before he moved from behind the horse, calling to Baby. The dog slunk over, dragging Ty's shirt in her mouth.

"Thank you, Baby," Ty said, snapping the shirt into place. "Now, the rest of my clothes, if you please."

Baby ran off, returning with Ty's jeans, socks and underwear. He hurriedly dressed, hoping Lexi was teasing about leeches.

The last one in the door for dinner, Ty looked around when the conversation stopped as he sat down at the table.

"Dude, how was your day?" Jimmy asked with the glint in his eye which meant Ty was in for some teasing.

"Just fine. Yourself?"

"Dandy. But then I didn't have an afternoon swim or spend time mooning the boss, either."

Ty's head snapped up and he glared coldly at Jimmy across the table.

"If ya know what's good fer ya, ya better shut yer trap, Jimmy boy," Swede said, putting a restraining hand on Ty's arm. He could feel the muscles tense beneath his fingers. He knew there was one thing Ty wouldn't take any teasing about and that was Lex.

"Aw, I was just funnin' with you. The boss said she caught you at the swimming hole and that monster ya'll call a dog ran off with your clothes. Looks like you found them," Jimmy said, helping himself to a heaping portion of mashed potatoes and gravy.

"Baby brought them back to me," Ty said, trying to bank his anger and irritation. He should have known better than to go skinny dipping in the pond. That was one mistake he'd never make again.

"I bet the boss would have been more than happy to help you. I bet she would have…" Jimmy's teasing was cut short when Ty jumped up and grabbed his collar from across the table, bringing Jimmy to his feet.

"You can say whatever you want about me, but you leave her out of it," Ty ground out, giving Jimmy a shake before turning him loose and storming out the door.

He stalked to the shop and slammed the door, thoughts and feelings swirling through his head. If the hands were making comments about him and Lexi, maybe he needed to pack up and leave. It was the very last thing he wanted, but he didn't know what else to do.

The sun was starting its evening descent when Swede came in the shop, shaking his head.

"Son, I don't know what's eatin' at ya, but let's get it out here in the open where we can clobber it down to a manageable size. Jimmy was just funnin' ya."

"I know he was," Ty said, not looking up from the part he was putting back together. "I didn't mean to lose my temper."

"Well, I suppose he should be glad all he got was a good shake rather than a fist to that smarty mouth of his," Swede said with a grin.

Ty looked over at him and nodded his head, a small smile working at his lips.

"I'll apologize to him when I go in," Ty said, carefully tightening the nuts into place then wiping his hands on a rag.

"Thet would be good. He thinks the world of ya and he's plumb beside hisself thet he made ya mad," Swede said, sitting down on a stool and staring at Ty. "Ya might as well git whatever is makin' ya tied up tighter than widow Johnson's knittin' off yer chest. Out with it."

"What makes you think something's bothering me?" Ty asked, cleaning up the workbench and putting the tools away.

Swede liked that about Ty. He always put everything back in its place and made sure his work area was clean before he called it a night. He did it in the shop, and anywhere else on the ranch they asked him to work. Most of the boys weren't as careful in keeping things clean and put away.

"The way I see it, somethin' happened when ya went with Lex to the rodeo a few weeks back. Ya been avoiding' thet gal like she is a live carrier of the plague ever since and it ain't right," Swede said, giving Ty a fatherly scowl. "What'd she do to deserve the cold shoulder?"

"She didn't do anything wrong, Swede," Ty said, sitting down on stool near the foreman and running his hands through his already mussed hair. "It isn't about what she's done, it's me."

"Well, what about ya?"

"It's… I don't…" Ty got up and paced around a bit. "I just can't talk about it. For Lexi's sake, though, I need to keep our relationship strictly professional."

Ty looked up surprised when Swede cackled at him, shaking a gnarled finger his direction.

"It's way too late for thet, pard. Way too late. In case ya ain't noticed, ya both have fallen in too deep to try and go back now. If'n it were me, I'd keep right on swimmin'."

"You don't understand," Ty said, shaking his head. "Lexi's association with me isn't ever going to be beneficial for her."

"Who are ya to decide thet? Did the boss tell ya thet?" Swede asked. When Ty shook his head, Swede continued. "Thet is for Lex to decide, not yerself or nobody else. Give her the choice. Yer breakin' thet sweet lil' gal's heart an I can't hardly stand to watch. She cares for ya, son, more than ya realize. Don't let what others think influence yer decision. Sometimes ya jes got to follow yer heart. Believe in yerself and follow yer heart."

Swede got to his feet and headed toward the door. "Jan saved ya some dinner and a big piece of pie, if yer of a mind to come get it."

"Thanks, Swede. I'll be right in."

Follow his heart. Ty mulled over that idea as he finished cleaning up for the night and closed the shop door. It was much easier said than done because following it would lead him right to Lexi's arms.

A few days later, on a sweltering afternoon, Ty was working in the shop making repairs to the older farm pickup they used to run around the ranch. Cal, who seemed to be particularly hard on equipment, busted a tie rod that morning and they needed the truck back into service sooner rather than later.

Pounding out his frustrations in repairs suited Ty just fine. He turned up his music, playing John Waite's *Missing You* over and over, missing Lexi more each time the song repeated.

He was nearly finished with the repair when he heard Baby barking outside. Wiping his greasy hands on a rag, he stuck his head out the door but didn't see the dog anywhere.

After the encounter at the pond, he carefully avoided being around Lexi if at all possible and knew she was staying close to the house today. He didn't want to run into her, but Baby's insistent barking was calling to him to hurry.

Rushing out the door, he followed the sound of her barking to a small shed behind the ranch house where Lexi kept garden tools and the lawnmower. Baby was standing in the open doorway barking and whining.

"Baby, I told you to hush," Ty heard Lexi caution. "I'll get myself down just fine."

Peering inside the shed, Ty saw Lexi's jean-clad legs hanging over the edge of a small loft. With no windows in the building, he didn't know how she could see anything up there with the minimal amount of light that came in through the door. He looked around and saw the footstool she'd used to climb into the loft had tipped over. Stepping inside, he righted the stool and turned his face up toward Lexi just as the door banged shut, leaving them in darkness.

"Oh," Lexi said, startled by the sound and the lack of light.

Ty put his hands on her legs causing her to scream.

"It's just me Lexi Jo. I've got you," Ty said, sliding his hands up to her thighs and tugging. She stopped screaming, turned over, and scooted to the edge of the loft trusting Ty to catch her as she pushed herself off the small landing.

She felt him pull her to his chest and put her hands out, catching herself on his strong shoulders.

Sliding down the length of him, she held her breath and thought she might pass out from the sensations rocketing through her. When her feet touched solid ground, he let her go.

284

"Didn't mean to startle you," Ty said, taking a step back. Feeling behind him, he pushed on the door, but it wouldn't budge.

"Thanks. I didn't expect the door to slam shut," Lexi said, reaching toward the door and finding it stuck in place.

"It appears to be stuck," Ty commented.

"Baby! If you're blocking this door, you're going to be in so much trouble. This is not okay, Baby. Move!" Lexi ordered, pushing against the door and getting nowhere. If the dog was on the other side of the door, she wasn't making a sound.

"Well, what do we do now?" Ty asked, afraid to move too much. There was barely room for one body to maneuver around in the small shed and everything from rakes to shovels hung on the walls on pegs. The riding lawnmower, a rototiller and weed eater took up what little floor space was available.

"Wait, I guess," Lexi said, both annoyed and pleased with the dog. She could think of worse things than being locked in a shed with Ty. "Since we aren't going anywhere anytime soon, how about we finish our talk from the other day?"

"I don't think so," Ty said, trying to distance himself from Lexi and knocking a garden hoe from the wall. He caught it before it maimed either of them.

"Well, I do," Lexi said, leaning against the lawnmower. Enough light snuck in around the edges of the door, she could make out Ty's form even if she couldn't clearly see his face as her eyes adjusted to the darkness. "Talk to me Ty. Tell me what I did so wrong that you can't stand to be with me anymore."

"Lexi," Ty growled, unable to stay away from her any longer. He lifted his hands and softly rubbed them up and down the length of her arms. "You didn't do anything, babe. It's all me."

"What's you, Ty. Please, tell me what's wrong so we can make it right," Lexi pleaded, stepping closer to him. "I miss you."

Lexi's scent filled Ty's senses, her warmth seeped into his soul, and he felt his resolve weaken. He hadn't counted on being this close to her. Resisting her when she was so real, so inviting, was impossible.

"Warm in here, isn't it?" Ty asked, running his hand through his hair and feeling like he was suffocating. Steadying himself against the door, he yanked off his coveralls in an effort to cool himself down, but it wasn't helping. Ty felt his temperature spike higher when Lexi leaned into him, wrapping her arms around his waist and holding on.

"Ty, just talk to me," she whispered, absorbing his strength, his vitality, his very essence. He wore a tank top and she could feel every deliciously carved muscle through his damp shirt. "Please?"

"You need to forget about me, Lexi. And if you need me to leave for that to happen, then I'll move back to Portland. I have to let you go," Ty said, in misery. He didn't want to leave. He didn't want Lexi to let go of him, ever.

"Why? Why do I need to forget about you Ty? Tell me why. There must be some reason," Lexi asked, desperate to know what had driven this wedge between them.

"It's me, Lexi. Can't you just leave it at that?"

"No, I can't. Everything was fine until we were coming home from the rodeo. Did Uncle Rob say something to upset you?"

Ty sighed and ran his hands through his hair again, even though Lexi still held to him tightly.

"No. No one in your family said anything," Ty said. "None of the guys said anything."

"Then who did? Who upset you?"

Trapped like they were in the shed with Lexi's persistent questioning, Ty decided to tell her the truth. "I don't know."

"What do you mean you don't know? You have to know," Lexi said, trying to make sense out of what Ty was saying.

"I overheard a couple of guys talking outside the café. What they were saying wasn't very nice about you and me... us," Ty said, trying to keep from getting angry all over again. "I don't want people to think I'm dating you because of who your dad was or how much money you have. The rumor seems to be that I charmed my way into your good graces just to get an easy ride. That isn't true, Lexi. I don't care if you're penniless. I …"

"You what?" Lexi asked.

"I wouldn't do that," Ty said, still trying to keep from revealing his heart to Lexi. If he did, he was afraid there'd be no turning back and he just couldn't do that to her. He didn't want her to feel obligated to him in any way.

"I know you wouldn't," Lexi said, hugging him and resting her head against his chest. She could feel his heart pounding fast beneath her ear. "I never thought you would, Ty. Why are you wasting so much time and effort in worrying about what other people think? It isn't any of your business, anyway. The only person you need to worry about is you."

"I know that, but what other people think can sure make things hard or easy on a person and I don't want things to be hard for you."

Lexi took Ty's face in her hands and breathed in his scent. "Look, buckaroo, if I'm hearing you correctly, you've spent the last month making us both miserable in some gallant, though completely idiotic effort to protect me from gossiping nitwits?"

"When you say it like that it sounds stupid," Ty said, growing agitated. He needed out of this shed. He needed

Lexi out of his arms. He needed... to kiss her so very badly.

"What's stupid is you letting this go on for a month when we could have had this conversation the day you got upset. So, now that I have assured you the gossiping doesn't bother me at all, are you done sulking?"

"I haven't been sulking," Ty argued, turning around and knocking a shovel and rake off the wall. He caught the handles before they smacked into Lexi. It was dangerous to be in the shed locked up in close proximity and that danger had little to do with garden tools and much more to do with his ability to maintain his control with Lexi. "And I can't date you anymore."

"Why not? Do you find me that disgusting? Unappealing? Annoying? What is it about me that's driving you away?" Lexi yelled, slapping at Ty's chest. She'd been down this road with men before. Eventually something turned them away from her, usually her heritage, although she wouldn't expect that from Ty. "What, Ty? Just tell me!"

"Nothing, babe," Ty said, gathering her into his arms and giving in to his desire to kiss her, just one more time. He devoured her lips, drank deeply from the honeyed sweetness that was all Lexi, and felt drunk from the experience. Finally breaking the contact, he put a hand to the back of her head and pulled her against his chest, holding her close. "There isn't a single thing about you that I don't find appealing. You drive me wild, Lexi Jo Ryan. Every laugh, every smile, every toss of your raven hair, every swing of that perfect posterior, every touch from your hand, and definitely every kiss. You make me forget anything else exists."

"Ty," Lexi breathed his name on a whisper, on a prayer. "Then what's the problem?"

"Me. The problem is me," Ty said, letting out long sigh. "There isn't a single thing, not one, that I can ever give you that you don't already have or can't buy yourself. I can't provide for you. I can't offer you anything. Except me."

"That is the only thing I'm ever going to want from you, Ty. Just you. I don't care about that other stuff. All I want is you."

"Lexi," Ty said, lowering his head to hers again, nearing the point of surrender.

"Ty, I think I'm falling in love with you," Lexi whispered, giving in to the temptation to bury her hands in Ty's hair and kissing his cheek.

"Good," Ty said, hugging her close again, pressing his lips to her neck. "I don't have to think, Lexi Jo. I know I'm in love with you."

"You are?" Lexi said, pulling back. "Really?"

"Yes, really. Do you think I would say it if I didn't mean it?" Ty asked, pulling her flush against him. The heat between the two of them might soon cause the shed to combust in flames.

"No, you generally say what you mean," Lexi said, resting her head on his chest again. "I'm so glad, Ty. I never expected to feel like this with anyone."

"Me either."

"So what are we…"

Whatever Lexi was going to say was lost when Ty kissed her urgently, passionately, wrapping his hands around her waist, drawing her so only a breath of space separated them. A spare garden hose slithered off a hook and wrapped around their feet.

Ty smiled against her lips. "The first thing we are going to do is bust out of here if I have to drive the mower through the door. It's hotter than a hat maker's box on the 4th of July, as Swede would say, and I'm going to be beaten to death by your garden tools if we don't leave soon."

Lexi laughed and stepped back into the rototiller.

Ty stood at the door and tried to decide if the dog was still sitting in front of it.

"Baby, I'm coming out so you better move. I'm not kidding around," Ty cautioned before giving the door a hard shove. It flew open and banged back against the front of the shed. Fresh air flooded over him and he sucked in a big gulp.

Looking behind him, he held a hand out to Lexi. She grinned and took it, tugging him toward the house with the promise of some iced tea and cookies for his trouble.

Going in the back door to the kitchen, Ty washed up while Lexi filled glasses with ice and poured tea. He sat down at the counter on a bar stool while she put cookies on a plate. When she tried to sit down beside him, he pulled her onto his lap and nuzzled her neck.

"I don't want you that far away," he whispered in her ear, making her shiver.

She held her glass of tea to her throat, trying to cool herself down, although with Ty alternately nibbling cookies and her ear, it was difficult.

"What were you doing in the shed, anyway?" Ty asked, taking a deep drink of the tea.

"I found another clue," Lexi said, digging a scrap of paper from her pocket. She laid it on the counter and Ty read the note:

Mowing Away the Competition

"I assumed it meant something to do with the lawn mower or the garden shed," Lexi said, looking at Ty. Staring into his hot, bright eyes, she forgot about the lost money, about their lost month together and enjoyed being right where she was at that very moment.

"It would make sense," Ty said, studying the words. From past experience, he knew what Lex wrote wasn't necessarily what he meant. "Beyond the lawn mower, what things mow here on the ranch?"

"The swather, the weed beater we use on the ditches, the cattle themselves mow down the grass. Why couldn't he just have left a note that said, 'I hid the money in a box. Here's the map. Good luck.'"

"I think your dad was having a little fun with you," Ty said with a grin.

"This is ridiculous and insane," Lexi huffed, frustrated. Each time she found a clue, she thought it would be the last one. It just led to another and another.

"How about I help you go look again? I'm assuming you weren't quite through when Baby ran her little play on us," Ty said, finishing his tea and intently focusing on placing as many kisses as he could on Lexi's neck before she began squirming on his lap.

"That would be great," Lexi said, jumping to her feet. "Let's go."

Ty kissed her again, so thoroughly Lexi felt her knees tremble.

"Come on, Nancy Drew," he teased, taking a series of deep breaths to cool his ardor as he led her out the door.

Taking a flashlight to the shed, Ty climbed up to the loft area and looked around. One small tool box was the only thing of interest to him and he handed it down to Lexi. The lid was padlocked shut so they took it to the shop where Ty cut it off.

Inside the box was an assortment of antique hand tools and a small envelope.

Lexi took the envelope in her hand and sighed, looking over the tools.

"Those belonged to my great-grandfather," Lexi said, running her hand over the motley assortment of once useful pieces. "Daddy said he learned how to use a tool properly by playing with these as a boy."

"That's a box full of your family history, Lexi. Just think of the hands that smoothed these handles," Ty said, reverently picking up a hammer. The handle was grooved from being held in sweaty hands for so many years.

"Let's see what this says," Lexi said carefully opening the envelope. A small slip of notebook paper was tucked inside.

Don't Mess with the Boss

"Well, isn't that helpful," Lexi said dryly, angry at her father over the latest set of clues. Anyone who knew Lex already knew no one messed with the boss. She liked to think her hired hands followed that rule with her as well.

"Don't discount it yet," Ty said, holding the paper in his big hand. "It could mean more than you think it does."

Rubbing her hands across her eyes, Lexi released a tired sigh.

"I can't keep chasing something that isn't there, Ty. I give up. Maybe someday we'll find the money, maybe we won't, but I give up."

"No one said you had to find it right now, did they? If finances are tight, cut my pay. I can work in the evenings for some of the neighbors doing repair jobs if you need extra money," Ty said, giving her a comforting hug.

"Ty Lewis, you can't be real." Lexi looked at him with teary eyes. He had just proven to her that he truly loved her. Not her money, not her ranch, not her supposed social standing. He loved her. "Thank you for the sweet offer, but we aren't hurting for money, buckaroo. It just bothers me to have it hanging out there. I'm afraid of what could happen if someone else found it."

"Then I guess we'll just need to work closely together to figure this out sooner rather than later," Ty said, thinking he had a few ideas on what Lex was really trying to tell them.

Lesson Eighteen
Never Stop Learning

*"If there's somethin' ya don't know,
git out there and find out all ya can about it."*

"It can't be as bad as all that," Jan commented to Ty as he lingered over his cup of breakfast coffee. "She'll be home soon enough."

Ty lifted his head and looked at the housekeeper as she finished her own coffee and carried dirty dishes to the kitchen sink.

"How'd you know?" Ty asked, picking up a stack of dishes and carrying them in for her.

"I may be older, but I was young and in love once. I also raised five kids. I know the signs," Jan said, giving Ty a pat on his back. She knew she shouldn't play favorites but the big, quiet man was always so thoughtful and helpful. As Swede would say, he was just a good egg. It didn't hurt that his smile could charm the birds out of the trees or the blue of his eyes could entrance any female regardless of her age.

Ty grinned and helped finish clearing off the table before he went out for the day. Things were pretty quiet on the ranch right now.

According to Swede, they'd start haying again in about a week and things would really get busy. The guys were caught up on fence repairs and Ty was finished with equipment repairs, unless Cal tore something else up today.

Those without anything better to do were mucking stalls, cleaning tack, and riding horses that hadn't been ridden as much as they should.

Gus volunteered to work around the ranch yard pulling weeds and tending to the landscaping. Ty thought it was the notion of being closer to Jan, not the flowers that sparked Gus' sudden interest in staying closer to the home place.

Swede gave Ty permission a couple of months ago to work on a surprise for Lexi in his spare time. So without her knowing about it, he had been slowly restoring her dad's old mustang.

Lexi left three days ago for a cattleman's meeting near Pendleton. She was going to spend a few days visiting with Bertie and Linc before the meeting began then come straight home afterward.

Ty missed her more than he thought he could possibly miss anyone with her gone. It had been two weeks since he came to his senses and told her he loved her. Without ranch work to keep him busy and distracted from his thoughts of Lexi, he decided to work on the car.

Swede thought it was a great project and helped him tow the car into the shop before the dust from Lexi's truck quit swirling down the driveway. Lex had, at some point before he died, ordered all the necessary repair parts, including a new engine for the car as well as new upholstery and interior linings. Although he'd made a lot of headway in his spare time restoring the car, it would be a lot easier to get the job done in the shop.

Able to finish up everything that needed done under the hood before he went to bed last night, Ty and Swede took the car for a quick test drive.

"Woohee, son, this ol' car is smooth. I'm not sure she sounded this good brand spankin' new!" Swede said as they pulled out on the highway. Ty slowly worked up to speed, but then let the accelerator hit the floor and they zoomed across the desert highway. "I plumb forgot what a fun car this was. I don't remember the seats being so almighty lumpy, though."

Driving back to the ranch, Ty could hardly go to sleep when he finally got to bed. He was too wound up about finishing the restoration project.

Now, with the early morning light sending the dust motes into a frenzied dance in the shop, Ty tackled the interior work. The final touch would be a paint job. Swede found someone in Burns who could do it and the car would go in first thing in the morning. The shop promised to have it done so they could bring it home the following day before Lexi returned to the ranch.

Smiling as he started pulling up the ratty carpet from the floorboards, Ty listened to his music and mused about how much his life had changed in such a short period of time.

Taking a break to gulp down water and stand in front of the air conditioner in the shop window, he called Beth to check in with her. She was on her morning break and rushed, but she made time to visit with him for a few minutes.

"Lexi will be so surprised about the car, Ty. I think it's just great you are doing this for her," Beth said, enjoying the unexpected call from Ty.

"I hope so. I wanted to do something nice for her. Something unexpected," Ty said, wiping the sweat from his forehead onto his bare arm. He'd taken to wearing sleeveless coveralls with a tank top as the summer heat permeated every building on the ranch. "I wish Mom could see this car, Beth. She would have loved it. You know how she always had a thing for muscle cars."

"Yeah, she did. I don't know what it was with her and the cars and the rock music. Guess that's why you turned out the way you did," Beth teased.

"What's wrong with that?" Ty asked, trying to sound wounded.

"Not a thing, sweet brother, not a single thing. Now tell me what is so special about this car, other than Lexi's dad owned it."

"It's a Mustang Boss. Limited production. It could mow down the competition without even…" Ty stopped when all of the puzzle pieces Lex left behind suddenly fit into place. So excited, he could barely stand still. "Say, Beth, I just realized I've got something I need to take care of, but thanks so much for your help."

"My help?" Beth asked, confused. "But, Ty…"

"Love you, Bethie, I'll talk to you soon. Give Jax a hug from his favorite uncle."

"Okay, bye."

Ty mentally ran through all the clues Lex left behind. How did he not see this before, especially with the last clue about not messing with the boss? Standing next to the car, he wondered where Lex hid the money. He knew it wasn't under the hood because he had been through every square inch of space there. It had to either be in the trunk or inside the car.

Deciding to just continue on with what he started, Ty worked with a renewed purpose and vigor that soon had the carpets ripped out. He removed the dash and door panels, the fabric lining of the roof and saved the seats for last. It would be easier to take the seats out to recover them so he loosened the bolts and soon had the front driver's seat out of the car.

Moving over to the front passenger seat, it felt heavier than the driver's seat. Tipping it forward to drag it through the passenger side door, he laughed when he saw a lumpy duffle bag stuffed up inside the seat. No wonder Swede complained about it being uncomfortable the night before. It looked like Lex cut a hole beneath the seat, pulled out some of the foam and stuffed in the bag of money.

Clever as long as Lexi didn't get rid of the car, which Lex must have known she would never do.

Pulling out the bag, Ty gasped when he opened it to be greeted by stacks and stacks of $100 bills. He'd never dreamed of seeing so much money in one place in his entire life and took a moment to look at it. He wondered how Lex had acquired all that cash. It surely didn't come from banks in Burns. Did the sick man drive to Bend to do his banking? He surely didn't walk into one bank and tell them he wanted to cash $500,000 in checks. Even if he had it electronically deposited to his account, how did you go in and request half a million dollars in cash?

His palms began to sweat as he zipped the top on the bag. The big question now was where to stash the money until Lexi got home and he could hand it over to her. It needed to be somewhere secure. Somewhere no one would look. Holding the bag in one hand as he looked around the shop, Ty felt a warm presence bump his leg.

"Hey, Baby. What are you doing?" Ty asked, absently rubbing her head. Baby sniffed the duffle bag and whined, looking up at Ty with big, sad eyes.

"I know you miss him, Baby," Ty said, patting her sides and stroking her head gently. "Where shall we hide this for Lexi? Where's a good hiding spot, Baby?"

The dog barked and looked in the direction of Ty's tool chests. Of course! They locked, no one bothered them and the money should be perfectly safe there until Lexi returned. Taking out his keys, he unlocked one and moved his tools around until he could get the bag inside, then locked it up.

He'd barely returned the keys to his pocket when Swede came whistling in the shop door.

"Look at thet. Yer really makin' headway, dude."

298

"I'm trying," Ty said, trying to hide his nervousness. He didn't know why, but finding the money and having it in his possession was causing him feel a sense of panic. What if he lost it? What if something happened to it?

He didn't want to be responsible for all that money and wished Lexi would just hurry up and come home.

"Need any help?" Swede asked, looking at the seat that hung part-way out the door.

"Sure. I'm trying to get the seats out of the car so we can put new upholstery on them. It shouldn't take long to do it if you have time to help me."

"Let's git 'er done," Swede said, rolling up his shirt sleeves and grabbing one end of the seat.

By lunch time, they had the front seats finished and were part-way done with the back. Ty made sandwiches from the supplies he kept in the shop fridge and he and Swede sat drinking icy-cold pop while Baby sat at their feet whining.

"What's wrong with the dog?" Swede said, rubbing her back with the toe of his boot.

"She's been whining like that since she came in the shop. Maybe it's the car. I'm sure she connects it with Mr. Ryan." Ty didn't know a lot about animals, but Baby seemed to have many of the same emotions as a human. He'd seen her happy, sad, pouting, teasing. It made sense that she would miss her master, too.

"Yer probably right," Swede said, finishing his sandwich and dusting off his hands. "Let's git back at this. We should be able to git the inside done before dinner time, don't ya think?"

"I do. And I appreciate your help. I know this doesn't have anything to do with ranch work, but…" Ty started to say, but Swede didn't let him finish.

"It'll make the boss happy and thet's more important than anythin'. I'm as anxious as a pig at a bacon factory to git this thing done and back in the garage before the boss gits home," Swede said as he and Ty got back to work.

Swede followed Ty into town early the next morning to drop off the car to be painted. The shop owner couldn't stop gaping at the car when Ty drove up.

"Man, if you ever need a job, let me know," the guy said, taking the keys from Ty. "Ol' Lex wasn't sure he'd ever get this thing running again and you've got it purring like a kitten. I'll make sure it gets painted exactly like he would have wanted."

"Thanks," Ty said, getting in the ranch pickup with Swede. They stopped and picked up some supplies at the feed store before heading back to the Rockin' R.

They repeated the trip the next morning and Ty couldn't stop smiling when he saw the car wearing a new coat of black paint that matched the original color. Driving down the street to the tire store, he put four new tires on the car, made a couple other stops, and then drove it home.

Lexi was due to be back late that afternoon and he had more than one surprise he was planning for her.

Ty was just closing the garage door when Lexi sent him a text message.

"Buckaroo, miss you! Can't wait to see you."

Grinning, Ty texted her back. *"Miss you, too. Call me when you're an hour out."*

"Okay! Love you!"

Looking at his watch, Ty needed to hurry through his list of duties for the day if he was going to have everything ready by the time Lexi got home.

Lesson Nineteen
Ask and Ye Shall Receive

"Ya want something, ya can't pussyfoot around it.
Ask for what ya want from the git-go."

Taking a deep breath, Ty looked around Lexi's kitchen and hoped she wouldn't mind him invading her home and making dinner. By the time the evening was through, he was pretty sure she wouldn't care at all.

Earlier in the afternoon, he spent some time prepping what he could of the meal, putting together a green salad and making a batch of fudge brownies. Ty set the table and made sure his surprises were in place for the big evening ahead.

When Lexi called to say she was almost to Burns, Ty hustled to the bunkhouse, took a quick shower and shaved, then returned to Lexi's where he made spaghetti carbonara and tried to calm his nerves.

He knew Lexi would probably want a shower when she got home, so he planned to have the food ready to eat about thirty minutes after her arrival.

Wiping down the counters, making sure everything looked perfect, he heard Lexi drive up in her dad's pickup. He smiled as he remembered her saying it wouldn't do at all to show up to a meeting of good ol' boys and cattlemen driving her little sports car.

Drying his hands, he waited for her to come in the door. She walked in dragging her suitcase behind her.

SHANNA HATFIELD

Dressed in a business suit with her hair piled into a French twist on her head, she looked tired and overheated.

Lexi pulled up short when she saw the table set for dinner and turned with a surprised smile as she noticed Ty standing in the kitchen.

"Welcome home, Lexi Jo," he said opening his arms to her. It was all the invitation she needed to drop her purse and step into the warmth and wonder that was Ty.

"I missed you, buckaroo," Lexi said, kissing his jaw and inhaling deeply of his fresh, clean scent. She could also smell something delicious cooking and raised an eyebrow at him. "Did you make me dinner?"

"Yeah. I hope you don't mind. I didn't want to have to share you this evening," Ty said, nodding toward the stove. "It won't be ready for a few minutes. I thought you might like a little time to freshen up before we eat."

"You read my mind," Lexi said, giving him a kiss that let him know just how much she had missed him. "I'll be right back."

Lugging her suitcase to the stairs, Lexi hauled it up as fast as she could, giddy at the idea of spending the evening alone with Ty.

The past couple of weeks with him had been the happiest of her life. Although they didn't have much time for dating, they managed to do something together every day even if it was riding out to check fences or her handing him tools in the shop as he made equipment repairs.

She knew without a doubt she loved Ty and wanted him to be a permanent part of her life.

Hurrying to the bathroom in her room, Lexi took a fast shower and washed her hair. She towel dried her raven tresses, letting the waves and curls do what they willed. Putting on mascara, lip gloss, and a few strategic touches of perfume, she slipped on a cotton summer dress and wedge sandals before going down the stairs.

"I hope you made plenty. I'm half starved, buckaroo," Lexi called as she took the last steps of the stairs and returned to the kitchen. Ty had drawn the shades and darkened the room so that the candles flickering on the table created a warm, romantic glow. Two plates piled with pasta, bowls filled with green salad, and a basket with warm bread waited at two place settings.

"I did," Ty said, turning from where he was pouring sparkling lemonade into two flute glasses. When he saw Lexi he almost dropped the glasses. She looked so fresh and pretty in her light yellow dress, especially with the way it contrasted against her bronzed skin. "Wow, Lexi! You look beautiful," he said, handing her one of the glasses.

"Thank you, kind sir," Lexi said, threading her arm through his as they walked to the table. He pulled out her chair and waited for her to take her seat before he sat down beside her. She waved her arm around the table. "So what is all this for? What are we celebrating?"

"You," Ty said, rubbing a thumb over her high cheekbone before giving her a soft, gentle kiss. He tipped his glass to hers in a toast.

Lexi's eyelids lowered as she savored his touch. "Why me?"

"Why not?" Ty asked with a teasing smile. "Come on and eat my feast before it gets cold," he said, taking her hand and offering grace for the meal.

Ty asked about her conference, how Bertie and Linc were doing and anything interesting she saw while she was gone. She asked him about what he'd done while she was out of town and things about the ranch that Ty was sure Swede already told her.

Finishing up their meal, Lexi leaned back in the chair, full and happy. Unable to keep her gaze from Ty's bright blue eyes, she took in his hair that had been trimmed since she left. His eyes were glittering with warmth and love while a smile teased the corners of his mouth.

Surprisingly, he was wearing the blue-striped western shirt that was her favorite because it brought out the color of his eyes. Jeans and boots, polished to an impressive shine, completed the all-too enticing package that was Ty.

Expecting him to be wearing a T-shirt, shorts and flip flops, Lexi wouldn't complain at all about Ty's current attire. She loved it when he dressed in cowboy mode, as he called it. She was pretty sure if Wrangler ever ran out of models for their jeans, Ty would do a great job representing them.

"Lexi Jo," Ty rumbled, staring into her gold-flecked green eyes and falling into the inviting depths. He wanted to show her exactly how much he missed her when she was gone, but decided to behave himself. For now.

Drawn to him by a force she couldn't explain, Lexi leaned toward him until she felt their lips connect and explosions of fire and ice burst around them. She didn't know how it happened, but her next thought was that she liked being on Ty's lap, closely wrapped up in his arms as he kissed her face and neck before returning to her lips.

Suddenly, he pulled back, burying his face in her neck. He said something she couldn't hear so she lifted his head up and looked into his eyes, now ablaze with fire and longing.

"I couldn't hear you," she said, kissing him again.

Nipping at her bottom lip, he took another kiss from her before setting her on her feet, getting up, and taking her hand.

"Let's do these dishes then I might have a surprise or two for you," Ty said, carrying plates to the sink.

"You mean this fantastic dinner wasn't my surprise?" Lexi asked as she helped place dishes in the dishwasher and put leftovers away.

"No, ma'am. That was just a prelude to the real surprises," Ty said with a mischievous grin.

"That was a pretty awesome prelude," Lexi said as they finished the dishes and dried their hands. "You can cook for me anytime, buckaroo."

"I have a very limited collection of recipes, so don't get any wild ideas about my cooking abilities," Ty said, taking her hand and escorting her back to the kitchen table where the candles still flickered. Kissing her cheek, he smiled. "Now cover your eyes and you can have your first surprise."

"How many surprises are there?" Lexi asked, wondering what had gotten into Ty. She'd never seen him act like this before. He seemed excited, nervous, and happy all at once.

"Three," Ty said as he picked up the duffle bag with the money from the pantry where he hid it when he came in to cook dinner. Carrying it to the table, he set it down in front of Lexi. "Okay, open your eyes."

Lexi looked from the duffle bag to Ty and back again, confused.

"Just open the top," Ty said, fighting the urge to unzip the bag for her.

"Ty, what could you…" Lexi asked as she tugged on the zipper then gasped as she realized she was looking at a bag full of money. Her dad's hidden money. Turning bright eyes to Ty she grinned. "You did it! You found the money!"

Throwing her arms around his neck, she hugged him tightly before turning her attention back to the money. "Where did you find it? How did you find it? Does anyone else know?"

Ty laughed at her excitement and gave her a moment to get used to the idea of having half a million dollars on the table in front of her before he said anything.

"No one else knows about it. Beth said something that finally helped all the clues make sense and it didn't take long to find it after that," Ty said, taking Lexi's hand and pulling her to her feet before blowing out the candles on the table. "Where I found it has something to do with your second surprise. Would you like to see?"

"Yes, please," Lexi said, watching as Ty zipped up the bag and returned it to the pantry. She was still processing the idea that the money had finally been found. And it was in a duffle bag. In her pantry.

"No sense tempting anyone," Ty said closing the pantry door and leading Lexi outside around the house toward the garage.

Fortunately, none of the other hands seemed to be out and about so they made it to the side door without interruption. Ty had no doubt they were all sitting in the bunkhouse watching out the windows.

"So my second surprise is in the garage?" she asked, wondering what could be in the garage. There wasn't anything in there but her car and her dad's rusty old mustang. "No one messed with my car, did they?"

"No, nothing like that," Ty assured her as they stepped inside. Ty and Swede carefully covered the freshly painted car with a new cover, instead of the raggedy one that had covered the mustang for way too long.

"You bought a new cover for dad's car," Lexi said, immediately noticing the change.

"Yes, I did, but that isn't the surprise," Ty said, trying to keep from bursting with excitement.

"You found the money in here? In the garage?" Lexi asked, looking around.

"No," Ty said, drawing out the suspense.

"No? Then what are we doing in here?" Lexi asked, wishing Ty would just tell her where he found the money. She was dying to know and she wanted to get on with the rest of her surprises. Lexi didn't know how he could top finding the money, but she was game to let him try.

"I found the money in your dad's car. Think about the clues, especially the last one about not messing with the boss," Ty said, walking Lexi over to the mustang. "It all made perfect sense once I figured out it was the car."

Lexi stared at him and shook her head. How had she missed what her dad had been saying all along? How had she missed finding the money in the car? She'd gone over it with a fine-tooth comb when she first started looking for the money and never found a thing.

"Where was the money hidden?" Lexi finally asked as she pulled on the car cover. She sucked in a gulp of air and her eyes grew wide in surprise as she took in the shiny black paint. She assumed the car looked just like it did when her dad drove it off the lot brand new. No wonder he'd loved it.

Ty yanked the cover all the way off the car so Lexi could get a good look at it. When her eyes filled with tears, he walked over to her, pulling her to his chest.

"You like it?" he asked quietly, gently rubbing her back and shoulders.

"Ty, when did you… how did you…," she tried to ask around the lump in her throat. She had no idea when Ty found the time or money to restore the car her dad loved so much. It meant more to her than any gift he could possibly give her. Finally, she let out a ragged breath. "Thank you."

"You're welcome, babe," Ty said, kissing her forehead and turning so they were both looking at the car. It did look good. Really good.

"Come on, you have to check it all out," Ty said, opening the driver's door so she could look inside.

"Where did dad stash the money?" Lexi asked sitting down on the smooth leather of the driver's seat, inhaling the scents of new upholstery and carpet. She took in the new dash and door panels. Ty had even put in new lining along the roof, new rubber seals around the doors and somehow managed to get all the goo off the gear shift that accumulated there after years of use.

"Under the passenger seat. He cut out some of the foam and stuffed the money up in there. Unless you removed the seat, you would never have found it," Ty said, leaning on the door and soaking in the pleasure lighting Lexi's big green eyes. Looking up at him she grinned.

"Well, I think we should take it for a spin. I want to see how good this mechanic is that worked on it. Everyone keeps bragging about his talents, but I want to see for myself," Lexi teased as Ty winked at her and closed her door. He opened the garage doors and waited for her to back out before climbing in the passenger side.

"You better buckle that seatbelt, buckaroo," Lexi teased as she put the car in gear and gingerly drove down the driveway. She waited until they were out on the open road to put the car through its paces. She liked the way it handled every bit as much as her Nismo.

They drove almost to Hines before Lexi turned around and headed for home.

"I can't believe you did all this," Lexi commented to Ty as they turned off on the ranch road. "It means so much to me."

"I know, Lexi," Ty said, taking her hand in his and kissing her palm. The touch of his lips to her hand sent a shiver racing through her and she turned her warm gaze his direction. He met her eyes with a hot blue light shining in his own. "Swede helped me, though, so he gets half the credit."

"I know he didn't do half the work. He can barely figure out how to use a wrench, let alone anything else mechanical," Lexi said as they neared the ranch yard. The hands came running out to admire the car and for the next several moments, Lexi let them all take turns sitting in it and commenting on the car. Swede finally herded them all back toward the bunkhouse with a wink Ty's direction.

Lexi drove the car back into the garage while Ty closed the door then helped put the cover back over the mustang.

Walking out the side door, Lexi looped her arm through Ty's and leaned her head against his shoulder.

"You're amazing, you know that?" Lexi said as they strolled back through the yard and up the porch steps.

"Nope," Ty said, holding open the back door for her.

"I don't know anyone else who could have done what you did to dad's car. It would have cost me a fortune to have someone restore it," Lexi said, walking into the kitchen and pouring them both glasses of iced tea.

"It was a labor of love," Ty said with a smile that nearly made Lexi drop her tea. Getting a better grip on the cold glass, she held it to her throat, hoping to cool off a bit. Her insides felt like they were on a slow simmer, getting hotter and more molten by the minute.

"Want some dessert?" Ty asked, washing his hands at the sink and sliding a foil-covered pan across the counter in her direction.

"Sure," Lexi said, reaching for the pan. "What did you make?"

"Brownies. Special brownies," Ty said, taking a plate out of the cupboard and setting it down by the baking pan Lexi was uncovering.

"What's so special about them?" she asked. Before Ty could respond, Lexi took off the foil and set it aside, picking up a knife. Holding it poised over the pan of brownies, she slowly set it back down on the counter and looked from the pan to Ty and back again.

"Do you mean it, Ty?" she asked, unbelieving of what she was seeing. There, in the chocolate frosting covering the brownies, Ty had spelled out "marry me" with M&Ms.

"Absolutely," Ty said, removing his hand from where it was fishing in his pocket and dropping to one knee. He took her left hand in his and slid a ring on her finger that fit perfectly. "Lexi Jo Ryan, I love you more than anything in this world. I can't live without you and I don't even want to try. Will you please marry me? I don't have a thing to offer you except my love. I hope you'll accept it for the rest of your lifetime."

Lexi couldn't speak, could barely think. She pulled on Ty's hand, and he got to his feet, looking at her expectantly. Instead of answering him, she threw her arms around his neck and squeezed, laughing and crying against him before covering his face in kisses.

"Does that mean yes?" Ty asked with a deep chuckle that made Lexi's knees wobble.

"Yes," she whispered. "Yes, forever yes. But on one condition."

"What's that?" Ty said, pushing her back far enough so he could look in her eyes.

"Soon," Lexi said with an impish grin. "I don't want a long engagement. The sooner I belong to you, the happier I'll be."

Ty looked at her in surprise then pulled her flush against him, sealing the deal with a kiss that left them both breathless.

"I'd be happy to oblige, ma'am," Ty said, in his best imitation of a drawl. "Ya'll just tell me when and where to show up."

"You can count on it, buckaroo."

Lesson Twenty

Happily Ever After Isn't Just for Fairytales

*"Woohee, pard! Ya been worse than a love-sick pup
since ya set eyes on thet sweet lil' gal."*

The last Saturday in July, a day according to Swede
that was hot enough to make a cactus sweat, was a perfect
day in Ty's opinion.

At eleven that morning, Lexi would march down the
aisle set up in the yard at the ranch house and vow to love
him until death do they part.

It was a quarter past ten now and Ty had been forced
to stay in the bunkhouse by Jan so he wouldn't catch a
glimpse of Lexi before the ceremony.

He didn't bother to tell the woman that he'd talked to
his bride-to-be no less than five times that morning already
and she'd sent him three text messages.

Sitting down with a glass of tea and a cookie, Ty
mused over how much his life had changed in such a few
short months. In February he was homeless, desperate and
without a plan for his future. Now he had a job he enjoyed
in a place that he never wanted to leave with a woman who
whispered to his soul.

A firm slap to his shoulder brought him out of his
musings and nearly made him choke on the cookie.

"You ready for this?" Nate asked as he took a cookie off the platter on the table and helped himself to a glass of tea.

"Absolutely," Ty said with a grin. He was so glad Nate, Beth and baby Jax were able to come for the wedding. Nate would serve as his best man while Beth stood up with Lexi. The ceremony was going to be small and intimate with a larger gathering of neighbors and friends for the reception that would immediately follow.

Large tents were set up around the ranch yard with plenty of room for everyone. The reception was to begin at noon, giving the bridal party time for photos to be taken before all the guests arrived.

There would be a catered barbecue meal and a dance floor had been set up, even if Ty couldn't imagine anyone would be crazy enough to dance out in the heat today. Although large fans were blowing air around in the tents, Ty figured they better have plenty of beverages and ice on hand because people were going to get overheated.

When he proposed to Lexi a month ago, he wasn't sure what she meant by wanting to get married soon. He had no idea he would be anxiously awaiting the moment he said "I do" just four weeks later.

Thinking about how she tackled the wedding with the same organized, get-it-done attitude she brought to everything made him smile. She included him in the plans, of course, but he didn't care what she wanted to do as long as the end result was them being married.

Keeping his hands off his very tempting fiancée had been an excruciating challenge, but he made it.

At three o'clock, no matter who was there or what was going on, they were leaving for a four-day honeymoon in Sisters, Oregon, where he reserved a romantic cabin right on the edge of the Deschutes National Forest. While wildlife lingered just steps away from the patio door, the property where they were staying offered a resort complete with a spa, movie theater and restaurant. He didn't think they would suffer from a lack of things to do, should they find the need to leave their room.

Thoughts of the honeymoon must have made him flush, because Nate grinned at him and slapped his back again.

"I see you're concentrating on all the really important details of today," Nate said with a teasing grin. "You sure you're grown up enough to be a fit husband?"

Ty glared at his brother-in-law and friend.

"You know I'm kidding with you," Nate said, taking another cookie. "Your sister is about to bust her buttons, she is so proud of you and excited for you. We both are."

"Thanks, man," Ty said, leaning back in his chair. "Of all the places I thought I'd end up, I never imagined it would be here."

"Yeah. Who could have predicted you'd be a homeless man living in your pickup, move to the middle of nowhere, fall in love with a beautiful cowgirl and somehow talk her into marrying you."

"Why does it not sound quite so fantastic when you put it like that?" Ty said with a chuckle. "Lexi likes to make it sound like a fairytale. You know, happily ever after and all that."

"I know," Nate said. "Of all the people who deserve to be happy, Ty, you are at the top of the list."

"Now, don't go getting all mushy on me like the girls," Ty said, imagining the female emotions on the rampage up at the ranch house.

Not only was Beth there with baby Jax, but all of Lexi's female cousins, aunts and grandmother Sunny were there as well.

Sunny flew in to Redmond three days ago and Lexi and Ty picked her up at the airport. Ty wasn't sure what to expect, but he would have known the older woman even if she and Lexi hadn't been waving to each other, laughing and crying. They looked exactly alike. Realizing with a smile that his soon-to-be-wife was going to be a very lovely woman even in old age, Ty waited for Sunny to finish hugging and kissing Lexi before she turned her attention to him.

"Well, good gracious, girlie, you certainly picked a looker, didn't you?" Sunny said studying him for a moment. "Give your new grandma a hug, sweet thing."

Ty gently hugged the vivacious woman, inhaling the soft scent of roses and absorbing her welcoming warmth. Before he could let her go she pulled his head down and whispered in his ear. "You're going to take good care of this girl of mine, aren't you, Tyler?"

"Yes, ma'am. I plan to cherish her every day for the rest of our lives," Ty whispered.

"Good boy," Sunny said, kissing his cheek and threading her arm through his. Squeezing his bicep, she glanced up at him with a saucy grin Ty had seen before on Lexi's face. "Nice guns."

"Grandma!" Lexi exclaimed, shaking her head at her grandmother.

"Oh, hush, girlie," Sunny said stepping away from Ty and walking around him in a circle, surveying him like she would a prized bull. Ty was dressed in Wranglers, a snap-front shirt, polished boots and his Stetson. Anyone unaware of his background would never know he wasn't an authentic born-to-ride cowboy.

Pursing her lips together, Sunny nodded her head approvingly. "I do believe, Tyler Lewis, that you will more than do, especially with a tushie like that."

"Grandma!" Lexi said, her face flaming red as she grabbed her grandmother's arm and nearly dragged her out to Ty's pickup. Ty picked up Sunny's luggage, hiding his embarrassment, although he was pleased that he had passed the older woman's inspection.

In the few days she'd been out at the ranch, Ty had felt a connection to Sunny. Maybe it was because he missed having a grandmother or because they shared the same sense of humor, or because she and Lexi were so much alike. Whatever it was, they hit it off and had spent many hours laughing and joking, much to Lexi's enjoyment and dismay when the teasing turned to her.

Now, as Ty and Nate sat waiting for the signal it was time to assemble in the yard, Ty couldn't help but wonder what Sunny was saying to Lexi.

"Aren't you nervous, girlie?" Sunny asked as she helped Lexi settle the veil on her head. Standing before the full-length cheval mirror in the master bedroom, Lexi sighed with contentment as her grandmother leaned over her shoulder and peered in the mirror with Lexi.

For Lexi it was looking into her future, for Sunny it was a chance to see into her past. They both smiled warmly.

"Why would I be nervous?" Lexi asked adjusting the veil so it sat more firmly on her head. Her grandmother had chased everyone else out of the room so they could have a moment together. Lexi appreciated the quiet after having her aunts and cousins flitting around her all morning.

Sunny fussed with her skirt then stood back and surveyed the picture Lexi made in her white taffeta mermaid-style gown. With cap sleeves and a simple bodice, the skirt was made of crisp individually sewn pieces of taffeta in a layered pattern that hugged her trim figure before belling out at mid-thigh. Lexi's luxurious raven hair was piled high on her head in a profusion of curls with tendrils escaping down her back. A diamond necklace that belonged to her mother encircled her neck. It

315

had been the gift her dad gave her mom on their wedding day. Her bouquet was a simple bunch of coral roses.

"I'd be nervous if I had a man as fine as that Tyler Lewis waiting downstairs to wed me," Sunny said, fanning her face with a lace handkerchief. "My stars, but he is a handsome thing. And such a big man, to boot. Now your grandpa, he was quite a catch in his day, too. I was more wound up than a prize heifer in a bull pen the day we got married. I suppose you already know what you need to know about the honeymoon. If not, I'll give you some pointers."

"Grandma!" Lexi said trying to hide her smile. She thought she'd said it a hundred times if she'd said it once in the last few days. Her grandmother had a habit of saying the most shocking things, or at least they were supposed to be shocking. Lexi was silently amused much more than she should have been. Especially by the way her grandmother and Ty got along so well. That pleased her more than anything.

"Honestly, honey, are you scared or nervous?" Sunny asked, taking Lexi by the shoulders and looking her in the face.

"No, Grandma," Lexi said, smiling dreamily, thinking of her groom. "I can't wait to marry him. We're going to be wonderfully happy together."

"I quite think you will be, sugar. You couldn't have found a better man to marry."

"Thanks, Grandma. That means a lot to me," Lexi said, starting to feel emotional.

"Before we make our mascara run, let's just cut this off right now," Sunny said with a choppy laugh. "I'll go find your aunts and see if they are ready to get this show on the road. It's almost time."

Lexi gave her grandmother a warm hug just as Beth knocked on the door and came in, carrying Jax.

"Oh, give that precious boy to me," Sunny said, sweeping him up on her way out the door. "I could just eat you up, little man."

Beth handed over the baby and smiled at Sunny's back as she hurried out the door.

"Your grandmother seems to have decided Jax is part of her brood as well," Beth said, staring at Lexi. She didn't think she'd ever seen a more beautiful bride. Ty was going to hyperventilate when he saw Lexi. Just thinking of his reaction made Beth smile widely.

"Yes, Grandma thinks you all are special," Lexi said, smiling back at Beth and stretching out a hand toward her. "Thank you for standing up with me. I feel like we've already become good friends and I'm so excited to finally have a sister."

"Me, too," Beth said, carefully hugging Lexi so she didn't crush her dress.

"Are you ready for this?"

"Absolutely," Lexi said, giving one last glance in the mirror, hoping Ty liked her dress and the way she looked.

"Swede has been pacing a groove in the floor waiting for you to come down," Beth said, helping Lexi adjust her gown as she strode out the bedroom door. "I think it is so sweet you asked him to walk you down the aisle.

"Well, I couldn't very well ask one uncle and not all of them," Lexi whispered as they walked down the stairs. "Besides, he's been like a second father to me since I was born."

As they reached the bottom step, Swede turned and a look of fatherly pride settled on his weathered face.

"Woohee! If ya don't look like somethin' out of a magazine, I don't know who does," Swede said as his eyes got moist. "Yer daddy would be so proud, boss. Ya done good in yer choosing."

317

"Thank you, Swede," Lexi said, kissing his cheek. "And thank you for everything, including walking me down the aisle."

"I'm right honored ya asked," Swede said, straightening his jacket as he held out his arm.

"That tux looks really nice," Lexi said, knowing Swede had originally balked at the idea of wearing a "monkey suit," as he called it.

"It does, don't it," Swede commented as he led her toward the front door.

Lexi's Aunt Bertie waited for the signal to begin the processional music. Lexi would walk down the front porch steps on Swede's arm, across the lawn and down the aisle created with a gossamer runner to where Ty waited with Nate and the pastor beneath the rose arbor.

Taking a deep breath, Lexi nodded her head and Bertie began. Beth went ahead of the twosome, smiling as she walked down the steps and through the yard with a sweet little girl who belonged to one of Lexi's cousins. The miniature princess followed Beth, throwing rose petals out of a white wicker basket.

Not to be left out of the fun, Baby, who had a bath and a brushing at a groomer's the day before, wore a big coral bow around her neck and carried the rings tied to a satin pillow down the aisle. She stopped beside Nate and wagged her enormous tail. When he took the pillow from her, Baby flopped down to watch the proceedings with a goofy grin on her doggy face.

Ty smiled at Beth as she walked toward them, her heart in her eyes as she shared in this day of love and celebration. They both knew if their mom could have been there, she would have loved Lexi.

The flower girl took her place beside Beth then all eyes turned to the porch as Swede and Lexi came down the steps.

Drawing in his breath, Ty felt waves of emotion roll over him with such force he thought for a moment he might be ill. Nate put a steady hand on his shoulder and squeezed, understanding all too well what Ty was experiencing.

Lexi had never looked more beautiful than she did at that moment with the sun picking rich highlights of midnight blue out of her raven curls. The dress fit her to perfection, showing off her womanly curves while a veil hid her face from him. He could imagine the tears glistening in her big green eyes, the edges of her tempting lips curling up in a smile while her cheeks glowed pink.

Suddenly the crowd disappeared and Ty was focused solely on Lexi, on her soft floral scent teasing him, her warmth reaching out to him, her love enveloping him.

When Swede stopped and placed Lexi's hand on Ty's, it was all he could do not to shout, "She's mine, she's mine!"

Instead, he tried to bring his thoughts back into line and smiled down at her with all the love overflowing from his heart.

Lexi glanced at Ty and lost herself in his bright blue eyes the minute they turned down the aisle and she could clearly see him. She knew Ty and a tuxedo would be a lethal combination to her system, but she had no idea exactly how potent it would be.

Dressed in a black tuxedo with a vest and silk tie, Ty looked like he could have come right from some celebrity party with his rich wavy hair carefully combed into place, his new black boots polished to a high shine and the coral rose boutonniere bringing a pop of color to his ensemble. The blue of his eyes and the white of his teeth were accented by the tan of his face.

When her eyes connected with his through the veil, she could feel the heat radiating between them with a force she thought might make her already weak knees lose the ability to function at all.

As Swede passed her over to Ty, she lightly squeezed his hand, hoping her love was conveyed in her touch. At his wink, she knew it was.

Together they turned and faced the pastor who did his best to keep his face impassive but couldn't hide his smile from this couple he had come to know and enjoy having in his congregation.

The first Sunday Ty joined Lexi for church, the pastor wasn't sure what to think, but it was soon apparent that Ty was genuinely interested in attending, not just in sitting in close quarters with Lexi.

The ceremony went quickly and flawlessly. Braced for the passionate kiss that was sure to come, the pastor grinned at the look that passed over Ty's face when he announced it was time to kiss the bride.

Not one to hurry moments of pleasure, Ty slowly lifted Lexi's veil and carefully folded it back. He had worried about doing it properly and Beth gave him plenty of pointers and practice in the two days they had been at the ranch.

Staring into Lexi's eyes, deep green orbs reflecting the love, joy and longing in his own, he smiled at her from his heart.

She smiled back at him as he gently brushed his thumb across her cheek, her chin and finally a fleeting touch across her lip before he dropped his head to hers. Planning on a brief touch of the lips, especially in front of the yard full of her family and the ranch hands, Ty quickly lost himself in the sensations and emotions of the moment.

Gathering Lexi in his arms, their kiss was deep, strong, and filled with promise. Nate finally bumped him on the shoulder while the pastor cleared his throat and Swede cackled loudly.

Lexi's face was fiery red when they turned to greet their family and friends as Mr. and Mrs. Tyler Lewis, but neither of them seemed able to stop grinning.

The wedding party just finished posing for photographs when guests began pouring into the ranch yard, bearing gifts, cards and smiles.

After a tasty barbecue lunch, those who had the energy got out on the dance floor.

Thanks to Beth, Ty was a passable dancer. He danced with his beautiful bride as long as he could before her many male relatives demanded a turn. With a jaunty smile, he wandered off to dance with her aunts, cousins and eventually Sunny.

"Thank you," he said as he respectfully held Lexi's grandmother during a slow dance.

"For what, sweet thing?" Sunny asked, tipping her head back to look at her handsome new grandson. For sure, her Lexi girl knew how to pick a real man. Not only was he drop-dead gorgeous, he was also kind, loving, a hard worker, and funny.

"For Lexi," Ty said with a warm smile. When Sunny looked at him confused, he continued. "The first time I was in the ranch house, she showed me your painting above the fireplace. I could see immediately where she got her pretty face. After meeting you, I know she got not only your outward beauty, but your inward beauty as well."

"Oh, you're going to make my mascara run and who wants to dance with a raccoon-eyed grandma?" Sunny said, swiping her finger under her eye to catch the lone tear that escaped. "I'm proud to have you in our family, Ty. I know you'll cherish Lexi as much as her grandpa cherished me and her daddy cherished her mama."

"Forever and always," Ty said, giving Sunny a hug as the song ended. He walked her back to where Bertie and Linc were sitting at a table in the shade of the tent by a big fan.

"Well..." Bertie said, looking at him expectantly. "Did she do it?"

"Who do what?" Ty asked, playing dumb. He knew what Bertie was after.

"Did she brand you?" Bertie said with a mischievous glint in her eye. "I told her she should months ago."

"Lexi sent a brand to me this morning with a note to wear it," Ty said, looking a little embarrassed. "It's one of those rub-on tattoo things."

"We'll let's see it," Bertie said, waiting for Ty to roll up his shirt sleeve. He'd long ago abandoned his jacket, vest and tie.

"No, ma'am," Ty said with a wicked grin. "The only one who's seeing that part of my anatomy is my wife."

Linc and Sunny laughed as Bertie's cheeks turned pink.

Glancing at his watch, he knew they were down to just a few more songs before Lexi would be whisked inside to change and they'd head off to Sisters by way of Bend.

Before he could ask anyone else to dance, Lexi came and took his arm. "Come dance with me," she said, dragging him on the dance floor. He laughed as the country band they'd hired began playing Bryan Adams' *Can't Stop This Thing We Started*. It was the perfect song to play as they prepared to leave the reception. Holding Lexi close as they danced, he smiled down into her sparkling eyes.

"That was a great song to pick, babe."

"It seemed fitting, considering your love of eighties music," Lexi said, leaning back in his arms as they danced to better admire the face she loved.

"There's a county song I wouldn't mind seeing you dance to again, if you're ever in the mood to shake that fine fanny of yours around the kitchen," Ty growled as he bent down to her ear. "In fact, maybe I need to download it to my phone so you can dance for me later."

"I don't think so, buckaroo." Lexi blushed and smacked playfully at his arm. "In case I didn't mention it before, I love my ring."

"I'm glad," Ty said kissing her cheek.

"It's absolutely perfect," Lexi said, turning her fingers so she could admire the white gold band on her finger.

Ty had a friend in Portland who was quite talented at designing jewelry. Deciding he was going to propose to Lexi, he called Kye and begged for a rush job. Having a general idea of what he was looking for, Kye guided him through the design process which resulted in a white-gold ring featuring a running rope pattern that looped into hearts.

The really fun part about the ring was that Ty had it made so that the engagement ring and wedding band had to be together to see the whole pattern. He'd made Lexi give him back the engagement ring a week ago so he could have the two bands permanently connected. On the inside of the band, he inscribed, "Hearts tied forever by love."

"Did you read the inscription?" Ty asked as he twirled Lexi around.

"Of course!" Lexi said with a laugh. "Roped, tied and yours forever!"

"Forever," he agreed, kissing her neck then her lips as they danced.

Those watching the couple could see the love on their faces. Sunny and Bertie smiled when Ty bent down and whispered something that made Lexi blush.

When the song finished, Sunny and Bertie, along with a few of Lexi's cousins swooped in and took her in the house to help her change.

The newlyweds were taking her car, but she had agreed to let Ty drive. Giving up on keeping it from being festooned, it now sat at the end of the walk, with crepe paper streamers and a big sign in the back window that said "just married." Thankfully, no one felt inclined to tie tin cans to the bumper.

Finished saying goodbye to Beth, Nate and the baby as well as the hands and Swede, Ty waited impatiently for Lexi by the front door.

Hearing a noise at the top of the stairs, Ty looked up to see Lexi on the landing sandwiched between Bertie and Sunny. She wore high wedge sandals with a hot-pink summery dress that skimmed her curves and accentuated her bronzed skin. Her hair was still piled on her head and she wore an indulgent smile as Sunny kept an arm around her waist.

Reaching out to her as she came down the last step, Sunny gave his hand a playful smack and engulfed Lexi in a hug.

"Congratulations, girlie, you made an excellent choice. I expect you two to come visit me this winter. Promise?" Sunny said, whispering in Lexi's ear.

"I promise, Grandma. Thank you for coming and for welcoming Ty to the family," Lexi said, hugging the older woman back. She was glad for the momentary distraction from Ty. He wore jeans and boots with a new blue western shirt that brought out the intense color of his eyes. The sleeves, rolled up past his elbows, revealed his tan, muscular forearms and a peek of his impressive biceps. Good gracious, all that virile, gorgeous man now belonged to her.

"Well, why wouldn't I welcome him, honey? He's a keeper for sure," Sunny said, kissing Lexi's cheek before turning her over to Bertie for another round of hugs.

"Baby girl, we're so proud of you," Bertie said, snuffling back tears. "You go have a wonderful time with this handsome husband of yours."

"I will Bertie. Thanks for everything," Lexi said, grateful to her family for their help in making her wedding something she would always remember.

"You bet. Give us a ring when you're home and ready to be part of the regular world again," Bertie teased as she pushed Lexi away. Turning she gave Ty a quick hug and kiss to his cheek then stepped back, letting Sunny have a turn.

"Sweet thing, you take good care of my granddaughter," Sunny said, hugging Ty one last time. "I expect to see that good looking face of yours in Florida before spring."

"Yes, ma'am," Ty said with a grin. He reached out and pulled Lexi to his side before anyone else could distract them.

"You ready to go Mrs. Lewis?" Ty asked as he opened the front door.

"More than you know," Lexi said with a flirty grin as they ran down the porch steps and to her car. Well-wishers blew hundreds of bubbles at them and tossed rose petals while cheering and waving.

Baby sat near their car, wagging her gigantic tail and barking. She licked their hands as they gave her a pat on the head and told her to be good while they were gone.

A few hours later, they pulled up at a resort at the edge of Sisters. While Lexi was immersed with wedding details, she asked Ty to be in charge of the honeymoon. He knew they couldn't be gone very long and he didn't want to spend too much of their precious time traveling, so after doing some online searching he settled on the cabin at Sisters. It was convenient, romantic and looked perfect on the website.

Walking into their secluded cabin at the back of the property, he decided it lived up to all his expectations of providing a romantic getaway. From the huge sunken tub big enough for two by a fireplace to the plush king-sized bed, it was just what he was hoping for.

He set down their luggage then hurried back outside where Lexi was looking around, taking in the beautifully landscaped grounds.

Ordering ahead when he made the reservation, the fridge in the room held an assortment of sodas and juice as well as a meat and cheese plate. A basket of fruit sat on the coffee table and a box of specialty chocolates waited for Lexi to take a sample.

Watching his beautiful bride as the sun sent shimmering rays dancing around her, he had to remind himself that all this was real, that she was real. She was finally his.

Feeling his gaze, Lexi turned and offered him a smile that shot straight to his heart.

"Ready to go in?" he asked as she held her hand out to him.

"Sure," she said, turning toward their cabin. "Want to get some dinner?"

"No, ma'am," Ty said, turning over her hand and kissing her palm, keeping his blue eyes focused on her green ones.

"Aren't you hungry?"

"Famished," he said, the heat in his gaze increasing.

"Then let's get you something to eat," Lexi said, turning toward the restaurant on the edge of the property.

"Nope," Ty said, sweeping her into his arms and carrying her into their cabin, pushing the door shut behind him with his foot.

Lexi was still catching her breath from being swept into his arms and hurried inside. With her arms looped around his neck, her lips were just inches from his and suddenly the thought of eating didn't hold as much appeal as it had a few minutes earlier.

"I thought you said you're starving," Lexi whispered, not quite sure what Ty was thinking.

"I am," Ty said, his voice dropping in pitch as he held her tightly to his chest. "Starving for you. Famished for your kisses. Hungry for your arms around me. Dying to taste every little bit of you."

"Oh," Lexi said, whooshing out her breath as Ty captured her lips in a kiss unlike any she'd ever known. It was wild, demanding, urgent and the most wonderful thing she had ever experienced. Heat and electricity exploded between them with a brilliant force of unrestrained passion. Lexi wasn't aware of anything except the feel of Ty's arms around her, his body pressed against her, and his lips moving insistently on hers.

"Ty, I love you," she whispered as he carried her into the bedroom and let her slowly slide to the floor.

"I love you too, Lexi. More than anything," Ty said, stepping around her and unfastening the hook at the top of her dress. He tugged gently, then impatiently on the zipper. As it finally started sliding down, his warm breath caressed Lexi's neck. "Thank you for marrying me."

When her dress was unzipped, Ty pulled it off her shoulders then held her hand while she stepped out of it and kicked off her sandals before turning around to him.

Lexi wasn't sure what to expect, but it wasn't the undiluted look of pure wanting on Ty's face.

"You are so beautiful, Lexi Jo. Absolutely the most beautiful woman I've ever seen," Ty said, trying to keep his passion in check and finding it more difficult with every passing second.

There had been moments in the last month when it taxed every bit of self-restraint to keep from taking things too far with Lexi, but he held on for this moment. The moment when she would finally be his.

The aching need that had started in his gut had now grown to a throbbing desire that encompassed his entire being. Taking in the sexy white lingerie Lexi was wearing, the gentle curves and softness of her skin, along with the pink blush in her cheeks, he was nearly undone.

His fingers shook as he quickly pulled the pins from her updo and watched the mass of curls tumble around her shoulders and down her back.

Burying his hands into her hair, he pulled her close and breathed deeply of the scent that was solely his wife – a combination of her warm, floral perfume, her sweetness, and the lingering hint of outdoors and sunshine.

"Oh, babe," he moaned, kissing her neck, worrying her earlobe, searing her with his kisses.

"Ty," Lexi whispered, wrapping her arms around his neck and savoring every touch, every kiss from this man who had so quickly sauntered into her life and claimed her heart for his own. Raising her lips to meet his, their kiss was filled with wanting. Lexi felt her insides grow molten, her limbs languid. Breaking the contact, she gave Ty a seductive smile. "I don't think this is quite fair."

"What's that?" Ty asked, running his hands over her exposed skin in delirious pleasure.

"You're still fully dressed and I'm not," Lexi whispered, feeling suddenly bold and brazen as she quickly untucked his shirt and in one smooth motion yanked the snaps free. Pushing it off his shoulders, she took a moment to admire Ty's rock-hard chest and arms, tanned by the summer sun.

While she was lost in the wonder of Ty's physical beauty, he pressed hot kisses down her neck, across her collar bone to her shoulder.

"Is it my turn again?" he asked, sliding his fingers down her back toward the hooks that kept him from treasures he could wait no longer to explore.

"Not yet," Lexi said with a saucy grin, pushing him backward onto the bed and grabbing his foot. She took off his boots and socks then divested him of his belt and jeans.

By the time she was done, they both were trembling from sensations passing between them.

"Aunt Bertie said you put on the brand but would only let me see it. Care to show it off?"

"Yes, ma'am." Ty looked up at her with such heat in his eyes, she thought what few clothes she had on might melt into a lacy puddle at her feet. Licking her lips nervously, she couldn't muster the strength to draw her eyes from Ty's.

She let out a whoosh of air when one of his strong arms snaked out and grabbed her waist, tumbling her down beside him. Unable to restrain his desire any longer, Ty rolled on top of her, ravishing kisses down her neck, rapidly removing the last bits of fabric separating him from his blushing bride.

"Lexi," Ty whispered in her ear. "I love you so much."

"Are you sure we have to go home already?" Lexi asked as they put the last of their bags in her car and looked fondly at the resort. "It seems like we just got here."

"Time flies when you're having fun," Ty said, wrapping his arms around her from behind and nuzzling her neck. When she turned to look at him, he waggled his eyebrows at her suggestively.

"You!" she smacked at his arm playfully then kissed him on the lips. "Promise we'll come back here at least once a year."

"I promise," Ty said, holding her car door as she climbed inside. "At least once a year, my beautiful bride. Maybe next time we'll even get to see something beyond the resort."

Ty waited until she had her seatbelt fastened then ran around to the driver's side and got in the car.

Lexi held out her left hand, studying her unique and lovely wedding ring.

"What are you doing?"

"Thinking about how glad I am you answered that classified ad," Lexi said, grinning at her new husband. "I had no idea what a bargain I was getting."

"A bargain?" Ty asked, looking at her curiously.

"Sure. I got a wonderful husband, a mind-blowing lover, a true friend, a great mechanic, a hard-worker, someone willing to learn the ropes, and the only guy Baby likes," Lexi said, squeezing Ty's hand. "Not to mention you are quite possibly the most handsome man I've ever seen with that bad-boy aura, sexy eyes, tempting hair and undeniably fine caboose."

Ty grinned at her. "Is that so, Mrs. Lewis?"

"That is so. Just ask Aunt Bertie. Besides, when I turned around that first day and saw you standing there by the corrals, you completely took my breath away."

"You not only took my breath," Ty said, his eyes glowing bright with warmth and love as he kissed her hand. "You took my heart. Forever and always, Lexi Jo."

Reaching into her purse, Lexi held out a tiny box to him, tied with a black ribbon.

"What's this, babe?" Ty asked with an indulgent smile, taking her hand in his and kissing her palm with moist lips, making tingles begin at her toes where they worked their way up to her head.

"A wedding gift," Lexi said. "Open it."

Ty opened the box to find a set of car keys attached to a keychain with the Rockin' R Brand. He knew the keys went to the Mustang.

"Are you serious?" he asked, studying the keys in his hand.

"Dad would want the car to be yours," Lexi said, leaning over to kiss his cheek. "Besides, if you have it to drive, you won't hog my car."

"But Lexi Jo, I just…" Ty took a breath and smiled at his wife. "Thank you. This is perfect, but as you know, I can't give you anything but my love and me."

"I thought of something you can give me no one else can," Lexi said softly, love making her eyes glow. Ty could see flecks of gold dancing in the mossy green pools.

"What could I possibly give you?" Ty asked, kissing her wrist and working his way up her arm. He stopped when he got to her elbow and looked at her, feeling surrounded by her love.

"A baby."

###

Spaghetti Carbonara

1 pound spaghetti
1 tbsp. olive oil
1 tsp. salt
6 slices bacon
4-6 sausages
1/2 cup cream
1/2 cup Parmesan cheese
2 eggs, beaten
2 tbsp. fresh chopped parsley

Bring a large pot of water to a boil with salt, add spaghetti and cook until al dente. Drain well. Toss with olive oil, and set aside.

Chop bacon into small pieces and fry in a large skillet until slightly crispy. Remove from skillet and drain. Set aside.

Using remaining bacon grease, fry sausages until brown on all sides, then cover with water and simmer for about 12-15 minutes until cooked through. Italian sausages would be best but you can use whatever you have on hand.

When sausages are nearly finished cooking, add beaten egg, Parmesan cheese and cream to noodles, stirring vigorously to keep the eggs from getting all funky on you. Add bacon and return to low heat, stirring to coat all noodles and to make sure eggs are cooked before serving.

Sprinkle fresh parsley (or dried if you don't have fresh) over the top, serve and enjoy!

Polenta Alla Romana

1 pound of bulk sausage (use Italian if you want a little more spicy kick)
2 cups of cooked chicken, cut into bite-sized pieces
1 cup grated Parmesan cheese
2 cups of sauce (tomato or Alfredo)
2 cups of chicken broth
1 tube of Polenta
1 tbsp. butter
parsley (optional)

In a heavy-duty skillet, brown the sausage. When it is cooked, add the chicken, one cup of the chicken broth and sauce. Simmer about 10 minutes until sauce starts to thicken.

While the sausage is cooking, break the polenta into small pieces and place in a skillet with a cup of the chicken broth and a tablespoon of butter. Simmer on medium heat until liquid is absorbed and polenta breaks down smoothly (about 10 minutes). Use a potato masher to get out all the lumps.

Spoon polenta onto a plate and top with the sauce, then sprinkle with Parmesan cheese and, if you like, parsley.

Chocolate Bundt Cake

1 chocolate cake mix
1 small box of instant chocolate pudding
1 cup sour cream
1/2 cup water
1/2 cup oil
3 eggs
1/2 cup chocolate frosting
berries (optional)
whipping cream (optional)
mint leaves (optional)

Combine all ingredients in a large mixing bowl and pour into a greased and floured bundt pan. Bake at 350 degrees for one hour or until edges start to pull away from the pan. The batter will seem oddly thick, but that is how you want it.

You can use a fun bundt pan shape to make this cake look like you went to a lot of work (when you really didn't). I like to finish the cake with some pre-made chocolate frosting (yes, right out of the can) that has been warmed. Use about 1/2 cup and microwave for 10-15 seconds, just until it starts to melt. Pour over the top of the cake. You can dust it with powdered sugar, cocoa powder or top with festive sprinkles. You can also pour caramel sauce over the top and serve while the cake is warm. This is especially tasty when served with a side of Dulce de Leche ice cream. Trust me. It will nearly make you faint with bliss.

I like to make the cake the day before, frost it then refrigerate and serve chilled. My favorite presentation is to serve it with a dollop of whipped cream and fresh raspberries.

Available now!

Savvy Summer Entertaining - The savvy hostess will find all the hints, ideas and recipes needed for a fun and successful summer entertaining season!

From Savvy Entertaining's blogger, this book includes her favorite tips for celebrating summer!

Coming Fall 2012!

The Cowboy's Autumn Fall - Brice Morgan thought love at first sight was some ridiculous notion of school girls and old ladies who read too many romance novels. At least he does until he meets Bailey Bishop at a friend's wedding and falls hard and fast for the intriguing woman.

Bailey Bishop attends her cousin's wedding with no intention of extending her brief visit to Oregon. Married to her career as an archaeologist, Bailey tries to ignore her intense attraction to her cousin's best friend, Brice. Ready to return home to Denver, Bailey is offered the opportunity to explore a new archeological dig not far from the family's ranch in Grass Valley.

Can she keep her feelings for Brice from derailing her plans for the future? As the autumn season arrives, love falls on willing hearts at the Triple T Ranch.

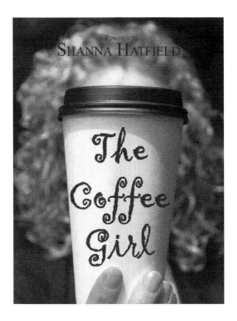

Coming August 2012!

The Coffee Girl – Almost thirty, Brenna Smith isn't sure how much more off-track her life could be. She certainly never pictured herself living at home with her parents, working in a job she dislikes for a loathsome boss. The only bright spot in her mundane existence is the cute guy she runs into every morning as she stops to get coffee.

Brock McCrae has worked hard to be able to manage his own construction company. Handsome, successful and full of life, he finds his world turned upside down as he falls for a woman he knows only as The Coffee Girl.

Is there something more than a shared love of coffee brewing between these two? Find out… in August 2012!

by
SHANNA HATFIELD

An excerpt…

The Coffee Girl
Copyright 2012
by Shanna Hatfield

Shanna Hatfield
shanna@shannahatfield.com
shannahatfield.com

Special thanks to Colleen Brady for her help with the cover of this book.

Chapter One

Listening to the rain pelt against the windows of the coffee shop, Brenna Smith held back a long-suffering sigh as she impatiently waited in line.

Knowing how busy the shop was early morning, she should have skipped the coffee or left the house five minutes sooner. If the line didn't start moving a lot faster than its current snail-like speed, she was going to be late for work at her office in Portland and being late wasn't an option.

Skies the color of cold gunmetal coupled with the cold drizzle of rain didn't help her dreary state of mind this morning. Unwilling to think about what the day would bring, she rolled back her shoulders, closed her eyes, and took a deep breath.

The delicious scent of cedar wood, warm musk and, not surprisingly, rich, dark coffee filled her senses. Taking another deep breath, she opened her eyes, fastening her gaze on the back of the man in line in front of her.

It was him.

Brenna first noticed the man in the coffee shop several weeks ago. She could always smell his unique, outdoorsy scent before she saw him. How had she not noticed he was standing right in front of her today?

Dressed in a canvas coat, jeans, work boots and a ball cap, seeing him brought the hint of a smile to Brenna's face.

The guy wasn't movie-star handsome, but he was ruggedly good-looking and from the way his coat stretched across his broad shoulders, she assumed he would be fit. He was probably around five-ten with an easy smile, and she liked the way laugh lines framed his bright hazel eyes. She guessed him to be around her age.

Placing his order, Brenna tried not to stare too intently at his back or listen too attentively to the smooth cadence of his voice.

Turning around, he handed her a cup of coffee with a wink and a smile before walking toward the door.

"Thank you," Brenna called to his retreating form. He waved a hand in response as he strode out of the coffee shop.

Brenna's thoughts tumbled around the man while she took a sip of her coffee. Biting back her grin, she wondered how he knew she always ordered a chai latte.

Rushing out the door, she stepped off the sidewalk only to be splashed by a car speeding through the parking lot.

Staring at the car with something akin to murderous fury in her eyes, she dashed across the parking lot and got in her car grumbling. Her momentary euphoria at having the cute guy purchase her coffee was quickly dissipating.

"Just perfect," Brenna muttered to herself as she got back on the highway, heading north into Portland.

Putting her foot down on the accelerator, she kept her speeding just shy of going over the point that would get her a ticket.

Letting out the sigh that had been building since she got up that morning, she gripped the steering wheel in frustration.

She hated this rush to work every day. Hated her job. Hated pretty much everything about her current existence. In a few weeks she was going to turn thirty and this was not how she pictured her life as she hit that milestone.

Pulling into the parking lot, one car among hundreds at the company where she worked as a research analyst, Brenna hurried in the doors and tapped the toe of her high heel as she waited for the elevator to take her up to her office. She'd worked long and hard to make it to the position of a senior manager but the job no longer held any joy for her.

Racing down the hall and past the receptionist, she threw her rain-splattered trench coat on the rack just inside her office door, grabbed notes and a folder from her desk, and hurried to the early morning staff meeting. Sliding into her chair with two minutes to spare, she took a breath, closed her eyes and tried to center herself.

Her hot-shot boss came swaggering in five minutes late sporting sun glasses and a hangover. If he wasn't a nephew to one of the big-wigs in the executive suites upstairs, Brenna was certain he would have been fired long ago instead of promoted to his current position that allowed him to run rough-shod over a good team of people.

The last year had been a game of cat and mouse for her, trying to stay off his radar. Any time he focused in on her, she found herself popping antacids like they were candy. He was rude, obnoxious and arrogant, and that was when he was having a good day.

From the wrinkled appearance of his suit, that looked suspiciously like the same one he had on the previous day, Brenna knew today was not going to be good.

Sinking a little lower into her seat, she wished she had some magic way to become invisible.

"Well, kids, what's shaking?" Wesley Mettler asked as he took his seat at the head of the table and looked around the room. Not giving anyone time to answer, he motioned to a new intern sitting close to the coffee and pointed his direction. "You, coffee."

When the young man looked around uncertain, someone discretely pointed at the coffee pot on the table and Wesley. Jumping up, Tony poured the coffee and quickly walked it down the long table to the boss.

Instead of saying thank you, Wesley glared at Tony over his sunglasses then sat back in his chair taking a long drink.

"Which one of you is going to make me look brilliant today?" Wesley asked, looking around the room.

Brenna kept her eyes glued to the legal pad in front of her, hoping Wesley wouldn't notice her. She thought she was safe until she felt his gaze boring into the top of her head and fought the urge to squirm in her seat.

"Ms. Smith, what can you share with the group this morning?" Wesley asked, a snide tone in his voice. It wasn't a secret to anyone that he disliked Brenna. Maybe it was the fact she was conservative. It could have been that she wasn't one of the office beauties. Some chalked it up to her intelligence and competence that constantly made him feel threatened. A handful liked to think it was the way she turned him down with such vehemence the one time he propositioned her that he didn't try again.

Taking a deep breath to calm down, Brenna tried to gather her thoughts. "We finished researching the site retargeting project. It's definitely something we don't want to waste time considering. We need to move on this one while we can maintain an edge. I'll have a report with a proposed action plan ready by the end of the week."

"No, you won't," Wesley said, swiveling his chair back and forth, sunglasses still in place as he rested his elbows on the chair arm and steepled his soft fingers together. "I want it before you leave today."

"But, Wesley, that's not possible. It will take several days to compile the information, create the graphics, write the…" Brenna's explanation was cut short when Wesley sat forward, lowered his glasses and gave her a cold stare.

"Today, Ms. Smith. It will be on my desk before you leave today and I don't care how long it takes you and whoever can help you to get it done. You've got until 11:59 p.m." Turning from Brenna, he moved on to his next victim and the meeting adjourned a few minutes later.

One of the first to leave the meeting room, Brenna hurried back to her office, ignoring the sympathetic looks of her coworkers.

Quietly shutting her door, Brenna would rather have slammed it. Her heart was still pounding and she felt a headache coming on. She knew from experience there wasn't a thing any of them could do about Wesley. The last person who complained was fired before the day was through and escorted out to her car by security.

Deciding she might as well accept the inevitable, Brenna lost herself in frantically preparing the report as the hours flew by. She doled out parts of the project to her team members and together they might get the project finished before Wesley's ridiculous deadline.

It was well past noon when a quick knock sounded on her door.

"Come in," Brenna called, looking up from her computer long enough to acknowledge her good friend Kathleen with a warm smile.

"Did you come bearing gifts?" Brenna asked, continuing to type as she watched Kathleen stride across her office carrying a bag from the deli down the block.

"I brought you some lunch," Kathleen said, setting the bag down before perching on the corner of Brenna's desk.

"Better not let Weasel Wesley see you doing that," Brenna said, digging a chef's salad out of the bag.

"I'm not worried about him in the least," Kathleen said, crossing her legs and swinging one foot defiantly.

Kathleen didn't need to be worried because her grandfather was one of the big wigs in the executive suites as well. He wouldn't allow Wesley to get Kathleen fired, although he did expect her to work her way up through the company and pull her own weight.

With her looks, attitude and intellect, Brenna didn't think it would take Kathleen long to have her own office up near her grandfather's. She was tall and lithe with flowing black hair, snapping green eyes, and carried herself like royalty. She was also sharp, fearless, and one of the best friends Brenna had.

They met the summer they both were interning with the company. The internships led to part-time jobs while they were finishing their college degrees and they both started climbing the corporate ladder. It had been a hard climb, especially in a company that still functioned with the mentality that women should be secretaries and errand-girls while men did the rest.

Working their way into senior management positions was quite an accomplishment for them both.

"Maybe you aren't, but I am. You know what happens when he gets tired of employees. Before you know it, you're packing up your personal belongings and out the door," Brenna said, eating her salad.

"The company knows how valuable you are, even if Wesley doesn't. They aren't going to let him chase you off like he has the rest," Kathleen said, stealing an olive out of the salad.

Brenna looked at her friend and smiled.

"Thanks for bringing me lunch. I needed a little break."

"No problem," Kathleen said, staring at Brenna's computer screen where multiple windows were open as she worked on piecing together her report. "I heard what Wesley did this morning. Is there anything I can help with?"

"No. My team is working on the charts and graphics while I write the technical details and formulate the battle plan. I'll probably burn a little midnight oil to get this on the weasel's desk as requested, but I'll manage."

"You always do," Kathleen said, sliding off the desk and adjusting her slim skirt. "Just don't stay too late and for goodness sakes, make sure you put your name in that report. He always takes credit for your efforts even though everyone knows who really does the work. Call me if you need anything."

"I will, Kat. Thanks," Brenna said, waving a hand at her friend as she walked out the door, shutting it behind her.

Hours later, Brenna got up to stretch the kinks out of her neck and back and noticed the sky was no longer gray, but black with approaching darkness. She waved away her team at five, telling them to go home and enjoy the evening.

Picking up the phone, Brenna called her mom and let her know she was going to be late.

"Well, how late, honey?" asked Lettice Smith, better known as Letty. "We can wait dinner for you if you'll just be a little while."

"No, Mom. I've got a couple more hours of work to do before I'm finished, so don't wait on me. Please. I'll grab something to eat on my way home," Brenna said, staring into the watery darkness outside as she leaned against the desk.

"Well, drive careful. I hate you making that long trek to and from work every day," Letty said.

"I know, Mom. See you in the morning," Brenna said, disconnecting the call.

Growing up in Silverton, Oregon, just an hour or so south of Portland, Brenna and her family didn't think anything of the trip whenever they needed to run into the city. It was something else entirely when you had to make the drive every day in heavy traffic.

During college and right up until about six months ago, Brenna lived in a cute little apartment with two roommates not far from her office. When the owner of the apartment building decided to sell it to a developer for a new retail center, the tenants were given a month to get out. Without time to hunt for a new apartment, Brenna moved back home temporarily.

Yeah, that's how I've always envisioned my life, she thought sarcastically: a 30-year-old living at home with her parents, in a job she barely tolerated working for a boss she loathed in a city she often felt was sucking the life-blood right out of her.

Someday she'd follow her dreams, but today was not that day.

Her sister Avery kept telling her to stop waiting for someday and do it now, but Brenna was too cautious, too responsible, to throw caution aside and plunge blindly into the future.

She had a nice little nest egg, a good start on her retirement, and a few close friends she enjoyed. But none of that erased her longings or the loneliness that sometimes threatened to overwhelm her.

When she closed her eyes, she could see a sweet little cottage-style home, a man with broad shoulders and dark hair and a gangly mutt. The smell of coffee and fresh baked pastries hung in the air, along with a hint of cedar and some other scent that drifted just out of her mind's reach.

That picture was one she'd seen for years, but she had yet to see the house, the man or the dog. So she'd just go on dreaming.

Opening her eyes, Brenna returned to her paperwork with a sigh. She was exhausted, her back was killing her from sitting at the computer all day, and she was hungry. Pushing all that aside, she buried herself in her work.

A few hours later she neatly bound the report in a presentation folder. Gathering up her coat and purse, Brenna turned off her office equipment and lights, shut the door and walked down the hall to Wesley's office. The door was open so she went in and dropped the report on his desk.

It was when she turned to leave she saw Wesley sprawled on the couch with an empty bottle of whiskey on the floor beside him. She shook her head and quietly walked out, knowing by his snores he had no idea she'd been in the room.

Hurrying out of the building, she asked one of the night security guards to walk her to her car. She wasn't overly paranoid, but she'd rather be safe than sorry. As they walked past two homeless men begging for change, Brenna was glad for the escort. He waited until she was safely buckled into her seatbelt before returning inside.

Brenna's stomach growled as she headed south on the freeway. She planned to swing by one of her favorite restaurants closer to home, so she kept on driving.

Mentally exhausted, she was tired of playing the office games, tired of putting up with Wesley, and tired of having no life outside of her job.

Maybe it was time to think about making a change.

Brenna was mulling over that thought when she heard a loud pop and her car pulled to the right. Of course her tire would blow when she had just driven past an exit. Carefully driving the car onto the shoulder of the road, Brenna turned on her hazard lights and jumped out of the car into a steady fall of bone-chilling rain. Hurrying around to the passenger side, she could see her tire was not only flat, but missing a piece or two of rubber.

Perfect.

The flat tire unraveled the last thread that was holding Brenna's frustrations in check. Running back to the driver's side, Brenna slid behind the wheel and burst into tears.

ABOUT THE AUTHOR

SHANNA HATFIELD spent 10 years as a newspaper journalist before moving into the field of marketing and public relations. She has a lifelong love of writing, reading and creativity. She and her husband, lovingly referred to as Captain Cavedweller, reside in the Pacific Northwest with their neurotic cat along with a menagerie of wandering wildlife and neighborhood pets.

Shanna loves to hear from readers:

Blog: shannahatfield.com

Facebook: Shanna Hatfield's Page

Pinterest: Shanna Hatfield

Email: shanna@shannahatfield.com

Made in the USA
Middletown, DE
22 September 2015